DEVIL
IN THE
DETAILS

QUENTIN SECURITY SERIES
BOOK TWO

MORGAN JAMES

Devil in the Details
Copyright © 2020 Morgan James.
ISBN: 978-1-951447-08-3

All rights reserved. No part of this publication may be reproduced, stored or transmitted in any form or by any means, electronic, mechanical, photocopying, recording, scanning, or otherwise without written permission from the publisher. It is illegal to copy this book, post it to a website, or distribute it by any other means without permission.

This novel is entirely a work of fiction. The names, characters and incidents portrayed in it are the work of the author's imagination. Any resemblance to actual persons, living or dead, events or localities is entirely coincidental.

Morgan James has no responsibility for the persistence or accuracy of URLs for external or third-party Internet Websites referred to in this publication and does not guarantee that any content on such Websites is, or will remain, accurate or appropriate.

Designations used by companies to distinguish their products are often claimed as trademarks. All brand names and product names used in this book and on its cover are trade names, service marks, trademarks and registered trademarks of their respective owners. The publishers and the book are not associated with any product or vendor mentioned in this book. None of the companies referenced within the book have endorsed the book.

Editing by Hot Tree Editing

DEVIL
IN THE
DETAILS

CHAPTER ONE
Lydia

"Dirty, low-down, lying, cheating son of a..." I tossed the drink back and set the glass down on the sticky bar with a little more force than necessary. Okay, maybe a lot more than necessary. But I needed to take my aggression out on something. Here I sat, at my cousin's bachelorette party of all things, only weeks after my own fiancé had walked out. This party should have been mine. Instead, I was now bridesmaid instead of the bride.

With our pending nuptials less than a month away, Shawn had gotten cold feet—or so I thought—and run off. But not alone. Oh, no, that would have been far less complicated than the truth. He'd taken off with one of my best friends. Needless to say, that relationship of twenty-some years was dead now, too.

Our breakup was really a blessing in disguise, though I hadn't been able to admit it at the time. It had felt like a betrayal and, in truth, the rejection still stung. We'd both been under pressure to marry, from both my mother and Shawn's father. I didn't resent him for finding happiness; I did, however, begrudge the fact that he'd chosen to cheat on me instead of ending things amicably.

Though he hadn't admitted it, I even knew why he'd cheated on me. Every waking moment was spent in my bridal salon, trying to get it off the ground. I'd opened Something Blue only eight months ago and, while we were doing well so far, I still had a long way to go. Shawn had been extremely jealous of the shop, as if it were a living, breathing thing that took my time away from him. In a way, it kind of was. It was my baby, and I loved the salon far more than I'd loved Shawn.

My mother, Jolene, met Shawn through the law firm where he worked. When she suggested I go out with him, it was easier for me to just agree than fight it. While my feelings for Shawn were only lukewarm at best, Jolene had been enamored of the charismatic young man on a fast track to be a lawyer at his father's firm in Dallas. Shawn did all the right things, said all the right words. But something had always seemed… off. When he proposed after only a year, Jolene was thrilled. My friends loved him, and I began to question whether something was wrong with me. Despite my reservations, I accepted his offer.

So here I was, eight months later, alone in a bar in godforsaken Las Vegas. The land of weddings and huge jackpots. I rolled my eyes. Maybe I could buy a groom. Someone tall, dark, and handsome with—

"He was an asshole."

I startled, nearly falling off my stool as I whipped toward the deep, masculine voice. "I'm sorry?"

My gaze swept over the equally sexy body attached to the voice as the man slid onto the stool beside me. Even seated, he was a head taller than me. Golden blond hair crowned his head, cropped close to his skull, and a day's growth of whiskers adorned his square jaw. The sight sent a tingle of pleasure straight to my core. If there was one thing in this world I couldn't resist, it was a man with sexy scruff. It got me every time.

"The asshole you've been muttering about over here. Sounds like a dickhead."

I stared in open-mouthed fascination. Or horror. I wasn't sure which. "You heard me?"

The man chuckled. "Oh, darlin', I heard ya. The lying, cheating fool." My cheeks burned with embarrassment, and I dropped my gaze to the bar. I could feel the man's eyes sliding over me, but his voice was still a surprise when the rough drawl rumbled from his throat. "There's just one thing I can't figure out."

I looked up at him in question. Blue eyes met mine before sliding over my face, then lower. His intense perusal sent a tendril of heat curling through me, and my skin flushed. I reciprocated the gesture and looked him over. He was tall. Like tall-tall, probably a good six or seven inches taller than my own stopped in here tonight." A smile split his face, showcasing a row of even white teeth. He held out a hand. "Alexander McLean. My friends call me Xander."

I slipped my palm into his. Immediately, the warmth of his touch enfolded me, and the feel of his rough callouses turned my cheeks crimson. "Lydia Dawson."

"My pleasure, Miss Dawson."

I heated under his gaze, his smooth, cultured words rolling over my body, practically caressing my skin. What was it about this guy? My fingers tingled where they lay in his, and awareness streamed through my body as if I were hyperaware of his every movement. He casually stroked the back of my hand with a thumb before releasing me and reaching for his whiskey.

"So, that's some getup, girl."

I glanced down and wrinkled my nose. "My cousin, Rose, is getting married. I was kind of obligated to come here for the bachelorette party."

"Would that happen to be Rose Norman?"

I turned surprised eyes on him. "You know her?"

Xander dipped his chin. "She's marrying my friend Aaron."

"Small world." I grinned. "Is that what brought you here, too?"

"It is. Are you a bridesmaid?"

"Yep." I rolled my eyes. "I don't even know why I'm here. We've never even been that close. I'm only here to round out the dozen attendants she needs." I made a face. "Seriously, who does that? A dozen bridesmaids and groomsmen?"

Xander's eyes twinkled with mirth. "It's a hell of a lot, that's for sure. Thank God I'm not in the wedding."

My heart dipped, and I pushed the irrational pang of disappointment away. "You're not?"

He rolled the glass between his hands. "Nope. I ship back out of here in a couple days."

I digested that bit of information. "Are you in the military?"

"Yep. So why aren't you out with the girls?"

I blinked at the abrupt change of subject. I'd learned from past experience that men generally loved to brag about themselves, especially hunky alpha males such as Xander. He'd thrown me for a loop twice tonight already, and he intrigued me five-foot-seven frame and built like a Norse god. I allowed my gaze to roam the broad shoulders encased in a short-sleeved button-up shirt, the muscles of his biceps popping out under the sleeves. I dragged my eyes back up to his face. The pale blond of his hair enhanced his sharp cheekbones and straight nose, and his cerulean eyes drilled holes through me like he was staring into my soul. A strange feeling coursed through my body. I would have blamed it on the alcohol, but I wasn't that drunk. Yet.

He gave his head a slight shake, like he just couldn't quite wrap his mind around whatever he was thinking. Finally, he spoke. "Why the hell would a man cheat on you?"

"I guess I just couldn't compete." I shrugged, aiming for nonchalant. In truth, it hurt to even say the words aloud. "He ran off with my best friend."

The man's eyes widened, and his mouth dropped open in an 'O' of shock. "I... don't even know what to say to that. Seriously?" He threw me a bewildered look, and I nodded solemnly. "I just... Jesus. The man obviously wasn't right in the head to leave you, let alone betray you like that. Fucking hell." He tossed back his drink and I smirked.

"Well, that part was probably my fault. I didn't love him as much as I should have."

The man studied me. "Doesn't make it right, either way. You're still better off without him."

"Oh, I know. It was more than just that." I lifted one shoulder offhandedly. "I may have also mentioned something about him being a pretentious, self-absorbed, scum-sucking lawyer trust fund baby."

The man threw back his head on a shout of laughter. "Good for you."

"Yeah, well, it wasn't much of a consolation." I tossed back a shot of tequila.

He nodded once. "What he did was low. But"—he shrugged—"it's a good thing you figured it out before you married the idiot."

I laughed. "Thank God. I'd rather marry some stranger off the street than spend one more single day with that selfish prick."

He gestured at the bartender to refill our drinks before turning his attention back to me. "You have no idea how glad I am I on multiple levels. Turning my attention back to him, I jerked a thumb toward the Strip. "They hit up a gentleman's club down the block. I decided I've seen enough penises this year."

A deep chuckle fell from his lips. "Sweetheart, that's the saddest thing I've ever heard."

A smile lifted the corners of my mouth. "Sad but true."

"Maybe you'll change your mind."

Was that an invitation? I quirked a brow at him. "And what about you? Not hanging out with the guys?"

His shoulders tensed the slightest bit. "I... don't do well in loud, crowded spaces."

Right. Sympathy swelled in my chest and I glanced around the bar. "If you want to leave—"

"No way." He bumped his shoulder against mine. "I'm having a good time right here."

I dipped my head, heat blossoming across my cheeks at his compliment.

"Anyway." He seemed to struggle for something to say. "That's quite a dress."

Back to that again? Admittedly, I'd drawn several sets of eyes when I walked in here, though probably not in a good way. I was pretty sure more than one guy thought I was for hire. I almost regretted not changing, but if this gorgeous man next to me wanted to discuss my chosen attire for the evening, I was game. I grinned cheekily. "You don't like it?" Those gorgeous blue eyes followed my movement as I ran a hand over the tight bodice and ruffled skirt that flared around my thighs. "It's ridiculous, but she wanted us all to match."

"It's a little much." Xander laughed. "Don't get me wrong, darlin', you're killing that dress. I think every man noticed you the second you strolled through the door."

I blushed and covered my smile by taking a sip of my drink. "I'll take that as a compliment."

"Good, I meant it as one. Lucky me, I beat them all over here." His eyes bored into mine, and I squirmed under the scrutiny. The man exuded sex appeal, and my mind automatically strayed to steamy nights and rumpled sheets. He'd be a fantastic lover—strong, sure, and confident. He'd be able to pick me up with no trouble at all. I didn't have much time to contemplate the thought as he spoke again. "I like you, Lydia. Tell me more about yourself."

"Well." I bit my lip for a moment. "I own a bridal salon back home called Something Blue. It's fairly new, so it takes up a lot of time. But I love it."

"Ah, a romantic." He shot me a grin, and I couldn't help but smile back.

With a conciliatory shrug, I admitted it. "I love helping women find the dress of their dreams. It's symbolic in a way, I think. The perfect dress is the beginning of a good marriage. As a woman, I know what makes me happy—what makes me feel good. I think the same should apply to a marriage. Communicating how you feel and never settling for less than what makes you happy."

Xander nodded appreciatively. "I can see that. So you were engaged to the lyin', cheatin' fool?"

"Unfortunately." I made a face. "He was more my mother's type than mine. She seemed to think he was perfect for me."

"So why did you go along with it?" Those bright blue eyes drilled into me, and I nervously licked my lips. Clearing my throat, I shifted my gaze away from him.

"I don't know. I just… everyone kept saying how wonderful he was, and I thought maybe it was me that was wrong. He looked so perfect on paper, I had to be missing something. I kept waiting to feel more for him, but it just never happened. My mother told me I wasn't trying hard enough, that I was being blind and stupid."

Xander lifted a brow. "I have a feeling that you're a lot of things, Lydia." His voice was low and gravelly, and the sound curled around my heart. "But stupid is most definitely not one of them."

"Well, Jessica obviously saw something in him that I didn't."

"Yeah. The dick she was sucking," Xander deadpanned. I couldn't help the snort that rose up, and I covered my mouth with one hand to stifle my laughter. He grinned back at me, then the smile slipped away. "Seriously, though. You're better off without him."

"I know." It was true, and I felt no remorse as I made the admission.

"I have a personal question for you, if you don't mind."

"Um… okay?" My brows lifted the slightest bit at his serious tone, and unease skittered down my spine.

Xander studied me. "I can understand why that would hurt you. But you don't seem… heartbroken."

"I guess I'm not really," I admitted. "I kind of knew deep down something was wrong. I just didn't know it was… that," I finished lamely.

His eyes narrowed on me, and he picked up my hand. "You're a smart, beautiful woman, Lydia. You said it yourself—you know deep down what you want. And it wasn't him. Your mother said he was perfect for you. But what did *you* feel? Did you really think he was the right man?"

"I…" I bit my lip. Was he right? Maybe in the back of my mind, I'd been hoping that, with enough time, Shawn and I could work things out. But in my heart of hearts, I had to admit—it wasn't true. I didn't love him. I swallowed hard and said what I'd never admitted out loud. "No."

"Well then, here's to a fresh start." He gestured to my glass, and I touched it to his. Xander's arm muscles rippled as he lifted his glass to his lips, and I couldn't tear my eyes from his neck as he swallowed the fiery liquid. Good Lord. He had muscles everywhere. Even his muscles had muscles. What would it be like to have those arms wrapped around me? The thought sent a shiver down my spine.

With a sudden start, I realized I was staring. I snatched my gaze away, turning my focus instead to the shot glass in my hand. "To fresh starts."

Xander, I learned, was Texas born and bred, hence the sexy-as-sin drawl. He'd enlisted in the Army and had completed his training in special forces just a few years prior. He'd been deployed all over the globe on missions he couldn't speak of, to places he never wanted to see again. But he was doing it for the greater good. His parents had both been big into charity and had died on a mission trip almost a decade earlier.

"I figured going into the military was my way of giving back," he said. "We help eliminate these terrorist cells that control people and take innocent lives."

I tossed back my third shot—or was it my fourth?—and laid a hand on his knee. "I think that's fantastic. You're a good man,

Xander."

"You think so?" His gaze slid over me, and my body warmed from the inside out.

I nodded. "You're a total catch. Any woman would be lucky to have you."

"Yeah?" A sexy little grin tugged at the corners of his lips.

Warning bells went off in my mind, but fuzzy from the alcohol, I tuned them out. "I deserve to let loose and have some fun, don't I?" I stared at Xander and he looked back, his expression a mixture of amusement and concern.

"Of course you do, darlin'. What did you have in mind?" He turned to face me, one foot planted on the floor, and extended a hand to help me off the tall barstool.

I stepped down and moved into the vee of his legs. He watched me with an eagle eye, and his hands moved to my hips, gripping me tightly. "You all right there, beautiful?"

I grinned up at him and he pulled me closer, lifting my arms to loop around his neck. "Perfect now." I leaned my body into his and rose up on my toes, pressing my lips to his. He reciprocated, his lips soft and warm, the kiss demanding. I pulled back just enough to speak against his lips. "The night is young, cowboy. What do you say we get into some trouble?"

at least passably sober—as much as I was, anyway—I led her outside. Lights winked at us overhead, and we strolled leisurely down the Strip in comfortable silence. Once in a while she'd point or pull me to a stop to take in some attraction. Mostly, though, we just enjoyed being together. I focused on the feel of her pressed against my side, the soft curve of her hip beneath my palm. I splayed my fingers, pressing ever so gently into her flesh. She tipped her chin up at me, a beautiful smile lighting her face.

I couldn't help it any longer. I pulled her to a stop and cupped the back of her head in my hand. Holding her, I dipped my head and brushed my lips over hers. Everything around us disappeared the moment we connected, bleeding into the distance. Lifting my head, I stared into those pretty eyes. The same ones that had drawn me to her in the first place. Only, instead of sadness, they now held hunger. Lust.

I liked the feel of her next to me. I liked her quiet, composed demeanor. I liked Lydia—really liked her. It was a stupid, senseless thought, but one I couldn't help nonetheless. I could see myself with someone like her. I could see myself with her. From what I could tell, she was smart and business savvy. The fact that she was gorgeous was just the cherry on top.

I was fucking tired of being alone, of having no one to come home to. Lydia was still hurting from a betrayal she'd never seen coming—not only from the idiot she'd been engaged to but her best friend as well. I couldn't imagine the damage that would do to a woman.

"You deserve better."

A tiny line appeared between her eyebrows. "Um... okay?"

"I would never cheat on you." I startled both of us with my statement.

Her mouth formed a perfectly round 'O' of surprise. "I don't... I don't know what that means," she whispered.

Of course she didn't. We'd known each other for a couple hours, but I felt... *something* when I looked at her, when I touched her. And she'd already admitted earlier that she was attracted to me. I only had one more tour—I needed to put in another year, then I'd be out. Lydia had her business—she'd have something to focus on while I was gone. Then we could find out if this

CHAPTER TWO
Xander

Goddamn. This woman was something else. And she sure as fuck deserved more than the stupid shit who'd run her through the emotional wringer. What a fucking tool. I was pissed on her behalf that he'd led her on, letting her think she wasn't good enough when he was the one who'd been at fault. Who the hell cheated on a woman like Lydia?

Her warm, lithe body pressed to mine felt like absolute perfection. Her heels boosted her a couple extra inches, bringing her forehead right in line with my lips. I felt huge next to most girls, awkward and ungainly. But Lydia was the perfect height, and I knew she'd fit my body like a glove. I wondered if I'd ever have the chance to feel her next to me, my scarred, tattooed skin sliding against her creamy white flesh.

That sexy-as-fuck grin slayed me, and I slipped off the stool. Holding my arm out to her like the gentleman I most certainly was not, I asked, "Where are we headed?"

She curled a hand around my bicep and fell into step next to me, then against me. She dissolved into a fit of giggles as she righted herself. "Oops! Sorry!"

"You good?" I slipped a hand around her waist to steady her, my fingers curving into the soft flesh of her hip.

"Never better." She tossed me a sexy, sultry smile, and I studied her.

We'd shared a few drinks at the bar, but she'd taken her time with them, and she wasn't slurring her words. Deciding she was thing between us was worth pursuing.

I couldn't believe I was even considering this. Feeling her out, I squeezed her hand. "Have you ever considered a long-distance relationship?"

Her eyes darted to mine, wide with surprise. "Xander…"

I tugged her closer and framed her face with my hands. "I know it sounds crazy, but Liddy…" The nickname slipped off my tongue like silk. "I like you a lot. You already know I'm attracted to you." She blinked up at me, her mouth parted slightly as she digested my words. "We haven't spent much time together, but you just… I feel this connection with you. Do you feel it too?"

She swallowed hard, then nodded hesitantly. "I… I think so."

I took her hands in mine, heedless of the people funneling around us on the sidewalk. "I will always take care of you. I'll do everything in my power to make you happy."

"Are you… You're serious?"

I almost cringed at the incredulity in her tone. Was that a good sign or bad? I pressed on, determined to feel her out. "Only if you want to. You deserve so much better than that asshole. Let me be that man," I begged.

"But… why? Why me?" Genuine confusion filled her eyes, as if she had no idea why I was even asking. Was she really so insecure?

"I know you don't know me—but I know me. And I know what I want, Lydia. I want you."

She stared up at me for a long moment, unblinking. Every muscle tensed as she opened her mouth to speak, sure she was going to shoot me down. Her mouth closed, and she gave a little nod instead. Hope and lightness filled my heart. "Is that a yes? You'll give me a chance?"

She licked her lips, eyes never leaving mine. "Yes."

My mouth broke into a huge smile, and I moved my hands to frame her beautiful face, her expression still a bit bemused. I crushed my mouth to hers, my tongue slipping between the seam of her lips, tasting every inch of her. The kiss was hot and hard and insistent, and I broke away, breathing hard. I pressed my forehead to hers, my nose brushing hers as I spoke. "I won't let you down, Lydia Dawson. You're mine now."

CHAPTER THREE
Lydia

My mouth was dry, my eyes heavy. I felt like I'd been hit by a freight train. I shifted in an attempt to stretch my stiff, fatigued muscles, but I couldn't move. Apparently, the tequila train had run me over, then backed up to park on top of my chest.

I blinked rapidly to dispel the last vestiges of sleep and blearily took in my surroundings. The room was unfamiliar, and it took several seconds for me to realize I was in my hotel room. The heat at my back and the heavy arm draped over my waist—my *naked* waist, I realized as I peeked below the covers—told me that I had indeed indulged in a Vegas moment. I remembered the man from the bar, but not much after that. We'd obviously had sex, or so I assumed. There wasn't a whole lot of room for doubt, considering we were both naked. I could feel a hard ridge pressing against my bottom, and I resisted the urge to press my hips backward.

What the hell else had happened last night? We'd left the bar and headed down the Strip, stopping to watch the fountain at the Bellagio, then… Then what? My memory was foggy after that. I stole a glance over my shoulder and caught a glimpse of him sprawled out behind me, his head inches from mine on the pillow. The sight sent a momentary pang of longing through my heart. Last night, he'd been sweet and sexy and so gorgeous it hurt to look at him. The lines of his face were softer in sleep, making him look sweet and almost innocent.

I vaguely remembered our discussion of a serious relationship as we'd walked, giddy and half-drunk, down the Strip. We'd had an amazing time, our passion and lust fueled by the romantic, sparkling lights of the city and the novelty of something new. Despite our initial connection, I knew it would never work.

Trying to avoid the awkward, after-random-hookup moment, I untangled my limbs from his as gently as possible and slid toward the edge of the bed. His thick forearm tightened around my waist and pulled me back to him.

"Where do you think you're going, beautiful?"

He nuzzled my hair, and I melted a bit. So maybe our morning wouldn't be so awkward after all. We were both adults; we would part amicably, maybe even trade numbers for later. I almost laughed aloud at the thought. Because he was in the military, he was probably never in one place very long. I would never see the man again after I left this hotel room. I let out a soft sigh. It was really too bad. Come checkout time, my Vegas man would have to stay right here where he belonged. In the meantime, though, he felt too good. I snuggled up to him, shimmying my hips closer to him.

Well, good morning. "Happy to see me?" I wiggled my bottom against his morning erection, and his deep laugh rumbled over the back of my neck.

"I think you already know the answer to that."

"What are you going to do about it?" I gasped as he lightly bit my shoulder, then chuckled, the sexy rumble sending a sensual sensation skittering down my spine.

"I have a couple ideas." His hand left my belly and slid up over my ribs, then cupped my breast. A rough thumb flicked over my nipple, and I shifted my legs restlessly, fighting back the urge to moan in pleasure. He rolled me to my stomach, and I pressed my face into the pillow, letting out a soft cry as his fingers slipped lower, teasing my slick folds.

My legs parted of their own volition as he toyed with my cleft and moved between my legs, his arousal prodding my entrance. I lifted my bottom as his thumb brushed my clit, and before I could speak, he thrust inside with one hard stroke, filling me to the brim.

Lost in the heady sensation, I pushed against him, finding a steady rhythm, grinding my hips against his. His cock stroked in and out, teasing the bundle of nerves with each pass, and the fire burning low in my belly consumed me with its intensity, causing me to cry out. Burying my face in the pillow, I screamed as I came, my muscles contracting around him, triggering his release.

Xander let out a groan as he thrust twice more, pulsing inside me, his weight heavy as he slumped over my back. He trailed kisses over my nape before pulling out of me and tucking me into his side. I lay with my head on his chest, my fingers trailing over his lower abdominal muscles, feeling the hard ridges in the dim light.

He lazily stroked my shoulder with one hand, and the feel of smooth metal caught my attention. I reared back, mouth agape, frozen in shock.

"Is that a wedding band?!"

He looked up at me, his face impassive. "Yes."

"How could you?" I snatched the sheet off the bed and wrapped it around myself.

"Lydia—"

"Don't 'Lydia' me, like I'm the one at fault here!" I clambered from the bed. "I can't believe this. You lied to me. You told me you weren't seeing anyone."

Fury mixed with shame caused tears to burn the backs of my eyes. How could he? And how could I have missed something that obvious? My passion-fueled happiness from the past few minutes melted away, replaced by humiliation. Why? Why were men so shitty? First Shawn, then Xander. He'd seemed so sincere last night, so genuine when I'd told him about Shawn. He'd even denied being attached to anyone when I'd asked. I wanted so badly to believe I was mistaken, but the gold band on his finger made my heart clench.

He opened his mouth to speak, but I had to know. The words spilled from my mouth. "Is it true? You're really married?"

Cerulean eyes staring intently into mine, he nodded. I sucked in a sharp breath, pain exploding in my chest, and my legs turned to jelly. Oh, God. What had I done? I tried to snatch my hand back when he grasped for it, but he was too strong. "Don't you dare touch me! What are you—"

"Lydia."

I jumped at the commanding tone, his intense blue stare pulling me under. His eyes dropped meaningfully, and I followed his gaze to my own left hand. I stared stupidly at the thin gold band that matched his. My heart stuttered, my brain rejecting the idea even as snippets of memory flashed into focus. Were we…? Had we…?

"Lydia… *we* are married."

CHAPTER FOUR
Xander

"Oh, my God. This can't be happening."

I studied her. "You don't remember."

It wasn't a question so much as a statement, but I said it anyway. She hadn't been that drunk, had she?

"Of course not!" Her face twisted into an expression of rage. "I can't believe you talked me into this! I was drunk and you took advantage of me!"

"Oh, no, darlin'. Don't you lay that on me. You were the one saying last night how much you wanted a real man and suggested we get married."

"I most certainly did not!"

I lifted a brow at her. "You did. Multiple times, in fact."

"I would never do that!"

I shook my head. "Really? Then how, exactly, did we end up married if you were so dead set against it?"

Her jaw dropped as she stared at me. "I'm not opposed to marriage as a whole. I would just never marry a stranger." Her eyes narrowed on me. "Clearly you tricked me."

I couldn't hold back the laugh that bubbled up in my throat. Lydia glared down at me, and I swung my legs over the bed, not giving a shit that my junk was on full display. Not like she hadn't seen it—several times. And wasn't that a kick in the nuts? Best sex I'd ever had, and the woman didn't even remember. I shook my head as I pushed to my feet.

Her jaw almost hit the floor as she covered her eyes. "Oh, my

God! What are you doing?"

I batted her hands away. "Little late for that, isn't it?" Grabbing one hand, I dragged her to the table in the corner of the room and picked up a small packet. "You want proof? Here ya go, darlin'."

Her chin notched up as she snatched the folder from my fingers. She extracted the marriage certificate, and a photo fell out and landed faceup on the laminated wood tabletop. I felt more than heard her gasp.

It was a fantastic photo, really. We'd left the hotel bar and walked down the Strip, talking about how we'd stay in contact while I was away, when suddenly Lydia had stopped in the middle of the sidewalk and turned to me, looping her arms around my neck. *Why wait?* she'd asked. She wanted me. And I wanted her. God knew I was attracted to her—our chemistry was so fucking potent I could damn near smell it smoldering between us.

I couldn't explain it, but I felt like I knew her. Not just the tidbits I'd picked up in the short time since we'd met, but really *knew* her. It was crazy to think, and even crazier to say out loud, but I swore I could read her soul. I knew the kind of person she was, the things she wanted out of life. She deserved the best and, while I wasn't the best man for her, I'd spend forever trying to be the one she needed me to be.

So when she'd asked why I wasn't married, I'd told her the truth—that I'd been waiting for a woman like her. I'd been waiting *for her*. After almost three decades on this earth, I'd never met a woman like Lydia, never felt so much for someone I'd just met. But she was different in so many ways. She was kind and sweet and beautiful, sexy and smart and so fucking amazing. She made my heart race, turned my blood so hot, my body so hard I thought I'd explode into a million pieces.

When her smile stretched across those gorgeous lips of hers, her eyes pleading for me to listen, I couldn't say no. Instead, I'd laced my fingers with hers and speed walked to the nearest chapel. Although it wasn't Elvis who married us, it still had Las Vegas flair. The officiant was a burly biker guy with tattooed sleeves running down both arms. The witness was his mother, barely five foot tall with a cotton candy pink beehive tall enough to rival that of Marge Simpson.

In the photo, Lydia had her arms wrapped around my waist in an intimate embrace. Her eyes were on the camera, a dazzling smile on her face. My eyes were on her, an admittedly besotted look on my face, and the photographer had captured the moment forever.

She ran a finger over the photograph before pulling away and retreating into herself.

"I think you should go." She pulled the sheet tighter around herself, refusing to look at me.

"Lydia, let's talk about this."

"Please go."

With a sigh of frustration, I bent to pick up the jeans I'd barely been able to strip off before we'd made love last night—the first time. I pulled them on and shrugged my rumpled shirt over my shoulders, leaving it partially unbuttoned. My wallet and keys lay on the table next to the discarded manila envelope, and I snagged those up, shoving my wallet into my back pocket. Swiping my phone from the nightstand, I turned to her.

"I'm going to go grab us some coffee. I'll be back in twenty minutes. Then we're going to talk."

She nodded absently, her posture rigid, and I let out a soft sigh. I wanted to pull her close, reassure her that everything would be fine, but I knew she wouldn't appreciate the gesture. My touch might push her over the edge, and I didn't want to risk losing her. For now, I'd give her some space, a few minutes to herself, then we could clear the air, fully caffeinated and conscious.

I strode to the door of the hotel room and pulled it open, then took one last look at Lydia before I stepped into the hallway and closed it behind me.

Damn it. I should have waited and done things the right way—should have wined and dined her, won her over the old-fashioned way, let us get to know each other a little better first. But damn it, I didn't have time for that shit. I had to nail her down while I could. But the effects of alcohol combined with Lydia's natural allure meant I hadn't been able to deny her. We had a special connection, something I'd determined within just minutes of meeting her. Despite our unconventional start, I was looking forward to getting to know her better, learning all the things about her that made her tick. I wanted to know about her childhood, all her memories, her hopes and dreams.

Now we were stuck in this boat that was sinking perilously, insecurities flooding in faster than I could bail them out. I grimaced. I was never impetuous like this, had never done anything this crazy. I was a good soldier, always following orders and doing the right thing. So, what the hell had happened last night? I'd completely lost my head, been swept away by a pretty face—a beautiful woman who happened to have no recollection of the events that had taken place.

I liked the idea of having someone to come home to after a mission. Someone to talk with, share my life with. Start a family with. And the more time I'd spent with Lydia last night, the more I began to imagine coming home to her. Seeing her in my house, pregnant with my children. It was crazy, I knew. Who in the hell thought those things as soon as they met someone? But wasn't that precisely why people dated in the first place—to see if someone would be a compatible partner? I'd just accelerated the process a little bit. Okay, maybe a lot.

Stabbing the button to summon the elevator, I shifted on my feet. I'd give her some space, let her clear her mind and come to terms with what had happened last night. Then we could discuss how to proceed from here. I'd be leaving soon on another deployment, anyway. I wanted to see more of her before I was shipped off this time, and I hoped after she'd had some time to think things over that she'd come to the same conclusion.

The ding from the elevator doors opening disrupted my thoughts, and I stepped inside, punching the button to the lobby. Doubt started to creep in. Maybe this was a terrible idea. As much as I'd wanted her last night—still wanted her—would we have enough in common? We'd seemed to get along so well last night. Even when we hadn't agreed on something, it had been more of a friendly debate rather than staunch refusal to see the other's point of view. That was refreshing. I'd dated several women who thought their opinions were the only things worth believing. I liked a woman who knew what she wanted—just not a woman who thought her opinion was the only one that mattered. Talking with Lydia last night, I felt that she genuinely seemed to care about my thoughts and feelings on things.

I shook off the negative thoughts as the elevator doors parted, and I strode across the gleaming, freshly polished floors to the coffee shop in the corner of the lobby. Reaching the counter, I let out a mirthless laugh. This was one of the problems of being impetuous. I had no idea how she took her coffee. Shit. Did she even like coffee, or did she prefer tea?

I scanned the board, debating my options. Finally, I ordered a black coffee, a chai tea, and some frou-frou vanilla-flavored drink, just in case. As the barista whipped up the drinks, I automatically scanned my surroundings. A woman, her long red hair a halo of crazy, frizzy curls drifting around her head, sat at a table in the corner, phone in hand. Her eyes met mine, and I offered a small smile, then continued to rove the room. People bustled back and forth, busy even for eight o'clock on a Sunday morning. But that's Vegas—some people were starting a day of sightseeing and tourist activities. Others were just now spilling back into the hotel after a long night out on the town.

I smiled. The thought of doing something domestic like that appealed to me. I didn't take much time off, and I'd like to take Lydia around a bit, explore the sights. We were only here for our friends' bachelor and bachelorette parties, but Lydia had divulged that she hadn't seen much of the town. I didn't care all that much to see the sights; I just wanted to spend some more time with her before we had to part ways. She hadn't mentioned when she was leaving. Maybe we could spend the day together. Ideas spun through my mind. My imagination must have been running overtime, because the woman stepping off the elevator reminded me of Lydia, right down to a pair of long, slender legs that I'd thoroughly enjoyed having wrapped around my waist last night; she was practically a doppelganger for my new wife.

My brows pulled together as I looked closer. Large sunglasses covered the woman's eyes, and she moved at a fast clip across the lobby, pulling a small suitcase behind her, a powder-blue garment bag hooked over one shoulder. My eyes narrowed, and the words Something Blue jumped off the pale blue fabric. *Son of a bitch!*

Striding across the lobby, I caught up to her on the sidewalk just as she'd stepped outside. I reached out and grabbed her wrist, bringing her to a halt. Lydia jumped and let out a high-pitched squeak. I almost felt bad for scaring her—almost.

"What the hell do you think you're doing?" I growled.

She slapped one hand over her heart. "Oh, my God, Xander! You scared the life out of me!"

I snorted. "Well, it's nice to know you at least remember my name, even as you're trying to run out on me." Anger seeped into my tone, and Lydia's face contorted in aggravation.

"Come on. You and I both know this is best. We did something stupid last night that both of us regret."

My grip on her wrist loosened, and I ran my fingertips up to her elbow, then back down, slipping her palm into mine and lacing our fingers together. "I don't regret it." Or I hadn't anyway, not until I saw how much it bothered her. Did she really want away from me so badly that she'd run off without even saying goodbye?

"Xander…"

I knew I'd have to act fast if I had any chance of keeping her. "Listen. I ordered us some coffee. Let's just go sit down and talk for a while."

She glanced indecisively over her shoulder toward the parking garage, and my voice turned hard. "You at least owe me that. If you want a damn annulment, you can spare ten minutes of your precious time."

I released her arm and turned on my heel, stalking through the lobby to the coffee shop. At my approach, the barista picked up my carryout container with the three drinks and set it on the small side counter. She started to smile as we made eye contact, but she froze when she saw my face. I could only imagine the thunderous expression; I could feel the scowl pulling at my mouth. Quickly averting her gaze, she moved to the back counter and busied herself with one of the machines. I picked up the container and strode to a table tucked into a corner furthest away from the comings and goings of the early morning crowd.

Kicking out a chair, I placed myself with my back to the wall and sat heavily. My eyes stayed glued to the coffee cups in front of me, but I saw her approach. No, that wasn't true. I felt her. As if my body was attuned to her, I knew the second she drew up next to the table. She stood there for a moment before pulling a chair out and sitting primly on the edge of the seat.

I pushed the tray of drinks across the table, angry at her but mostly at myself for being such an idiot. "Coffee, tea, or some girly thing."

One corner of her mouth kicked up in a tiny smile. Her voice was soft when she spoke. "Tea, please."

I rolled my eyes. Tea. Go figure. That was just one of the many things we didn't know about each other, wasn't it?

Lydia plucked the cup labeled Tea from the container and sipped tentatively. I snagged the plain black coffee and set it in front of me, transferring it from hand to hand to keep my body busy. My brain wouldn't stop, and I needed something to do with my hands.

Maybe this had been a fucking stupid idea. She didn't want to be with me, that much was clear. No matter how well we'd gotten on last night, come morning she was already regretting our decision. Hell, she didn't even remember it. And that fact alone made me believe that maybe I'd begun to regret it, too. It'd been rash, but I'd expected her to at least talk to me, not run away.

We sipped our drinks in silence for several moments, and I listened to her breaths moving in and out of her chest. The tension between us continued to grow. What the hell had we been thinking? I almost snorted at the thought. Clearly, we hadn't. We'd been more than half-drunk on alcohol and sexual attraction.

"What's your favorite color?" Her voice cut through my musings, and I lifted a brow at her. Lydia just shrugged.

"Green." Although as I stared into her gray eyes, I began to reconsider. My new favorite color was platinum—bright and untarnished, just like her big, beautiful eyes, surrounded by those thick, dark lashes.

Said lashes swept against her cheeks as she glanced down at her cup. "Mine is red."

Interesting choice. Such a bright, vibrant color for a subdued woman like Lydia. But she'd surprised me on multiple levels last night. With me, she'd been completely uninhibited, free of her mother and dickhead ex. She'd come completely out of her shell when we'd made love, her passion lighting a fire deep inside me. We'd destroyed the bed once we'd stumbled back into her room late last night—or was it early this morning?—then repeated the act when we'd woken. Hell, had that really been less than an hour ago?

I couldn't get enough—being even just a few feet away from her made my blood boil with lust. All I wanted to do was kiss away her reservations, take her back to bed and treasure her for the next several hours until life came calling. And it would, all too soon. Within a week I'd be off on another deployment, she'd be back at work in her bridal salon, and… then what?

"Favorite movie?"

The corners of her mouth tipped up. "*Overboard*."

The irony was not lost on me. She suddenly sobered as our situation bore down on her. She hadn't fallen off a boat and been picked up by a near stranger, but the similarities were there. We'd been thrust together, and now we had two options: fight to make it work or walk away. I wasn't a quitter—never had been, never would be. But I couldn't do it alone; it would take both of us to work this out.

I rolled my shoulders. "What do you want, Lydia?"

Her eyes widened a fraction before dropping back to the table. "Xander, I—"

"Listen. I'm leaving in just a few days." Her gaze snapped back to mine. "Tell me what we're doing. Are we going to make this work, or are you going to walk away?"

"That's hardly fair." Her gray eyes narrowed to slits and her lips thinned. "This is crazy. We live in different cities; we like different things. We don't even know anything about each other. What if we're totally different?"

"What if we're exactly alike? What if we're perfect for each other? Maybe we don't like the same things. Do all couples agree on everything?"

"No, but—"

"What are we going to do, Lydia? I will do my damnedest to make this work if you will. What's it going to be?"

Her grip tightened on the coffee cup, and my gut clenched as I watched her chest rise and fall, her breath unsteady.

"I just… I can't." The words floated out on a whisper, and my heart fell to my toes. I should have known better. Why would a beautiful woman like Lydia want a hardened, battle-scarred soldier like me? I was too hard, too rough, and she was too delicate. Maybe she was right. She was perfection, and I was lethal, deadly. I didn't deserve to breathe the same air as her, let alone have her for myself.

I let out a harsh laugh. "Of course not."

Pushing back my chair, I stood abruptly and strode to the counter to pull a napkin from the holder. I scribbled down an address and stalked back to where Lydia sat. I could feel her eyes on me, but I refused to meet her stare. I dropped the napkin on the table in front of her. "Send the paperwork here."

Without another word, I spun on my heel and left, my long-legged stride carrying me quickly through the lobby and into the bright sunshine outside. I turned to the right and stormed toward the parking garage that housed my rental car, silently berating myself. One thing was for certain: I would never do anything impulsive like this again—never let a woman make me feel like I wasn't good enough, worthy enough.

I didn't slow even when I heard her calling my name, didn't turn around. I didn't know exactly where I was going, but it didn't matter. I could come back for my clothes later. Right now, I just needed to put some distance between us. Because if I saw her again, I wouldn't be able to control myself. I'd beg her to think things over and give me a shot. But I'd already given her a choice, and she'd made her decision. She didn't want me, and I didn't need her.

I rubbed a hand over my heart. Too bad I didn't believe it.

CHAPTER FIVE
Lydia

TWENTY MONTHS LATER

I spread out the cathedral-length lace train and smiled at the effect. It was beautiful. The dress was gorgeous, the veil was stunning, and everything looked perfect—so long as you didn't look at the bride's face.

"It looks like a tail." Caryn Anderson's nose scrunched up in disdain, and I repressed a heavy sigh, just barely refraining from rolling my eyes.

"It's very classy. It will look perfect in St. Mary's as you walk down the aisle. The effect will be very dramatic."

If there was one word in the English dictionary that Caryn was familiar with, it was drama. The woman was full of it. She was full of something else, too, but I kept that thought to myself. Caryn came from money, and lots of it. Her great-great-grandfather had owned several steel mills, and her family had made a fortune over the last couple centuries. As the demand for US steel died away, the family moved into other ventures, including technology. The woman never let me forget that I was "lower" than her, treating me like a servant more than a successful business owner.

I'd been tempted more than once to escort the woman from the shop, but, unfortunately, she had too much influence in the area. One negative word from Caryn Anderson and my shop would fold within a month. And I needed her income now more than ever. With that thought, I squared my shoulders and lifted my chin.

"Of course, we could go with a smaller train, something less... noticeable." I knew the strategic wording of my statement would catch Caryn's attention—and not in a good way. Predictably, the woman's head snapped toward me as I continued. "Lauren—" I let out a small cough as if covering a mistake. "Um, *another bride* had a train this length a few months ago."

Caryn's eyes narrowed. Lauren Weaver-DiDonato was the woman's archrival, and she had just been married three months earlier to the oldest son of the current Italian president. Lauren, unlike Caryn, was the sweetest person I had ever met. Although both women were socialites, Lauren devoted her time to multiple charities and organizations. Caryn devoted her time to, well, Caryn. Although she was the face of a local organization to end hunger, I'd never seen the woman lower herself so much as to walk past one of the food banks. They weren't exactly in a part of town that Caryn frequented. In fact, she was notoriously picky. I'd heard that Caryn sent back meals every time she went out to eat, and local restaurants feared her presence. They, like me and every other small business owner in the area, were forced to play nice or suffer the consequences.

A sneer curled over the woman's face. "My wedding—and my dress—will be better than that tramp's." Caryn flicked the train behind her. "Everyone knows he should have been mine. I won't let her steal my moment."

She studied her reflection in the mirror for a moment. "More. I want it longer. I want the veil longer, too. And more crystals."

Good God. The dress already weighed damn near forty pounds. Caryn, with her usual dramatic flair and less-than-ideal sense of fashion, had demanded the most over-the-top of styles for her dress. The cathedral train extended six feet behind her, and the expensive, delicate lace flared around her feet in a mermaid style before skimming up her body, hugging her curves. The sweetheart neckline clung to her generously enhanced breasts, dripping with hand-sewn Swarovski crystals. Three thousand and eighty-two. I would know—I'd counted every damn one. My assistant Gwen and I had taken turns sewing them on two weeks ago when Caryn had made her latest demand. Now she wanted more? She was going to blind every person in that church when she walked down the aisle.

I attempted to do some damage control. "We could add more, but I think this understated look is perfect, don't you?"

It wasn't understated by a long shot, but classy wasn't exactly in her vocabulary.

Caryn rolled her eyes. "Of course you would. You wouldn't understand what someone like me needs. I'm held to a higher standard, you know. People look to me to set the bar. Everyone loves me."

Everyone loved to hate her, that was for sure. I refrained from rolling my eyes. "What did you have in mind?"

"I just told you. More crystals, as big and as many as you can fit on here. All over the train, too."

My eyes widened. "Well, if you want the train to be longer, I'll need to order more lace. As for the crystals, we'll need to stick to smaller clusters. If we put too much strain on the lace, it'll rip."

Caryn whirled on me, her finger hovering in my face. "You're just lazy and incompetent. You don't want to do any more work. All you've done since I walked through the door is talk down to me and tell me what I can and can't do." She poked her finger at me, her long, manicured nail coming perilously close to my chest. Could I sue her for assault if she stabbed me with one of those damn things? "I'm the bride. I make the decisions here. I want more crystals, and you're going to make it happen."

I clasped my hands together at my waist and clamped down on my anger. "We can do whatever you'd like. I'm just trying to avoid you having to spend your wedding day with a hole in your dress."

Caryn's eyes narrowed, and her lips pressed together firmly before stalking off of the small platform. "Fix this."

"Can I help you take the dress off?"

"You've done enough." The words were a snarl as she slammed the dressing room door behind her. I gritted my teeth and curled my toes inside my shoes, forcing myself to stand still instead of barging into the room behind her and ripping every perfectly dyed blonde hair from her head. I couldn't wait for this wedding to be over. It was still a month away, which was far too long in my opinion. I wondered how the poor groom felt.

With a shake of my head, I made my way to the front of

the shop, straightening gowns as I went. Though we kept many designers' samples, most people came to me for my unique designs. A fiancée of a local baseball player had come to me a couple years ago and, after trying on almost twenty gowns, had looked despairingly at me and said she just wasn't finding the one. Eager to help, I sat down with the young woman and sketched out some ideas. Two months later, the woman got married in my first gown made by hand. The bride sang my praises, and Something Blue was now sought-after for custom gowns.

Brenda, the receptionist, popped her head over the desk. "Is it safe to come out now?"

A grin tugged at the corners of my mouth. "Not quite. She's—" A commotion came from the back of the shop. "—on a rampage again, apparently." I walked quickly toward the back.

"Stupid dressing rooms are too small. Ugh!" Caryn threw the dress on the ground just as I came around the corner. The woman glared at me. "And this fabric is cheap. It ripped right down the back as I was taking it off!"

I locked my hands together in front of me and squeezed tightly, drawing in a deep, calming breath. *Don't kill her. She's not worth it.* I had to reorder more lace anyway to adjust the length of the train, so I would fix that at the same time. I'd just tack the price on to Caryn's ever-growing bill. Thank God the bridesmaids had already purchased and picked up their gowns. The only thing left for them to do was have a few minor alterations done, and they had those scheduled for just a couple weeks prior to the wedding. After this wedding was over, I'd never have to see the supercilious, self-righteous woman again.

Caryn shot me a challenging look, and I pasted on a tight smile, refusing to let her ruffle my feathers. "Just leave it there and we'll take care of it."

Aggravation flashed on the woman's face; she was obviously disappointed that she hadn't been able to get a rise out of me. With a huff, she stomped toward the front of the store, designer handbag swaying at her side. "I'll be in touch. Maybe next time you can get it right," she sneered.

The doorbell jingled a happy little tune as it closed behind her, and I shot a glance at Brenda, who flashed both middle fingers at the woman's retreating form.

"Good riddance."

I laughed. "She's a handful, that's for sure. Can you imagine what the poor groom must feel?"

Brenda shuddered. "She either has him completely whipped or he's just as much an asshole as she is."

I made a small sound of commiseration. "Maybe he'll come to his senses."

"Then what?" Brenda turned to me. "Can you imagine having to deal with that woman a second time around?"

Now it was my turn to shudder. "God, no. I'd talk to the groom myself, convince him to keep her."

Brenda laughed. The sound was drowned out by the jingling of the bell over the front door. A familiar young woman walked into the salon, and my stomach dipped. I'd forgotten that she was coming to pick up her final paycheck today.

Megan had been my employee since the salon opened almost three years ago. She'd been reliable—up until about a week ago. Megan was getting married this summer, and I'd gotten complaints recently that, when working with bridal parties, she talked more about her own wedding than the customer's. Not to mention the money. Megan was my third key—the backup to Brenda and me. We rotated opening and closing the store each day. Unfortunately, the last several times Megan had closed by herself, we'd found money missing from the drawer the following morning. It was never anything major—five dollars here, ten there—but it was the principle of the thing. Megan still denied any involvement, but I'd had to cut her. If nothing else, I had to make an example of her so my other girls would know they couldn't get away with it.

I rounded the desk and greeted her with a polite smile. "Hello, Megan. Let's head back to my office."

I shot Brenda a quick look. "Call if you need me."

Megan sullenly followed me to the back of the salon and preceded me into my small office. I took a seat and gestured for her to do the same. Her paycheck was locked in the top drawer, and I retrieved it, handing it to her. She snatched it from my hands, a nasty sneer on her face.

"I still think this is crap." She stuffed the envelope in her purse and crossed her arms over her chest.

"I'm sorry," I said softly. And I meant it. She'd really been a great addition to our team, and I'd miss having her.

"I didn't take your money," she said adamantly.

I took a deep breath. "Unfortunately, that's not what the computer log says," I stated. "I looked back through the transactions and found that your code was entered to unlock the register each time."

Her shoulders dropped. "That's not possible. I swear I didn't do it!"

I resisted the urge to rub my temples. She'd been singing the same song for a week now, and if I didn't know better, I'd swear she was telling the truth. But numbers didn't lie. Right before she left each night, she'd entered her six-digit code to open the register and count the money—and skim a small portion off the top.

I sighed. "I'm sorry, Megan. I don't know what else to tell you."

"Well, you're blaming me for someone else's mistake." She shoved her chair back and stood. "Whatever. I don't need this job anyway."

I pressed my lips together and held back an eye roll as she stormed from my office. There was a niggling doubt in my stomach that said she was telling the truth, but I just couldn't prove it. Either way, she had to go. I didn't like to fire people—in fact, I'd never had to do it before now. But I was sure it wouldn't be the last time. So, steeling my shoulders, I grabbed my purse, then locked up my office and headed back to the front of the salon.

Brenda slid a wry look my way. "Sounds like that went well."

I lifted one hand. "You know how it goes."

"I do," she said. "I'm sorry."

"It is what it is." I drummed my nails on the counter for a moment. After that little episode, I needed a pick-me-up. "Well, since we don't have any more appointments for the afternoon, I'm going to go see my favorite person. Gwen and I will put in some extra hours later."

"What do you want me to do with the witch's dress?" Brenda called.

I turned around, walking backward toward the front door. "Leave it there for all I care. She wasn't too worried about it!"

Pushing my concerns away, I climbed into my car and headed home. My heart lightened considerably as I unlocked the door and stepped inside. Soft music drifted from the living room at the back of the house, and my feet carried me in that direction.

My eyes landed on the towheaded baby girl seated on the floor, clapping her hands in time to the lullaby playing on the TV. At the sight of me, Alexia clambered awkwardly to her feet.

"Ma-ma-ma!"

A grin split my face. How had I made something so perfect?

I dropped to my knees and scooped my baby girl into my arms. "Hey, baby. Mama missed you."

She gave me a wet, smacking kiss on the lips before planting her chubby hands on my chest and shoving herself away, eager to get down and play some more. It simultaneously made me proud, yet sad. It almost made my heart hurt to see my daughter's fierce independence. It was something she'd so obviously gotten from her father.

I turned my attention to the older woman on the couch. "How was she today, Darlene?"

"An angel, as always."

I chuckled. "I don't believe that for a minute."

At only eleven months, Alexia was stubborn and determined. She'd begun eating solid foods at three months and taken her first steps only days after she'd turned nine months old.

Darlene just winked at me. "Doesn't matter. She could be an absolute terror and I'd still love her like my own."

I smiled at the older woman. Darlene and her husband had come into my life just when I'd needed them most. They lived right next door, occupying the other unit of the duplex I currently rented. Within only a couple months, George and Darlene had become the family I craved.

Over the past year and a half, Darlene and I had become extremely close, though I'd never disclosed the full truth about my relationship with Xander. The older woman knew that Alexia's father was in the military and spent much of his time overseas. I'd never once mentioned that we'd divorced after our very regrettable Vegas wedding and that he knew nothing of his daughter.

Warmth spread around my heart as I watched Darlene pull Alexia close and press a kiss to one chubby cheek. Alexia jerked away as if offended to have had her personal space invaded. She framed Darlene's face in her little hands, then returned the favor with a sloppy, wet kiss of her own. The interaction brought a smile to my face. We weren't perfect, but we had everything we needed. My daughter filled so much of my heart, but there was a tiny little corner that remained empty—and I feared it would feel that way forever.

CHAPTER SIX
Xander

I stared out the small oval window of the airplane, nervous anticipation racking my body as the familiar landscape came into view. Over the loudspeaker, the captain announced our descent, and something inside my chest tightened. It was good to be home. Not that I'd be here long. Just over a week from now I'd be packing up and heading to Dallas to start my new job anyway.

Through a friend I'd learned of Quentin Security Group, a private firm that focused primarily on personal security detail. Just getting off the ground, QSG was open to anything they could get their hands on. An ex-Marine himself, Connor Quentin looked for the brightest and best to bring various skill sets to the team, giving ex-soldiers something to do besides sit behind a desk all day. And the fact that QSG was located in Dallas was an added boon—because *she* was there. The past two years felt like a blur of activity, throwing myself from one mission to the next, but I hadn't stayed quite busy enough to keep my mind from drifting back to a certain brunette.

I knew the likelihood of running into Lydia in a city that size was slim to none, but my heart raced every time I thought about her—with anger, anticipation... lust. I'd had time to reevaluate my life after I left Vegas—and Lydia—behind. She might have been thousands of miles away physically, but she was never far from my mind. There was something about her that called to me, something biological that had been a perfect complement to me. But she hadn't wanted any of it. Or maybe she'd been denying herself.

Still, I couldn't turn off the feeling that she was more than a one-night stand. I'd really connected with her. She was smart and sexy and easy to talk to, and I'd appreciated that more than anything else. For a moment, I allowed my thoughts to drift to her once more, wondering what she was doing right now. I hoped her business was doing well. I knew from the way she'd spoken that she truly loved her job, and, even though part of me was mad at her, I wanted to see her succeed.

She'd be two years older, probably getting ready to settle down. Was she dating someone? Married? My hand clenched into a fist where it rested on my thigh, and my gut twisted into a knot at the thought of her with someone else. Part of me wanted to look her up, to see if we still connected as well as we had that night in Vegas. The other part of me dreaded seeing her. Did I really want to know if she was married to some nine-to-five desk jockey, living in the suburbs with a white picket fence and a baby on the way? Fuck no. Maybe it was time to bury the past and move on.

The plane bounced several times on the runway before coming to a stop, and people slowly began to file off. It seemed to take forever to deplane, my nerves growing increasingly agitated with each moment that passed. I grabbed my beat-up bag from where it was stored overhead then slipped into the flow of passengers headed toward the exit. A familiar face so much like my own stood near the doors of the airport.

I flashed my brother a grin and strode toward him, wrapping him in a tight hug.

"How was the flight?"

I yanked on the strap of the duffel, pulling it higher on my shoulder as I made a face. "Long."

I'd spent the past twenty-six hours either in the air or wandering airports, and now all I wanted was to get home. Somewhere familiar. Abel led the way to his truck, and I tossed my stuff in the back before climbing into the passenger seat. "How's Emily?"

A bright smile lit my brother's face. "Good. About five months along now." Pride had his chest puffing out. "It's a girl."

"That's awesome, man. I'm happy for you. You sure you guys

don't mind me crashing for a couple days?"

"Naw." Abel flipped on his blinker to merge onto the highway. "Em can't wait to see you. We've still got all your stuff packed up in the basement, so all you have to do is call the U-Haul."

"I appreciate it."

Abel and Emily had moved into our parents' home after they'd been killed, and so many mementos of our childhood remained in that house. I knew I'd find my old baseball glove and cleats buried in one of those boxes, and it brought a smile to my face. It was the kind of home I wanted for my family one day.

My smile slipped away as a pair of steel-gray eyes invaded my memory. Trees and telephone poles sped by in a blur as the miles bled away, taking me back to that night in Vegas with the woman I'd never forget. Even the smallest things reminded me of her, and I wondered if that would ever change.

Dust rose behind the truck as Abel churned down the old gravel road to the farmhouse, and I rolled the window down, breathing in the fresh air. There was something so pure, so clean about country air. It wasn't tainted by fumes or thick humidity or the sand that rose into the atmosphere, earth splintered apart by land mines.

Thank God that part of my life was over. I was honored to serve my country, but now I was ready for the next phase of my life—settling down, starting a family. I looked back on my mistake with Lydia with a sense of resigned bitterness. I'd have probably made her a shitty husband anyway. She would've been stuck home alone while I was halfway across the world, going to sleep every night wondering if I was safe—alive.

She'd reached out to me a couple times—short, succinct emails asking to talk. I'd almost given in. But it would've been pointless. I wasn't good enough for her then and I sure as hell wouldn't be now. Besides, I'd seen this before; it was nothing more than a case of misplaced guilt. Women felt bad for breaking things off right before their husband or boyfriend was headed right back into the heart of danger, and they'd beg for reconciliation without really meaning it. I had no desire for Lydia's sympathy. As she'd requested, I'd signed the damn annulment papers and done my best to push her from my mind. It was better for both of us this way not to drag it out.

I'd seen too many failed marriages between my friends and their wives and girlfriends back home. No, when I married, I would do it right. I'd take my time, make sure that we were compatible on all levels, that we were on the same page and wanted the same things out of life. I would be there for my wife and kids, be home for dinner every night. I didn't want to miss birthdays and anniversaries and watching my baby's first steps. I just needed to make sure I didn't make the same mistake as I had two years ago. I'd let a pretty face and intense chemistry sway my emotions.

I was looking forward to settling down, but I could still feel the barb in my heart from Lydia's rejection. Sometimes I resented her for turning me away. Part of me prayed she wouldn't sign the papers; despite her insistence that we annul the marriage right away, it'd taken damn near a year for her to file. I deserved someone who was willing to meet me in the middle, but Lydia hadn't even been willing to try.

But... then why reach out to me? It was a question that had nagged me over the past couple years and, if I was really honest, it was quite possibly a huge reason I hadn't allowed myself to move on just yet. Deep inside there was still a small sliver of hope that maybe—just maybe—she regretted walking away from me. Unfortunately, I had a feeling it was too late for all that. Why would she wait for me when I'd been too much of a pussy to even respond to her?

I could've emailed back, but what would I have said? That I still loved her? She'd have laughed in my face—metaphorically speaking. Had I ever actually loved her? Maybe not. But she was the type of woman I could have come to love. Or was it a fleeting moment of passion that had ended too soon? We hadn't parted on the best of terms, but what exactly did she expect from me? Did she want an apology, an affirmation that what we'd done was wrong? Because I wasn't completely sure it was. For that brief moment in time, I'd been happy. She was different, special, and she made me feel like no other woman ever had. What I wouldn't give to go back in time to do things over, do things the right way.

When I got to Dallas, I'd look her up... eventually. I didn't exactly relish the idea of seeing her with another man, but I had a feeling it was the only thing that would give me the kick in the ass I needed to let go once and for all. It sounded stupid to my mind, but my heart needed the closure. I needed to see for myself that she'd moved on so I could do the same.

It may have been the best sex of my life, but it wasn't enough to make a marriage. Lydia's molten gaze tormented me, the memory of that night still fresh in my mind. The thought of her made me hard, and I willed the arousal away as Abel pulled the truck up alongside the barn. Goddammit. I needed to scrub the memory of her from my brain. How was it possible that a woman I'd been with once could still tempt me more than I thought possible?

A couple of dogs bounded over as I pushed open the door, and I bent to pat one on the head. The screen door slammed, and I glanced over to the house where Emily stood on the front porch, drying her hands on a dishtowel. She caught my gaze and waved, a huge smile on her face. I grabbed my things out of the back, then followed Abel up to the house. I watched as my brother and Emily exchanged a heated glance, one of his hands going to her softly rounded stomach as he dropped a kiss on her upturned mouth.

Jealousy swirled in my heart, curdling deep in my stomach. I wasn't envious of my brother—not exactly. I desperately wanted what Abel had—a beautiful wife, a baby on the way. A home. Emily and Abel had eyes only for each other, and I felt like an asshole for breaking the moment.

"Hey, Em."

A vibrant smile lit her face as she opened her arms for a hug. "Hey, yourself. You home for good?"

I pulled her into an awkward embrace, careful not to put any pressure on her swollen stomach. "For a bit. Got a job lined up in Dallas."

She stepped back, and Abel held the door for us. "Come on in and tell us all about it."

I dropped my things in the spare bedroom, then meandered back down to the kitchen. Fifteen years later, it still looked the same as it always had, with its sturdy oak cabinets and faded, peeling wallpaper. I knew Abel's job at the mill paid okay, but I wondered if I should offer some money. Almost immediately, I dismissed the idea. A man's pride was a fickle thing, I thought with a grim smile. Whether it pertained to women or wallpaper, no man wanted to be wrong.

A stack of mail lay on the corner of the table, and Abel tipped his chin toward it. "That came for you. Figured I'd keep it here rather than forward it on. God knows it woulda just ended up back here anyway."

"No doubt." As often as I'd been moved around, it took the mail awhile to catch up to me sometimes. Picking up the dozen envelopes, I flicked through them until a familiar name caught my eyes. Walker & Raines. And just like that, any hope I'd harbored for getting back together with Lydia sputtered out, leaving my heart feeling empty and cold. My thumb traced the return address of the envelope from the attorney. It was over. Here in my hands, I held the proof that she'd never wanted me after all.

A myriad of emotions welled within me: anger, humiliation, rejection. But one reigned supreme—disappointment. Damn. I wished… I wished a lot of things. But none of it mattered now. I was holding the paperwork that separated me from Lydia, severing any last tie I may have had to her. It was over. I tossed down the unopened envelope. I didn't need to read what was inside. Maybe one day… but not yet.

Pasting on a smile and steeling my spine, I flicked a glance at Abel, whose intense eyes were focused on me. My brother never missed a thing, and I'd surely have to explain later. But now wasn't the time. I slid into my seat—funny how I still thought of it as "my" seat after all these years—and turned my attention to my brother and sister-in-law.

We chatted amiably over dinner, and I finally retired to my room as the sun began to set. After being awake for damn near three days, I was ready to crash out for the foreseeable future. I showered and fell into bed, asleep minutes after my head hit the pillow, gray eyes filling my dreams.

CHAPTER SEVEN
Lydia

The front door slammed, and I jumped at the resounding bang. I clenched my eyes closed and ground my back teeth together, instantly regretting ever giving my mother a key to my place. The tap-tap-tap of expensive heels drew closer to the living room, and I pasted on a smile. I pushed to my feet just as my mother breezed into the room, looking elegant as ever.

"Hi, darling." Jolene Lowell-Dawson-Carrick-Ronstadt graced me with her signature aloof smile.

"Hello, Jolene."

I couldn't remember a single time when she hasn't been Jolene to me. Never mother, definitely not mom or mama. Just... Jolene. She brought to mind the old Dolly Parton song—beautiful Jolene, who always got what she wanted, whenever she wanted it. I loved my mother, I really did, but Jolene was a force to be reckoned with. She operated under the policy that everything was her way or the highway. The only things that mattered to her were image and money—and lots of it. She'd cultivated both over the past several decades, moving up the ranks from husband to husband.

For a brief period of time when she was younger, Jolene had been a nurse. It was at the hospital where she'd worked that she met my father, Lyle Dawson, an esteemed surgeon. Their marriage had fallen apart when I was only six, and Jolene had immediately moved on to investment banker David Carrick. She'd put in a whole twelve years with him before things began to decline. I had a feeling she'd met someone else, but I never said as much. When I was twenty, Jolene married Roy Ronstadt, the lawyer who'd presided over her divorce from husband number two. That had lasted barely two years, bringing the grand total up to three marriages.

For the past year and a half she'd been dating someone new—a man whose name I couldn't remember—and I assumed wedding bells wouldn't be far away. As soon as the thought crossed my mind, I cringed. My mother wasn't a bad person, exactly. She just... wasn't good at being alone. Ironically, she wasn't good at relationships either—not with any of her husbands, and not with her only child. Personally, I thought she needed the security of money and social status more than she needed someone who cared about her.

Jolene was always far more interested in herself than anyone else, and I thought a huge part of her regretted having me. Hence me calling her Jolene—she never wanted to acknowledge that she was actually old enough to be a mother. She'd resisted any real involvement in my life, instead hiring a nanny to look after me during my early years. It had been a point of contention between my father and her, and it was a huge part of why he'd left her. Not that he'd had time for me, either. My father spent every waking moment of my youth trying to establish his practice, and he had little time for a child or wife. But we rounded out the image he desired, and my mother reaped the benefits while she could.

Unfortunately, the fighting over my mother spending money unnecessarily still rang in my ears to this day. Why would my mother hire someone to look after me when she herself didn't work? She'd quit nursing the moment they'd tied the knot. After having me, she'd pawned me off on a caretaker, gotten back into shape and, consequently, the dating pool.

Jolene was all about image. She was a beautiful woman, and she knew it. But that didn't stop her from seeking constant reinforcement from anyone and everyone who would give it to her. She was a shameless flirt, but her husbands had allowed it because she made the ideal trophy wife. She looked pretty on their arms and, after cultivating relationships with the upper crust for years, she had plenty of connections.

I couldn't remember the last time I'd spoken with my father. Last I'd heard, he was also on wife number three, who was just a year older than me, and they were having the time of their lives traveling Europe. Both of my parents were self-absorbed serial daters, concerned with only themselves. Was it really any wonder I was so jaded?

Yeah, I sold women the gowns of their dreams, but I didn't really envision that for myself. I'd had a good dose of the realities of marriage. Maybe I just wasn't cut out to settle down and marry and be happy. I hadn't exactly had the best role models. If I ever did marry again, for real this time—and that was a big if—then it would be only for love. I couldn't stand the thought of jumping from partner to partner in search of the biggest bank account. Alexia was the only bright spot in my life, despite the grief Jolene had given me when she'd found out about my botched Vegas wedding and fatherless child.

In the heat of the moment, I hadn't fully considered the ramifications of having unprotected sex, something I'd always been incredibly diligent about. I'd scheduled a test once I'd arrived home to make sure I hadn't contracted anything, but it had come with a huge surprise. My hormones must have still been in flux, because it was evident I was pregnant just a few weeks after I returned home from Vegas. I'd stopped taking birth control when Shawn and I became engaged, then resumed as soon as we'd split. Regardless of Jolene's feelings on the subject, I couldn't bring myself to regret getting pregnant. I loved that little girl with all my heart.

I waited a beat, irritation pulling at me. Figured that my mother would show up now, just before bedtime. It was her MO, after all. She'd stay for ten minutes, just long enough to take a handful of pictures of Alexia, deliver some passive aggressive insults my way, then escape. God forbid should she actually spend some quality time with her granddaughter, I thought bitterly.

I bit my tongue, trying desperately to tamp down my incredibly uncharitable thoughts, and pasted on a smile. "What brings you here, Jolene?"

Jolene waved airily. "I hadn't talked to you for a while. I just wanted to see how you were doing."

A tight smile lifted the corners of my lips. "We're fine. Just getting ready for bed in a minute."

"I figured. I just wanted to bring a few things by for Alexia." She turned to the little girl, her voice several octaves higher. "Look what Mimi brought."

Only by the strictest measure of control did I manage to not roll my eyes at the ridiculous nickname. At least she hadn't insisted on being called Aunt Jolene. She opened the large bag slung over her forearm and produced several toys and frilly dresses.

"She's not even one, Jolene. She doesn't need all that stuff."

"Come now," my mother chided as she held a ruffled pink dress up to Alexia's tiny body. "I like to spoil her."

I refrained from saying anything, because refuting the statement would be pointless. Jolene only knew how to buy happiness and love. It was a shame, really, that my mother was too blind to see what was right in front of her. Children didn't need to be bought. They offered love and affection unconditionally. But I knew better. After fifty years on this earth, my mother wasn't likely to change anytime soon—or ever.

I shook off my irritation and tried to swallow my bad attitude. I hated feeling indebted to anyone, even if it was just my mother—especially if it was my mother. Because Jolene never did anything out of the goodness of her heart. No, there had to be an ulterior motive. I just needed to find out what it was. "How have you been, *Mother*?"

Her eyes flashed with irritation. "Wonderful. How's your little shop?"

Whether she meant it or not, I heard the thread of condescension in my mother's voice, and it set my teeth on edge. Nothing was ever good enough for Jolene. It was the exact same reason she'd tried to pawn me off on Shawn several years ago. He'd been exceptionally good-looking, not to mention the fact that he was now partner at a prestigious law firm.

I was proud of what I'd accomplished all by myself, regardless of the fact that my mother constantly made her wishes known that I should hand the reins over to someone else. It baffled me sometimes, my mother's attitude toward the workforce. She herself had been a nurse—but that had only been a means to an end.

Jolene should really have never reproduced. She wasn't maternal in the least, and I sometimes wondered how I'd managed to turn out as normal as I had. Not that I was catch of the year—far from it. But I at least wanted more… attainable things out of life. I wanted to be happy and healthy. If I made a little money along the way, great. My bridal salon would never bring in millions of dollars, but it made me happy to help women find the dress of their dreams, and that was enough for me.

Jolene still scorned the situation and offered her opinions freely. I, for the most part, gritted my teeth and bore it. I wanted Alexia to know her only close relative, and I couldn't bring myself to turn my mother away. If Jolene had her way, I would be married off already to give the impression of a happy little family, regardless of my feelings on the matter. To my mother, everything was for show. She had to have the best clothes, drive the nicest cars, and she had to project the image of the perfect family—even if what lay beneath the surface was more than murky.

I never questioned it, but I knew my father—and stepfathers—probably hadn't been faithful to Jolene. She was a difficult person to get along with, critical and overbearing, and I could understand from their perspectives why the marriages hadn't lasted. But Jolene seemed to get whatever she wanted for whatever amount of time they were married, and I assumed she didn't ask too many questions. As long as she was given the lifestyle she desired, it didn't matter what—or who—they did in their free time, so long as it was done discreetly.

I wanted more for myself. Being a single mother had never been on the agenda. It was far from a perfect situation, but seeing my little girl every day, holding that bundle of perfection in my arms, made my worries disappear. I was confident everything would work out the way it was meant to. I just needed to be patient.

"Business is doing well. In fact, we secured a pretty high-end client a few weeks ago." Knowing that it would raise Jolene's esteem, I let it hang in the air for a moment until my mother's head swiveled toward me. "You've heard of Caryn Andersen?"

Her mother's eyes lit up. "Really?"

I nodded, a smile cracking my face. It would give my mother

something to gossip about over seventeen-dollar salads with her friends at the country club next week.

"Well, that's very impressive." My mother paused, and unease settled in my gut. Somehow, I predicted the words before they even left her lips. "You know, you should really consider getting married."

I opened my mouth to respond, but Jolene cut me off. "Being a single mother is hard work. I did it for years."

I bit the inside of my lip and just barely managed to refrain from voicing that Jolene had endured motherhood with more help than most people had, even between marriages. And by most people, I meant everyone. I'd had a nanny until I was out of middle school, and after that I'd spent so much time between ballet and junior league charity events that I'd never had a moment to myself. It wasn't like Jolene had really been overwhelmed by the whole parenting thing. It was the same reason she refused to be called anything as crass as "grandma." The best part of having a grandchild, in her eyes, was being able to brag to all of her friends about how cute Alexia was, how precocious, how smart.

My mother's fakeness irked me to no end, but I'd learned over the past twenty-six years to just ignore it. Sometimes it was just easier to let my mother say her piece and move on. She would head out soon, leaving us in peace for another week or two before she descended again like a virus one couldn't quite fight off. All I had to do was get through the next few minutes without killing her.

I turned to my mother. "I don't think I'm ready for that just yet."

Jolene rolled her eyes. "It never should have happened in the first place, but I think you're looking at this the wrong way. Wouldn't it be so much easier? You could spend your days with Alexia, hire a few more people to help out in the salon."

I shook my head. "I can afford to hire someone else if I wanted to. I like being involved. I enjoy what I do."

Jolene's lips turned down for a moment as if gathering ammunition for her parting shot. "Well, if nothing else, think of Alexia. It would be good for her to have a father figure in her life." She studied Alexia for a moment. "She didn't get a single drop of your genes."

I gritted my teeth. "She's perfect."

"Of course, of course," Jolene soothed. "It's just a shame she doesn't look anything like you."

It was true, of course. Alexia was her father's daughter through and through. The only thing she'd inherited from me was her steely gray eyes. She had Xander's flaxen locks, so pale they were almost white. She had an innate ability to sense distress or change of emotions, and I felt a stab in my heart.

I drew a deep breath. "If anyone ever asks, I just tell them she looks like her father."

Most everyone knew he was a military man, but few knew the whole story. As far as anyone knew, we'd married after a brief affair—understatement of the year—and he was serving overseas. I wouldn't trade Alexia for the world, but I couldn't help but wish the circumstances had been different.

"Do you remember Roy's partner, Albert?" Jolene suddenly spoke up.

My eyebrows drew together. "I think so. I know the name."

"Well, he has a son about your age."

Oh, God. Now I knew where this was going. Before I could even open my mouth to protest, Jolene kept going.

"He asked about you, was hoping to take you on a date."

"Oh, I don't think—"

"It's perfectly fine." Jolene waved her concern away. "He knows all about Alexia, of course. I took the liberty of accepting for you."

"What?"

Jolene speared me with a withering look. "It's one date, Lydia. I'm sure you can pry yourself away from your precious business for a few hours."

I ground my teeth as she rolled her eyes, my ire with her growing. "Most everyone believes I'm still married."

"Oh, I took care of that."

I froze. "What does that mean?"

Jolene lifted a shoulder. "I told him you were a widow."

"What?! Oh, my God. You can't lie to someone like that!"

"It's better than the truth," my mother shot back. I dropped my gaze, tears gathering in my eyes. Once more, I felt like the little girl I'd been all those years ago, never quite good enough. My mother pressed her lips into a firm line and stared me down. "It's really the least you can do."

Of course. She never hesitated to throw that in my face, did she? It seemed I had a lifetime of favors to make up for. I never should have asked my mother for help when I'd opened the salon; it was like making a deal with the devil. "Fine. I'll be there."

"Anyway." Jolene patted Alexia on the head and stood, brushing her skirt into place. "Reservations are for seven o'clock this Saturday." She breezed out just as quickly as she came in, leaving a wake of distress behind her as usual. I heaved a sigh.

"Come on, missy." I scooped Alexia into my arms. "Bedtime."

Despite my attempt to push my mother's words from my mind, I couldn't quite dispel the nagging inadequacy. I'd tried to contact Xander to let him know, but he'd washed his hands of me—of us—a year ago. I didn't ever want to put myself—and especially not Alexia—through that again. I'd go on this date, certain nothing would come of it. It'd been a long time since I'd been with a man. Twenty months, in fact. I missed the intimacy, missed the calming contact. Most of all, I missed being a desirable woman. If nothing else, this date would give that back to me for just a few brief moments until I had to return to reality—and loneliness.

CHAPTER EIGHT
Xander

I broke down the cardboard box and set it beside the back door to put out with the recyclables, then swiped the back of my wrist across my forehead. Damn, I hated moving. I should be used to it by now, but it never seemed to get easier. I'd learned after the first two or three times to keep only what I needed, so I'd downsized considerably over the past ten years. Still, I'd brought all my childhood mementos that Abel and Emily had packed away. I'd have to go through that stuff at some point, but for now I shoved the boxes in the spare bedroom.

"Where you want this stuff?"

Clay brought in the last box, and I gestured to the counter. "Anywhere over there is fine."

He slid the box across the cheap tan Formica, then leaned a hip against the counter and rubbed the back of his forearm along his sweaty forehead.

It was hot as fuck outside, and the air-conditioning of the small apartment was welcome. I reached into the fridge and snagged two bottles of beer. Clay tipped his head in gratitude as I passed one to him. "Thanks for your help today, man."

I glanced around the tiny two-bedroom sublet. I'd been lucky enough to find one already furnished, so I'd only had to bring my things. Still, it'd been easier with Clay's help. He was another member of QSG, an ex-marine who I'd met on a mission back in Kabul. It was the same time I'd met Con. The different branches of military all intermingled, each focused on their part of the mission, but we'd become fast friends—or as close to friends as any military man could have. We'd bonded during some downtime over a game of poker and *The Walking Dead*.

Clay Thompson himself had just been discharged and had only been with QSG for about two weeks now. He seemed to be enjoying it so far, which was a good omen for me. Like every other soldier who'd spent several tours overseas, I was worried about returning to civilian life. People didn't understand how fucking different it was. Every time I came home, it was like culture shock; I didn't know where I fit in or how to act. I was hoping that this gig with QSG worked out. Almost every member was ex-military, though I knew from what Clay had said that there was an ex-FBI agent there as well. I assumed that had been strategic on Con's part.

Over the course of the morning, Clay had caught me up on some of the jobs the other guys were working. Though I wasn't technically scheduled to start for another week, I was ready to hit the ground running. I glanced at the clock. Just after six. Motion from the corner of my eye caught my attention, and I turned back to Clay. He pulled a small stack of mail from his back pocket and tossed it on the table. "Grabbed those off the seat of your truck."

"Cool. Thanks, man." I'd been studiously avoiding that particular stack of mail for a week, and I wasn't any closer to addressing it now. I cleared my throat. "Plans for tonight?"

A grimace broke over his face. "Nothing good."

I lifted an eyebrow. Clay always had a woman lined up. Saturday night and he had no plans? I wasn't buying it. More likely, he just didn't want to share. "Wanna grab a beer?"

Clay shook his head. "Nah. I'm headed over to the Hilton to do some grunt work."

"What the hell's going on there?"

He rolled his eyes. "Cheating husband. I have the pleasure of getting proof of his infidelity for his wife so she can screw him in the divorce."

I winced. "Good for her, I guess."

Swallowing the last of the beer, Clay glanced over at me. "Sure you're good here?"

"Yeah." I walked him to the door. "See ya next Monday."

Clay gave a mock salute before jogging down the steps, and I shut the door with a sigh. What the fuck was I going to do for the next day and a half? I could wander the city a little, but the idea held little appeal. My gaze fell to the envelopes sitting at the edge of the counter, taunting me, Lydia's pretty face flashing in my mind's eye, turning my stomach to knots.

As I did every time I began to feel anxious, I pulled the deck of cards from my back pocket. I'd picked them up in Vegas the day I'd met Lydia. They'd been used at a table in the Bellagio, and they were punched through the middle with a round circle. It was the very same deck I'd used when I first met Con and the guys, and they stayed on my person at all times. I shook them out of the box like a smoker with a pack-a-day habit and began to shuffle. The familiar motion helped to soothe my nerves.

A harsh breath escaped my lungs, and I shoved the cards back into the carton then tucked it away in my pocket. Snagging another beer from the fridge, I snatched up the stack of mail and headed to the living room. No time like the present. If I was going to have to rehash my depressing past, I may as well be drunk for it. Maybe it would dull the pain of regret and failure that had followed me for the past year and a half.

I chugged the remainder of the beer and cracked the top off a new one, tossing the cap on the coffee table. Sinking into the soft cushion of the couch, I settled the beer between my thighs and flicked through the envelopes, trying to stall as long as possible. With a sinking sensation in my gut, I finally ripped open the remaining letter. It was fairly hefty, and the pages curled from being folded in half. I slipped them from the large mailing envelope and skimmed the front page. My entire body stilled, my mind halting as I tried to process the words on the page.

Hands shaking, I flipped several pages to the tabbed documents, and my heart thudded to a stop, the papers fluttering to my lap.

Holy shit.

How was this possible? This had been taken care of nearly a year ago... hadn't it?

Unable to comprehend the words, I reread the missive twice more. I ran my fingers over the hard creases as I folded it and slipped the papers back into the envelope. Tapping it against my palm, I debated what to do. It seemed Lydia Dawson-McLean and I had some unfinished business. Because, apparently, according to the paper in my hands… we were still married.

CHAPTER NINE
Lydia

I drummed my nails on the counter, my mouth set in a straight line. "I feel terrible leaving you guys here alone."

Despite the fact that it was already four o'clock and the salon would close in an hour, I was desperately trying to put off going home to get ready for my date tonight.

"Please." Brenda waved a hand. "You just don't want to go."

No kidding. I rolled my eyes. "*Of course* I don't want to go. My mother set this up; it's inevitably going to go badly."

The ladies knew of my tense relationship with my mother, and they were always more than supportive of me. At least—they were usually. This time, however, it seemed as though Gwen and Brenda had teamed up against me. "Why do you want me to go on this date so badly?"

"You deserve it," Brenda said, leaning her elbows on the counter. "It's been..."

She trailed off, and I stiffened. I knew exactly how long it'd been. I let out a sigh. "I know, but—"

"Come on," Gwen cut in. "It's just dinner. How bad could it be?" I shot her a withering glare, and Gwen's mouth tipped up in a rare smile. "Okay, so it is a blind date your mom set up...." She laughed when I cringed. "But you'll never know unless you try. Right?"

I pinned her with a stare. "If it's a disaster, I'm firing you," I joked.

"Whatever." She laughed again. "You wouldn't get rid of me."

And wasn't that the truth? She was far too invaluable for me to toss her out.

"Fine." I tipped my nose up in mock disdain. "Then I'll hijack your Tinder profile."

She cracked a smile. "I don't think my boyfriend would like that."

Her statement took me by surprise. In the time that I had known her, I didn't think I'd ever heard her once talk about having a boyfriend or going on a date. She was quiet and reserved, but she was a hard worker, a trait that I most admired in her. "I had no idea you were seeing anyone."

She gave a jerky nod, her eyes dropping self-consciously to the floor as a fierce blush stole over her cheeks. "About eight months."

It was so hard to interpret Gwen. She was barely a year younger than me, but she seemed so naïve, almost sheltered sometimes. About a year and a half ago, she'd come into the shop asking about employment. With her quiet demeanor, I knew she wasn't cut out to be a saleswoman. When I asked if she had any sewing experience, she'd sadly shook her head and said no. There was something about her that pulled at my heartstrings, and I felt compelled to give her a chance.

Although she was self-taught under only my direction, she'd come a long way in her short time here. She started with small jobs, repairing rips and tears and loose beads on the stock gowns. As her confidence and skills grew, she began to help with custom gowns. It was infinitely easier with her help and since then, we'd designed nearly two dozen for various brides. With my designs and Gwen's attention to detail, everyone loved us. They flocked to us to make their dream gown, and Gwen and I made a great team.

To hear that she was seeing someone was a surprise, but she seemed to hold her cards close to the vest. She was almost painfully shy sometimes, and I wanted to ask a million questions about the guy who'd apparently won her heart. The last thing I wanted to do was embarrass her though, so I clamped down on them and veered back onto the topic at hand. "Really, I can cancel, it's no big deal."

Brenda propped her hands on her hips. "Don't you dare stand

that poor man up."

I rolled my eyes. I was sure, if he kept company like my mother, then he was far from a "poor man." Still, I let the comment slide. "Fine." I held my hands up in surrender. "I'm going."

Brenda clapped her hands like a schoolgirl, and Gwen offered me a smile. "I'm sure you'll have fun."

I wasn't so sure, but I didn't have much choice. They were right—I couldn't back out now. "Maybe," I conceded. Maybe this wouldn't be so bad. As Gwen said, it was only dinner. But something about this whole situation just felt… off. I couldn't explain it, but the nervous butterflies in my stomach had kicked into a flurried frenzy. I took a deep breath and placed my hand over my middle to calm them. Dating sucked. Besides, I didn't need a man to make me happy. My attention was better spent on my daughter. I hadn't gone on a single date since Alexia was born, and my last date—if you even wanted to call it that—had been with her father. And look how that had turned out.

Shaking off the thought, I lifted my chin and steeled my spine. "I promise, I'll try to relax and enjoy myself."

A soft smile curved Brenda's face. "You deserve it, dear. You work so hard, and you're such a good mom. But you deserve to have some time for yourself, too."

I looked around at my employees—and friends. They were closer to me than my own family, and I appreciated them more than I would ever be able to tell them. I knew what they said was in my best interest, and despite the tingle of unease in my heart, I knew it was the right thing to do.

"You're right." I smiled at the two of them. "Thank you."

Pushing away from the counter, I gave a little wave. "I'll see you on Monday."

I headed out in the afternoon, my thoughts clouded and murky as I drove home. I generally tried to avoid talking about my marriage if at all possible, but I'd told friends and family members that Xander and I had eloped during a trip to Vegas. The romanticism seemed to appease people without giving away too many details.

Whenever someone asked, I told them that Alexia's father had been a soldier in the Army. And it wasn't a complete lie. He *had* been in the Army—at least when I knew him. I didn't know if he had been discharged since, but the night we shared together, he told me he had to complete one more tour. I didn't know much about the military, but I assumed that was usually a year or two, depending on the situation. I'd told my mother the truth out of necessity when I'd broken the news that I was pregnant. After I'd finally filed the paperwork for the annulment, I'd told Brenda and Gwen, needing to vent and get it off my chest. It made me feel like a failure that Alexia might never know her real father. Now, nearly two years later, part of me wondered what might have happened between Xander and me.

For those first few months, I scoured the newspaper and internet for information on what was happening overseas. Even though things hadn't worked out between us, I still prayed every day that he was safe. There were times when I regretted walking away from him. The last two years had been incredibly difficult, and on the nights I cried myself to sleep, I wished he was there to hold me. It was crazy and stupid and more than a little selfish of me. I'd been the one to push him away, but part of me was still mad at him for not responding to any of my pleas.

He'd never returned any of the emails, and I couldn't help but wonder if he'd given me false information so he wouldn't have to see or hear from me again. I knew the address that he gave me was correct at least, because he'd signed the papers. But when I checked the White Pages, the phone number was listed under Abel and Emily McLean. The knowledge was like a knife to the heart. I had absolutely no way to contact him.

The packet from our lawyer was in my bedroom at home, tucked away in my underwear drawer. I'd cried myself to sleep the day I received it two months ago, so much so that I hadn't been able to bring myself to open it. I'd just stashed it away like the dirty little secret it was. I knew it was my fault, but it seemed like one more failure to add to a lifetime of mistakes.

I knew I worked too much, trying to grow the business so that Alexia and I could have a comfortable life together. It was a hard balance, and I regretted not being able to spend as much time with her as I should. I hated to see my little girl grow up without a father. Maybe it was time to do right by her and give her a father figure to look up to. I needed to set aside my own insecurities and focus on what was best for Alexia

CHAPTER TEN
Xander

I glanced up at the small shop front on Belleview Avenue. It was cute in a quaint sort of way. Not that I knew shit about bridal salons, but it was blue—just like the name—and it looked homey. In fact, it looked very much like an old house. Situated only a block down from the park, I had a feeling most of these businesses had been homes decades ago before commerce came in and swallowed them up.

Mounting the wide concrete steps two at a time, I threw the door open. The bell above the door jangled crazily, and several sets of eyes turned in my direction. I closed the door much more softly than I'd entered the place so the women wouldn't think I was a complete madman.

Glancing around, I made for the first saleswoman I saw. Dressed in a suit, she appraised me carefully. "Can I help you?"

"I'm looking for Lydia..." I paused, and the girl tipped her head in silent question. "Um, yeah," I finished lamely.

Did she still go by her maiden name, or did she use her married name? It was something I probably should have figured out before now. But that letter I'd opened an hour ago had propelled me from the chair without a second thought. I still couldn't fucking believe it. According to the letter dated just a couple months ago, we hadn't signed the necessary papers. I'd forgotten a signature on one, while she'd missed signing another. Evidently the documents had then been misplaced internally by a new paralegal, and the lawyer apologized for the delay, saying that he'd returned one copy to me to sign while the other had been sent to Lydia. It was almost completely unheard of, and I marveled once again at the coincidence.

I'd thought of her constantly while overseas. Maybe this had happened for a reason. What were the odds that—despite demanding an annulment—she'd missed signing the document? I didn't know what my excuse was. In all honestly, I thought it'd been taken care of. I was sure I'd checked and double-checked, but maybe a small part of me had hoped something like this would happen. I couldn't be sure. All I knew was that Lydia and I were still married. And I needed to know how she felt about that. Had she chosen not to sign? The thought made my heart flip over in my chest.

The salesgirl rolled her lips together in thought. "I believe she left for the day. You can check with Brenda to be certain." She lifted a hand and gestured toward a counter along the opposite wall. "The woman in blue."

"Thank you." I tipped my chin at her and made a beeline across the room. I shifted impatiently as the two women in front of me paid for their purchases, gossiping all the while. Finally, they left in a flurry of colorful fabric, and I stepped forward. Before I could speak, however, a petite young woman with short brown hair rounded the desk. She passed a dress to Brenda. "When you get a chance, can you please see if we can still get this in periwinkle?"

"Of course. I'll let you know in just a moment."

The young woman turned and caught my gaze, freezing like a deer in headlights. My collar suddenly felt a little too tight. I was as out of place in here as a bull in a china shop, and I was ready to find Lydia and get the hell out of here.

The older woman—Brenda—smiled at me in welcome. "What can I do for you, sir?"

"I'm looking for Lydia."

Her brows drew together as she peered over the counter at me. "I'm sorry, she's not available at the moment."

"Is she at home?" I still had her address somewhere, but I thought for sure she would still be at work.

"I can't say."

More like she refused to. Agitation pulled at me. "Where the hell is she?"

The petite woman's eyes grew wide, and her hand fluttered to her throat. Brenda darted a look at her before returning her gaze to me. "If you'd like to speak with her, you're more than welcome to come back on Monday when she returns."

Her tone told me I was welcome to take a flying leap off a bridge, too, but there was no fucking way I was waiting all goddamn weekend to find her. I leaned forward and leveled her with my most imploring stare. "I need to speak with her right away."

She sniffed, not at all affected by my plea. "Is this an emergency?"

She had no idea. I snorted. "You could call it that."

She lifted an eyebrow. "I can pass along a message if you'd like." She picked up a pen, the tip hovering over the pad in front of her. "What's your name?"

"I," I bit out, "am her husband."

Her mouth formed an 'O', but no words came out. For a single second, I felt a stab of vindication. Refusing to linger on it, I pressed forward. "I need to speak with her. Please."

"I… um…" Brenda darted a glance at the younger woman, and I searched for a name tag.

"Gwen." I appealed to her, hoping she would take pity on me. "Please. I need to know where she is. I have to speak with her."

She bit her lip. "Well, um…"

What the fuck was going on? Why the hell was everyone being so secretive? I let out a little growl. "Where the hell is my wife?"

Gwen wrung her hands at her waist and shot a look over at the older woman before meeting my gaze again. "Eros," she whispered. "She's on a date."

The fucking hell she was. Red creeped into the edges of my vision, and I managed a curt nod before spinning on my heel. I didn't have a fucking clue where this Eros place was, but if Lydia was there, I was going to fucking find it.

I googled the address, then set the GPS to direct me to the restaurant.

I had no idea what I was going to do, but one thing was for certain—Lydia was still my wife. And I'd be damned if some other man was going to touch her. Ever.

CHAPTER ELEVEN
Lydia

My hand on the handle of the huge front door, I halted in place and drew in a deep breath. I really did not want to do this. I'd never been good at dating, and, especially after my debacles with Shawn and then Xander, I had no real desire to deal with men ever again. I glanced through the glass at all the people seated inside. Who was he? I literally knew nothing about this guy. Was he divorced, or had he been single his entire adult life? Was he as uncomfortable with this arrangement as I was? Would he be offended if I cancelled and told him I wasn't feeling well?

Immediately, guilt assailed me. It wasn't this guy's fault that my previous relationships had all crashed and burned. I at least needed to give him a chance. Determined to try to be more positive, I pulled open the door and stepped inside. Tamping down my unease, I smiled shakily at the hostess. "Hello. I'm here to meet with Harvey Levenstein."

The hostess returned my smile. "Right this way, miss."

I followed her to the back of the restaurant, weaving between tables full of people. Groups of men who I assumed were holding business dinners were interspersed between couples seated intimately in a dimly lit dining room. The restaurant itself was beautiful. It was upscale without being overdone, the lighting soft and flattering. Large frosted chandeliers in a circular shape approximately five feet wide hung from the ceiling over various parts of the room. They cast their soft glow over the patrons, lending to the ambience.

The hostess halted beside a chair and shot me another smile. "Anything else, miss?"

"No, thank you," I replied.

Across the table, Harvey didn't bother to stand. In fact, he barely looked away from his phone. I settled into my seat as the hostess made her way back to the front of the restaurant. Finally, as if just noticing my presence, he lifted his head and smiled at me. A mixture of surprise and pleasure lit his eyes. "Wow, you're a lot prettier than dad let on."

"Um... thanks?" I wasn't sure if that was a compliment or not.

The waitress came by and Harvey dove right in, ordering a bottle of red wine. I barely held back a grimace. I hated red wine, even the sweet stuff. I didn't drink very often, but when I did it was usually a white dessert wine that tasted more like Kool-Aid than rotten grapes. Without giving me a chance to look at the menu, he went ahead and placed our orders. The waitress gave a perfunctory nod and strode back toward the kitchen.

I didn't recognize the name of whatever he'd ordered, and I barely managed to tamp down my irritation as I turned my gaze back to Harvey. "I don't think I've had that before."

I wasn't terribly picky, but it was the principle of the thing. I hated that he felt like he had the right to order for me.

"Oh, don't worry," he assured me, "you'll love it."

I sat back in my seat, not entirely convinced, but unwilling to fight over it. My phone buzzed as a call came through, the vibration pulsing through my purse where it hung over the back of my chair. I leaned over and peeked inside just in time to see the salon's number flash across the screen. I briefly debated answering then decided against it. Brenda was probably calling to make sure everything was going okay, and I was determined to make it through this date if it killed me.

Silence fell between us for a moment before Harvey spoke up again. "So, you run a bridal shop?"

"Actually, it's my shop. I own it," I clarified.

"Ah, I see," he said as he winked at me. "You're one of those women."

I bristled at the statement, but I tried my best to keep my face expressionless. "What kind of woman would that be?"

"Oh, you know." He waved a hand in the air. "The kind of woman who wants a fairy-tale wedding. Prince Charming on a dashing horse and everything that goes along with it."

I tried not to be insulted by the statement. "Actually, no," I responded. "I don't think marriage is in the cards for me just yet."

"Oh, come on," he scoffed, giving me a knowing look. "Every woman wants that. Actually, I think it's great," he commented. "I can make that happen if that's what you want."

Who did this guy think he was? I opened my mouth to shoot him down, but he continued, barreling right over me.

"Not that I'm proposing," he said, lifting his hands. "Not yet."

Was this guy for real? My stomach roiled as he shot me another wink, and I forced myself to take a drink of water to keep the contents of my stomach from ending up all over the table. It'd be a cold day in hell before that happened. The waitress arrived by the table and uncorked our wine, then poured a bit into Harvey's glass.

I watched as Harvey swirled the deep red liquid around the glass, then inhaled deeply. He took a tiny sip and seem to chew on it for a good ten seconds before finally swallowing. Pressing his fingers to the base of the glass, he slid it toward the waitress. "That'll do."

Oh, God. Figured the man would be a wine connoisseur. I barely managed to hold back my eye roll. I knew this date hadn't been a good idea. Still, it was the first time I'd been out in months, and I was determined to enjoy it despite the poor company. Harvey prattled on, making small talk, and I made noises at the appropriate times to acknowledge his statements. I allowed my mind to wander, thinking about next season's fashions and the samples that I wanted to order. The new Marchesa was to die for, and I couldn't wait to get it in my shop. I needed to make sure I ordered some new shoes too, since the style had changed from spring and we were moving now into summer and fall wear. I also needed a couple new headpieces—

I jumped in my seat, ripped away from my thoughts as Harvey let out a cringeworthy guffaw. My shoulders shot up to my ears, and I fought the urge to look around the room to see if everyone's eyes were on us.

God, the man had the worst laugh *ever*.

Thankfully, we were saved seconds later by the waitress delivering our meals. "Anything else?"

"No," Harvey responded for both of us. I was too busy eyeing my food to formulate a thought. Bones stuck up out of a cut of meat that looked less than appetizing. I picked up my fork and poked at it. "What did you say this was again?"

"Osso buco." Harvey gestured with his chin. "It's good, you'll like it."

"Right…" I drew out the word as I cautiously cut into it. "But what exactly is it?"

He looked at me like I'd just asked what year it was. "Veal."

Nope. Just… nope. I set the knife at the edge of my plate and speared a potato, then popped it into my mouth. I liked hamburgers at a backyard barbecue. I even loved the occasional steak once in a while, though it wasn't really in my budget these days. But I drew the line at eating meat from baby animals.

I watched, stomach churning, as Harvey turned his attention back to his own plate and dug in. The clatter of silverware against porcelain filled the air as he cut into it with vigor, and I dropped my gaze away. I didn't care if I offended him by not eating it—he hadn't bothered to ask my opinion before ordering, anyway. At least the vegetables were good. I'd grab a snack before bed once I got home.

I pasted on a polite smile and forked up a carrot, counting the minutes until I could escape. Maybe not out the front doors—because that would be rude, right? Hell, at this point, I wasn't sure I even cared. I'd been on a handful of bad dates in my life, but this one took the cake. His sheer obnoxiousness grated on my nerves, and I gritted my teeth before setting my fork on the edge of the plate. I glanced around, desperately trying to catch the eye of our waitress. God willing, she'd take pity on me and bring the check so I could get the hell out of here.

All I wanted to do was go home, kick off my heels, and have a glass of wine. Or maybe the entire bottle. And not the crappy red that I could smell from here, the smell of fermented grapes so potent it permeated the air. I sighed. Though it sounded nice, I knew I would never do it. Being a single mom, I always had to think about Alexia first. What if there was an emergency in the middle of the night? I hadn't drunk a drop since I'd found out I was pregnant, wanting to always be coherent in case something happened.

Suddenly, the hairs on the back of my neck stood on end, and I had the sensation of eyes burning a hole in the back of my head. I glanced surreptitiously toward the tables to my left, then right, but everyone was busy eating or talking. Unable to seek out the source of my unease, I picked up my fork and speared another stalk of asparagus.

"Do you need something?"

The sound of Harvey's voice jerked my attention across the table. I opened my mouth to speak just as I realized he was looking over my shoulder.

"Yeah."

That voice... Deep and masculine, I was sure I had heard it before. That same tingly sensation skittered down my spine as I slowly turned toward the man hovering beside my chair. I took in the thick, muscular thighs and a snug black T-shirt that if I looked closely enough—and I totally did—I could just barely see the outline of the man's abs. Thick, corded arms and broad shoulders came into sight next. Then something caught my eye. The neckline of his shirt played peek-a-boo with a dark tattoo that I swore I'd seen before. My eyes lifted to the man's face, over beautiful lips curved into a smug smirk, a nose that I was sure had seen a fist or two, then...

My heart thudded to a stop as my gaze collided with a pair of blue eyes—eyes I hadn't seen for almost two years. He knew the moment it clicked; I could see the satisfaction in those glimmering depths. I was dimly aware of the fork falling from my fingers, the clank of silver on porcelain muted as blood thrummed in my ears, blotting out everything else.

Oh, God... Why was he here? What did he want?

His smile changed, becoming more predatory as he seemed to read my mind. "My wife."

CHAPTER TWELVE
Xander

My heartrate increased the closer I got to the high-end restaurant. Pulling up in front of the imposing stone façade, I threw the truck in park and hopped out. The kid at the valet stand passed me a ticket and I shoved it in my pocket, not missing a stride as I pushed through the front door.

I was already three steps into the room before common sense kicked in. What the hell was I doing? I had no idea what her reception to me would be. Did she even know we were still married? I had to imagine she didn't; otherwise she would have hounded me for the annulment.

My gaze slid over the dim interior, searching for a familiar face. As if my eyes were drawn to her and her alone, I zeroed in on the elegant slope of her shoulder, made more prominent by her hair pulled severely away from her face. Though her back was mostly to me, it was undeniably her. My breath caught at the sight of her. Suddenly, time slipped away, and I was back in that bar with her, throwing back shots of tequila. I narrowed my eyes as I studied her. She sat ramrod straight in her chair, one hand placed in her lap as she ate, the perfect picture of grace and propriety. Something else occurred to me in that moment. She looked… uncomfortable.

I waved off the hostess at the stand, and, ignoring the curious stares from the patrons around me, I cut right through the middle of the room. As I neared the back of her chair, I heard the man across from her speak in his nasally tone. He flicked a glance toward me as I neared the table, his brow puckering with a combination of concern and confusion. I rested one hand on the back of Lydia's chair and speared him with a glare.

"Do you need something?"

"Yeah." Lydia turned toward me, and I watched her expression as her eyes glided over me, starting at my midsection and working their way up. She still hadn't figured it out yet. What would she say? My heart pounded against my ribcage as her gaze traveled over my chest and shoulders, then finally up to my face. I felt a little surge of smug satisfaction as she met my stare, her eyes widening comically. A clatter filled the air as the fork slipped from her fingers.

My smile probably spoke more of a wolf preparing to pounce on its prey than a friendly greeting, but I was here for one reason and one alone. "My wife."

"What?" I dragged my gaze away from Lydia and back to the man across the table. One perfectly plucked tawny eyebrow lifted, and his lips twisted into a sneer. "Who are you?"

Stretching my hand across the table, I offered it to him. "Nice to meet you. I'm Xander. Lydia's husband."

His mouth dropped open, but he ignored my outstretched hand. I couldn't hold back a smile at the ridiculous sight of him gaping like a fish. Dropping my hand back to my side, I shot him a sly wink. "Thanks for taking care of her for me. I've got it from here."

I turned back to Lydia, who had been strangely silent up to this point. Wide gray eyes bored into mine, and she blinked slowly, as if to make sure I wasn't an apparition. Pulling out the chair beside her, I sank down and crossed one ankle over my knee. Angling myself toward Lydia, I directed my next words to her. "How ya been, darlin'?"

My words seemed to snap her from her trance, and her pretty gray eyes narrowed. "What are you doing here?" she hissed.

"Came to find you, of course," I replied. "Heard you were here, and I had to come see for myself."

The guy leaned across the table. "Who the hell is this, Lydia?"

She darted a quick glance at me, then back to him. "It's... This is Xander. He's..."

"Her husband," I supplied helpfully.

She shot me a withering glare, and the man huffed. "What the hell is he doing here?"

"*He*"—I stressed the word as I threw a look at the man—"is busy reuniting with his wife."

"I'm not your wife," she hissed at the same time the man spoke.

"I thought you said you were a widow?"

I turned a bewildered look on Lydia, who at least had the good sense to look ashamed. "You told him I was dead?"

"I didn't…" Her hands moved agitatedly in front of her face. "It wasn't… Never mind."

I couldn't fucking believe it. She couldn't even own up to our marriage. And to tell people I'd died? "That's a little cold, even for you, Liddy."

Her guilty flush deepened with anger. "First of all, my name is Lydia. Not Liddy. Don't call me that. Second, I'm *not* your wife." She turned to the man. "I'm so sorry. I have to go."

She jumped up, grabbed her purse, and was gone in a whirl of black skirt before either of us could say another word.

"Hey!" the guy called to her back. "The check!"

I turned a disgusted look on him. "Seriously? What kind of man takes a woman out and makes her pay?"

The asshole had the nerve to prop his hands on his hips. "It's expensive."

"What the fuck ever." I pulled out my wallet and tossed a fifty on the table as I flicked a glance at her nearly untouched plate. "She eats like a fucking bird. I'm sure that'll cover it."

I followed Lydia, determined to catch her before she could ditch me again. Luck was on my side, and I spotted her by the valet stand just outside. She threw me an aggravated glare as I stepped up beside her.

I remained silent for a moment, allowing my gaze to skim down her body. She'd filled out since I'd first met her, but it looked good on her. Healthy. Her bust and hips had rounded a bit, but she was still as beautiful as ever. Maybe even more so. I wanted to reach out and touch her, let my fingers trail over each dip and curve to see if they really were as addictive as I remembered or if my memory had played a trick on me. Shoving my hands in my pockets, I rocked back on my heels. "So."

She redirected her gaze across the street, trying her best to tune out my presence.

"You drove separate."

Her brows drew together. "I don't see how that's any of your concern."

"The fact that you're not leaving with that prick"—I hitched a thumb over my shoulder toward the restaurant—"means a hell of a lot. Believe me."

"Your opinion means nothing to me." She lifted one elegant shoulder. "Harvey is..."

She trailed off, either unwilling to finish or unable to come up with anything flattering. From the little I'd seen, I was more than willing to bet it was the latter. As if her words conjured the idiot, he came barreling through the door of the restaurant barely a second later. Placing himself between us, he addressed Lydia. "Can we reschedule?"

I snorted. "So you can split that tab for that meal, too?"

She glanced at me over the man's shoulder, her face twisting into an expression of incredulity. "What? Never mind." She held up a hand and met the guy's gaze. "I'm flattered, but I don't think so. Now excuse me while I go settle my check."

He threw me an angry glare before stomping off, and Lydia turned toward the restaurant, muttering under her breath, "Asshole."

I caught her elbow and dragged her back to me. "I took care of it."

Her pretty lips formed a small 'O' before she caught herself, and her face settled back into an expression of annoyance. "Well." She cleared her throat. "Thank you."

One foot tapped an impatient rhythm on the sidewalk as if it would magically conjure the valet so she could escape my presence.

The thought alone pissed me off. Shoving my hands back in my pockets, I studied her. "We need to talk, Lydia. You're still my wife and—"

Her chest rose on a sharp inhale, and she spun toward me. "I am *not* your wife."

I let out a mirthless laugh. "Really? Because I have papers that say otherwise."

"That's impossible," she scoffed.

"Really? You sure about that?"

Her shoulders tensed. "Of course. Why wouldn't I be?"

"You ever read the documentation that the lawyers sent back?" Though she refused to look at me, I read the hesitation in every line of her body. "You didn't, did you?"

The blood drained from her face, giving me the answer I'd been looking for. I sighed. "We apparently both forgot to sign one of the documents."

Cold expression firmly back in place, she glared at me. "Fine. Let's take care of it, then. I'll sign it right now." She began to dig around in her giant purse, probably looking for a pen.

I was fucking tired of fighting. I set a hand on her arm to halt her frantic searching. "Come on, let's go somewhere and talk."

An alarmed expression moved over her face. "N-no. I can't—"

"Lydia." She froze at my exasperated tone. Searching her eyes, I softened my voice. "I just moved in, so my place is a mess, otherwise I'd invite you there. Let's just go back to your place and—"

"No!"

She said it much too quickly, and my eyes narrowed. "You don't trust me to come home with you?"

"I-It's not… I can't…" She stammered over her words and fell back a step, her hand moving to the base of her throat. So she was fine speaking to me in public, but the second I mentioned going somewhere quiet, she freaked out. Why?

She whirled away, stumbling much too close to the curb. I caught her elbow and yanked her back just as the valet pulled up with a compact black car. "Jesus, Liddy!"

Tearing herself from my grasp, I watched as she practically ran around the vehicle and threw her bag on the passenger seat as she clambered inside. The valet held the door for her and she ripped it from the poor guy's hands, slamming it shut and throwing the car in gear.

What the fuck just happened?

The valet watched with a combination of surprise and dismay, jumping back as she peeled away from the curb. For some reason, I felt the need to apologize. "I'm sorry." Digging a twenty from my wallet, I handed it over to him. "She's a little… frazzled."

That was a fucking understatement if I'd ever heard one, and I was at a loss as to how to proceed. The look on her face had spoken less of hate and more of… fear? Was she so afraid of me that she'd damn near thrown herself in front of a moving vehicle? Propping my hands on my hips, I stared after the red taillights disappearing into the distance.

I'd give her a couple days to calm down. Then Lydia and I were going to have a serious discussion.

CHAPTER THIRTEEN
Lydia

I bit my lip, blinking away the tears burning the back of my eyelids. This was the absolute last thing I needed this morning. I'd been an emotional mess the past two days, snapping at everyone and ready to cry at the drop of a hat. Seeing Xander the other night had thrown me completely off balance, but that was nothing compared to what I'd experienced over the past few days.

Nothing. Nada. Not a phone call, no emails, not a visit to my house or the salon. It was extremely unnerving, and I didn't believe for a second that he would leave well enough alone. He was biding his time, waiting to swoop back into my life and ruin everything. The possibility of him popping up unexpectedly hung over my head like a black cloud, and I was stressed almost to the point of breaking. Brenda had asked about him once but promptly dropped the subject when I practically bit her head off.

I needed to tell him about Alexia. There was no putting it off any longer. I'd allowed myself to fall into a state of complacency for the past year, but that had dissipated in a matter of minutes. Now that Xander was back, it felt as if the ground of my perfectly constructed world was crumbling beneath my feet. I could only imagine his reaction. He would be *furious*, and I wasn't quite ready to deal with it just yet.

"This is horrendous. I don't understand why you can't figure out..."

I whirled at the sound of Caryn Anderson's voice and steeled my spine, lifting my chin as I stared her down. With everything spiraling out of control around me, I finally reached my wits end. I was done with this woman throwing her weight around. "Caryn, I appreciate your business, but clearly we are not seeing eye to eye. I think it'd be better if you went somewhere else."

The other woman's mouth dropped open in shock. Likely it was the first time anyone had stood up to her. "Are you kicking me out?"

I clasped my hands in front of my stomach and affected my most calm but firm expression. "I think it's in everyone's best interest to find someone better suited for your needs. Someone who can make your vision come true."

Good freaking luck to whomever that might be. The woman was hell on wheels, and if I never had to see her again, it would be too soon.

Her jaw dropped open, gaping like a fish. The sight would have been comical if I weren't so pissed off and frustrated with our constant battling. "You can't just quit! Who the hell do you think you are?"

I spread my hands wide. "I don't believe I'm the best person to design your dream dress. You said so yourself."

Caryn threw the dress on the floor. "I'm not paying you a dime. Your work is—"

"Actually," I interjected, holding up my index finger, "your contract states that you're required to pay for the amount of work that has been completed. However," I cut Caryn off again as she opened her mouth to protest, "I'll cut that number in half as a courtesy. I'll mail you the bill next week."

I didn't care what the hell I had to do to get rid of her, I just wanted the woman out of my salon and out of my life.

The woman's eyes narrowed to angry slits. "You'll regret this."

"I seriously doubt it." I smiled serenely. "Best of luck to you."

Throwing her giant designer handbag over one twig-thin arm, Caryn stomped off the dais—taking care to grind her stiletto-clad heel into the delicate lace of the dress on her way out. I closed my eyes at the sight, anger simmering deep in my belly. I clenched my hands together in an effort to refrain from leaping over the dais myself and strangling the woman. The bell over the door jingled, announcing Caryn's dramatic exit. The slam of the door made me flinch, my shoulders jumping to my ears.

"That woman could piss off a nun."

A smile cracked my face, and, relaxing, I turned to Gwen. "Amen, sister. She's a walking nightmare."

"Is that salvageable?" Gwen pointed to the fabric puddled on the floor, and I scooped it up, inspecting it.

"I think so. Except where Queen Bitch ripped a hole in the lace."

"I'll take care of it."

I passed it over with a smile. "You're a saint, you know that?"

"Better believe it." My assistant shot a cheeky smile my way and cradled the dress in her arms. "I'll see if I can work some magic, and we'll use it as a display."

"Sounds great. Thank you."

Gwen headed toward the back of the salon, and I took a moment to compose myself before striding to the welcome desk. Brenda sat behind the computer and swiveled toward me as I approached. "You okay?"

I offered a small smile. "I'll be fine. We shouldn't hear anything from her anymore, I hope."

Brenda chuckled. "She certainly left in a huff. Looked like someone pissed in her Cheerios."

I smothered a giggle behind both hands. "That's awful."

"No," Brenda deadpanned. "*She* is awful. I'm just honest."

"Fair enough," I said on a laugh. "I'm going to straighten up a bit before the next appointment."

I paused in front of the large glass window overlooking the street, watching the world outside. What made women like Caryn so cold? She'd been raised with a silver spoon in her mouth, had everything handed to her on a platter, while I'd scrimped and saved and sacrificed everything. Despite all that, I wouldn't trade it for a thing. The struggle I'd endured made it all worth it.

I shook my head and turned away with a sigh. Meandering the display room floor, a sense of pride swelled deep inside. My fingers trailed over the sleek satins and delicate lace as I fluffed the skirts, carefully arranging the fabric.

The shattering of glass behind me ripped a small scream from my throat, and I instinctively covered my head with my hands as

I dropped to one knee. A full second of silence ensued before chaos broke out across the salon.

"Lydia!"

"What happened?"

"Are you okay?"

Voices assaulted my ears from every direction, and I opened my eyes. Tiny shards of glass littered the floor at my feet, and, dazed, I turned toward the window. The sounds from outside filtered in through the gaping hole in the lower portion of the window. What remained of the pane was splintered, looking like jagged teeth ready to chomp down on its next victim.

There was only one reason it would have exploded like that. rushing forward, I braced one hand on the sill, carefully avoiding the shards of glass. Leaning out, I scanned the sidewalk to my left and right, looking for anyone, anything, responsible.

Cars whizzed past, and a couple people ambled around the corner farther down the sidewalk, but whoever had broken the window was long gone.

Shaken, I turned back to the group of women gathered around, watching me intently for guidance. Placing one hand over my still racing heart, I pasted on a soothing smile. "Everything's fine. It just scared me."

"What happened?" Brenda asked, concern evident on her face.

"I'm not sure." I debated voicing my fears but decided against it. "Whatever it was, I'm sure it was just an accident."

"Mhmm." She hummed a low sound in her throat, and the rest of the ladies exchanged uneasy glances.

I reached for patience. "Maybe someone was mowing the grass and it ricocheted through the window. Or something fell off a truck."

None of the ladies seemed to like either of those explanations, but it seemed to calm them at least.

Gwen rounded the corner but came to a dead halt when she saw us. "Is everything okay? I heard a commotion, and—" Her eyes rounded as they moved over my shoulder to the shattered window behind me. "Oh, my gosh! What happened?"

I held up my hands. "Just an accident. Let's get this cleaned up, then—" My words were cut off as the bell over the front door jingled, and we collectively turned toward the sound.

Please, God, no.

I stared at the one single person on earth I had no desire to see—one far worse than Caryn. I'd been dreading this moment, waiting for him to walk through that door and change my life forever.

My heart dropped to my toes, and a steel band constricted around my lungs as blue eyes cut to me, sending a fiery sensation through my body that I didn't understand. God surely hated me. There was no other explanation for it.

CHAPTER FOURTEEN
Xander

A cacophony of chattering female voices met my ears as I entered the small salon. The tinkling of the bell over the door announced my presence, and several sets of eyes swiveled toward me. The only ones I cared about, though, were the steel gray pair that met mine, turning my blood to fire. The stormy depths registered agitation and... worry?

Immediately on guard, my gaze swept over the scene before me, taking in the broken window behind the three women as well as the glass littering the pale blue carpet. Shit. I'd been so preoccupied on my way in that I hadn't even noticed.

Lydia straightened and directed her attention to the women gathered in a semicircle around her. "Gwen, would you please bring me the vacuum? And Brenda, could you please make some calls to get this window replaced or at least covered for now? I think our next appointment is due in about an hour."

The women avoided me completely, scattering like pigeons as Lydia dismissed them with a gentle smile.

I lifted a brow at her. "What happened here?"

She drew in a shaky breath and waved me off. "Something broke the window, but it's nothing, I'm sure."

"Hmm." I hummed a noncommittal sound before venturing closer, examining the gaping hole in the lower corner of the window. "I can get some plastic sheeting and cover this for you."

"That won't be necessary." Her voice was clipped, and her immediate refusal had my hackles raising.

I turned to her and crossed my arms over my chest. "Looks like you have a penchant for pissing people off, Liddy."

Her pretty gray eyes narrowed on me. "First of all, don't call me that. Secondly, I didn't do anything." She lifted a hand and gestured toward the street. "It was probably some kid playing or… something."

I didn't like that tone at all, or the worried look in her eyes. I was willing to bet there was a hell of a lot more to the story than whatever bullshit she was feeding me.

"Did you find whatever came through the window?"

"Not yet." She shook her head. "I was more worried about getting the glass cleaned up and the window covered before our next clients get here."

I nodded and bent to a knee, searching beneath the ruffled folds of white fabric.

"What are you doing?"

I tipped my head up to meet her curious gaze. "I'm looking for whatever they tossed in here." I swept my arm under the low-hanging dresses on the rack, and my fingers brushed something hard and rough. I stretched my fingers and snagged the large rock, then climbed to my feet. I held it out for her inspection. "Found the culprit. What the…?"

Her eyes widened, and she snatched the rock from my fingers just as I noticed the word scribbled in black marker across its smooth surface.

Fraud.

She clutched the rock close to her chest, her whole body trembling as she glanced worriedly out the window. What the hell was going on here?

"Lydia."

Her gaze jumped to mine, but she remained silent.

"What is that?"

She swallowed hard, then reluctantly passed it back to me. I shot her a hard glare before redirecting my attention to the rock in my hands. I turned it over, but there was nothing else. Just that one word. What did it mean?

"Any idea who may have done this?"

Her brows furrowed, and she chewed her bottom lip in thought. Finally, she gave a little shake of her head. "No."

"You sure you haven't pissed anyone off lately—besides me?"

Her angry glare threatened to cut right through me, and I felt a sudden stab of guilt. I hadn't come to provoke her; I'd just wanted to talk things out a bit. With Lydia, though, things never went as planned. It occurred to me that she might be more accommodating if I showed her I wasn't the bad guy here. I held up my hands in a placating gesture. "I'm sorry. I shouldn't have said that. You should tell the police about this."

She gave a derisive little laugh. "So they can do… what? Post someone out front to make sure no one throws another rock through my window?"

She had a point. There wasn't a hell of a lot they could do. "They can at least file a report. Have you had any trouble recently?"

She froze, her mouth parted slightly as if something had just occurred to her. Almost immediately she snapped it closed, and her expression shut down. "No."

I didn't believe that for a second. If I pushed any harder, I'd be calling her a liar, and I didn't want to drive the wedge any further between us. If she wasn't going to open up to me, I'd just have to do it my way. "What can I do to help?"

"Don't worry about it." She turned to leave, but I reached out and caught her shoulder. Her muscles tensed under my touch, and I could feel the faint vibration of her body as I slowly spun her around to face me. Her gaze collided with mine, and I studied her expression. Fear warred with trepidation in those liquid depths, and remorse seized me. She was obviously shaken from the incident, and I'd made the situation worse.

I stroked her shoulder lightly with my thumb. "Why don't you let me fix this up while you clean? If you have any plastic sheeting, we can get this covered up until someone can get out here to replace the glass."

She looked torn, and her gaze darted to the back of the salon. "We have another appointment coming in soon, and—"

"Let me take care of it," I cut in. "Please."

Her teeth sank into her bottom lip, and she wrapped her arms around her waist before finally relenting with a single jerky nod. "We should have some in the back. I'll go check." She shrugged out of my hold and took a couple steps away before angling back to me, her voice as soft and uncertain as her gaze. "Thank you."

The corners of my mouth lifted. "Welcome."

I watched her slink from the room then turned back toward the window, inspecting the rock still in my hand. If this was an accident, I would eat the boots on my feet. The park was too far away and, though a kid may have been involved, it was surely no accident. I'd have to chat with the neighbors, see if anyone heard or saw anything.

Noise from behind prompted me to turn around, and I saw the younger woman standing there, watching me closely. I recognized her face—she was the same one I spoke with the other night, the one who'd told me where Lydia had gone on a date. And thank God she had. I owed her a sincere thank-you for that. What the hell was her name again? I offered up a small smile and thought I saw a faint blush stain her cheeks, but my attention was diverted as Lydia came around the corner.

She held a large piece of plastic in one hand and a roll of duct tape in the other. She shrugged. "Fixes everything, doesn't it?"

I quirked a grin at her. "Damn near everything."

We remained that way for a long moment, each of us absorbed in the other. A throat cleared from behind Lydia and she jumped, breaking the moment. "I'm sorry, I'll take that."

She extricated the vacuum from the other woman and set it aside. "Gwen, can I borrow you for a second?" Her gaze flicked to me. "I'll be back in just a minute."

I dipped my chin at her. "Take your time."

Lydia led the other woman around the corner, her voice hushed as she gave instructions, and I turned back to the window. There was still something between us, some indefinable quality that tethered her to me. The feeling had awoken the moment I'd laid eyes on her four nights ago, and it refused to let up.

The papers I'd brought with me burned a hole in my back pocket. I'd brought them somewhat out of obligation, but now I prayed I wouldn't need them. I couldn't bear to leave whatever was between us unexplored. I'd fallen hard in lust with her two years ago, and it seemed I was on the same track now. I wasn't ready to let go of her.

I applied the last strip of tape to affix the sheeting to the window frame, then turned to find Lydia watching me. She chewed that full bottom lip, looking unsure as hell as she reluctantly met my eyes. "Thank you for doing that."

"It was no big deal." I shrugged. "Didn't take much effort, and it'll at least get you by until someone gets out here to fix it."

"Well, um..." She shifted nervously, and I chanced a tiny step closer.

"Can we talk?" She opened her mouth, but I cut her off. "I know you've had a crazy morning. Tomorrow, maybe?"

"I suppose," she hedged. "I might be able to make time in between appointments..."

She said the words like they had to be pulled from her, and I barely managed to bite back my smile. A victory was a victory, no matter how small. At this point, I'd take whatever I could get.

"Perfect." I stepped forward, bringing myself to an arm's length away. "I'll bring us lunch."

"Oh, no, that won't—"

Her mouth snapped shut as I reached out and brushed a single strand of loose hair from her cheek. She seemed so uptight, everything perfectly in place, as if nothing dared defy her. Each time I'd seen her recently, she'd been buttoned up, her hair pulled ruthlessly away from her face. Even on her date, she'd been dressed primly, almost businesslike—not the way most women dressed, in my experience. Most tried to show off their tits and legs to their advantage; not Lydia. She was confident exactly the way she was, and I fucking loved that about her.

The sleek chignon she now wore showed off those gorgeous cheekbones and luminous eyes, but I wanted to see it down again. I remembered the way her hair had fallen in tousled waves and draped over my chest after we'd made love, the sexy tendrils tickling my skin. I wanted to run my hands through the long, silky strands and wind it around my wrist, bending her to my will as I made love to her mouth.

My gaze dropped to her lips, slightly damp from where she'd run her tongue over them, and my groin tightened in appreciation. Fuck. I shoved away the dirty thoughts tickling the back of my mind and dropped my hand away. "I'll see you tomorrow around lunchtime."

She nodded jerkily, and I could feel her eyes on me as I made my way to the front door. I risked one last glance as I exited and met her gaze. Pretty gray orbs narrowed on me as I shot her a wink, then hopped down the few steps and strode to my truck, humming softly and debating just how to win my wife over again.

CHAPTER FIFTEEN
Lydia

The ringing of my phone on the bathroom counter made me jump, and I swiped mascara off the bridge of my nose. Glancing at the screen, I slid my thumb over it to answer the call. "Morning, Darlene."

"Lydia? I'm so sorry to do this to you, honey, but I can't watch Alexia this morning."

It wasn't her words so much that worried me, but the tone of her voice, laced with worry. "Are you okay? What's wrong?"

"George was having chest pains, so I called the doctor. He's worried George is having a heart attack; they're taking him to the hospital."

On cue, I heard the faint peal of a siren from outside. "Oh, my gosh, of course! Do you need anything, or want me to come with you?"

"No, no, dear. We'll be fine. And I'm so sorry—"

I cut her off. "Don't you worry about a thing. You get George taken care of and let me know what the doctor says."

We hung up, and I quickly finished my makeup, then scrambled to get a diaper bag together. Tossing in diapers and a couple changes of clothes, toys, and baby food, I gathered Alexia. "Come on, sweetness. You're coming with me today."

It wouldn't be the first time she'd come to the salon with me. The women all loved to play with her in their spare time, but it was exhausting trying to keep a one-year-old occupied while running my business. Today, though, I couldn't summon the energy to let it bother me. All that mattered was that George would be okay.

As soon as I got to the salon, I got Alexia settled in the back. We had a changing room right off the alterations room that was carpeted and surrounded by mirrors. The alterations room also connected to my office, so she could easily be relocated if we had any incoming clients. The ladies and I took turns watching her and playing with her over the next few hours.

Around noon, I pulled my phone out for the hundredth time, checking for any update on George. I couldn't turn off my worry. The bell rang as a customer strolled through the front door, and I barely managed to swallow a moan when I saw who it was. Oh, God. I'd completely forgotten about Xander coming for lunch today. His gaze narrowed on me like I was the only person in the room.

He stepped close, much closer than I was comfortable with. "Is everything okay?"

After everything else that had happened this morning, I wasn't ready to deal with him just yet. I still hadn't heard anything from Darlene, and Alexia would be waking up from her nap soon. I'd been keeping on eye on her using the video baby monitoring system that connected with my phone, but she'd been snoozing away in her pack and play for the past hour.

Oh, God. Just the thought of Xander and Alexia—the daughter he knew nothing about—in the same building was almost enough to make me hyperventilate.

I bit my lip. "This really isn't… It's been a bad day. Can we reschedule?"

"Have you eaten yet?"

Food had been the last thing on my mind today. "No, but—"

"Come on." His voice was soft and convincing, tempting me to just let go and give in to this ridiculous feeling flaring between us. "You need to eat something."

I worried my lip, debating. I needed to get him out of here, but… I also needed to talk to him. I at least had to make plans to see him later. I prayed that, if I was at least accommodating, our next conversation wouldn't go so badly. I would just have to allude to Alexia's presence, tell him that there was something he needed to know. And wasn't that the understatement of the year?

"Just… just give me a second."

I hustled to the dressing room where Gwen was just finishing up an alteration consult, and I pulled her aside. "Can you do me a huge favor and take Alexia to the park for a little bit? I hate to ask."

"It's no problem at all. We'll head right over."

"I really appreciate it." This would buy me half an hour at least. Anxiety gnawed at my stomach. I hated deceiving him, but this was the only way. I took my time walking back to the front of the store, giving Gwen plenty of time to get Alexia and escape out the back door.

Xander still stood at the counter, and guilt sliced through me as he turned a smile on me. God, I was such a terrible person. My heart was beating so hard, I was sure he could hear it from where he stood several yards away. The stress of the day was going to kill me.

Steeling my spine, I pasted on a smile and gestured with one hand. "We can go to my office."

He nodded an affirmation, and I turned, acutely aware of his gaze firmly fixed on my back.

"Lydia?"

I turned at the sound of Brenda's voice. "Yes?"

"I have Ms. McCoy on hold. Apparently there was a mix-up with one of her bridesmaid dresses."

I slapped a hand over my forehead. "Damn. Yes, I completely forgot." I turned to Xander. "Can you find your way back by yourself? I'll be there in just a moment."

"No problem at all."

I smiled gratefully. "It's the plain white door on the back wall. Can't miss it."

"I'll find it."

I threw a glance over my shoulder and watched as Xander made his way to the back of the store. By now, Gwen should have Alexia outside, and Xander would never know the difference. Worst case, he would just see a woman carrying a baby outside. No big deal. Crisis averted.

My heart raced in my chest, and I pressed a hand over it as if I could physically will my pulse to slow. I was furious with myself for letting him affect me so deeply. I couldn't deny that I was still attracted to him—too much, in fact. I hadn't really taken the time to study him during our last two encounters, but I did now. He walked with a confident swagger, a man who had no qualms about who he was. He seemed larger than life, completely out of place in my feminine boutique.

He was bold, rugged manliness, from his broad shoulders down to the thick, muscular thighs encased in his dark jeans. The bag of takeout food swung at his side, and my heart fluttered a little bit at the sight. I thought he'd been joking when he alluded to a lunch date, but to see that he'd actually brought food touched me. It was a genuinely sweet gesture, and I deeply appreciated it. It also made me feel even more guilty about what I was about to do.

I bit my lip. Honestly, I didn't have a good plan for this. Even after agonizing over the past four days, I still hadn't devised the best way to tell him he had a daughter. I wanted to have a private moment with him, but part of me also longed for the safety of a public setting. I knew without a doubt, though, that I couldn't do it here. That conversation was *not* going to go well, and I didn't need a battle raging in my place of business. And there was no doubt in my mind that that was exactly what would happen. Xander was a military man; he undoubtedly believed in honor and integrity above all things. I'd done him a horrible injustice by withholding information from him.

My cheeks flamed as I turned around and caught Brenda watching me, a tiny smile playing on her lips. I knew I looked as guilty as a kid caught with her hand in the cookie jar, because Brenda let out a little laugh as I made my way around the counter.

"It's okay to look. Hell, girl, everybody else is doing the same thing." I noticed with a little pang of jealousy that she was right. The eyes of my salesgirls and the ladies seated around the dressing rooms followed Xander as he meandered through the shop. Brenda bumped my shoulder conspiratorially. "Boy has nice assets."

She emphasized the word *ass*, and I lightly backhanded her arm. "Be good before I have to fire you for sexual harassment."

She laughed. "If you're going to fire me, I'll at least make it worth my while. Did you see his biceps? They look like boulders." I nodded. Unfortunately, I knew from experience just how hard he was all over. Almost against my will, memories of that morning in Vegas came flooding back, and heat raced through my veins.

Pushing the thought away, I turned my attention back to Brenda. I found what she was looking for and handed it over with a smile. "Do me a favor and let everyone know I won't be available for the next half hour or so."

Smoothing one hand down my skirt, I pulled my shoulders back and prepared to face Xander by myself. I walked with purpose toward the back of the store but stopped short as I rounded a corner and saw Gwen. My eyes widened, and hers did the same. It took me less than half a second to realize that Alexia wasn't with her. And if Gwen and Alexia hadn't left yet, that meant…

I raced toward my office, Gwen on my heels.

A soft voice floated down the hallway toward me, and I recognized Xander's low, deep rumble. Except it was softer, somehow, almost as if he were talking to…

Oh, God.

CHAPTER SIXTEEN
Xander

Lydia was impeccably dressed in another dark suit, hair pulled back, looking elegant as ever. Still, something didn't feel quite right. I took in the set of her shoulders, the tight lines of her expression. Despite her well put together appearance she seemed... frazzled.

My mind immediately jumped to the worst. I noticed that the window had been fixed, so I assumed someone had been out first thing this morning. Had something more dire happened in the meantime, or was she still concerned over yesterday's incident?

I pondered her demeanor as I wandered to the back of the salon, easily finding the door to her office. I set the brown bag of food on the desk, then glanced at my watch. Just after noon. Settling into the chair by Lydia's desk, I propped one ankle on the opposite knee. Last night, I'd thought a lot about exactly how to proceed. Lydia obviously didn't trust me, though I couldn't say I blamed her. Two years ago, we'd done things all wrong.

Leaning back, I laced my fingers together and rested them on my stomach. I could hear the faint voices coming from the salon, punctuated by the occasional laugh. I hoped to hell Lydia would hurry up so we could get on with it.

A soft scuffling noise drew my attention to the connecting door, and I waited to hear the sound again. A second later the door handle jiggled. Perplexed, I stood from the chair and headed straight to the door. Placing my hand on the doorknob, I gave it the slightest twist and found it locked. I really shouldn't open the door since it was Lydia's space. But someone was obviously trying to get in, and if they were trying to do so without her knowledge, I was going to find out who it was. Leaning closer, I pressed my ear to the door but heard nothing from the other side. The person on the other side was being extremely quiet, and my instincts flared.

One hand on the knob, I used the other hand to flick the lock. In one smooth motion I unlocked the door and threw it open. Surprise rooted me to the ground when I saw nothing—until I dropped my gaze. A tiny toddler cowered behind the door frame. I glanced inside the attached room full of dresses but saw no one. Maybe she had escaped one of the brides from the salon. I was sure someone would be looking for her soon.

Dropping to my haunches, I lowered my tone and spoke soothingly to her. "Hey, little one. How did you get back here?" She peeked one eye around the doorframe, and I gently coaxed her out. "Come here. I won't hurt you." After a moment, she took a tiny step toward me. I held out my hands and waited. "I'll bet someone's missing you." Tentatively, she took another step closer, inspecting me with a wariness only a baby could manage, before apparently deciding I was safe enough. Her tiny hands stretched upward, and I carefully lifted her into my arms.

"You lost, little one? I think we should go find your mama."

The baby reached out with jerky, uneven motions, grabbing for my face, and her mouth tipped up in a huge smile. I knew nothing about kids, except for the fact that I eventually planned to have some of my own. A handful of teeth dotted her mouth as she grinned at me, and I couldn't help but smile back. How old were kids when they got their first teeth? I figured she was maybe a year old or so, since she could walk.

"Who do you belong to, huh?" The baby tugged at my ear, and I grimaced as her tiny nails dug into my skin. As gently as possible, I extracted them and clasped her hand in my own. I felt a little silly carrying on a one-sided conversation with this tiny little girl who probably didn't understand a damn thing, but I loved the smile it put on her face. From out in the salon area, I could hear the rapid approach of footsteps and voices, one of which I recognized as Lydia's. The other I assumed belonged to the baby's mother.

I smiled down at the little girl in my arms. "Not gonna answer me? That's okay, I think I hear your mama now."

My eyes swept over her delicate, tiny features. Pale blonde hair, straight as a pin, capped her head, and icy gray eyes bore into my own baby blues. My gaze narrowed just as the office door swung open and I came face-to-face with a breathless Lydia. Fear and another emotion crossed her face when she saw the baby in my arms. I glanced between her and the infant, cataloging their features.

Lydia's assistant popped around her seconds later and immediately began to apologize. "I'm sorry. I looked away for two seconds, I swear…"

"It's fine." Lydia didn't even bother to glance at the younger woman, just kept her gaze fixed on me.

The assistant wrung her hands together for a moment, then started toward me. "Here, let me take her."

Some irrational anxiety had me tightening my hold on the little girl, who squirmed within my grasp. I reluctantly passed her to the young woman. "I'd like to speak with Lydia for a moment. Alone."

Lydia's eyes flared at that word, and her muscles went rigid with tension. The assistant hesitated, then finally bobbed her head and turned to leave the room, the baby on her hip cooing and babbling incoherently. Lydia reached out a hand and stroked down the baby's spine before turning her attention back to me.

For a long moment, I just stared at her. There was an explanation for this. There had to be. Fury and anticipation warred within me, the emotions threatening to bubble to the surface. My body flushed hot, then ice cold, rendering me numb. "Whose little girl is that?"

"Mine." She looked tired, defeated. And scared. There was no mistaking the fear in her eyes.

Deep down, I knew the answer to the question I was about to ask. But I wanted to know—I needed to hear it come from her mouth. "And her father?"

I held my breath, suddenly terrified to hear the answer. I wanted her to say it out loud, yet at the same time I didn't want to acknowledge the possibility.

She bit her lip and glanced at the ground before meeting my gaze again, moisture clouding her eyes. Her voice was whisper soft. "She's yours."

For a moment, everything went completely still around me, and I felt my mind go blank with shock. I misheard her—I had to have. Yet, I'd held the proof that what she said was true. I inhaled deeply and speared Lydia with a sharp look. "You need to explain what the hell's going on. Right now."

Her teeth sank into her lower lip as her face twisted into an expression of remorse. "I didn't want you to find out like this."

"You didn't..." I gave my head a little shake, still trying to digest everything. I had a kid. "What the fuck, Lydia? Why the hell didn't you tell me?"

She flinched at my words. "I tried!"

"You tried?" My eyes narrowed to cold, angry slits. "Explain to me how the hell you 'try' to tell someone they have a daughter?"

"Please, I—" She reached one hand toward me, but I evaded her grasp.

"Tell me, Lydia, because I'd love to know. How could keep this from me?"

"I don't know!"

I refused to be moved by the tears welling in her eyes. "I can't fucking believe this."

I'd missed out on everything. Lydia's pregnancy, my daughter's birth, her first steps... My throat tightened as cold settled in my bones. I fought to keep my voice even as I spoke. "You condemned me years ago, chalked me up as bad husband material. And now you've hidden my daughter from me?"

"I didn't mean—"

"You did, Lydia. You had every fucking chance to tell me, but you never said a word. How could you?"

Tears slipped down her cheeks, and despite my anger with her, my chest tightened at the sight. "Please, Xander, I swear I'll do whatever you want. Just don't take her away."

I stared at her, rooted to the floor as her words sank in. "Jesus, Lydia. Do you really think I'd do something like that? You really think I'm so horrible that I'd take a little girl away from her mother?"

I shook my head in disbelief. "I can't be here right now. I need to leave. But we are not fucking finished, know that right now. You don't get to make the decisions anymore."

I stomped through the salon, and the women scattered as I made my way toward the front door. My entire body felt hot with anger, fit to burst. How the fuck could she do this to me? I replayed the moment in my head over and over again, seeing those blonde locks and big gray eyes for the first time. I couldn't believe I didn't figure it out sooner. She was an exact fucking replica of both of us—mostly me—and it was like a spear to the heart. How the hell had I not known I had a little girl? How could Lydia not tell me? It was the ultimate betrayal, and I was tempted for a moment to turn around and confront her again, but I forced myself to walk out the front door before I did something stupid.

Out on the sidewalk, I seethed. What she'd done was completely unacceptable. She'd had a million opportunities to tell me about the baby, yet she'd been too much of a fucking coward. In that moment, I hated her. I wanted to lash out and hurt her, and I felt the need to physically restrain myself. Pulling the deck of cards from my back pocket, I shuffled them mercilessly. Pedestrians veered in a wide arc around me as I glared straight ahead. I probably looked like a crazed person, a scowl on my face as I pushed onward, but I couldn't bring myself to care.

A thousand thoughts bombarded my mind, echoing in my ears and drowning out the sounds around me. I'd missed everything. Lydia's pregnancy, the birth of our baby girl... Jesus. I scrubbed a hand over my face. In my fury, I hadn't even thought to ask the little girl's name. Guilt prompted me to turn around and go back, but residual anger pushed me to keep walking and blow off some steam.

I drew in a deep breath, forcing my heartrate to calm. Anger warred with confusion, and my fury won out. I'd missed almost an entire year with my daughter, and I wanted to punish Lydia for keeping her from me. One thing was for certain though. I was never going to miss another day in my baby's life, whether Lydia wanted me around or not.

The monotonous act wasn't nearly satisfying enough. My trigger finger twitched, and my hands ached for the familiar weight of a pistol. Still too pissed to think clearly, I did the only thing I could do at the moment. Spinning on my heel, I headed down the street to where my truck was parked and hopped behind the wheel. I needed to channel some of my negative energy, and I didn't want to be alone. Steering onto the main road, I headed toward headquarters.

Thirty minutes of navigating through bumper to bumper traffic later, I turned into the parking lot behind the large brick building and cut the engine. Closing my eyes, I tipped my head back against the seat and remained there for a long moment. A thousand thoughts flitted through my brain. I traveled back in time to those first few months after we had parted. She'd emailed several times. Why hadn't she given any indication then? She asked to talk, but nothing more. How could she keep something like that from me? Why the hell hadn't she said anything?

Rationality slipped away as anger took hold again. My jaw clenched and my eyes popped open as my fingers gripped the steering wheel, my knuckles white with tension. I forced them loose and took a deep breath before climbing out of the cab. I jiggled my keys anxiously as I rounded the building and shoved the front door open. Connor's little sister, Abby, sat behind the reception desk to my right, and she pasted on a smile as I stepped inside. She opened her mouth to speak, but then closed it again upon seeing my expression.

Dismissing her without a thought, I strode down the hallway toward our offices. I made my way to the very end and stopped at the last door on the left. Con sat at his desk, head bent as he watched something on the tablet in front of him. His eyes lifted to mine as I walked inside and shut the door. Steepling my fingers together, I pressed them to my mouth and leaned against the cool wood of the door. I took a deep breath before meeting his expectant gaze. "Hit the range with me?"

Barring the rifle that had been an extension of myself for the past twelve years, I needed the familiarity of a weapon. I needed the weight of it in my hands, needed to feel the recoil, the smooth coldness of metal. It was the only stress reliever I knew, and it grounded me in a way nothing else could.

As if sensing something was not quite right, he nodded silently and stood. I followed as he moved to a door on the wall to my left, which housed QSG's small armory. Con tapped in a five-digit security code, and the door let out a soft beep as the lock disengaged. We grabbed our guns and ammo, then locked up. We remained quiet until we made it out the back door and climbed into Con's truck. The silence pressed in on me, the weight of it like lead over my shoulders, the words clawing at my throat, desperate to be let loose.

I wasn't particularly close to Con, but I needed to vent to someone and get this off my chest. He was a marine, but we'd served together on a couple different missions overseas, along with another member of QSG, Blake Lawson. While working together, we developed a sort of kinship and we had stayed in touch. Though we'd conversed through dozens of emails about him forming QSG, I really knew little about him. Still, I knew I could trust his opinion. I knew he would listen without judgment. Blowing out a hard breath, I pushed the words from my lips. "I have a kid."

Con's face remained impassive, and he just waited for me to continue.

I shook my head, still trying to wrap my mind around the thought of the little steely-eyed blonde I'd held for the first time this morning. It had taken a moment for me to process exactly what I was seeing, but looking at that little girl was almost like being transported back in time. Packed away in a box somewhere, I had baby photos that looked identical to Lydia's daughter. *My* daughter.

I started from the beginning, telling him of my stupidity in Las Vegas. A few minutes later, we sat in silence, absorbing the information. There wasn't much to the story, since Lydia hadn't shared much with me. In her defense, though I hated to admit it, I hadn't stuck around long enough to really listen. I planned to rectify that in the near future, but I wanted to do so with a clear head. My mind was still in a bad place, and her betrayal hurt my heart more than I thought it could.

A look at Con told me he wasn't surprised in the least. I knew he was jaded from a previous relationship, though I didn't know the whole story. He sat there quietly, the only indication of his agitation the slight drumming of his fingers on the steering wheel. Taking his eyes off the road for a second, he threw me a look. "And?"

My lips curled up in a smirk, though I felt no humor. "I didn't choke the life out of her, if that's what you're worried about," I remarked dryly.

He cocked an eyebrow at me. "Why?"

I read between the lines. Why had Lydia not said anything? That same question had played on a loop in my mind over the past half hour. "I have no fucking idea. It's—*she's*—a kid, for Christ's sake. That's not something you should keep from someone."

"That's pretty low," he agreed. "How old?"

Fuck, I had no idea. "Young." I thought back to how long ago that'd been, mentally calculating the months between my cousin's wedding and now. "One, maybe?"

He didn't say anything, only nodded. The gesture pissed me off. "What?"

"Nothing. When did you get back?"

A little over a week ago. "Doesn't matter. She still should've said something."

"Not arguing. What kind of woman keeps a father from his kid?"

Hearing Con's disapproval was both gratifying and unsettling. Part of me wanted to speak up in Lydia's defense, while the rest of me still wanted her to hurt, too, just the way I did. Still, I'd liked her at one point and was still technically married to her. I couldn't stomach the thought of anyone speaking badly of her. "She emailed a couple times."

"Hmm." I shot him a glare, and his gaze flicked to mine before meeting the road again. "So, maybe she tried?"

"Trying isn't the same thing as doing," I snapped. "She should have tried to call or email every day until I answered."

Even as the words left my mouth, I knew I was being unfair. I should have reached out to her before now. If I had, maybe we could've avoided this whole ordeal. I tried to see the situation from her point of view. It couldn't have been easy for her to find out that she was pregnant while I was half a world away. Would I have told someone that kind of information via email or phone call? I would've loved to say yes, but I seriously doubted my conviction. How could you drop that kind of bomb over the phone?

Con turned into the range, and we hopped out of the car. Dark thoughts plagued my every step, dragging me down. I didn't know who I was more pissed at—her or myself. I was furious at Lydia for keeping the baby a secret. But, like the idiot I was, I'd ignored her emails, scared of what she had to say. While I'd reluctantly signed the papers to annul our marriage, I'd never dreamed something like this could have happened.

I didn't like to admit it, but as a man, my word was everything. I took pride in accepting responsibility for my actions, and I'd let her down by being a coward. It was one thing I had always promised I would never do, yet I had when the most dire opportunity presented itself.

A few hundred rounds later, I felt better both mentally and physically. The exertion had helped to focus my mind and release the tension I'd been carrying in my muscles all morning. We'd both made mistakes, and now we needed to be accountable for our actions. Tomorrow I would go speak with her, and we would have a rational conversation about everything that had transpired. I couldn't take back what had happened—but together, we could change the future.

CHAPTER SEVENTEEN
Lydia

The near-slam of the door punctuated his exit, and I slumped back against the wall as tears poured down my cheeks. A sob welled up in my throat, and I covered my mouth to keep it from escaping.

I swore my heart threatened to stop beating when I saw Alexia in his arms. It was the worst possible scenario, and I'd run a thousand of them through my mind. For nearly the past two years, I'd wondered how I would tell him about his daughter if I ever saw him again. I never wanted him to find out like this.

Inwardly, I seethed. I was furious with the entire situation—with Xander for never responding to my emails, with Gwen for not following directions and putting us in this predicament. But the truth was, the only person truly responsible was me. I knew I should've come clean with him before but I was so worried about his reaction. Rightfully so, I guessed. While I'd played it out a thousand times in my head, it was worse than I ever imagined—so much worse. I didn't blame him for being pissed at me; I deserved every ounce of his anger.

Forcing myself to calm, I took a deep breath and swiped the tears from my cheeks. A thousand emotions swirled in my stomach. Guilt, sadness, anger, humiliation. I knew Xander hated me for what I'd done. But it'd never been intentional—surely he knew that, right? Somehow I'd make him understand.

I fanned my face, knowing my cheeks were blotchy and red. Drawing in another breath, I tried to clear my muddled mind and ventured out into the salon. Gwen was still by the front desk speaking with Brenda, and I approached quietly, my eyes on Alexia.

I took her from Gwen's arms and cuddled her close. Beside us, Gwen shifted awkwardly, wringing her hands in front of her, her gaze pinned to the floor at her feet.

Desperately trying to rein in my anger, I spoke in a low, calm voice. "I need you to please explain to me exactly what happened."

"I…" Gwen began, then trailed off, biting her lip. Her gaze moved to mine, searching imploringly. "I left her in the back for just one second. I wanted to grab her sippy cup from the fridge before we left. I didn't want to carry her through the salon and risk him seeing her, so…"

I inhaled sharply through my nose. Well, that hadn't worked out at all the way she'd planned. "It was less than a minute, I swear."

I briefly closed my eyes, forcing myself not to lash out at her. Gwen was only a year or so younger than me, but she didn't have kids of her own. She had no idea what could happen in the blink of an eye. I also couldn't discount the fact that this was mostly my fault. I met her gaze. "I know she's barely one, but she's starting to climb and get more curious. She can't be left alone, especially not back there where she can get into something and get hurt."

I searched Gwen's eyes to make sure she understood, and she nodded vigorously. "I'm sorry, it won't happen again."

I sighed. "Thank you. And I'm sorry, too, for putting you in this position."

From behind the counter, Brenda spoke up. "You know we don't mind having her, honey."

I shot her a grateful smile. "I know. But she's my responsibility. Maybe I really need to look into day care."

I'd initially discarded the idea because of the cost as well as some of the horror stories I'd heard. When Darlene had offered to stay with her, I'd jumped at the chance. Unfortunately, it had come back to bite me in the ass—big time.

"What are you going to do?" Brenda's voice was soft, and I knew she wasn't referring to day care.

I slid one hand over Alexia's pale locks, and she snuggled against my shoulder. Closing my eyes, I pressed a kiss to her forehead before meeting Brenda's worried gaze. "For right now, I think I need to go home. I'm sorry to keep doing this to you guys, but—"

Brenda held up a hand. "We've got it covered. You need this. You need to be with her."

Brenda was right; I did. All I wanted to do was go home and cuddle my baby close, let her sweet laughter push away the worry and fear that hovered over me like a thick, dark cloud.

He'd glared at me like I was lower than dirt, and I felt like it. I felt horrible for keeping it from him, for depriving him of all the little moments I'd been able to capture over the past year and a half.

*

Muscles coiled with tension, my body was wound so tightly that the jingling of the bell over the door made me jump. Dread congealed in my gut, and my heart skipped a beat. In that moment, I hated the tinkling sound that had once seemed so cheery and welcoming, because this encounter would be far from either of those things. I didn't even glance over—I didn't have to. We opened barely fifteen minutes ago, and we didn't have an appointment scheduled until 11:30. I knew exactly who I would find in the doorway.

I focused my eyes on the computer screen in front of me, desperately trying to maintain my composure as he drew near. I felt him more than saw him, as if his presence was larger than life. He seemed to fill the entire room, and it sent a tingling sensation through my body. I swallowed hard, willing my heart to slow where it thudded painfully in my chest. I was sure Xander could hear it pounding from where he stood barely three feet away from me. I briefly closed my eyes as he cleared his throat, the sound both demanding and understated.

Reluctantly, I glanced up into those blue eyes that did funny things to my insides. I withdrew my fingers from the keyboard and curled them into fists by my sides, steeling myself for the conversation ahead. After the way he left yesterday, I had a feeling this wasn't going to be even remotely civil. Fire filled his eyes, and I had to fight to keep from taking a step backward.

His voice was pitched low. "We need to talk." I nodded, unable to speak over the lump that had formed in my throat. He stared down at me for a moment then tipped his head toward the back of the salon. "Is she here?"

I shook my head and swallow it before speaking. "No, she's at home with Darlene."

He lifted an eyebrow, his inquisitive gaze demanding I explain. "Darlene is a neighbor," I offered. "She watches Alexia during the day."

"Except yesterday." Xander's voice was deceptively soft.

I dipped my head in the barest of nods. "Yesterday was a fluke. Darlene's husband had a health issue, so Alexia stayed here instead."

He tipped his chin in understanding but remained silent otherwise. We stood there for a long moment in the silent standoff, and I shifted nervously on my feet. "Did you... did you want to talk?" I asked hesitantly.

"I want to see my daughter." His commanding tone brooked no argument, and it sent a little shiver of unease down my spine.

"I can't—" I started, but he cut me off.

"She's my daughter, damn it!" He punctuated the statement by jabbing one index finger against the counter. "I'll be damned if I let you keep her from me anymore."

I raised my hands in supplication, already taking a step backward to put more distance between us. "That's not... I didn't mean..." I drew in a shuddering breath. "It's not my intent to keep her from you. I promise," I rushed on when he gazed suspiciously down at me. "Brenda will be here in just a few minutes, then I can take you to see her."

He studied me for a long minute, then, as if gauging my sincerity, he nodded. "Fine."

I waited for him to leave, but he remained steadfast by the counter. His presence was unnerving, and I tried to block it out as I went back to work. Nearly at my breaking point, I almost cried with relief when Brenda and Gwen walked through the door barely ten minutes later. I flicked a glance at Xander. "Let me grab my things and then we can go."

I hurried over to Brenda as she started toward the staff lounge. She glanced over my shoulder and caught sight of Xander. Her brows lifted, and I shook my head. "I'll explain in a second."

Inside the staff lounge, I grabbed my things from my locker, then pulled Brenda aside. "I hate to do this, but I need the morning off."

Brenda patted my shoulder. "Don't worry, dear. We'll take care of everything for today. Just take your time."

I shot Brenda and Gwen a grateful look. "Thank you, guys. I owe you."

Making my way back to the front of the store, I stopped in front of Xander. "Do you want to ride together, or do you want to follow me?" The thought of being confined in close quarters was enough to unnerve me, and I prayed that he would turn down my offer to drive. I shouldn't have worried about it, because he spoke over me.

"I know where you live." He said it so impassively, so matter-of-factly, that I didn't doubt it, and a tiny spark of anger shot through me.

"Fantastic." I couldn't conceal the sarcasm in my tone, and the corner of his mouth twitched up into a small smile. I was momentarily arrested by that tiny smirk, the first sign of humor I'd seen from him. When we first met, he'd given his smiles freely. I felt terrible for taking that away from him.

I felt Xander's eyes on me the entire time as he followed me outside to my car. He stood beside the driver door, watching me like a hawk, as if waiting for me to run. Finally I could take it no more. "What?" I snapped.

Xander gave a little shake of his head. "Nothing. Just making sure you get to your car okay."

"Oh." Well, I hadn't expected that. Off guard, I didn't know what to say. "Thank you."

He gave one more abrupt nod before striding off and climbing into the cab of a large silver truck. I started the car and rubbed my sweaty palms on my skirt, trying to relieve the tension strumming through my body. My heart raced the whole way home, and by the time we got there, I was ready to climb a wall. Worry and nervousness sluiced through me, and I watched with trepidation as Xander's truck pulled into the driveway and parked right behind me. I avoided him as I climbed from the car and made my way to the front door. With trembling hands, I fumbled the keys as I tried to unlock the door. They slipped from my hand and landed with a clatter at my feet. Flustered, I bent to retrieve them, but a large hand beat me to it. Wordlessly, Xander scooped up my key ring and held it out to me. Pushing my hair back from my face, I stood and finally managed to slip the key inside the lock. It let out a soft click as it disengaged, and a shaky breath left my lungs.

Whatever happened next would change everything. I fought the sudden tears clouding my eyes. Taking a deep breath, I swung the door inward and stepped inside, then held it for Xander. His penetrating gaze swept over the interior as he stepped inside, and I was sure that he had my house memorized by the time I closed the door behind him. He gave the impression of a man who missed nothing.

"Home, sweet home," I said softly.

He flicked those blue eyes to me and gave a slight nod. No words, no reaction, just an unsettling stoicism that seemed so at odds with the man I'd once known. I stepped out of my heels and left them on the mat beside the door. "You're welcome to take your shoes off, too," I said, though I immediately regretted the words.

It felt awkward inviting him into my home, like he was insinuating himself within its very walls just by being here. This was my space, and I felt as if he was infringing on it. I didn't want him to take his shoes off. I didn't want him to make himself at home. The very idea of having him here made me nervous and uncomfortable. It wasn't that I didn't trust him, but there was something else below the surface, something I couldn't identify sparking between us. Having him here was too… intimate. His nearness reminded me of the night we spent together nearly two years ago, but so much had happened since then.

I snapped back to reality when he shook his head. I should've been thankful he didn't make any indication that he would be staying for an extended period of time, but I couldn't help the tug of disappointment in my heart. He said he wanted to meet Alexia. Was this just a one-time thing? If he didn't plan to stay, then why was he here? Anger and irritation replaced my nervousness. My daughter deserved better than someone who would flit in and out of her life.

My tone was brusque as I spoke. "Come on."

He lifted one eyebrow but followed me past the stairs, toward the back of the house. The narrow hallway emptied into a small but comfortable kitchen, and off to the right, it connected to our living room. Darlene sat on the floor, surrounded by toys, while Alexia continue to empty her toybox. Laughter floated toward us, and I couldn't help but smile at the sound of that sweet little voice. There was absolutely nothing more precious than the baby's deep belly laugh.

Darlene, finally noticing my presence, turned to me. "Lydia, honey, I didn't expect you so soon." Her head tipped in confusion, then her eyes widened as they skipped over my shoulder and took in Xander standing behind me. The older woman pushed to her feet, and Xander followed me as I approached her.

"Ma-ma-ma!" Alexia toddled toward me, her arms outstretched, and I scooped her up, cuddling her close to my chest.

"Darlene, this is my husband, Xander." Alexia squirmed to be put down, and she took off toward her toys as soon as her toes touched the ground.

"Oh my, I've heard so much about you!" Darlene exclaimed.

My lips pressed into a tight smile as I felt Xander slide a sharp look at me. Floundering for words, I took a moment to compose myself as they shook hands. "Xander… um… just got home."

"That's right," Darlene remarked with an appreciative nod. "Thank you for your service."

"Thank you." Something about Xander's tone drew my attention to him. The words were quiet, and his shoulders were set in a rigid line, as if he was uncomfortable with the praise.

Darlene smiled. "No need to be self-conscious," she said. "My George was a Green Beret."

Surprise snapped my eyebrows toward my hairline, and I glanced at Darlene. "You never told me that." Though I'd only known them for a little over a year, I had only ever seen George putter around the garden and flowerbeds behind their house.

I don't know why, but with George's calm, quiet disposition, I assumed he'd been a shopkeeper or laborer. He didn't exude the same confidence and bearing that Xander did.

Darlene nodded. "It's been many years. He came home after Vietnam when our second was born." For a few more moments she reminisced about the past, then turned to Xander. "I'm glad you made it home safe, young man. There's no better place for a man than with his family."

Darlene's words slammed into me, making my stomach twist with guilt. I wrapped one arm around my waist, feeling almost sick with it. I couldn't undo the past year and a half, but I prayed that someday he would be able to forgive me.

CHAPTER EIGHTEEN
Xander

I glanced around the room, taking in every detail. The house was small but tidy. Cozy. It was the perfect place for Lydia and the baby. The neighbors obviously watched out for one another, though Lydia could certainly use more security. I hadn't seen an alarm at all when we'd entered the house, nor did I see one by the door off the kitchen, where I assumed the garage was located.

"I'll be home the rest of the day," Lydia said to the neighbor, "so you can go home if you'd like."

I didn't miss Lydia shuffling nervously in my peripheral vision. Darlene studied us with speculation, a sly look entering her eyes. She probably thought we were eager to be alone. Poor old woman. If she only knew.

"Of course." Darlene smiled. "You have a lot of catching up to do."

That was a fucking understatement if I'd ever heard one. Still, I pasted on a polite smile as the woman made her way to the sliding door.

Darlene slipped outside with one last little smile, and I turned my attention to the baby in the living room. A combination of fear and awe gripped me as I stared down at a tiny version of myself. With hair so blonde it was almost white, and a fair complexion that made those gray blue eyes stand out, she was the most precious thing I'd ever seen. "I can't believe how much she looks like me."

"Yeah. I know." Was that disappointment in her voice?

I couldn't help the bitterness that crept into my tone. "I should've known."

I knew I shouldn't have said it, but being here, seeing my daughter in her element, pissed me off all over again. I had a *kid*. She was mine, yet I didn't know a goddamn thing about her.

Beside me, Lydia stiffened, her chin jerking up, her eyes going flat and cold. I should want her to feel bad; I should want to hurt her for keeping my daughter from me. Instead, I regretted saying the words as soon as they left my mouth. I wanted her to feel guilty, but I didn't want to cause her pain.

I couldn't reconcile my emotions. Part of me was still angry—furious, in fact. At the same time, I was completely awestruck that we'd made something so beautiful, so precious.

As if she knew Lydia and I were talking about her, my daughter turned those big eyes on me, and my heart thudded to a stop in my chest. Was it possible to fall in love in a single moment, with a single glance? Because I knew, right that second, that this little girl already had me wrapped around her finger.

Amid the toys and blocks she'd been playing with, she picked up a stuffed elephant and toddled toward me. Did she recognize me from yesterday? I sucked in a breath as she stopped directly in front of me and held her arms up. I'd held her before, but somehow this was vastly different. It felt like a momentous occasion was occurring between the two of us, though she was too young to know it. Bending down, I slipped my hands around her tiny body and lifted her to my chest. She laid her head on my shoulder for a second, and warmth spread through my chest.

Lydia watched silently. Her eyes were slightly misty, though she quickly blinked it away. Something flitted across her expression before I could tell exactly what it was. I wished I could tell what was going through that mind of hers. As if she knew she was giving too much away, she crossed her arms protectively over her chest. I wasn't stupid. This couldn't be easy for her either.

The baby squirmed in my arms and held the small gray elephant up for my inspection. She chattered on in her childish gibberish, and a broad smile wreathed my face. Her little body wiggled again, demanding to get down, and I set her on her feet. The moment those tiny toes touched the ground, she bolted away again, back to her toys.

I turned to Lydia. "She's so small. I didn't expect her to be so…"

"Mobile?" Lydia let out a small laugh. "She started walking at nine months and hasn't stopped since. She must get that from your side, because I didn't walk until I was well over a year old."

I absorbed that, mentally doing the math in my head. "So she's almost one?"

A soft smile curved her mouth. "Her birthday's next month—the eighth."

Her smile dissolved as I stared at her. There was so much between us, so many things that need to be hashed out, but I couldn't think of a single one of them right now with her in front of me. Just as beautiful as she'd been two years ago, she stopped me in my tracks. Even when I'd been overseas, she filled my dreams. We'd had a connection once—I knew I hadn't imagined that. I'd thought I'd lost her, but in a strange twist of fate, we were now tethered together for life.

My heart softened just the tiniest bit toward her. The anger was still there, the faint sting of betrayal, but now lust overrode the other emotions. My fingers twitched with the need to reach out and touch her face. A lock of nearly black hair had fallen across her cheek, and I wanted to brush it away, tuck it behind her ear. In the end, I did none of those things.

I'd been hoping to win her over again, but knowing I had a little girl changed things. If Lydia still wanted an annulment, I would grant it to her. No matter what happened between us, the only truly important thing now was our daughter. I wanted to make sure she grew up knowing that she was loved and cherished, and I planned to start right now.

Moving toward the living room, I ventured closer. The baby's little head snapped up as she watched me curiously. I knelt and handed her a block; giant gray eyes met mine before she reached out and took it from my fingers, then placed it at the top of her tower. We continued like that for several minutes until she lost interest in the blocks and toddled off to find something else. A smile curved my mouth, and I winked at Lydia as she maneuvered around the couch and sat watching us. Once again, I wished I could read her mind. Her face was a mixture of emotion, but I'd be lying if I didn't see the sadness deep in those eyes.

Was she worried that I would leave again, or was she concerned, like she stated yesterday, that I would try to take our daughter away from her? I'd been upset—understandably—but I deeply regretted my words. I would never be selfish enough to try to split up mother and daughter. I said things I shouldn't have in the heat of the moment, and I owed Lydia an apology for that. But not now. I'd save that for later, when it was just her and me.

I thought back to the emails she'd sent more than a year ago. Maybe Lydia really would've told me. I'd never know. The important thing now was our daughter; from now on, I was going to be involved in her life as much as possible. I was around to stay—whether Lydia liked it or not.

CHAPTER NINETEEN
Lydia

I darted a glance at Xander from the corner of my eyes. His cockiness had leached away, giving him a softer look. He sat at Alexia's level, watching with a smile as she dragged toys out of the bins in the corner. She brought him her fuzzy yellow duck and a handful of other toys, depositing the gifts at his feet.

I grinned and picked up a toy phone. "This is her favorite. She doesn't talk much yet, but she loves to pretend."

Holding the phone to my ear, I carried on an imaginary conversation with the peppy mechanical voice on the other end. Alexia held her hand out, fingers grasping for the device, and I passed it to her.

Xander was quiet for several minutes, just watching our daughter before he finally turned to me. "I'm really angry with you, Lydia."

My cheeks burned, and I dropped my gaze to the floor so he wouldn't see the tears burning my eyes. I'd regretted not telling him—really, I had. He'd never truly believe that, though. And I deserved his scorn. Although I'd tried to contact him a couple times, it wasn't enough. I should have tried harder, should have made it a point to tell him he had a daughter. It was the absolute least he deserved.

"I'm sorry."

He must have heard the remorse in my voice, because he cleared his throat as if to swallow down whatever retort had sprung to the tip of his tongue. It was another long moment before he spoke. "I feel like an asshole for having to ask, but… what's her name?"

Shock and surprise jolted through me, but I immediately schooled my features. It was my own fault, after all, that he didn't know. I smiled softly, attempting to set him at ease. "Alexia Laureen."

He turned a startled gaze on me, and I just shrugged in response. "It seemed to fit."

He nodded slowly, testing the name on his tongue. "Alexia. Alexander and Lydia. Makes sense."

I dipped my chin in acknowledgement. "She's ours. Both of us." I felt the weight of his gaze but couldn't bring myself to meet his stare.

"That she is." He paused. "Why Laureen? It's not exactly a common name."

I bit my lip. Did I dare tell him the truth? Once I'd found out I was pregnant, I'd wanted to incorporate him into Alexia's life, even if not physically. I'd been intensely curious about the man I'd married and had done hours of research trying to dig up his past—where he'd come from, what his parents had been like. I'd found an article detailing his parents' deaths on a mission trip to Africa almost two decades ago now, and I'd felt a strong urge to link our daughter to them. I wanted Alexia to know about her grandparents and what good people they'd been—though I personally had never met them—and I'd decided that Xander's mother's name was perfect.

I lifted one shoulder. "I came across it online."

He raised a brow but didn't say a word, and he turned his attention back to Alexia. His words soon cut through the silence. "I stormed out yesterday, so we didn't have much time to discuss anything like I'd originally planned."

I stiffened at the statement, unsure as to where he was going, and I responded cautiously. "We can talk now if you'd like."

Seeming almost hesitant, he withdrew a sheaf of papers from his back pocket and handed them over. Before my fingers even touched the heavy envelope, I knew what it was. Xander cleared his throat, avoiding me.

I ran a fingertip over the edge of the envelope. "Have you signed yet?"

"Not yet." He shook his head, then turned to face me. "I have a proposition for you."

My breath caught in my throat and my heart skipped a beat as his intense gaze captured mine. God, when he looked at me like that, it was as if time had slipped away. I remembered how charming and funny he'd been the night we first met.

"I'll give you what you want if you give me what I want."

I sat frozen, digesting his words, trying to shake off the memory. What the hell did that mean?

As if reading my mind, he continued, "I'll grant you the annulment if you still want it. But I want time with Alexia."

My vision turned hazy and my heart raced, my entire body going completely lax. Thank God I was sitting, otherwise I probably would've collapsed in a very undignified heap on the floor. My mind couldn't quite comprehend what he was saying. Did he want custody? Of course he would. He had every right to her, I knew he did, but... How could I give up my little girl, even for a few days here and there? I'd been the only person in Alexia's life for the past eleven months, not including, of course, Darlene and the ladies from the salon who watched her now and then. I'd rocked her to sleep, comforted her when she cried, held her hand as she'd learned to stand and then walk. Before I even realized what I was doing, I found myself shaking my head. "I..."

Xander's eyes turned cold. "We can do this the easy way or the hard way, Lydia. You won't keep my daughter from me anymore."

I pressed a hand to my chest, my lungs and heart aching so badly that it hurt to breathe. I finally forced words up and out of my throat. "I just... She's my baby—"

"Don't give me that shit," he hissed. He pointed at the little girl playing with a stuffed lamb. "Do you even understand how I feel? Do you know what you've taken from me? You've deprived me of a year, Lydia. A whole fucking year of my daughter's life. I missed *everything*."

His voice got louder and louder, and I stretched out a hand, laying it on his arm. "Please, keep your voice down.

Alexia turned, as if sensing the discord between us. She climbed to her feet and toddled toward us. It was like a knife to my heart to see my baby girl head straight for Xander, and hot tears clouded my eyes.

Xander's attention was fixed firmly on me. "I want to spend time with her; I want to be involved."

"Xander…"

"Damn it, Lydia." Fury filled his eyes and he jumped to his feet. "She's my daughter too and—"

His words were drowned out by the high-pitched cry that split the air as Alexia burst into tears. Throwing herself at me, she turned her face into my shoulder, sobs wracking her tiny body.

A mixture of horror and guilt flooded his expression, and Xander reached out to soothe her. "I'm sorry, baby girl."

Alexia peered up at him but flinched, looking away again with a whimper as he reached out and gently stroked her back.

"Shh." I shushed Alexia, rubbing a hand over her back in soothing circles. "It's okay, sweetheart. Xander…" My gaze darted to him, and I bit my lip before correcting myself. "Daddy didn't mean to yell."

He stiffened at the word, every line of his body going completely taut.

"I'm sorry." I shot him an apologetic look as he dropped his arm to his side. "She's not used to men. Maybe we should table this discussion for another day."

After what seemed like a long internal debate, he finally relented. "Fine," he snapped. "I'll be back tomorrow."

I held Alexia close and allowed my tears to finally break free as the door slammed behind him. Maybe this time he'd stay away for good. As soon as the thought crossed my mind, I regretted it.

"Mama's here, baby," I crooned to Alexia. "I'll always be here for you."

As I held my baby close, I realized it was the only certainty in life. Regardless of what happened with Xander, I wouldn't let anyone disappoint us—and I especially wouldn't let anyone hurt Alexia. It was me and her against the world. And I was just fine with that.

CHAPTER TWENTY
Xander

"You here for good, McLean?"

I paused, turning my attention away from the box I'd been unpacking to Con, who leaned against the edge of my desk. "Sure."

I originally hadn't been scheduled to start until next week, but I needed something to take my mind off the situation with Lydia.

"Thank fuck." He pulled a chair closer, then sank down and propped his feet on the edge of my desk.

I lifted one brow. "Make yourself at home."

Turning my attention back to the box in front of me, I continued to unload its meager contents. A few books, a picture from when I'd been in the Army. I held the frame in my hands, not really seeing the picture inside.

It still hadn't fully sunk in that I had a daughter—a tiny little girl who looked just like me. If things had been different, would I be holding a picture of her right now instead? Would I see her precious little face staring back at me from the corner of my desk instead of my brothers? Better, even, would Lydia and I be in the frame as well, like a real family?

My family.

The words settled in my heart, dissolving some of the anger that still resided there. Nearly two years ago, Lydia and I had shared a wild night of intense passion and chemistry like I'd never known. Now we shared more than desire—we had a child together.

The memory of our night together had kept me sane and driven me to distraction in equal measure while I was away. I'd been terrified those couple times when she'd attempted to reach out to me. I thought maybe she'd moved on, found someone else. But the fact that she hadn't spoke volumes. And the paperwork for the dissolution being filed incorrectly? It had to mean something. In my estimation, all of these things had happened for a reason—Lydia and I were supposed to be together.

How did the expression go? Absence made the heart grow fonder? I'd felt something for her the night we first met—it was the whole reason I married her. I'd always been the staid, straitlaced one who never made one impulsive decision in my life. Yet, in that moment, I'd known it was right. Even just a few nights ago in the restaurant, lust had hit me like an uppercut to the chin. I still felt like it was right—but would I be able to convince her of that? Especially after yesterday. I'd lost my temper again, damn it, and it may have cost me both of them.

Con cleared his throat. "We've got a meeting in fifteen. Working a case in conjunction with Dallas PD."

Pushing the melancholy thoughts from my mind, I turned my attention back to my boss. "Go."

I listened intently as he briefed me on the situation. Over the past few weeks, a rash of burglaries had happened across the city. Reports had come from both wealthy residents and independently owned stores.

"Unfortunately," Con continued, "the only thing each victim has in common is that their security is lacking, if they even have it. A small jewelry store was broken into last week, but the perpetrator bypassed the security system so it never alerted the authorities."

My brows lifted at that news. That was pretty difficult to manage in this day and age. "And there are no common denominators?"

"Nothing that the PD or Jason have been able to find so far."

I would've suspected that the person responsible knew the places that he'd broken into. More than likely, he either knew the owner or spent a good deal of time there. "Ex-employee?"

"PD has cross-referenced employees from the stores and

checked into relatives of the homeowners. No matches."

Damn. "So what the hell are they doing with everything?"

I assumed this was more than a one-man operation, judging from the amount of work it took to accomplish something of this magnitude. Fenced items were much harder to get rid of than anyone realized. With technology, there was always a footprint somewhere online or a camera to capture someone's face.

"So here's the thing." Con half-laughed. "One of the victims is Alan Richter. Insanely wealthy, huge pain in the ass." Sounded about right. I gave a little nod of acknowledgement as Con continued. "A painting was stolen from his residence last week. Ironically, he also owns the jewelry boutique that was broken into."

"Sounds personal."

Con tipped his head. "That's why Richter is out for blood. He's certain he knows who took his painting."

I lifted a brow. "And that would be?"

"Oliver Eldredge. He owns an antiquity shop downtown. Unfortunately"—Con pulled a face—"Dallas PD questioned him and his employees but came up empty."

"What makes Richter so certain this Eldredge guy is involved?"

Con rolled his eyes. "An old feud, apparently. But, according to Phelps over at the seventh precinct, Eldredge was forthcoming and more than willing to help. Even offered to show them his home and warehouse where he keeps overflow."

Interesting. "They've checked all the local shops?"

Con nodded. "PD spoke with all local pawn shops, art galleries, other antiquities dealers... though they'd be stupid to take any of that stuff."

I snorted. "I would imagine. That's a lawsuit waiting to happen."

"Exactly." Con tipped his chin. "Doyle's been digging around online to see if there's been any recent mention of the stolen goods."

"Damn." That must be like searching for a needle in a haystack. But if anyone could find it, it would probably be Jason.

"Gets better." The promise in Con's tone had my ears perking up with interest. "We have a potential suspect. Ever heard of the Marvelous Maids?"

I blinked at him. "What the hell is that?"

A tiny smile quirked his mouth. "Cleaning service. Apparently, the regular cleaner who works for Richter remembers the painting that was stolen. She saw it across town yesterday in another client's house—Paul Mickelson."

"Oh, Jesus." Even I knew of that slimy fucker. His name was on every car dealership from here to El Paso, and he had a reputation to match his smarmy car salesman smile.

"Yep." Con tipped his chin. "PD interviewed him yesterday. He insisted on being guaranteed immunity for his cooperation."

I rolled my eyes. That son of a bitch could roll in pig shit and come out smelling like a rose. "Figures."

"Yep." Con scrubbed a hand over his face, and for the first time, I noticed the dark circles under his eyes.

"You look like shit."

He snorted. "Thanks, asshole. It was a long fucking night." I lifted a brow, prompting him to proceed, and he let out a sigh. "Lawson's girlfriend, Victoria, was attacked yesterday evening."

The news propelled me forward in my seat. "Jesus. She okay?"

Con waved me off. "She's fine, but he'll be out for a couple days with her."

I would hope so. The thought sent a chill through me. Lydia and I might not be on the best of terms at the moment, but I couldn't imagine someone hurting her. Or, God forbid, Alexia. I'd move heaven and earth to keep both of them safe.

I only knew Blake from brief interactions, and I didn't know Victoria at all. Still, the situation sucked. "They good?"

"I think so." Con lifted one shoulder in a shrug. "She's quiet. Been through a lot."

I nodded, my mind floating back to Lydia and Alexia. I'd been a fucking tool yesterday. I owed Lydia an apology for storming out—for the second time—and I needed to find a way to connect with Alexia without scaring the hell out of her again.

Con pushed up from the chair. "Conference room in five."

I nodded, my mind a thousand miles away. Pulling my phone from my back pocket, I tapped out a message to Lydia asking if I could come over tonight. I had no idea what I was going to do or say, but I had to make things right.

I nodded to the team as I slipped into the conference room

and took a seat next to Clay's twin brother, Cole. "Hey, man."

He tipped his chin at me as he relaxed into the chair. "You here for good?"

"Just in time for a party, apparently."

His attention jumped over my shoulder to Abby. "Thanks, beautiful." He winked at her, and she slapped his upper arm with the manila folder she held.

"That shit won't work with me."

He let out a laugh, completely unperturbed, and took the folder. Abby turned to me and held out another file. "Hi, Xander."

I accepted the folder. "Hey, Abby."

Cole twisted in his chair, his eyes following the petite brunette. "When you gonna let me take you out, Abs?"

She bared her teeth in a wicked smile. "You gonna make it worth my while?"

He grinned. "Always do."

"Knock that shit off," Clay barked from my other side.

I threw a look his way, but he kept his gaze firmly on the file in front of him. Beneath the table, though, his knee jumped anxiously, his hand curling into a fist on his thigh. Interesting.

Jason Doyle set his laptop down, dragging my attention to him. "Everyone ready?"

A low murmur of affirmation rose from the table, and Con nodded for him to begin. "As you all know, a painting recently stolen from Alan Richter's residence turned up in the home of Paul Mickelson. PD questioned him yesterday, and we finally got a lead."

That was good news.

"Apparently, the items are being auctioned off each Friday night. They're invitation only for only the wealthiest customers. New clients are referral only. Mickelson told them all about the process, but he swears he has no idea who's running them."

"Fuck." I leaned back in my chair. "So we've got nothing."

"IP address is different, and the signal gets rerouted all over the damn place. Website changes every week, and an invitation is sent out about an hour prior to the start of the auctions."

Con spoke up. "Apparently, two items were stolen from Richter's residence. The painting we know was purchased by

Mickelson. But he denies knowing anything about this." Con pressed a button on the remote and an image filled the screen, an ugly bust of someone that looked to be at least five hundred years old. "Richter is adamant we find it. He believes that Oliver Eldredge has it and plans to move it."

Con tipped his head my way. "Clay and McLean, you're on Eldredge. Basic recon. Dig into his background, anything you can find out about him. The PD have already been through the shop, but we'll need to get eyes on the warehouse, see if anything looks suspicious."

"I think we need to get into one of these auctions," Jason stated.

Con nodded. "Agreed."

He turned his attention to the other guys, and my attention drifted back to my wife and daughter. Alexia was mine, too, and what I'd told Lydia yesterday was true—I wanted to be involved in her upbringing. I replayed Lydia's reaction in my mind, her hackles rising, claws coming out. She was like a tigress, protective of her cub. I smiled at the image. That was Lydia, all right. Seeing her with the baby had made me want her all the more. She obviously loved our daughter and would do anything for her.

I was still angry with her—who wouldn't be?—but I couldn't deny that I still wanted her. It might require a lot of convincing on my part, but I'd just have to show her I meant every word of what I'd said before. I wanted Lydia and the baby, and I wanted to be part of their lives. I needed to make Lydia see that I didn't want to take the baby away—just the opposite, in fact. We could make this work. She wasn't going to give in easily, but I was going to win her over—one way or another.

CHAPTER TWENTY-ONE
Lydia

The doorbell rang, making me jump and causing my heartrate to double. Alexia continued to play on the floor, undisturbed by the sound. Pushing off the couch, I headed toward the front door, dread sitting like a lead ball in my stomach. Even through the narrow, frosted pane of glass in the door, there was no mistaking Xander's broad form.

Drawing in a fortifying breath, I unlocked the door and pulled it open. Xander stood there, larger than life, his presence dominating my entire front porch. Face unreadable, he silently stepped inside. Without waiting for an invitation, he toed off his boots, then turned to me, holding out a plastic shopping bag of Chinese takeout. A peace offering?

I slipped the handles from his fingers, careful not to touch him. "Thank you."

My stomach rumbled as the delicious smells wafted up to me. I'd gotten home barely fifteen minutes ago, giving me just enough time to change out of my work clothes and into a pair of comfy sweats and a T-shirt.

Closing the door, I flipped the lock, then gestured down the hallway. Instead of preceding me down the hall, Xander tipped his chin, gesturing for me to go first. I felt his gaze on me the whole way, like he was painting a bull's-eye on my back, just waiting for me to slip up. So far, nothing I had done was good enough. He hadn't allowed me to explain myself, had only thought the absolute worst.

Maybe tonight would go better since our previous two encounters had been less than successful—understatement of the year. Tonight he'd brought dinner. The fact that he'd gone out of his way to do something nice amped up my guilt. It was an uncomfortable situation at best, but I was determined to play nice, for Alexia's sake. If he could come halfway, I could too.

Rounding the corner to the living room, I saw Alexia was still in her spot, eyes glued to the cartoon playing on TV. I set the food on the counter and began to remove the containers.

I felt Xander come up beside me, his huge form moving into my peripheral vision. "You leave her alone like that all the time?"

I bristled at his words. *So much for that peace offering.* I wanted to speak up in my defense, but instead, I swallowed the words down. I knew he was still angry, but it wouldn't do either of us any good to feed into it. *Be the bigger person, Lydia.*

"I was gone for thirty seconds. Besides," I gestured around the room, "everything's babyproofed."

"It only takes a few seconds for them to get into something and get hurt."

I barely held back a snort. Now he suddenly had a wealth of knowledge about raising kids from some Google search he'd come across in the last two days? Was he out of his damn mind? What the hell did he think I'd been doing for the past year?

"You know, that never occurred to me. You're absolutely right." I turned toward him and pasted on a sweet smile, a direct contradiction to the sarcasm flowing from my tongue. "Next time, I guess I just won't answer the door."

Intense blue eyes narrowed on me, and I glared right back. If he thought he could just walk in here and start criticizing my parenting skills, he had another think coming.

I could practically feel the animosity vibrating off his tense body, and my gaze skittered away, back to Alexia. I'd hoped we could at least be civil for her sake, but gauging from the attitude he was carrying around, I didn't think that was very likely.

Appetite gone, I shoved away from the counter. Brushing him off, I made my way around the couch and settled on the plush cushion. My book still lay on the armrest where I had discarded it when the doorbell rang, and I picked it up and began to read again. For several long moments Xander stood rooted to the floor, and I could feel his angry gaze on me, burning into the back of my head. Finally, with an irritated sound, he entered the living room and settled beside me on the couch. My muscles tensed, acutely aware of him.

Finally noticing his presence, Alexia turned and peered warily at Xander. I watched surreptitiously over the pages of my book as she studied him. The sight sent a little pain of regret shooting through my heart. For both their sakes, I wanted her to be comfortable with him. I wanted Alexia to know her father, and he deserved to know his intelligent, sweet little girl.

With a soft sigh, I set my book aside. Infusing as much enthusiasm into my voice as possible, I directed my words to Alexia. "Why don't you come see Daddy?" Her eyes flitted to me for a moment before darting back to Xander, and she shook her head emphatically. Next to me, Xander tensed, his hands clenched into fists where they rested on his thighs.

"Don't take it personally," I said, gently resting a hand on his forearm. Thick cords of muscle tensed under my touch, and I pulled my hand away, tucking it into my lap. Xander leaned forward, bracing his elbows on his knees. For a long moment, he stared at the ground, then lifted his eyes to Alexia. His voice was quiet when he spoke. "I'm sorry. I've been an asshole." He spread his hands wide. "I don't have a good excuse. I'm just… lost."

I knew how that felt. "I understand."

He watched her for a moment before speaking. "What's she like?"

"Smart. Too damn smart," I smiled. "She watches everything and everyone. She loves to play, especially with things she can build."

A grin cracked his face, transforming him into the handsome man I remembered. "That's probably my fault. I was always that way, too."

Alexia continued to play on the floor, intermittently watching whatever was currently on the Disney channel. "She's always taken after you," I admitted. "Do you want to see some pictures?"

"Of course."

I couldn't tell if he was being genuine or just trying to appease me, but he moved closer regardless. I opened up the photo app on my phone and began to scroll. "Just so you know," I warned him, "I have a *lot* of pictures."

I started at the beginning, on the day she was born. Xander slipped the phone from my fingers and enlarged the image, a look of pure awe crossing his face. "She's changed so much."

A smile lifted my lips. "I know. It's gone so fast." My gaze darted to Alexia, her eyes glued to the TV. What would happen if Xander and I ended up sharing custody? He deserved to spend time with his daughter, but I couldn't imagine not seeing her every day. "She's constantly growing and changing. But there's no denying she got most of your looks with that hair."

I didn't mean for the words to come out so sad, but I felt Xander's gaze on me. "I see a little bit of you in her, too."

I rolled my eyes but managed a small smile. "Ha. Maybe a drop."

Xander shook his head. "I mean, she's pretty much my clone, but..." He laughed when I lightly backhanded his bicep, then sobered. "Seriously. She's beautiful and vibrant, just like you."

I felt my face heat as a blush spread up my neck and over my cheeks. Clearing my throat, I deflected his attention from me and back to the pictures on my phone. "Here's her first bath."

We sifted through hundreds of photos, dozens of frilly, cute little outfits and fluffy bows. I laughed as I pointed at a picture I'd taken around Christmas. "She was so good, letting me dress her up and change outfits a dozen times. I must have taken a hundred photos that day alone."

Xander smiled. "I'll bet."

Leaning back, he slung one arm over the back of the couch. Curled up on the cushion next to him, it brought me almost within his embrace, and my breath caught in my chest. We weren't touching, yet an electrical current connected us. I turned my head and found him looking right at me, those cobalt eyes cutting straight to my soul.

Suddenly, it was too much. I needed to put some space between us. "I—I should serve dinner."

I popped up from the couch, my heart beating a million miles a minute. I was terrified of Xander coming back into our lives and disrupting our peaceful environment. What scared me more than anything, though, was my reaction anytime he got close—and the fact that I wanted more of it.

CHAPTER TWENTY-TWO
Xander

Lydia hopped to her feet and practically ran to the kitchen, putting a healthy distance between us. Disappointment mingled with relief in my gut as I watched her move away from me. The air between us had been charged with lust, and my fingers still tingled with the need to reach out and touch her.

I curled them into a fist and gazed around the sunny, welcoming living room, taking in the comfortable furniture and décor. Although I'd been here just yesterday, I hadn't paid much attention to my surroundings. The house was homey and welcoming, trendy without being overdone. There was a faux stone fireplace situated against the far wall, and the couch was large and comfortable, the perfect size for cuddling up with a beautiful woman. Like Lydia.

Before the thought fully solidified in my mind, I heard the front door open then slam shut again. The hell? Someone had a key to Lydia's place? I threw a glance at Lydia, whose posture had changed dramatically. Because of me, or because of who the hell was here? She hadn't mentioned a roommate. A friend, maybe? Lydia's shoulders seemed to jump with each staccato tap of heels echoing in the short hallway as the visitor made her way toward the kitchen.

Still partially obscured by the couch, I watched the woman enter the room. She let out a huff and directed her wrath at Lydia. "I had to park on the street because of the behemoth truck blocking your driveway, and—oh, good Lord, what are you wearing?"

So, not a friend... My brows lifted at the woman's horrified gaze as it skimmed over Lydia, clad in the black sweats that hugged her ass and skimmed her legs. Not that I'd looked.

Lydia glanced down at herself with a shrug. "It's not like I'm going anywhere."

"How do you always manage to find the most horrendous things possible?" The woman shook her head as Lydia opened her mouth to respond. "Anyway. You know I can't stand this place. I thought you said your lease was up?"

My eyes narrowed as I studied her. Somewhere around middle-aged, I couldn't tell exactly how old she was. She was pretty enough in an overdone, high-maintenance kind of way, but that didn't explain how she knew Lydia or why she was here throwing insults around like it was her job. Was she a business associate? God, I hoped not. I wasn't gonna lie. Lydia wasn't exactly my favorite person at the moment, but I pitied her if she had to deal with this piece of work every day.

My eyes jumped to Lydia, who just shrugged sedately. "You know it suits us just fine. It's safe, and rent is reasonable."

The woman gave another little irritated huff and propped a hand on her hip. "Not if you have neighbors taking up all the parking space."

I stood and addressed the woman's issue. "Sorry, ma'am, that would be me."

Her surprised gaze snapped in my direction, just noticing me for the first time. Her lip curled slightly as she studied me, her gaze sliding over my standard issue black polo and TDUs. Almost immediately, she dismissed me and turned back to Lydia. "I didn't realize you were entertaining a... friend."

Anger rose up inside me. Above all things, I hated being disrespected. I somehow managed to bite my tongue for Lydia's sake. If she wasn't going to say anything, neither was I. The woman's gaze landed next on the Chinese food sitting on the counter, and she launched into an opinionated offensive. "I don't know how you eat that stuff." She shuddered. "It's revolting, and it's full of fat. You of all people should know better."

Had she just called Lydia fat? My Lydia, who was practically perfection, her tall figure rounded in all the right places? Who the hell did she think she was? Protective instincts flared to the surface, and I barely managed to tamp them down before I said something I'd regret. Well, that wasn't quite true. I wouldn't regret putting the woman in her place, but I had a feeling that Lydia might not like me speaking up on her behalf.

My brows drew together as I watched Lydia, waiting for her to defend herself. I couldn't understand why she let this woman walk all over her. So far, she'd had to audacity to insult Lydia's home, the food she ate, the way Lydia dressed, then dismissed me as if I were no better than common trash. I was already pissed off, struggling desperately to understand what was happening.

The open, relaxed expression Lydia had worn five minutes ago was long gone. If not friendly, exactly, she'd been polite and had even laughed a few times as we'd flipped through photographs. Now, though, it was as if she had literally flipped a switch. She'd shut every emotion down, defensive walls going up in their place. I hated seeing her like this, but I didn't know what to do about it. Why would she let someone speak to her this way?

The woman studied Lydia, then sniffed, as if not getting the reaction she'd hoped for. I didn't know what her angle was, but I was already ready to boot her out of the house. Lifting a shopping bag I hadn't noticed, she set it on the counter and begin to pull out tiny pink outfits. "I bought these for Alexia."

Lydia's shoulders slumped, and she seemed to soften. I watched the exchange with interest. Lydia's voice was quiet, almost resigned, when she responded. "Thanks, Jolene. I'm sure she'll love them."

The woman looked around. "Where is Alexia?" Her eyes lighting on Alexia, she strode into the living room and held her arms out. "Come here, baby."

Anger coursed through my veins as I studied the woman's features. Was Lydia related to this bitch? A sister, maybe? Jesus. My pity increased tenfold.

My daughter looked up at the woman—Jolene—for a moment, then redirected her attention to the blocks scattered around the floor. Jolene turned back to Lydia. "Have you spoken with the pediatrician lately? I still don't understand why she doesn't talk. And she doesn't make eye contact."

"It's perfectly normal," Lydia replied, her voice tight.

It was on the tip of my tongue to tell the woman that she was barely a year old and had the attention span of a goldfish, but her next words stopped me in my tracks, sending a wave of fury through me. "Are you sure there's nothing wrong with her?"

Red bled into my vision, anger threatening to explode outward. She thought she could walk in here and degrade my wife and child? She thought that bringing gifts could manipulate them into allowing her to spew her hateful opinions? Hell fucking no. I'd had enough. Drawing myself to my full height, I stared her down. "There's nothing wrong with her. She's perfect."

Jolene's gaze jumped to me, filled first with surprise, then loathing. "And who are you?"

Lydia tried to interject. "This is—"

I cut her off. "I'm Xander. Alexia's father."

Surprise flared in the Jolene's eyes, and she made a little sound of derision. "Of course. I should have realized. Too bad my grandbaby got all of your genes instead."

Wait… what? My mind spun. It took a moment for the words to register, then realization slammed into me, stealing the retort from the tip of my tongue. Christ Almighty. This just got worse and worse. This was Lydia's mother?

The bitch turned her attention back to Lydia. "How was your date?"

Just the mention of the man Lydia had been out with a few nights ago sent anger curling through me. Lydia shrugged. "We didn't really hit it off."

I snorted, then spoke the words I knew Lydia wouldn't. "That's an understatement. The asshole stuck her with the check."

Jolene threw a glare my way before dismissing me once more. "Well. Maybe next time."

Next time? How often did Lydia's mother set her up with assholes like the one I'd met Saturday night? Why did she feel it was her place to set Lydia up at all? And to mention it in front of me—Lydia's husband and Alexia's father—pissed me off more than I could say. "I think it's time to wrap up for tonight. It's almost Alexia's bedtime."

Jolene dug in her heels, not ready to give in. "You're staying?"

As much as I'd love to, I wasn't going to lie and tell her yes, make her think Lydia and I were sleeping together. From the distasteful look on her face, I figured that was probably the worst thing she could imagine. Didn't mean I couldn't stretch the truth a little. "You're blocking me in."

Her eyes narrowed before she gave a haughty toss of her head. "Lydia, we'll talk later."

"Okay."

Lydia's eyes remained glued to the countertop, but I saw her flinch when the front door slammed, punctuating Jolene's dramatic exit. I stared at Lydia, willing her to meet my gaze. Finally, steel-gray eyes lifted to mine, and the words poured from my mouth.

"What the hell just happened?"

CHAPTER TWENTY-THREE
Lydia

Jolene happened. Like a hurricane, she swept into my life then left me to pick up the destruction she left in her wake. Inhaling deeply, I swallowed down my frustration. "It's fine."

"It's not fine." Xander eyed me like I had two heads. "She insulted you, insulted our daughter..."

I knew all that. I'd been dealing with the same thing for twenty-six years. If I'd learned anything during that time, it was that my mother loved to fight. She thought she was always right, and she'd argue until she was blue in the face—or until the other person gave up. Which happened far more often than it should. I had no desire to engage in any kind of confrontation with her. It was easier to just let her spout her opinions then leave.

I waved a hand. "It doesn't matter."

"It does matter."

I bristled. "She just..." She just what? Xander wasn't wrong.

He continued, undaunted, when I remained silent. "She's manipulative, and you don't have to put up with that shit. Especially from your own mother, of all people."

I could feel my emotions shutting down. Tired of conflict, I turned toward the sink and busied my hands rinsing the dishes. "Okay."

Xander let out a growl behind me. "Don't do that."

"What?" I heard the flat tone of my voice, but I refused to let him get under my skin.

All of a sudden, he was beside me. Cupping my elbow in one

huge hand, he turned me to face him. "Don't shut me out like that."

"Like what?"

"That same crap you just pulled with her where you close yourself off and say something just to appease me."

I dropped my gaze and studied the grain running through the wood planking beneath my feet.

"Lydia."

I flinched at his hard tone. "Please stop yelling."

Out of my peripheral vision, I watched Xander's mouth open, then slam shut again. His huge hands gripped my upper arms, demanding my attention, and I reluctantly lifted my eyes to his. "I'm sorry, sweetheart. I'm not yelling at you. I just… Help me understand. Because I don't get it. Why do you let her talk to you like that?"

"It's just how she is." I shrugged, and he released his hold on me. "She's done this for years. She has an opinion about everything."

"That's more than opinionated, and it's a bullshit excuse for her behavior." Xander pointed to the bag of frilly pink dresses on the counter. "She thinks that buying you things gives her the right to say whatever she wants. That's not okay. Love doesn't come at a price, Lydia. You do something nice for someone because you care—not so you can manipulate them."

I swallowed hard. "She likes to buy Alexia things…" Because it was all she had to offer. She didn't spend any quality time with Alexia, instead showing up with gifts, breezing in and out of our lives every week or so.

My mother was a pain in the ass. I knew it all too well, and now, so did Xander. She wasn't ever going to change, so I wouldn't waste my breath trying to reason with her.

"You're so smart and strong and independent." My cheeks heated as Xander began to speak. "You can't let her make you feel bad for any of those things."

My mother's words from the past came floating back to me. *I only want what's best for you.* But that wasn't quite true, was it? Jolene wanted what was best for *her*. Tears pricked my eyes and burned the back of my throat. Not because Jolene's words had made me angry or upset—but because of Xander. Even still mad at me, he hadn't hesitated to support me. It felt good to have someone to hold me up instead of tear me down.

He met my gaze, studying me for a long moment. He lifted one hand and brushed a thumb over my cheek. "Don't ever sell yourself short. You're incredible, Lydia, just the way you are."

I swallowed hard, completely unsure of what to say. No one had ever stood up for me this way before. Not even Shawn. He'd seemed to care for me, yes, but he had the same pretentious air that my mother did. He was constantly trying to change me.

"Thank you." I whispered the words.

He was silent for several beats. "You're her daughter; why would she think it's okay to talk to you like that?"

I hung my ahead, ashamed. "Because she can."

He eyed me for a long moment. "What is she holding over you?"

I took a deep breath. "She loaned me the capital to open the salon. I didn't want to lease the building, and I managed to negotiate a good deal to buy it right after the recession. But…" I blew out a breath. "I needed twenty percent down, and I didn't have it. There was no way I could've afforded it otherwise, and…"

Xander spoke up as I trailed off. "She offered up the money."

I nodded at the rhetorical statement. Jolene never failed to throw that back at me anytime she wanted something. "You have to give to get," my mother had remarked more than once. It gave her free rein to demand whatever she wanted, whenever she wanted, and expect me to jump at her whim.

"I should have known," I continued. "Maybe I did. I set up a payment schedule so I could pay her off a little bit at a time as I started making money."

"What do you owe her?" His brows drew together.

I shifted on my feet. "A little over fifteen thousand."

"I'll take care of it."

My eyes widened. "No." I held up my hands. "No way."

There was no way I'd ever let him offer up money. That would be like jumping out of the frying pan and into a freaking volcano. I didn't want to owe this man anything. There was already so much between us, I didn't need to muddy the waters more than they already were.

Xander reached out and grasped my hands. "As long as you

owe her, she'll control you."

She would always control me; that would never change. I'd made a deal with the devil just by accepting the money from her in the first place. Now she would forever be able to tell me that I owed her because she'd funded my salon. I needed to break free, but I couldn't. Not yet.

I shook my head and tried to pull away, but he held me firmly in his grasp. "I can't take your money."

Xander squeezed my hands. "You will."

"Please don't." My gaze skittered away, focusing on the wall behind him. "I don't want to fight."

"Lydia…" Xander trailed off, then drew in a deep breath. His thumb rubbed small circles over the inside of my wrist, right at the pulse point. "I'm not trying to fight with you. I want to do this for you."

"Why?"

"Because it's the right thing to do."

Blue eyes stared into mine, and my breath caught. His words from just a few moments ago rose up in front of me. *You do something nice for someone because you care—not so you can manipulate them.* Did that mean he cared about me? No, he couldn't possibly. He was only offering because I was the mother of his child. Shaking the stupid thought from my head, I refocused on the situation at hand. "I won't take money from you."

"Then don't. We'll make it a business arrangement." I barely refrained from rolling my eyes. Yeah, because that had worked out so well for me in the past. I was already shaking my head when he continued. "Here's what's going to happen. I'm going to give you the money to pay your mother back. I opened an account in Alexia's name at the bank. Each month, I want two hundred dollars deposited into an account until you pay off the original amount."

I felt my mouth fall open. Was he serious? He wasn't even getting the money back. "But—"

He placed one finger over my lips, silencing my protest. He shot a look toward the living room where Alexia played quietly. Cerulean eyes cut back to mine. "Let me do this. I missed so much with her, and I want to make sure she's taken care of."

Tears burned my eyes and clogged my throat. Unable to speak,

I just nodded. How could I say no to that?

Sensing my unease, Xander dropped his hand away and changed the subject. "So. Why does she hate this place so much?"

I let out a soft, unladylike snort. "Probably because it's not the half-million-dollar home that my ex had picked out." That seemed like so long ago now. He lifted a brow, and I continued. "My ex—Shawn—"

"The one who ended up with your best friend?"

My gaze jumped to him, startled. "You remember that?"

Cerulean eyes bore into mine. "I remember everything about you, Lydia."

Heat licked over my flesh at his statement. The words were so simple, yet there was a wealth of information lying just beneath the surface. I barely repressed a shiver as his gaze skimmed over me like a lover's caress. I couldn't lie—I still remembered the feel of his hands on my body, the way he touched me, demanding and impatient and tender all at once.

I cleared my throat. "Shawn was—is—a lawyer. That's how he and my mom met," I clarified at Xander's questioning glance. "He was one of the lawyers who presided over her divorce when she left husband number two."

His brow scrunched. "How many times has she been married?"

"Three."

He let out a little laugh rife with disbelief. "Jesus. She might want to make friends with the lawyer."

"Husband number three *was* the lawyer," I deadpanned.

A smile cracked Xander's face and he shook his head. "Unreal. Anyway, go on."

"Right." I took a deep breath. "So, Shawn made a good living and he'd bought this huge house for us when we got engaged. I never lived there—he moved Jessica in after…" I waved a hand, not wanting to think about it. It'd been two years, but the hurt was still there, just beneath the surface.

"After I got home from Vegas, I started looking for a place to live. You remember my neighbor Darlene from yesterday." Xander nodded. "Well, I met her at the salon about a year ago when her daughter got married. I was pregnant"—his eyes darkened a bit at the mention of my pregnancy—"and needed a place to live. She and her husband, George, own this duplex. She convinced me to come look at it, and I fell in love with it."

As I spoke, Xander cracked open one of the takeout containers. "She said she'd rather rent it to me than anyone else. Besides, her daughter and son-in-law were moving to Oklahoma to follow his job." I opened the cupboard behind me and passed him a plate. "She and George helped me out a lot, moving furniture and stuff."

Xander piled food onto the plate, then passed it back to me with a nod, indicating I should eat it. I handed out another plate, then slid a fork over to him. "When Alexia came along, she kind of became a surrogate grandmother."

He paused in the act of scooping rice out of a container and met my eyes. "I'm glad you had someone you could count on."

His words hit me like a blow to the chest, and guilt immediately assailed me. "Xander, that's not—"

He held up one hand and gave a curt shake of his head. "It's fine. And I mean that—I'm glad you have people here who care about you and Alexia."

I nodded, then silently dug in to the plate he'd thoughtfully prepared for me. Over the next hour we made small talk, sharing laughs and swapping stories until I glanced at the clock on the far wall.

"Oh, wow. I didn't realize how late it was."

Xander pushed up from the couch. "Guess I should get going."

The words sent a little pang of disappointment through me. I'd actually been enjoying myself for the first time in a long while, and I was kind of sad that it was over. We weren't perfect, but we'd come to a kind of understanding at some point during the evening.

Scooping Alexia up, I propped her on my hip and followed him to the front door. "Will you be stopping by tomorrow?"

I prayed he wouldn't hear the faint breathlessness of my voice, as if my reaction hinged completely on his response. He met my gaze and studied me for a long moment before giving a slight nod. "Same time okay?"

I swallowed hard, my throat suddenly dry. "Sounds good."

Xander stood in the doorway, illuminated by the glow of

streetlights behind him. He bent and pressed a kiss to Alexia's downy head. "Good night, sweet girl."

He lifted his gaze to me, those liquid blue eyes sending a spark of warmth through me. Silence, thick with anticipation, fell between us, and my heart raced. Was he going to kiss me, too? Finally he dipped his chin at me. "Night, Liddy."

My heart dropped to my toes, and I couldn't squelch the disappointment that assailed me. He wasn't going to kiss me after all.

Not bothering to correct him, I swallowed over the lump in my throat, my voice raspy. "Night."

Closing the door, I fought against the tears burning the backs of my eyelids. It was irrational, but I couldn't help it. Part of me wanted him to kiss me as he had years ago. I should be happy that he hadn't. Xander had been true to his word, spending time with Alexia, trying to get to know her and be part of her life. Yet, after spending time with him tonight, it seemed as if time had slipped away. I felt… something between us. Did he not feel the same?

Of course he didn't. Pushing down my insecurities, I shoved the thought away. I didn't need any more complications in my life.

CHAPTER TWENTY-FOUR
Xander

I spent the morning chasing down leads and interviewing Oliver Eldredge's friends and employees, and even some customers. A lot of the people I'd spoken with said that he was honest and affable; a handful of others, however, didn't share the same opinion. Several people who had purchased items from Eldredge said he was conceited and supercilious and had swindled them out of their money. It was no secret that Eldredge placed a premium price on his items, but I couldn't say I blamed the man for trying to make a living.

From the employee directory we'd gotten from the PD, I tracked down one of his employees, a young woman named Mary Beth. She'd reluctantly admitted that Eldredge was an asshole but that he paid her well, and she'd never seen anything suspicious. She worked in the shop full-time and was going to school for art history. She hadn't seen the painting and had no knowledge of the statue that was still missing. I'd thanked her and left empty-handed with no leads.

Mickelson hadn't been able to secure an invitation for this week's auction, so we were currently at a standstill on the tech side. Jason was still working his magic in the hopes of hacking in, but last I heard, he was having a bitch of a time.

The officers in the precinct had checked pawn shops around the city to see if any of the fenced items had popped up, but so far there'd been nothing. It sucked that we had to wait another week for more information, but hopefully we would be better prepared and get a better handle on it. The biggest problem was that we had no idea where to begin. With the items being auctioned off potentially all over the world, it was damn near impossible to find them.

It'd been tedious and frustrating, and all I wanted to do right now was relax and see Alexia—and Lydia. I strode up to Lydia's front door and rang the bell. She met me only seconds later, Alexia propped on her hip, cooing happily. Her gaze turned solemn when she saw me, though, and I pasted on a smile, ignoring the pang in the region of my heart.

Over the past few days, I'd stopped at Lydia's house after work, spending an hour or so with them each night before bedtime. Alexia was beginning to relax around me a bit, but she hadn't fully adjusted to my presence. Lydia's admission the other day filled me with a protectiveness I'd never felt. She'd admitted that Alexia wasn't comfortable around men, not used to them. She couldn't know it, but I was fucking ecstatic at that little tidbit. That meant there hadn't been many—if any—men in her life since she'd had the baby almost a year ago.

Despite everything that had happened, Lydia was mine, damn it. She still had a slightly guarded look about her, but she, too, had begun to relax in my presence. I moved my gaze from Alexia up to Lydia. "Hey."

"Hey." She smiled and held the door for me, her eyes dropping to the box tucked under my arm. "What's that?"

"Just a little something for Alexia." I stepped inside and toed my boots off while Lydia locked up behind me. Turning back to Alexia, I held up the box. "Brought you a present, baby girl."

She examined it, her big gray eyes curious but unsure. Lydia's voice made up for Alexia's lack of enthusiasm. "Come on, sweet pea. Let's go see what Daddy brought you."

Following them down the hall toward the living room, I let that word sink in. God, that sounded good. Lydia settled cross-legged on the floor, situating Alexia in her lap, and I knelt next to them. Placing the box on the floor between us, I gestured to it. "Want to open it?"

Alexia craned her neck, turning to Lydia as if asking permission, and Lydia laughed. "Go ahead, open it."

Lydia slipped one lean finger under the seam and tugged

gently. Enraptured by the ripping sound of the paper, Alexia turned wide eyes on the present in front of her. She let out an excited squeal as she tore one long strip of paper off and held it up in victory.

I laughed and settled on my side, content to watch her. Finally we got the box open and Lydia retrieved the fluffy pink bear inside. Alexia took one look at the bear, then went right back to the strips of paper littering the ground. Picking them up, she let them flutter down like confetti, her laugh infectious.

I turned to Lydia, taking in the smile on her face, unable to stop the grin covering mine. "I think she likes the wrapping paper better than the bear," I said wryly.

She let out a tinkling laugh. "Don't be offended. I bought her a doll a couple months ago, thinking she'd love to have a baby. I took the doll out of the box, and, yeah…" She rolled her eyes and lifted her hands in a shrugging motion. "Alexia tossed the doll aside to play with the box for half an hour."

Alexia turned toward me as I let out a loud laugh. This time, though, it didn't seem to scare her. She examined my face intently, then seemed to relax when she saw that I was happy. I watched as she pushed up from Lydia's lap and made her way to her toybox. She dug around for a minute, then brought me a soft gray elephant. She held it out, and I slipped it from her fingers. "Is this for me?"

She nodded solemnly, then plopped down next to me and picked up the pink bear I'd brought. Moving the bear around, she chattered happily in her high-pitched voice, the words slurred and unclear. I lifted my gaze back to Lydia. "Does she talk much?"

She shook her head. "A few words here and there. Pediatrician says it's normal."

I nodded. I hadn't spent any time around little kids, so I took her word for it. Dropping the bear to the floor, Alexia jumped back up and made a beeline for her toys. I watched as she lugged a drawstring bag over to me. She pointed to the strings, indicating I should open it.

"You want this open?" She nodded and pulled at the strings but couldn't figure out how to open it. "Here, sweet girl, let me help."

Working the strings loose, I watched as she upended the bag and dumped dozens of colorful blocks on the floor. She picked up a bright pink one and held it up to me, then reached for another. With each block I stacked, she handed me another. Soon we had a good-sized tower going that was taller than Alexia.

I threw a grin at Lydia. "Want to help?"

She let out a throaty little laugh that wrapped around my heart. "Hey, you're the one who said you liked to build things."

"Oh, come on." I lifted an eyebrow in challenge, and she just shook her head with a tiny smile, holding her hands up in front of her.

"No way, I'm staying out of the destruction zone."

Before I could process her words, blocks showered down around me as Alexia smashed her tower, demolishing it into a pile of rainbow-colored block rubble.

I let out a gasp of mock outrage and turned my gaze on Alexia, who stared back at me expectantly. "Oh, you think that's funny?"

She let out a tiny giggle, and I reared up on my hands and knees, slowly stalking toward her. She laughed as I neared, pushing to her feet and running in a wide arc away from me. I collapsed to the floor, playing dead, and waited a long moment with my eyes closed. I could hear the tiny patter of her footsteps as she got closer, and she let out a little shriek as I opened my eyes and reached for her, drawing her into my arms. A deep belly laugh filled the air as I tickled her tummy, her arms and legs flailing with delight. Just as quickly as it started, Alexia rolled from my grasp and held up a tiny hand in my direction.

"No!"

"No?" I asked.

"No." She crossed her arms over her middle and shook her head emphatically.

Biting back my smile, I pretended to think for a moment. "Well, then…" Out of the corner of my eyes, I spied Lydia sitting within arm's reach. Faster than a snake striking, I snatched her ankle and yanked her closer to me. Lydia let out a gasp, then dissolved into giggles as my fingers danced over her ribs, tickling her.

Alexia laughed along as shrieks for mercy interspersed with peals of laughter fell from Lydia's lips. It was such a welcome sound that I couldn't help the smile from forming on my face. I wondered when she'd last allowed herself to really have fun. Using my body to press her into the floor, I moved more fully over top of her, still tickling her. Her chest heaved as she drew in deep, gasping breaths, and I smoothed my hand down her side. Her humor quickly fled as she took in our precarious position, and those gorgeous eyes met mine.

Only inches away, I could have dipped my head and pressed my lips to hers. I wanted to. God, how I wanted to. But not here, and not like this. Without breaking eye contact, I slowly lifted my body away from hers and sat back on my heels. I offered a hand, and she slipped a trembling palm into mine so I could pull her to a sitting position.

Pushing to her feet, she murmured an excuse about getting dinner started and slunk off to the kitchen. I watched her go, my eyes glued to the slight sway of her hips as she put distance between us. I watched her surreptitiously from the corners of my eyes, rewarded when I saw her peek over at me a couple times. It sent a tendril of hope curling through me.

I wanted her to look at me with something other than wariness. I wanted her to look at me with longing and desire and lust—the way she had a few minutes ago. I wanted everything from her, and I was determined to get it.

CHAPTER TWENTY-FIVE
Lydia

Butterflies kicked up in my stomach as I peered through my lashes at Xander, Alexia settled in his lap, playing with his fingers. Fingers and hands that had touched me only moments ago, sending fire licking over every nerve ending.

I pulled a package of pork chops from the fridge, then seasoned them and placed them in the skillet to cook. Off to the side, I started a pot of noodles. It was simple, but I knew that Alexia would eat them, since the cheesy shells were her favorite.

In the living room, Alexia popped to her feet and wrapped one tiny hand around Xander's thumb, her grip barely encircling his broad finger. "Up!"

I smiled, watching as she urged him to his feet. He willingly followed as she tugged him into the kitchen. I leaned back against the cabinet as she dragged him past me. "Looks like she has you wrapped around her finger—literally," I remarked, and Xander shot me a smile.

He shrugged good-naturedly. "There are worse things."

My eyebrows pulled together as Alexia guided Xander over to the very last cabinet—the one where I kept her treats. One of her favorite foods recently was rice cakes, and I knew instinctively that's what she was going for.

"Alexia…"

She glanced up at my warning tone, then darted a look at Xander. "Cookie."

She pulled at the cabinet door but was hindered by the baby

lock I'd installed inside. She sent a pitiful look up at Xander, who crouched down next to her. "You need something inside there, baby girl?"

Alexia pointed to the cabinet again, and Xander shot a look at me. "What's in there?"

I crossed my arms over my chest. "Treats." Directing my next words to Alexia, I said, "I'm making dinner right now. You can have one later."

Alexia barely glanced at me, instead framing Xander's face with her tiny hands, staring imploringly up at him. "Cookie."

Xander cleared his throat uncomfortably. "Not right now, sweetheart."

His entire body went rigid as Alexia threw her head back on a wail, at the same time swooning into his arms. Her back arched as she pitched a fit, her tiny arms and legs waving erratically. Xander shot me a panicked look, and I bit the inside of my lip to keep from smiling at the sight.

"Don't even think about it," I replied. I'd been on the receiving end of more than one temper tantrum, and I'd be lying if I said I didn't relish this little slice of payback he was now enjoying firsthand.

Alexia tore herself from Xander's arms and launched herself toward the cabinet, pulling on the knob to no avail.

Xander started to grab for her as Alexia sank down on the ground, but I circled one hand around his wrist, stopping him. "Let her go."

"Cookie!" She drew out the last syllable on an exceptionally long and impressive wail. She cried pathetically, huge crocodile tears leaking from the corners of her eyes as she begged for treats. I almost felt bad—almost.

"Alexia Laureen." I gave her my best mom look, hand propped on my hip, completely unyielding.

Beside me, Xander twitched as if wanting to reach for her to comfort her. I tightened my grip on his wrist, my voice low. "Show no weakness."

"You make it sound like wrangling a wild animal," he murmured.

"Good analogy," I acknowledged. "And not far off the mark."

Alexia sagged against the cabinet and stared at me for a long moment before crossing her arms over her midsection and stalking from the room. Xander watched in fascination, and I rolled my lips together as the pads of her tiny feet slapped against the floor until she clambered up onto the couch and her focus was captured by the colorful cartoons on the TV.

I released my grip on Xander's hand. He turned to me, his expression a mixture of awe and amusement. "I can't believe that worked."

I lifted one shoulder. "She's a baby. She's still learning the rules—and trying to figure out how to break them."

He shook his head, a genuine smile on his face. "Little shit."

A laugh bubbled up my throat. "You're telling me." I lifted a brow and threw him a teasing glance. "Wonder where she gets that."

Quick as lightning, his hand whipped out and playfully smacked my bottom. I sucked in a breath—not because it hurt, but because something occurred to me in that moment. We were flirting. I felt heat creep up my cheeks as Xander studied me, waiting for my reaction. I could do one of two things right now: I could retreat as I usually did and close myself off. Or I could do what I really wanted—give in to the way he made me feel, open myself up to his attention.

His muscles tensed as I pulled a spatula from the drawer in front of me and brandished it in his direction. "Don't make me use this."

The tension drained from his body, the serious frown on his face replaced by a wicked smile. The tips of his fingers glided over my hip as he stepped behind me under the pretense of moving toward the living room. I shivered as warm breath hit my ear. "Be careful what you wish for, darlin'. I just might take you up on that."

CHAPTER TWENTY-SIX
Xander

I scooped the baby from her high chair, and she immediately grabbed at me, planting her cheesy sauce-covered fingers on my cheeks. I clenched my eyes closed and grabbed a tiny hand to keep her fingers from getting too close to my eyes. Her chubby hands felt so tiny, so fragile in mine, and I kissed her fingers before shifting Alexia in my arms and following Lydia upstairs.

Water was already filling the bottom of the tub, and Lydia looked up with a grin as we entered the small room. I passed the baby to her and watched as she stripped Alexia's tiny clothes off her body and deposited her into the tub.

"Is she safe in there?"

Lydia tossed a smile my way. "Of course."

Admittedly, I didn't know much about kids, but she looked so little sitting in the big tub all by herself. "What if she slips?"

"We're both right here. Nothing's going to happen to her."

I knelt beside her and leaned my elbows on the edge of the tub, watching as my girls splashed in the water, batting a yellow rubber duck back and forth. The baby could obviously sit up by herself. But I'd heard some crazy stories. "What if—?"

A soft hand landed on my forearm. "She's fine, Xan. Don't worry."

I glanced across my shoulder at the woman kneeling beside me, her attention back on our daughter. "You've never called me that before."

Her brows dipped together. "What?"

"You called me Xan."

Her cheeks pinkened, and she diverted her focus back to Alexia. "I'm sorry, I didn't realize."

I shifted, sliding into a sitting position and resting my back against the wall so I could examine her better. "I like it."

She shot me a shy smile, then continued to rub soapy bubbles all over Alexia's little body. "Can you get a towel, please?"

Lydia rinsed the baby, then lifted her out into my waiting arms. I wrapped the fluffy towel around the baby, and a corner drooped over her face. I lifted it away. "Boo!"

The baby screamed delightedly, and I exchanged a grin with Lydia. Dropping the towel back into place, I repeated the process several more times.

Much too soon, Lydia's voice intruded on our game. "All right, little lady. Time for bed."

My gaze found Alexia's, and I smiled conspiratorially. "Mommy's a buzzkill."

"Hey!" Lydia gently backhanded my bicep, and I let out a laugh. Alexia took a cue from us both and laughed, too, the childish peals making my heart swell. God, this felt so good. Being here, doing this together. My girls. I'd missed so much with them. Anger threatened to surge again, but I pushed the useless emotion down. Done was done. From now on, we were all in this together.

I passed Alexia to Lydia and followed her to the bedroom at the end of the hall. The calming smell of lavender mixed with baby powder enveloped me as I stepped inside. Taking a seat in the rocking chair in the corner, I watched as Lydia suited the baby up for bed. She slid the diaper into place, then wrangled each of the baby's unruly arms and legs into the one-piece pajamas. All the while, Alexia babbled incoherently, pointing at the pictures hanging on the wall.

"She's going to be a talker, huh?"

Lydia smiled over at me as she scooped the baby off the changing table. "She's trying. It'll come sooner or later."

I ran a hand over Alexia's silky white-blonde hair. "She's perfect."

"She is." Lydia's gaze met mine, and she returned my smile with a soft one of her own. "Would you mind if we stole the chair for a bit so I can feed her?"

I noticed the sippy cup full of milk on the nightstand for the first time, and understanding dawned. "Sure."

She settled in and cuddled the baby on her lap. After losing almost two whole years, first with the pregnancy, then Alexia's birth, I didn't want to miss another moment. "Would you mind if I stayed?"

"Do you want to feed her?" She studied me intently, a strange expression on her face. I felt for some reason like this was a kind of test.

"Absolutely."

A brilliant smile curved Lydia's mouth, making her look a thousand times more beautiful, and my heart damn near melted. She stood and gestured with her head for me to sit, then passed Alexia to me. The baby peered up at me curiously, probably wondering why I was here. "What do I do?"

"Just hold her. She'll hold the cup herself." Lydia handed the cup to Alexia, who snatched it up and began to greedily gulp down the contents. "Usually we read. She loves the pictures."

I chuckled as I watched her. There was so much that went into caring for a baby. How had Lydia done it alone? On top of that, she was still running her own business. I'd seen the dark circles under her eyes, the ones that told me she stayed up too late and woke much too early. Lydia was working herself to the bone, spending every spare moment sewing when she wasn't with our daughter. She was going to kill herself if she kept it up.

Alexia's eyes began to droop, and Lydia extracted the now-empty cup from the baby's slack fingers. "Can you put her in bed?" she whispered.

I stood cautiously, trying not to wake the dozing baby, and gently placed her in her crib. My breath caught as her eyelids fluttered open then fell closed again. Her arms and legs twitched, her muscles relaxing into slumber. I watched in fascination as her tiny mouth puckered, like she was dreaming of her late-night snack. I automatically slipped a hand around Lydia's waist. She stilled for a moment before leaning into my embrace, then rested her head on my shoulder.

I shifted her closer to me and set my chin on the top of her head. Staring down at Alexia, I couldn't believe that we'd made something so small, so perfect. "It still blows my mind sometimes."

Though I kept my gaze fixed on Alexia, I could feel Lydia tip her chin up to look at me. "Her?"

I nodded, my throat too clogged with emotion to speak. Reluctantly, I released Lydia and bent over the high wall of the crib to place a gentle kiss on my daughter's pudgy cheek. "Night, baby girl."

Lydia followed suit, then closed the door behind us. I caught her hand in mine, drawing her near. "I'm really proud of you."

Her eyebrows dipped. "For what?"

"This. All of it." I gestured with my free hand. "Your business. This house. The way you are with Alexia—especially the way you are with her. You're a great mom, Liddy."

She blushed. "It's no big deal."

I smiled down at her and tucked a strand of hair behind her ear. "I don't know how you managed."

Her expression immediately sobered, the smile sliding from her face. "I'm sorry," she whispered. "I can't begin to tell you—"

"Hey." I hooked a finger beneath her chin and lifted her glassy gaze to mine. "That's all in the past. You've done an amazing job, but I'm here to help from now on. Will you let me do that?"

She nodded jerkily.

"Good." I stroked a thumb over her cheek. "Come on."

Tugging on her hand, I pulled her toward the stairs. Once in the kitchen, I swiped two bottles of beer from the carton I'd stashed in there earlier. I twisted off the tops and passed one to Lydia, then nodded to the couch. "Let's sit."

She sank down next to me on the couch, her legs tucked beneath her as she half-faced me. "Thank you for this."

"The drink?" I took a long swig of mine and watched her do the same. "No problem. Thought you could use it to unwind a bit."

"It's been a while." Lydia's tongue darted out, swiping up the tiny drop of liquid hovering on her bottom lip. "Actually, I think the last time I drank was with you."

"You don't go out much?" I couldn't help the little flare of satisfaction when she shook her head. She'd said the dates she'd been on had all been orchestrated by her mother. Still, she needed some time to herself once in a while. "Why not?"

"Well…" She dropped her eyes and picked at the label before meeting my gaze again with a tiny shrug. "I didn't really drink a whole lot to begin with, but I stopped as soon as I found out I was pregnant. Then I started nursing, so…"

My eyebrows drew together as she trailed off. "Nursing?"

"Breastfeeding," she clarified, her cheeks turning pink.

My gaze automatically dropped to her chest, where her arms folded protectively around herself, obscuring my view. Knowing she was uncomfortable but not sure why, I lifted my eyes to meet hers. An unidentifiable emotion swirled in the stormy depths. Each time I felt like we were taking a step forward, she pulled back. Didn't she feel the same connection between us? Why wouldn't she open up to me?

Deciding not to push her any further for fear she might shut down completely, I changed the subject. "Can I ask you something?"

Her expression turned guarded. "Sure."

"I got your emails." It'd been bothering me for the past few days, but I hadn't found a good time to bring it up. "Were they about…?"

She swallowed hard, her voice barely a whisper when she spoke. "I couldn't figure out how to tell you. When you didn't email me back, I… I tried to find you." Her eyes stared imploringly into mine, begging me to believe her. "The address you gave me was listed under someone else, and I couldn't find a good phone number, and… I didn't know what to do."

Her words hit me harder than I expected. "It's my brother and his wife. I didn't have a permanent residence, so I used their address."

She nodded and bit her lip. "You'll never know how sorry I am."

I believed her; I should've known she needed something. "I'm sorry, too."

Now that I understood her a little better, I knew what I had to do. I needed to prove to her that I wouldn't leave her. I wanted to protect her, take care of her and show her it was okay to lean on me. I'd be here for Alexia—for Lydia—any time she needed me.

"Why don't you let me watch Alexia while you're at work tomorrow?"

She bit her lip, a mixture of emotion I couldn't read swirling in her pewter eyes. "Really?"

I nodded. "I thought maybe I could hang out here with her, since all of her stuff is here."

I had no idea what babies needed, but from the look of things, it was a hell of a lot. Lydia's place was packed full of stuff. A crib and stroller, a variety of bottles and cups and plates, tons of toys. I had no idea what some things were for, but I'd figure it out.

Truth was, I wanted to be here, in Lydia's house. It was more comfortable, felt more like home than my tiny apartment. Plus—the best part—she and Alexia were here. And the more time I spent here with them, the more I wanted to become a bigger part of their lives. I knew Lydia was still cautious, probably wondering what my intentions were.

Reaching out, I took her hand in mine. "I told you I wanted to be involved, Lydia. I meant that—I still mean it. I want to see our daughter every day."

It was on the tip of my tongue to tell her I wanted to see her every day, too, but I somehow managed to refrain. We'd flirted a bit over the past few days, but I had a feeling anything more serious would scare her away.

The attraction between us felt natural, as if we'd been together for years instead of just a few days. There'd been times on tour when I'd wondered if my memory had been playing tricks on me, if I'd overthought our time together. We'd had sex several times that night, but I recalled every passion-soaked second of it. Seeing her here, though, being able to touch her made me realize that, if anything, I'd downplayed my attraction to her. I wanted her more than ever.

CHAPTER TWENTY-SEVEN
Lydia

I yanked the door open before Xander even knocked, and the surprised look on his face would've made me laugh if I wasn't so stressed out. I quickly waved him in. Since he'd been here every day, he knew where most everything was, so I gave him a quick recap of her daily schedule.

"Her food is in the fridge. Just make sure to cut everything really well so she won't choke. And not too many treats." I shot him a look. "You know how well that went over last time."

He grinned and tweaked Alexia's nose. "We'll be good. Right, sweet girl?"

"Are you sure about this?" I asked.

"Yeah, of course."

"Okay." I wrung my hands together. "But if you need anything, Darlene is right next door, and you can always text me or call the salon. Anytime," I emphasized.

Xander jiggled Alexia where she perched on his hip and grinned at me. "I'm sure we'll be fine."

"Okay, but—"

"Liddy." A heavy hand landed on my shoulder, and Xander's intense blue gaze peered into mine. "Go to work, sweetheart."

I knew he didn't mean it as a dismissal, but it felt like one, and I automatically stiffened. He must've felt the tension in my shoulders, because he stroked his hand up the side of my neck, cupping it in one big palm. He dipped his head as if trying to capture my attention. "I promise. Everything will be just fine."

I nodded, my throat tight. It was hard as hell to hand over control. Alexia and I had a schedule all worked out, and I knew Darlene adhered to it when she was here. Xander had never spent any time around little kids before. Still, I knew I couldn't deny him this time with his daughter, and it was good for Alexia to get to know him too. Grudgingly, I swiped my keys out of the bowl on the kitchen counter and held a spare out to Xander.

"I'll… see you later." With one last kiss for Alexia, I reluctantly left.

The first part of my morning at the salon flew by. My ten o'clock bride tried on nearly twenty gowns before deciding on a custom design. We spent the next two hours poring over magazines, drawing up various examples of what she might like. Finally, she strode out the door just after two o'clock, a smile on her face. That made one of us at least.

After she left, my anxiety ratcheted up tenfold. My hands flitted to my pockets every two minutes or so, checking for messages. Xander hadn't called or texted yet, and I couldn't help but wonder what was happening back at the house.

Brenda shot me a look over the counter as I drummed my nails against the Formica. "Why don't you go home already?"

I let out an exasperated sigh. "You have no idea how much I want to. But I don't want him to think I don't trust him." It had taken all of my willpower not to call and check in with him over the past few hours. Xander was a responsible adult, and I knew that he wouldn't let anything happen to Alexia. I just had to trust that he would reach out if he needed help.

I wandered back to the alterations room to check on Gwen. "Need anything back here?"

Dark brown eyes met mine, and she shook her head. "No, thanks, I think I'm good."

"Okay." I stood helplessly, looking around the room, hoping that something would jump out at me. I wanted something—anything—to keep me occupied.

"You okay?"

I offered a little smile. "Just a lot on my mind."

She nodded, then set down the needle and lace she was holding. "Can I… Can we talk for a second?"

Her voice held a trace of seriousness, more so than usual, and

I pulled out a chair. "Of course. What's going on?"

Gwen bit her lip, looking unsure. "I really like my job here, and I appreciate you giving me a chance."

My stomach dropped to my toes, but I remained quiet. I had a feeling I knew exactly where this was headed.

She blew out a hard breath. "I've got some things going on in my life right now, and... I'm kind of looking for another job."

She refused to meet my gaze, and for a long moment I debated exactly what to say. I hated to lose her. "Is it the money?"

"No, I just..." She hesitated, then switched subjects. "Would you change your life for the person you love?"

Xander immediately came to mind, and I pondered her question for a moment before responding. "I think that finding love is a very special thing. And if you both care about each other, you should do what's best for both of you."

"I don't think I can stay here and be with him," she said, her voice sad, almost regretful.

"Does he not like you working here?" I couldn't imagine why not—unless he disapproved of her being around women getting married. Maybe he had no interest in marrying Gwen right now—or ever. It was no secret that a lot of women who worked in bridal wanted their own happily ever after. It was so easy to get swept up in the fairy tales and the happiness that others were feeling.

Honestly, until Xander had come back into my life, I'd been closed off to it. But recently I'd been seeing things in a different light. I saw each glowing bride with new eyes, so in love with her groom, ready to start their lives together. Could Xander and I have something like that? We'd flirted a bit, but I didn't know if that was enough. I knew one thing, though—he'd support me in whatever I chose. His actions with my mother the other night proved that. He would never hold me back from something I loved.

"I think there has to be compromise," I said slowly. "You have to work together and meet in the middle. That being said," I continued, "you'll always have a place here."

"Thank you," she whispered, still unable to meet my eyes.

"If you ever need to talk, I'm here." I stood and returned the chair to its position. Gwen nodded and picked up the fabric she'd been working on. I didn't want to push her too much, but I also wanted her to know that I was here to listen if she needed me.

Shoving down my feelings, I attacked the displays, waxing the steel rails so the hangers would slide better. When I was done with that, I meandered the salon, straightening gowns and reorganizing the jewelry shelves, determined to keep myself occupied. By the time four o'clock rolled around, I was ready to rip my hair out.

Sending an imploring gaze at Brenda, I admitted defeat. "I need to go home."

She let out a little laugh. "I can't believe you made it this long."

I drummed my fingers on the steering wheel as I drove home, anticipation and worry warring in my heart. All the while, I imagined dozens of scenarios of what I might find at home. The house would probably be a mess. Xander would probably be haggard, Alexia grumpy and crabby. He wasn't used to dealing with toddlers, and I could only imagine the crying and yelling that might have gone on today. Worry won out as I pulled up to the house and jumped out of the car.

The silence that greeted me when I pushed the door open was unnerving. I blew out a breath as I stepped inside and kicked out of my heels. Locking up, I made my way toward the living room at the back of the house. Xander had said something about going to the park; maybe they were still out. My brain froze and my heart tripped in my chest as I rounded the corner and took in the scene before me.

Xander's huge body was sprawled out on the couch, Alexia perched atop his bare chest, fast asleep. For a long moment, I remained frozen. Tears pricked my eyes and burned the back of my throat. They looked so perfect, so sweet together, and the sight sent my heart pitter-pattering against my ribs.

My eyes skimmed over his bare, well-defined pecs. Why was he naked? I ventured closer and barely held back a sigh of relief—or maybe disappointment. He wore a pair of black gym shorts that rode low on his waist, the band of his boxer briefs peeking out. His chest rose and fell on deep, even breaths as he slept. Alexia lay draped over him, held securely in place by Xander's hand firmly on her back. I didn't want to disturb them, but he couldn't be comfortable like that. I reached out to pick her up, but Xander's free hand shot upward. I let out a soft gasp of surprise as his eyes popped open and his fingers wrapped around my wrist.

"Shh." His voice was barely a whisper, the slight shake of his head stopping me. "Leave her."

"Are you sure? I can take her to her room."

His hand slipped down my arm until his fingers brushed mine. "I like her just like this. Why don't you go change, take a few minutes to relax and unwind?"

"Are you sure?"

"Of course." His thumb lightly stroked the back of my hand, sending tiny shivers of awareness through my body. He gave a gentle tug, and I sat on the edge of the couch, the flesh of my hip burning where it pressed against his.

I kept my voice soft. "How was she?"

"Perfect." A smile lit up his face before it twisted into a wry smirk. "Well, mostly. That last bottle of milk didn't sit well with her, so most of it ended up on me."

I pressed a hand over my mouth to cover my smile. "I'm so sorry."

"No, you're not," he teased softly, giving my hand a squeeze. "You're just glad it wasn't you."

I lifted a shoulder. "I'm kind of used to it. But, yeah, I'm kind of glad she puked on you and not me."

"Brat." He gave a little half-laugh, and the baby wiggled, one tiny foot twitching in her sleep.

Xander stroked one hand comfortingly down Alexia's spine, calming her. His palm covered almost her entire back, looking huge in relation to her small body.

A smile curved my mouth as I took in the stark contrast between Alexia's fair skin and Xander's swarthy, sun-kissed flesh. My gaze dropped to where our hands were still joined. It made my heart race in my chest, but I was reluctant to pull away. I liked the feel of his hand on mine, strong and warm.

"Whatcha lookin' at, darlin'?"

His thumb slid over the back of my hand again, and my cheeks flamed as I met his gaze. I shook my head. "Oh, it was nothing."

He lifted a brow but stayed silent.

"Well." I cleared my throat to rid it of the rasp choking my voice as I stood. "I, um… I guess I'll go change then."

Xander's clear blue eyes slid down my torso, leaving a trail of fire in their wake as they skimmed lower. Heat gathered in my core as his appreciative gaze slowly lifted to mine. "You better get out of here while you still have a chance."

I scooted from the room, tossing one last glance over my shoulder just before I headed down the hallway. Bright blue eyes were still locked on me, and my heart pattered away in my chest, filled with a happiness I hadn't felt in years.

CHAPTER TWENTY-EIGHT
Xander

We put the baby to bed, then I pulled Lydia down the stairs. I'd been hard as fuck since she got home this afternoon, and I needed her in my arms—right this second.

"Liddy?" Her gaze lifted to mine as I slipped one arm around her waist and eased her closer. "I really want to kiss you right now."

Her eyes dropped to my mouth, and she bit her lip before giving a single nod. I dipped my head low, brushing my lips across hers in a tantalizingly chaste kiss.

Her arms came up and twined around my neck, pulling me back to her as I started to break away. Happy to oblige her, I dropped another kiss on her plump lips. Her mouth parted, and I ran my hands down her back, brushing my nose along hers.

"We should stop, sweetheart."

Biting her lip, Lydia dropped her gaze to the ground, and her arms followed suit, slipping down my chest to rest at her sides. "You're right, I'm sorry. I—"

"Lydia." I infused just enough forcefulness into my tone to demand her attention. Her eyes met mine, a startling myriad of emotion in the pewter depths. I could see her need, her desire, and—beneath all that—her uncertainty. I wanted to wipe the slate clean, start fresh.

She beat me to the punch before I could say a word. "This is just... new for me. And scary, you know? You've been such a huge help the last few days, like today, when you watched Alexia.

And I love that you've been spending all this time with us. Not that you're here because of me, I mean, but Alexia deserves to have a father in her life, especially someone like you, and it's been really... great."

She took a deep breath for the first time, and I pressed my lips together to contain my smile at her rambling. She looked so fucking cute yet so heartbreakingly vulnerable at the same time it stabbed into me like a knife. I wisely kept silent as she bared her soul to me.

"I just don't know what will happen, and... that worries me."

I loved that she was concerned for Alexia's welfare first and foremost, but I knew deep down what else she was asking. "I'm here, Lydia—for both of you—as long as you'll have me."

"But—"

Her words abruptly cut off as I cupped her face in one hand. Using my thumb, I pressed up on the underside of her chin, forcing her gaze to mine. We locked eyes for a long, heart-stopping moment. Then I kissed her. Soft and gentle so as not to frighten her, I teased her lips with soft brushes of my skin against hers. She swooned against me, and I shifted her closer, locking one arm tightly around her waist. Restraint damn near killing me, I tugged gently on her lower lip, waiting for them to part and allow me in. With a soft sigh, she opened, and I swept my tongue inside, swallowing her shallow breaths.

When I finally lifted my head a minute later, her eyes were closed, her cheeks flushed the sweetest pink I'd ever seen. Big gray eyes blinked open and met mine. "Are you trying to distract me?"

A tiny smile quirked my mouth. "Maybe."

Unable to stay away, needing to taste her again, my mouth captured hers once more. This time, Lydia threw herself into the kiss, matching me stroke for stroke, her hands curling into my neck as if she never wanted to let go. She tasted of everything sweet and sexy and an innocence that was purely Lydia.

Her chest rose on a ragged inhale. "Was that a distraction, too?"

"That"—I kissed her hard—"was a declaration."

This close, I saw her swallow hard. "A declaration?"

I nodded solemnly. "I'm not going anywhere. I want to be

here for you—for Alexia."

Time stood suspended for several long moments as we both remained silent, breathless. Finally, she nodded, a tiny smile lifting the corners of her mouth. "That sounds… perfect."

An answering grin tugged at my lips, and the hope I'd harbored deep in my heart flowed to the surface. "No. You"—I punctuated each word with a light kiss—"Are. Perfect."

A pleased smile lit her face even as her cheeks flushed at my compliment. "I'm hardly perfect."

I slid my thumb over the apple of her cheek. "I disagree. But then, you already know that. I've been crazy for you since the moment we met." I watched her cheeks turn pink in the dim light, and I smiled. "I better get out of here before I do something I'll regret."

She peered up at me, her brows drawing slightly together. "Okay."

Her voice wavered, whisper-soft, and I pulled her into my arms. "I meant what I said, sweetheart. This time I'm going to do it right. I'm going to make you fall for me, Lydia Dawson."

It was on the tip of my tongue to call her by my name, but I stopped myself just in time. *Lydia McLean.* Had a nice ring to it.

A tiny tremor ran through her body, and her tongue darted out to wet her lips. "We'll see about that."

I couldn't tell if she was teasing or not. I decided it didn't matter. She might not believe me yet—but she would. I was going to do everything in my power to make my wife fall for me again.

I captured her lips in one last soul-searing, knee-buckling kiss, holding her tight as she swayed into me. I lifted away and stared into lust-filled eyes. I wanted so badly to scoop her into my arms and carry her to bed, but I clamped down on the urge.

I set her away from me, making sure she was steady on her feet before releasing her. "Night, beautiful."

I forced one foot in front of the other until I was safely outside and I could finally breathe again. Lydia did something to me that I didn't understand. Whatever it was, I wanted more of it—maybe even a lifetime's worth.

Chapter Twenty-Nine
Lydia

The vibrating of the phone on the nightstand jarred me from sleep. Groggily, I swiped at it and managed to unplug it from where it was charging. Mind muddled, I tried to place the number flashing across the screen. I debated answering, but I couldn't think who would be calling so early. A bad feeling in my stomach, I tapped the button to connect the call and held the phone to my ear.

"Hello?"

"Ms. Dawson? This is Maryann with Frontline Security."

Oh, God. Fear crawled up my throat, and I clutched at the phone with both hands. "What happened?"

"Ma'am, an alarm has been set off at 1095 Belleview Avenue. Can you please verify your password?"

"No." I shook my head to clear my foggy brain. "I mean—I'm not there."

"Thank you, ma'am. We've contacted your local law enforcement, and police have been dispatched to the location."

"Thanks."

Ending the call, I tossed the phone on the bed and threw the covers to the side, ready to pull my clothes on and run out the door. I'd just stepped into a pair of jeans when it occurred to me that it was the middle of the night. I froze, debating what to do. I didn't want to wake Alexia and take her with me, but I also didn't want to have to rouse Darlene from sleep. I knew she wouldn't hesitate to come help, but still…

I drummed my nails against the screen of my phone before tapping the number on speed dial. Xander's voice filtered over the line, raspy and sleepy. "Liddy. Everything okay?"

"There was a break-in at the salon, and I—"

His tone changed, instantly alert and ready to take charge. "I'll take care of it."

I could hear rustling in the background, and I imagined him rolling from bed, still warm from sleep. I could send Xander in my stead, but it was my shop. I was the one who needed to be there. "Actually, that's not what I wanted to ask. Can you come stay with Alexia until I get back?"

There was a pause on the other end, then— "Are you sure?"

"Yeah." I slipped my arms into a zip-up sweatshirt. "I need to be there to speak with the police."

"Okay." He seemed hesitant to agree. "I'll be at your place in ten."

Without another word, he hung up, and I shoved the phone in my back pocket. I peeked in on Alexia, and a couple minutes later I heard the front door open and close. Xander's voice floated toward me. "Lydia?"

"I'm here." Grabbing up my purse, I met him in the hallway.

He caught my arm as I approached, concerned eyes boring into mine. "I don't like this."

"I know," I replied. "The police are already on their way, so I won't be there alone. I'm sure they'll get it taken care of quickly."

"Call me as soon as you figure out what's going on," he said. His hand slowly loosened around my arm, as if he was reluctant to let me go.

"I will. And Xander?" His brows lifted in silent question. "Thank you." I stretched up on my toes and gave him a quick kiss.

The second my lips brushed his, an iron band came around my back, holding me close. His free hand cupped the back of my head, and his mouth pressed hard against mine. He lifted his head with a soft growl. "One more for the road."

He swept down, consuming me, pushing all thought from my head. I knew it was his way of offering reassurance, putting me at ease, taking my mind off the situation at hand. He grounded me, made me feel safe and protected—and I appreciated it more than I could say.

Breaking away, breathing hard, I clutched at his biceps. "Thank you. For everything."

He gentled his hold, allowing me to peel myself from his arms. Still lightheaded from that one last kiss, I grabbed my keys and headed out the door. I tossed one more glance over my shoulder before it shut behind me and found Xander's intense gaze fixed on me. It filled me with warmth and something more—something I had no business entertaining. The feelings he instilled in me weren't safe. He'd been back in my life barely more than a week, yet he'd destroyed nearly every defense I'd put in place after Shawn left me. I couldn't let myself fall for him—because he would consume me entirely, heart and soul. And once I gave him my heart, I knew I'd never get it back.

Nerves twisted my stomach into knots as I sped toward the shop, and blue lights pierced the gray light of dawn up ahead. By the time I pulled to a stop at the curb, I could tell it was more than a simple malfunction of the alarm. Three cruisers sat outside the shop, and the front door stood wide open. I couldn't tell if they'd found it that way, or if they'd left it open for ease as they made multiple trips in and out.

I made a beeline toward one of the officers standing out front and introduced myself. I followed him into the salon, my heart sinking at the destruction that greeted me. Dresses had been ripped from the racks and strewn about the floor. Accessories from the glass cases littered the carpet, and every shelf was completely bare, their contents swept onto the floor.

One of the officers guided me through the salon. "Are you able to tell if anything is missing?"

They had already begun to fingerprint the doorknobs and several other surfaces, the black dust stark in contrast to the myriad of white gowns littering the floor.

Trying not to touch anything, I examined the contents of the empty glass cases and jewelry shelves that now littered the floor. With a defeated shrug, I turned the officer. "It's hard to say, but I don't think we're missing anything. I would have to do a full inventory to check though."

He nodded. "I was afraid that would be the case." He popped his hands on his hips and looked around. "On the bright side, if there is one, it doesn't look like anything was truly destroyed."

As I gazed around the room, I realized he was right. Someone had made a hell of a mess, but they hadn't done a whole lot of damage. Thank God for that. I turned back to the officer. "What now?"

"We'll check with the surrounding businesses to see if any have security footage, but getting warrants for those will take some time, if they'll even approve it. We'll analyze the prints we picked up here to see if we can find a match. If nothing comes up…" He offered an apologetic shrug, and I knew without asking what he meant. If the perp wasn't in their system, and with no witnesses, they had nothing.

He took my fingerprints in order to eliminate them from the

dozens they'd collected from the doorknobs and other surfaces, then stowed them in an evidence bag.

Once that was all taken care of, I turned back to him. "When will we be able to get back in here?"

"We're wrapping up right now. Maybe half an hour or so."

I fired off text messages to my employees, letting them know that the salon would be closed today. I was drained mentally and physically and had no interest sticking around for several more hours to clean. Instead, I asked the girls to meet at the shop an hour early tomorrow to get everything back in order. I called Brenda and asked her to reach out to the clients we had on the calendar today and reschedule them.

I crossed my arms over my chest and stood off to the side, watching in despair. The shop was my baby. Who would do something like this? Immediately, Caryn Anderson's face came to mind. I shook it off. She was a royal bitch, but I doubted she would be caught breaking and entering.

As the officers completed their work, they began to pack their things away and file out the front door. Exhausted, I closed and locked it behind them. Once they were gone, I surveyed the mess before me with a grimace. Though I was dead tired, I hated to leave thousands of dollars worth of material just lying on the floor. Scooping a handful of dresses up, I flung them over my forearm and carted them off to the back room. Once everything else was cleaned up, I would have Gwen check the dresses and see if any were salvageable. Hopefully, whoever had broken in wouldn't have had much time to do a whole lot of damage. It seemed that whoever was in here had just pulled them off the hangers and thrown them on the floor. I hoped that was the case—it would be much easier to fix a few beads than have to damage out several dozen dresses.

I picked up the jewelry scattered on the floor and spent a good portion of time untangling the strands from each necklace before setting them aside to be checked for quality. Tears burned the back of my eyelids, and now that I was alone, I let them fall freely. I allowed myself only a couple moments of pity. I needed to get back home and take Alexia off Xander's hands. Almost as soon as the thought crossed my mind, I heard the soft rumble of an engine pull up outside then cut off. Craning my neck to look out the front window, I saw a familiar truck sitting at the curb.

I watched in fascination and relief as Xander climbed out of the driver seat, then opened the rear door of the cab. My heart jumped into my throat, and I burst out the front door and down the steps to meet him. I reached the truck just as Xander extracted Alexia from a bright pink car seat. It looked completely out of place in the huge truck, and I blinked at the sight.

"When did you get a car seat?"

A small smile tipped up the corner of his lips. "I called in a favor. Took me damn near half an hour to get the damn thing installed." His face contorted into a grimace. "Might not be able to get it out ever again."

I let out a laugh and took Alexia from Xander as she stretched her arms out for me. I cuddled her close, burying my nose in her fine blonde hair, soaking up her sweet scent. God, what was it about babies that smelled so good? It was like they were so clean, so pure that they took all the bad away. Holding her in my arms, Xander at my side, I felt the tension begin to leave my body.

Xander turned to me, his voice quiet. "How did everything go?"

Blowing out a sigh, I gave him a brief rundown of the past several hours. "They lifted some fingerprints and poked around a little bit, but I don't think they have anything concrete." I shrugged. He nodded but didn't say much as he reached into the cab for something.

I glanced up at him. "Why are you here?"

He paused his rustling around in the back of the truck and met my gaze. "Gonna do some work here, and I thought you'd like to see Alexia for a bit."

Immediately on guard, I examined him warily. "What do you mean, 'do some work?'"

My grip tightened on Alexia, and she squirmed in my arms, reaching for Xander. I reluctantly handed her back to him and watched as she snuggled against his broad shoulder. The sight caused a momentary pang in my heart, and I rubbed the heel of my hand over my chest.

Xander slammed the cab door and gestured with his chin to the small silver sedan that slowed to a stop behind his truck. A pretty, petite brunette climbed out of the driver seat, while a hulking giant of a man unfolded from the passenger side. It was almost comical to watch, and I couldn't help but smile. The man rounded the car and slipped an arm around the brunette's shoulders as they made their way toward us.

With Alexia balanced on one hip, Xander gestured toward the couple with his free hand. "This is Blake Lawson." The man nodded in greeting, and Xander continued. "And this is his girlfriend, Victoria."

The woman held out a hand, and I slipped my palm into hers. "Nice to meet you."

The confusion must've been evident on my face, because Xander laid a hand on the back of my neck and squeezed gently. He directed his words to Blake and Victoria. "Why don't you guys head inside, and we'll meet you there in a second?"

Victoria shot me another soothing smile before heading up the stairs. I watched as the man he'd called Blake placed a hand on Victoria's lower back and held the door of the salon open so she could enter. Why were these two here? The question weighed heavily on my mind, and after a long morning, I wasn't inclined to beat around the bush. "What's going on?"

CHAPTER THIRTY
Xander

I watched as the weariness in her eyes turned to outright suspicion. My hand still rested on the back of her neck, and I slid my thumb along the cord of her throat. "You've had a rough morning. I thought I would call in some reinforcements."

Her head tipped to one side. "What does that mean exactly?"

I lifted one shoulder. "They're good people, and I would trust Blake with my life. He works for QSG also, and Victoria is a psychologist downtown."

Lydia gave a jerky nod, still looking unsure as hell. She crossed her arms over her chest and shifted her weight from foot to foot. With a gentle tug, I pulled her closer until she was flush against me. Her hands moved so that one rested on my chest, the other on Alexia's back.

For a long moment I stared down at the two of them. I had a daughter. A wife. A family. It made me more determined than ever to fix whatever had happened this morning and take the worry and tension from Lydia's shoulders.

"You've been up for hours," I explained gently. "You have to be exhausted." Lydia made a little face, but she didn't disagree with me. I took that as a good sign as I continued. "Blake is going to help me set up some security cameras, and I thought Victoria could watch Alexia for a while. Maybe take her to the park and play for a bit, so you can go home and get some sleep."

Her eyes widened. "Cameras?"

I dipped my chin in acknowledgement. "So this won't happen

again. And if it does—"

She was already shaking her head. "Xander, I can't afford that."

"Hey." I bent my knees until I was eye level at her. "Don't worry about it. QSG had some extras in their stock, and Con was more than happy to help."

I knew her security system was pretty basic, intended to go off only if someone breached the premises. But the cameras would come in handy to help identify the perpetrator if it ever happened again, which I hoped it didn't. Still, better safe than sorry.

She bit her lip and her gaze moved toward the salon. "I don't know. I mean, Alexia doesn't know Victoria, and—"

"Liddy." I captured her gaze again. "Everything will be fine. I promise."

Her head tipped up, those pretty gray eyes staring into mine. "Are you sure?"

"Absolutely." I dipped my head and brushed my lips across hers. "I can see how exhausted you are. Let us take care of the baby for a few hours, then I'll bring her home for naptime once we're done here."

Lydia practically melted against me, burying her head against my chest. "Thank you."

I'd been in the salon before, but I wasn't sure where everything was located. I pressed a kiss to the top of her head. "Can you show me where your hookups are before you head out?"

"Sure. I have to get my purse anyway."

Alexia still cuddled high on my chest, I slipped an arm around Lydia's shoulders and together we headed inside. She spoke as we walked. "The electrical box is in my office." She paused to pick a couple stray dresses off the floor and draped them over her forearm. "What all do you need access to?"

I gestured at the drop-tile ceiling. "Actually, that should be good. We can run the wiring right over the tiles. My plan was to put a camera at each entrance outside and one at the front of the store near the register. Any problem with that?"

"No, that sounds great."

Lydia stepped into the alterations room to deposit the gowns on a worktable. "I'm not looking forward to fixing all those," she noted with dismay.

I rubbed a hand over her back. "Sorry, babe. I know it's been a shi—" I caught myself before I swore in front of Alexia. "Crappy morning."

"Yeah." She exhaled heavily. "It has. But I really appreciate your help," she added softly.

Sliding my hand up her back, I cupped the back of her neck and pulled her close. "Anything for you." I dropped a kiss on her lips. "Now let's get to that fuse box so you can get home."

She held out her arms for the baby, and I handed Alexia over, knowing that Lydia needed the physical reassurance right now. She made her way through the attached door to her office and pointed to a white door recessed along the back wall. "Right over there."

I poked around for a second. "Good deal. I'll take it from here."

Her lips turned up in a tight smile, and she hugged Alexia closer. "Okay. Well…"

I knew if Alexia started crying, Lydia would never leave. The dark circles beneath her eyes had intensified, her exhaustion apparent. "Let's get you home, sweetheart."

I followed her out to her car and kissed her goodbye, promising once more that everything would be fine. Juggling Alexia in my arms, we waved goodbye and watched Lydia's taillights disappear around the corner. I turned to my daughter. "Want to go to the park?"

I smiled as her little head bobbed enthusiastically. Back inside the salon, Blake and Victoria were seated in the chairs near the front desk. I introduced Victoria and Alexia and, after a few tears, they headed out the front door.

I'd met Victoria for the first time this morning, but I knew Alexia was in good hands. I'd called Blake just after seven o'clock and asked them to run to the twenty-four-hour department store to grab a car seat for Alexia. Sweet and subdued, Victoria was Blake's opposite in almost every way. Despite her obvious exasperation at his overprotectiveness, they fit like two pieces of a puzzle.

I tossed a look at Blake now that we were alone. I was surprised Victoria had offered to come along after the incident last week.

"She doing okay?"

He lifted one shoulder. "She says yes, but she's still having nightmares."

"Hopefully time will fix that." Blake just nodded, and I changed the subject. "She's good with kids. You guys have any?"

He pulled out a spool of wire. "Not sure she's ready for that yet."

I let out a short laugh. "I understand that. Hell, I didn't know I had a kid until last week."

His hazel eyes met mine. "Looks like it agrees with you."

"Scared me shitless at first, but now…" I shrugged. "I wouldn't change it for the world."

Blake hitched a thumb over his shoulder in the direction Victoria had wandered off. "Gotta talk this one into moving in with me first."

For the next half hour, Blake and I worked in companionable silence, running the wiring so we could affix the cameras to the walls. Deciding to tackle the outside first, we focused on the front and rear doors and getting the wires run across the building. I was standing beside the front door when a compact maroon sedan pulled up to the curb outside and parked. A young woman stepped out and glanced around before making her way toward the salon. She looked familiar, but I couldn't place her. Her short dark hair swung just above her shoulders as she approached the front door.

In an attempt to cut her off, I stepped outside and greeted her. "Sorry, we're closed today."

The girl paused on the third step and met my gaze with a shy smile. "I know, Lydia sent me a message a few hours ago. I felt bad and thought maybe you guys could use some help."

As I studied the girl, it finally hit me who she was—Gwen, Lydia's assistant. I held the door wide and allowed her to enter. "Lydia headed home to get some sleep. You just missed her."

"That's okay," Gwen replied as she stepped further into the salon. "I know she said there was a lot of damage, so maybe I can get a head start on the repairs."

I was grateful for anything that would help Lydia at this point. "That would be great," I replied honestly. "It's really nice of you to offer, thank you." I led her to the back room where I'd seen

Lydia stacking some dresses.

Gwen took a look at the white mound of fabric in the middle of the table and made a small sound of dismay. "Goodness."

"I know," I commiserated. "You don't have to do this."

Her eyes cut to me. "Oh no, I want to," she reassured me.

I offered her a smile. "Well, thank you. It means a lot."

Leaving Gwen to deal with that, I started back toward Blake. I scanned the salon, absorbing everything still in disarray. It was normally so neat and tidy, and even after several hours of cleaning this morning, things still looked out of place. Lydia hadn't told me much, other than that the place had been wrecked. Blake threw a look at me as I propped my hands on my hips and glanced around.

"What are you thinking?"

I wasn't honestly sure. "I kind of want to see a copy of the police report."

He lifted a brow. "Why's that?"

I shook my head. "I can't figure out why they didn't seem to take anything. And like Lydia said, that was an awful lot of damage in a very short amount of time. Any idea what response time was?"

"No, but I can find out." Blake pulled out his phone and tapped the screen a few times, and I assumed he was shooting off a text to our boss, Con. "It seems strange to me," he remarked. "Even the costume jewelry. It's not worth much, but it's still something. This just seems like somebody wanted to make a mess for the sake of makin' a mess. Somebody upset with her?"

I lifted my hands in a shrugging motion. "She didn't seem to think so. I'll run it by her again and see if she remembers anything else. According to Lydia, the only person she's had trouble with recently was a girl she fired a few weeks ago."

Blake nodded. "Maybe she held a grudge and wanted to get back at her?"

It was possible, though she'd be stupid to do so. She wouldn't have to worry about getting another job if she ended up serving time for a breaking and entering.

His phone beeped an alert, and he lifted a brow in my direction. "Response time was six minutes."

I surveyed the mess again. That was a hell of a lot of destruction with only six minutes to work with, plus time to get away. "Maybe multiple people?"

"Possible," Blake agreed. "Guess we'll see what turns up."

A couple hours later, I thanked Blake and Victoria for their help, as well as Gwen, then carried Alexia to my truck. By the time I got to Lydia's, she was fast asleep. I carefully carried her inside and tucked her into her crib before making my way down the hall to Lydia's room.

I smiled at the image that greeted me. She lay in the middle of the bed under a pile of blankets, wrapped up like a burrito. She shifted slightly as I settled on the edge of the bed, the dip of my weight causing her to roll toward me the tiniest bit. I could feel the body heat rising off her where she lay bundled up in the thick comforter.

Stretching out on my side, I propped my head on one hand and studied her. Her mouth was parted slightly, cheeks flushed a pale rose. Thick, dark lashes fluttered as I stroked my thumb over her cheek. I didn't think I'd ever get tired of looking at her. It hit me then just how much I craved her—I wanted her beautiful face to be the last thing I saw every night before I closed my eyes, and the first thing I saw each morning when I woke. I wanted her curled into my arms, her body fitted to mine. I still remembered the way she felt against me—and I was desperate for more of it.

CHAPTER THIRTY-ONE
Lydia

Something soft brushed across my cheek, and a masculine smell filled my nostrils. I breathed deeply, trying to draw in as much of the scent as possible. It was delicious—kind of watery without being overpowering. I let it wash over me, wanting to roll around in it until it wrapped around my body and sank into every pore.

"Hey, sleeping beauty. Time to wake up."

The sexy, raspy sound of Xander's voice tickled my consciousness, and I slowly blinked my eyes open. "Mmm... Hey."

He smiled down at me. "There she is."

"I—Oh!" The bright afternoon sunlight streaming through the windows caught my attention, and I bolted upright, automatically glancing toward the clock. "What time is it? Where's Alexia? What—"

"Shhh." Xander gently pushed me back down. "Alexia is taking a nap. Everything's fine."

"Oh, God." I fell back to the pillows with a soft groan and scrubbed a hand over my face. "I hate that feeling. Like I'm running late because I overslept."

Xander brushed a hand over my hair, the effect soothing me and calming my racing heart. "You're fine, sweetheart. Just relax."

I curled into him, enjoying the feel of his hand stroking lightly over my arm. My nose tucked into the crook of his neck, I inhaled deeply. God, he smelled so good. Xander's chest rose and fell on a chuckle. "Are you sniffing me?"

Even though he couldn't see my face, I bit my lip to hide a guilty smile. "No."

His hand slid up my arm and over my throat, cupping my chin and turning my face toward him. My gaze collided with his, eyes dark with desire. Dipping his head, he brushed his nose over my jaw, then spoke against my lips. "It's okay if you are."

"I don't know what you're talking about."

He smiled like he knew I was full of crap. "That's too bad. Because I love the way you smell. And taste."

His mouth covered mine, his kiss brutal and breathtaking. My lips parted, and he took advantage, sweeping his tongue inside. The hand resting at the base of my throat slid south, the heat of his fingers burning my skin through the thin material of my tank top. My nipples pebbled as he cupped my breast, his thumb brushing over the tight bud.

I let out a little moan, and he broke away from my mouth to kiss his way down my neck, over the swell of one breast until he reached the tight peak. His fingers slipped beneath the strap and slid it down my arm, pulling the fabric down to bare me to his gaze. He sucked and nipped at my sensitive flesh, and I arched my hips into him, heat flooding my core.

I flattened one hand on his chest and shoved gently. There was no way I could ever physically overpower Xander, but he allowed me to push him to his back and pulled me with him. I settled over his hips, my legs straddled wide over his. The ridge of his erection pressed up into me, and I let out a soft groan. "Oh, God, Xander…"

My words trailed off as I rubbed against him. The friction from his jeans rubbing against my thin panties lit a fire low in my belly. My breasts swayed inches from his face, and he reached out to fondle my achy flesh. A jolt of electricity shot from my breasts to my sensitive folds, stoking the inferno building within.

He lifted his head and wrapped his lips around one peak, his tongue circling the tight flesh. A soft moan welled up and out of my throat as his teeth grazed the sensitive nerves, and I tightened my legs around his. Xander's hands wandered over my hips and waist, and I could feel the hardened callouses on his fingers as he dipped beneath my shirt, stroking my sides and stomach. I rocked on top of him, trying to temper the ache building inside. My hips undulated back and forth, and pleasure swept over me as I rode the edge of orgasm.

"That's it." Xander's hand moved to my bottom, pressing my hips down so I rode him harder, faster.

I couldn't form words, couldn't even think as the tempo increased and a tiny spark shot through my belly. It flamed to life, growing stronger and more intense until I finally snapped. The orgasm washed over me, sending ripples of pleasure throughout my entire body. My toes curled under the force of it, my hands clenching the fabric of his shirt as I rode out the ecstasy before finally collapsing over his chest.

One hand coasted lazily down my back, along each bump of my spine, then over the globes of my bottom. His thumbs slipped beneath the lacy edges of my panties, and he gently stroked my skin. Warm breath hit my ear as he spoke. "That was sexy as hell."

I felt my cheeks flame as I buried my face against his throat, embarrassment turning my entire body hot. I'd never done anything like that before—certainly not in the middle of the day, and never fully clothed.

I let out a soft cry of protest as Xander shifted us to our sides and pulled back a bit to look at me. His gaze unerringly took in every line of my expression, and his fingertips trailed over the apples of my cheeks, down the line of my jaw and over my lower lip.

"Does that embarrass you?"

I dropped my eyes to his chest. "Kind of."

"Don't. I fucking loved seeing you come. It's been too goddamn long." My eyes snapped to his, and he let out a rough chuckle. "Yeah, I remember exactly what you look like. How you sound. That night in Vegas is burned into my memory."

I blushed fiercely. Though I'd never admitted it out loud, it was for me, too. It'd been the best sex of my life. At the time I thought it was just because I was upset over the debacle with Shawn. I thought that being with Xander reinforced my femininity, my desirability. But now, feeling whatever this was growing between us, I knew it was more. Gone were my insecurities and reservations. I'd wanted Xander like I'd never wanted anyone before. I wanted to feel that way again—cherished, loved. Desired.

As if reading my mind, he spoke. "Next time, though…" He slid one hand down my body and between my legs. He cupped me through the damp fabric of my panties. "You're going to come on my cock while I'm buried deep inside you."

His dirty words sent a shiver down my spine, and I arched toward him with a little whimper. "Xan—"

Alexia's soft cry cut through the air, and I fell to my back. "Shit."

Xander chuckled and kissed me one last time before pushing off the bed. "Don't worry, darlin'. I'll make it up to you later."

CHAPTER THIRTY-TWO
Xander

"Remind me why we're doing this again," Clay groused from the passenger seat.

My lips quirked up in a wry smile. "Because the client is always right."

Clay huffed. "This is bullshit."

I lifted one shoulder. "Probably, but he wants proof, so we're going to get him proof."

I couldn't imagine that Oliver Eldredge would have tried to move the statue just yet. Things were still too hot, and I doubted he wanted anything coming back on him. If the guy was even involved—and that was a big if. From what we'd discovered, he appeared to be squeaky clean. Didn't mean that was the truth, but so far, there was no evidence to the contrary. He'd been more than accommodating, and I was beginning to think that Richter was just salty about their past and still carrying a grudge.

Concealed in an alley diagonal from the back of the shop, I flicked a glance at the clock before returning my eyes to the back door. Kingsley was late. Only by a minute, but still. Oliver's white Mercedes sat in its designated slot outside the back door, so I knew he was still there. I just prayed we wouldn't miss our window of opportunity and have to do this shit all over again. I wanted to get this over with and get the hell home to Lydia.

As if my thought had conjured the man, his black Maserati pulled into the lot.

"He's here."

Clay glanced up from the phone in his hands. "'Bout time."

Seconds later, a voice crackled over the computer system as Kingsley synced up his comm device. "You hear me okay?"

"10-4," I responded, and then I turned my gaze to the computer on the console. "Ready when you are."

A new window popped up as Kingsley activated the microscopic camera to give us eyes inside the shop. The trident on the steering wheel came into view as he climbed out of the car.

He certainly looked nothing like the police officer I knew he'd once been. Police lieutenant turned real estate mogul, Bennett Kingsley probably owned half the buildings in the city. He dabbled in construction, as well, and had helped smooth the way for QSG when Con was first getting started. His job today was to go in and scope out Oliver's shop, see if he could dig up any information. In his pristine suit, Kingsley fit in much better than any of us ever would.

For a long while, all was quiet. Then, through the discreetly placed receiver, I heard a saleswoman greet him.

"Hello, sir. May I help you find something?"

"I'll let you know when I find it." His voice was aloof, almost self-righteous, and I rolled my eyes. Fucking rich bastards.

Silence descended again, and Kingsley leisurely strolled the shop, examining its contents. From what I understood, Oliver carried a variety of antiquities—everything from ancient artifacts to furniture he'd rescued and restored. I hoped to hell Kingsley knew what he was doing. Con seemed to have faith in him, so I forced myself to do the same.

Beside me, Clay shifted and pulled his phone from his back pocket. He swiped a thumb over the screen, then grinned as an image popped up.

"Everything good?"

He redirected his gaze out the windshield, his face impassive as he lay his phone face down on his thigh. "Yep."

I lifted a brow. "Is it serious?"

Clay's phone vibrated, and his fingers flew over the screen. He sent the message, then clicked it off again. "Is what serious?"

"The girl you're talking to."

"Nah."

And that, right there, told me just how much she meant to

him. Twenty bucks said Clay fell into bed with the mystery woman an hour from now and wouldn't surface until he had to report for work. A conspiratorial smile curved my mouth. "Fine, I'll let you keep your secret."

Clay lifted his middle finger in response but remained stony faced, and I laughed. "Whatever, man. Have your fun."

Kingsley's voice crackled through the comm unit. "I don't believe you have quite what I'm looking for."

Shit. What the hell was he doing? I leaned forward in my seat, unsure exactly what the hell I was going to do about it. I couldn't go barging in there, but this wasn't part of the plan. Clay shot me an alarmed look, and I opened my mouth to say something to Kingsley when a second voice rang out, this one masculine.

"Perhaps I can help with something?"

Kingsley turned, and Oliver came into view. Small and wiry, he looked even smaller in person than he had in his photos. Kingsley waved a hand. "You have some nice pieces, but nothing feels quite right."

The older man approached. "Perhaps if you told me what you're looking for…?"

I held my breath during the beat of silence before Kingsley spoke. "I was told I'd know it when I saw it."

Oliver's brows drew together. "Have we met?"

"Bennett Kingsley."

Apparently that was all the introduction Oliver needed, because a smile wreathed his face as he accepted Kingsley's outstretched hand. "Ah, yes." His brows drew together. "I thought your places leaned more toward the modern?"

Even I couldn't miss the suspicion in the man's tone, but Kingsley seemed unaffected. "Modern lines are fine for the condos, but in my personal home, I'm looking for something a little more… traditional."

Oliver's smile flared back to life. "I see. Couldn't agree with you more. Who likes all those stark spaces and steel structures?"

"So you understand my predicament."

"I do. And do you know what you're looking for?"

"Not precisely. Nothing feels quite… right."

Oliver eyed him. "Perhaps if I know what you like, I may be able to procure something for you."

Yes, I chanted silently. This was what we'd been waiting for. Even his vague implication had me ready to celebrate.

"Do you work with collectors?"

"I do," Oliver responded hesitantly. "Sometimes it's just a matter of how much it will take to convince them to part with something."

Kingsley chuckled. "As I'm sure you're aware, that won't be a problem."

I rolled my head toward Clay and caught the grimace on his face. He threw me a disgusted look, and I couldn't help but grin. I didn't know if Kingsley was as much an asshole as he seemed, but he did a great job acting like one.

Pushing Oliver any more would be a mistake, and Kingsley instinctively seemed to pick up on it. He handed over his card. "Call me if anything else comes in."

Kingsley strode outside, then climbed into his sleek little car and took off with a rumble of the powerful engine.

I turned to Clay. "Thank fuck. Let's get outta here."

I wanted to get home to my woman, and I knew Clay felt the same, even if he didn't want to admit it.

I stopped off at QSG to drop off Clay as well as our comm equipment. Though I knew the statue hadn't been in Eldredge's shop, I uploaded the file to my desktop and checked the recording one more time for good measure.

Once I was done, I headed toward Lydia's place. I unlocked the door with the key she'd given me, then slipped inside. Letting my eyes adjust for a second, I stepped out of my boots and quietly made my way to the back of the house. Lydia had left the light over the stove on, and it gave the room soft, golden glow. Disappointment hit me hard. She must be asleep. I turned to go, and something caught my eye.

Curled up in a tiny ball at the end of the couch, Lydia dozed, a worn paperback lying loose in her fingers as if she'd fallen asleep holding it. The sight brought a smile to my face. I lowered myself to one knee and carefully extracted the book from her hands. A soft sigh left her lips, and her eyes fluttered several times before popping open. Landing on me, they widened, and she bolted upright. "Xander!"

"Shh." I ran a hand up the outside of her thigh. "I didn't

mean to scare you. I just wanted to see you for a second before I headed out."

"Oh." Her face fell. "You can stay for a while if you'd like."

I eyed her. "Are you sure?"

"Yeah. I was actually waiting for you." She gestured to the book now lying beside her. "I thought I'd read for a bit, but I must've dozed off."

Sliding my hands beneath her legs, I scooped her into my arms and sank down on the cushion, still warm from her body heat, then settled her in my lap. She brushed her nose over the base of my throat, and I smiled as she inhaled.

This was the second time she'd done that, and I quirked a smile. "You must like the way I smell."

"Shh." She delivered a playful slap to my chest. "You're ruining it."

"Ruining what? You got some fantasy that I don't know about?"

"Mhmm… I was having the most amazing dream before you woke me up." For a moment, hope flared then crashed to the ground in a fiery explosion a moment later. "Dark hair…" Her eyes flitted downward for a moment, and I swore I could hear a hint of a smile in her voice when she spoke. "Sexy abs…"

I followed her gaze to the book lying beside me, a rugged Scot on the cover, tanned and bare-chested. *Brat.* I tightened my hold on her, shifting her the tiniest bit closer. She tipped her head up at me, the teasing glimmer in her sultry eyes telling me she was deriving a great deal of pleasure from yanking my chain. She ran one hand over my chest. "Chiseled pecs…"

I flattened my lips to keep from smiling. "Yeah? Anything else?"

"A kilt." She cracked a huge grin, unable to hold it back any longer.

I snorted. "Can't help you with that one."

She let out a dramatic sigh. "What good are you?"

Smart-ass. I let out a low growl, gratified when her pupils dilated, lust swimming in the dark depths. "Oh, sweetheart, I'll show you just how good I am."

Shifting her in my arms, I dipped her over my arm so her back was arched, her breasts pushed forward. Twin peaks pressed against the thin material of her camisole, begging for attention. Starting at her neck, I placed hot, open-mouthed kisses over the sleek column, swept my tongue over her sweet, salty skin, and bit down. She let out a soft mewl, her body writhing, her bottom wiggling against my hard arousal.

I trailed lower, over her collarbone and between the valley of her breasts until I met the lace edging of her shirt. Her nipples were hard, tiny nubs, and I took one in my mouth. The wet fabric clung to her, enhancing the sensual vision. Pulling the opposite strap down her shoulder, I bared the other breast. Gently kneading her soft flesh, I took the tip in my mouth and bit down gently.

I'd never tasted anything so sweet as Lydia, and I knew I'd never get enough.

CHAPTER THIRTY-THREE
Lydia

I tunneled my fingers through his hair, gripping his skull and holding him close. I loved the faint burning sensation as his beard grazed my skin, and the sensation sent a ripple of heat curling through my belly. Xander's mouth moved to my breast, and he suckled my nipple through the filmy fabric of my camisole. The scrape of the material over my hardened peak shot a current of electricity straight to my core, and I ground against him. Shoving my shirt up to expose my breasts to his view, Xander latched on to a tight peak, his teeth digging into the tender flesh just enough to elicit a sting of pleasure.

"God, baby, I want you so much." His words brushed over my skin, warming my heart. The arm around my back tightened as he lifted me to a sitting position. "Spread your legs."

His words penetrated the fog of lust that had settled over my brain, and I struggled to follow his whispered instructions. My legs shook, but I finally managed to move astride him. One huge hand cupped the back of my neck and pulled, bringing my head down to meet his. I let out a soft sigh as his lips molded to mine, soft yet demanding. As my lips parted, his tongue delved inside, stroking against mine in a gentle rhythm. The banked embers within me flamed to life, and I clutched him tightly, my nails digging into his triceps.

His hands roamed impatiently over my body, around the flare of my hips and the dip of my waist. His fingers delved under the hem of my shirt, and he broke the kiss only long enough to strip it over my head. Talented fingers tweaked my nipples, his mouth still teasing mine with seductive, demanding kisses. I wiggled to get closer, his cock pressing up through the fabric of his pants and brushing my thigh.

My breasts felt heavy and full in his palms, aching as his thumbs flicked over the sensitive tips. An intense pleasure bordering on pain shot through me, and I froze. Sitting here on display, the light from the kitchen spilling into the living room, washing over me, I was sure he could see every inch of me—every imperfection. And there were a lot of those.

Oh, God. "No!" Tears sprang to my eyes and I ripped myself from his embrace, covering my breasts with one hand while searching for my shirt with the other.

Xander climbed to his feet and stepped close. "Sweetheart, what's—"

My lungs heaved as humiliation coursed through me, and Xander's words felt as if they were coming from a thousand miles away.

Large hands grasped my wrists, demanding my attention. "Liddy, stop!"

"Please let me go." I fought against his hold, unable to look him in the eye.

"Stop fighting me."

I resisted for a moment, then went slack, pinning my gaze to his chest so I wouldn't have to look him in the eyes. After a long moment, he released me, and I automatically crossed my arms over my breasts. My chin dipped to my chest in defeat. Tiny pink lines spread over my skin like cracks in glass, the stretch marks from my body swelling and shrinking after Alexia's birth. I closed my eyes so I wouldn't have to see the very things I'd tried to hide from Xander.

"Hey." His hands lifted to frame my face. "Talk to me. What's wrong?"

I shook my head, tears spilling down my cheeks, and he brushed them away with his thumbs. "I can't."

"Why?" He gently pressed up on the underside of my chin, forcing my gaze to his. Concern lingered in the cerulean depths. "Tell me what's going through your head."

"I'm... not back to normal yet." I could see the confusion

in his gaze, and the words left me in a defeated rush. "From breastfeeding."

Understanding dawned. "Oh, sweetheart."

I'd never been enough—not pretty enough, not successful enough. I sure hadn't been for Shawn. So why would Xander be any different? Where he was hard and muscular and in shape, I was soft and curvy and flawed. "I'll never be the kind of woman you want."

"Lydia, look at me." Reluctantly, I dragged my gaze upward. Clear blue eyes bored into mine. "I wanted you two years ago, and I want you now." His hands slid around to my lower back, holding me close. "I will *always* want you, Liddy. You're the mother of our baby girl. My wife. There's nothing sexier than that."

At his words, my head dropped forward to rest in the crook of his neck, and I drew in a shuddering breath. "I'm sorry."

His chin brushed my temple as he shook his head. "Don't apologize, sweetheart. I can't imagine what you've been through. But you don't have to do this by yourself anymore. I'll be here for you. Always."

I lifted my head and gazed at him, absorbing the truth in his gaze. "I just feel… awkward."

His fingers dipped into my hair. "I don't ever want to make you uncomfortable, Liddy. I won't make you do something you don't want to do."

"I do want this." I took a deep breath and gestured between us. "Us. I... I missed you."

His lips captured mine, turning my blood to molten liquid. I kissed him back feverishly, swept away by the passion I felt for him. "I missed you so damn much."

The connection I thought we'd severed nearly two years ago was still there—I could feel it. The passion between us was stronger than ever, and desire danced along my nerve endings like fire. His touch burned me, the inferno inside my body raging with need. I wanted him, all of him. It'd been much too long since I'd been touched like this—touched at all, really. With Xander, it was as if we had never been apart. He did something to me that I didn't understand, sparked a need inside me that I'd never felt before. I'd spent hundreds of nights wishing he was by my side, and now it was finally coming true.

"I need you to tell me, Liddy. Tell me what you want."

What did I want? *Him*. My heart screamed for him, needed him like my next breath. "You—I want you."

His mouth came down hard on mine, and our tongues tangled together in an erotic dance as old as time as he palmed my ass and yanked me toward him. I wrapped my legs around his waist as he carried me to the bedroom, then set me on my feet just inside the doorway. Grasping eagerly at my clothes, he walked us backwards until my back hit the wall. Once my hands were free of the material, I looped them around his shoulders, catching the back of his neck. I loved the feel of his hair beneath my fingers, the silky strands longer than they'd been a year and a half ago.

Hooking his fingers in the waistband of my sweats, he dropped to a crouch and slid them down my legs. I braced a hand on one muscular shoulder as I stepped out of them. Leaning forward, he nuzzled my core through my plain white cotton panties. They were decidedly unsexy, but Xander made everything seem special—extraordinary. It didn't matter to him whether I was in sweats or sexy lingerie.

He kissed one thigh, then the other before working my panties down my legs. The second I stepped free, he pressed up on my leg, forcing my knee to bend. He placed it over his shoulder and ran one finger through my drenched slit. I bit the back of my hand to keep the gasp welling up my throat from escaping, well aware of the baby asleep in the next room.

"So sweet." Xander moved closer, his tongue dipping between my folds and nudging the sensitive bud. I let out a whimper, and he tightened his grip as my legs trembled. "I got you, babe."

Slowly lowering my leg, Xander pushed to a standing position and pulled me against him. Sliding his hands beneath my bottom, he yanked hard and lifted me to his chest. My legs automatically wrapped around him, the material of his pants rubbing against my exposed core. His lips crashed against mine as I shifted my hips, trying to get closer, trying to find fulfillment. I felt empty, and I needed Xander to make it better.

Laying me back on the bed, Xander reached over his head and yanked his shirt off before tossing it to the ground. He quickly shed his pants, rolled on a condom, then crawled between my legs. "We'll play later, but right now I need to be inside you. It's been fucking killing me."

I nodded, breathless, too turned on to even respond. I wasn't sure I could form words at this point, let alone an articulate response. I needed him just as badly as he needed me. I wanted to feel the way he'd made me feel two years ago. I wanted to lose myself in him, lose myself in the comfort and strength and care that he offered.

"What's the easiest way for you to get off?"

"Um..." I blinked at the sudden question. I had no idea. On the rare occasion that I'd had sex with Shawn, it had always been rushed, in bed with the lights off. If I didn't get off—which was most of the time—I'd roll over and slide my hand between my legs to relieve the ache myself. I stared up at Xander, who watched me with an intensity I'd never known. "Missionary?"

He cocked a brow. "Is that a question?"

I glared up at him. "It's been a while."

Immediately, his gaze turned hot and feral. "Fuck yeah, it has."

His words, spoken on a low growl, sent tendrils of heat curling through me. No one had ever talked dirty to me before—no one but Xander. And I loved it.

"I need to know because this time is gonna be fast," he warned. "I've been jerking off to thoughts of this gorgeous pussy for days now, and I don't know how long I'm gonna last."

His accent was accentuated when he was turned on, I discovered. The low words blended together in a silken slur. Knowledge that he'd been imagining me while getting off sent a wave of heat climbing over my face. "I don't... I'm not sure," I stuttered.

"Let's find out." Xander's hands moved to my hips, and I felt the unmistakable nudge at my entrance as he lined himself up. "I can't fucking wait to feel you again."

I sucked in a breath as he slipped inside one inch, then another. His hands tightened around my waist, and he let out a sound that was a combination of a growl and a low moan. "Fuuuck."

Lifting my hips a fraction, he thrust deep. The motion took my breath away, and I swore I saw stars as his cock stroked my inner walls. My legs curved around his, holding him close, my nails digging into the skin where I gripped his shoulders. He commanded my body, every nerve ending alive and screaming for him. He filled every inch of me—my core, my heart, my mind.

Xander stared down at me, blue eyes dark in their intensity. "Goddamn, babe. You feel so good."

My muscles clenched around him as he began to pull out, not wanting to let him go. Before I could call it back, a tiny whimper left my mouth, and I sank my teeth into my lower lip. One hand moved to my head, tunneling into my hair and turning my face to meet his. The kiss was demanding, ferocious. He devoured me like a starving man needs food to survive.

Hot, panting breaths collided as our tongues slid over one another, eager to taste. I tried to cry out as he slammed back into me, but Xander stole the sound from my mouth. His lips were bruising as they claimed mine, his hips pumping back and forth. Heat raced through me, and I shattered in an explosion of light. Xander slapped a hand over my mouth as a keening cry escaped. The muffled sound travelled up my throat and vibrated through my body to the tips of my fingers and toes, stealing every molecule of oxygen.

One hand still buried in my hair, the other slipped beneath my bottom, pulling my hips to his as he pounded into me hard and fast. Concentration lined his face and his lips pulled up in a grimace as I felt him grow even harder inside me.

"Fuck, baby... Yes!"

Our bodies rocked together as he slammed into me twice more, then let go with a hiss, emptying himself deep inside me. He slumped over me, our damp bodies sealed together. After a long moment, he pressed a kiss to my collarbone, then levered himself upward.

I reluctantly relaxed my legs as he started to pull out. I couldn't help the sense of loss as his body left mine. He seemed to understand, because he shifted onto his side next to me, then grasped my hip and pulled me flush against him. My nipples brushed his chest, we were so close, and the sensation sent a shiver down my spine. I pressed my legs together to stop the ache, but it only intensified.

Xander cupped the back of my head and pulled me in for a

leisurely kiss. His tongue swept over mine, slow and sweet. His hand slipped down the expanse of my back and over the curve of my hip to my bottom. He squeezed the round globe before giving it a light smack. I jumped in surprise, and a tiny smile lit Xander's face when we finally broke our kiss.

"Give me a few more minutes to recover, then you're all mine again."

CHAPTER THIRTY-FOUR
Xander

I stared down at the woman in my arms, her unruly dark waves tossed riotously over the pillow beside me. A few strands still clung to her face, and I brushed them away with my thumb. Her lashes fluttered, but her breathing never changed, and I knew she was out. She'd collapsed—literally fallen flat on her belly with a laugh, joking that I'd fucked her senseless—the last time I'd pulled out of her half an hour ago.

I'd tucked her against me as she snuggled close, not wanting an inch of space between us. I loved watching her, loved every sexy sound she made. One of these nights I wanted her wild and unrestrained. I wanted to hear her scream my name. Soon I was going to arrange for a babysitter to watch Alexia for a few hours so I could fuck her properly.

I reached over to the nightstand and flipped off the baby monitor that rested beside the clock. I was a light sleeper from my years in the service; as soon as Alexia cried out, I'd be up. I wanted Lydia to relax and get some sleep. The stress from the shop was weighing on her, I could tell. Lydia worked too damn hard, and I wanted to help in whatever way I could.

Closing my eyes, I let my thoughts drift for a moment, inhaling the sweet scent of the woman next to me before finally falling sleep. Not long after, my eyes flew open, and I immediately took stock of my surroundings, trying to determine what had awakened me. After a moment of silence, a strain of high-pitched chatter floated from Alexia's room. A smile curved my face, and I glanced at the clock. With any luck, Lydia would sleep for another hour or two before she had to get ready for work.

I carefully extracted myself from her lithe body, one lean leg wrapped around mine like a vine. A tiny whimper left her mouth, and I tucked the covers around her. At the feeling of security, she immediately snuggled back in and dropped off to sleep again.

Yanking on the pants I'd worn last night, I crept from the room and closed the door behind me before making my way down the hall to Alexia's room. She stood by the rail of her crib, talking softly to herself and bouncing on the squishy mattress.

"Hey, baby girl."

She peered up at me over the railing, a trace of confusion in her eyes. "Mama?"

Her question sent a little pang of regret through my heart. I hated that I hadn't been here for her—for either of them—when they needed me most. I hated that Alexia still looked at me sometimes like she wasn't quite sure what to make of me, like she didn't recognize me or trust me.

"Mama's sleeping. Come to Daddy?"

I held my arms out and waited for her to come to me. Though I'd spent most every night over the past week with her, she still hadn't opened up completely. When Lydia was around, Alexia seemed to sense that everything was okay. But she was reserved when it was just the two of us, like she was afraid Lydia wouldn't come back. Maybe it was exactly as Lydia said; Alexia had never been around men. We were big, scary, hairy creatures to be feared. I'd do anything to take that look of concern off her face.

She reached up, and I scooped her into my arms. Carrying her over to the changing table, I spoke to her while I changed and dressed her. "You hungry? Maybe we should make breakfast for mommy."

She looked up at me hopefully as I tossed her soiled diaper in the pail and picked her up. "Cookie?"

I laughed and cuddled her close, brushing my nose over hers. "Good try. No cookies. Eggs?"

Together we strolled downstairs, and I whipped up some scrambled eggs while Alexia watched from her high chair nearby. She attacked the eggs with gusto when I set them on her tray, though I was pretty sure more ended up on the floor than in her mouth. Once I had everything cleaned up and had prepared a plate for Lydia, I picked Alexia up from her high chair and scooped up the plate. "Nothing like breakfast in bed. Right, sugar?"

"Bed," she mimicked.

"That's right." A grin split my face. Lydia hated not being in control, but I hoped she'd at least appreciate the gesture. Cracking open her bedroom door, I spied her still curled up in a ball in the middle of the bed. Setting the plate on the nightstand, I used my free hand to part the curtains a bit and let the early morning sunshine spill through.

Settling on the edge of the bed, I set Alexia down and ran a hand over Lydia's dark locks. "Hey, beautiful. Time to wake up."

Sleepy gray eyes peeked open as Alexia crawled on top of her. Extracting her arms from the confines of the covers, she pulled Alexia into a hug. "Morning."

Her voice was rough with sleep and sexy as fuck. "Morning. I brought you some eggs and toast."

Her eyes widened in surprise. "You made me breakfast?"

Alexia pulled free of Lydia's hold and crawled over to lay her head on the pillow I'd vacated barely an hour ago, then closed her eyes and pretended to sleep.

"We made you breakfast," I corrected, holding up the piece of mangled toast Alexia had tried to grab on the way upstairs.

Lydia let out a laugh, the soft, sweet sound burrowing deep into my heart. Unable to stop myself, I dropped my head and kissed her hard. Off guard, she hesitated for a fraction of a second before responding, her lips moving against mine. Threading my fingers through her long locks, I angled her head up to mine. "You're so lucky our daughter is in here with us right now."

"I'll make it up to you later."

I tightened my hold on her hair and took her mouth in a brutal kiss. "Bet your ass you will."

I nipped her bottom lip before letting her go and wrangling a wiggling Alexia with one arm. "Come here, princess. The sooner Mama goes to work, the sooner she can come home. And the sooner I can get her back under me."

I shot Lydia a wicked smile, allowing my gaze to peruse

the parts of her exposed by the sheet that had fallen down. Memories of running my tongue over her collarbone and throat rushed back to me, and my cock twitched. "I want to take you on a date."

She blinked up at me. "Um. Okay."

Fuck. "I know it sounds dumb…" I started, then trailed off. What the hell could I say? This was probably the stupidest idea I'd ever had. We were doing everything backwards. I should have done this two years ago; I should have done a lot of things differently.

"No." Lydia pushed to a sitting position and brushed the hair from her eyes. "I mean yes. To the date. I… I'd like that."

Hope zinged through my chest like a pinball machine. I'd skipped this part last time—the part where I got to know every little thing about her, fall in love with her one detail at a time. I admired her intelligence and drive, and I knew she was a shrewd businesswoman. But I loved this side of her—the soft, sweet woman, the mother of my child. I wanted more of this. I didn't care what it took to win her over—I was going to do it. "What about tonight? Think Darlene will watch Alexia?"

"I'm not sure."

"I'll take care of it. You eat and get ready."

Lydia's smile turned wicked. "I'm ready now."

I pointed at her as I shifted Alexia to my hip. "Don't start something you can't finish."

Her lips turned down in a pout and she slipped from the bed, pulling the sheet with her. "But it's so much fun."

With two strides, I closed the distance between us and fisted my hand in the fabric of the sheet, then yanked her to me. "You better get out of here while you still can. I'm sure Darlene would be more than happy to take Alexia for a bit so I can fuck my wife before work."

Lydia inhaled sharply, but I couldn't tell if she was turned on or appalled at the fact that I'd called her my wife. That single word stood out in my mind. Despite everything good that had unfolded between us over the past week and a half, I still felt a black cloud hovering over us. Technically we were still married. But was that what Lydia wanted? Or was I just some fling until she found someone better? We hadn't talked about it at all, like the situation would just disappear if we ignored it.

I could leave well enough alone. I could pretend that we were both content to stay this way. But I needed to know. I needed to hear it from her lips that she wanted me in her life—as both her husband and father to our daughter. I didn't know what I'd say if she still wanted the divorce. Could I convince her otherwise?

I knew that whatever connection had been between us two years ago was still there. I'd felt something that first night. No, it hadn't been love, but it had definitely been lust. And appreciation. And chemistry. Fuck, we had that in spades. Every time we touched it was like lighting a torch drenched in kerosene. She made me feel things I'd only ever heard about. I wasn't into all the gushy, romancey shit that the movies talked about, but I did know one thing—whatever Lydia and I had was different. I didn't know if it would carry us the distance, but I knew for sure it was worth exploring.

Lydia didn't respond, and I spoke quickly to cover my faux pas. "Dinner and a movie. Then we'll see where the night leads."

She gave a little nod, and I slipped my hand up to cup the back of her head. I stared into her eyes for a long moment before dropping one last kiss on her full lips. Without another word, I left the room, praying I hadn't fucked everything up.

CHAPTER THIRTY-FIVE
Lydia

I studied Xander from across the table. Somehow he'd managed to sweet-talk Darlene into watching Alexia and putting her to bed tonight so we could have some time to ourselves. I both anticipated it and dreaded it—because I knew exactly what this would be about.

His words from this morning had weighed on me all day. He'd called me his wife… and I had no idea how I felt about that. I'd tried to push it from my mind, but now it flared up full force. I hadn't let myself dwell on it over the past couple weeks.

A tiny tremor of fear ran through me, but it was shadowed by a sense of contentment and excitement. Part of me was flattered; the other was scared to death. Dinner had been mostly silent, interspersed with small talk revolving primarily around Alexia. He kept most of his experiences from the Army under wraps, and I wondered if it bothered him more than he let on. I didn't know exactly what he did or where he'd been, and it felt like one more secret between us.

He cleared his throat, and my stomach hit the floor as I dropped my gaze to my plate. My hand clenched around the fork I held suspended over my plate as I waited for the shoe to drop.

"Have you given any more thought to what you want to do?"

And there it was. I feigned ignorance. "What do you mean?" His expression told me I was doing a piss-poor job, and I let out a sigh. "I don't know."

He leaned back in his chair and set his hands on his thighs as he studied me. His voice was soft. "That doesn't sound promising."

I placed my napkin on the table. "It's just... It's a lot to think about."

"It sounds like you've made up your mind."

"It's not that," I hedged.

His shoulders dropped a fraction and a muscle in his jaw ticked. "Right."

I bit my lip, my skin flushing cold as his expressionless gaze landed on mine. He had every right to be angry with me. I wrung my hands together and prepared to bare my soul. "I... I'm scared."

His brows drew together, twin lines forming in the space above his nose. "Why? What scares you?"

I took a moment to gather the words that needed to be said. "You. You scare me."

His head jerked back and his eyes flared wide at my admission. "I scare you?"

"Not that way. I'm not afraid you'll hurt me—not physically." I swallowed over the sudden dryness in my throat. "You're... different. You're not like anyone I've ever met. You make me..." The words eluded me. I couldn't begin to describe the way he made me feel. Thankfully he seemed to understand, because he nodded solemnly.

"Trust me when I say this, Lydia." He leaned forward and braced his elbows on the table. "I feel a connection to you that I've never experienced with another person. I felt it when we first met, and it's still there now. All I'm asking for is a chance."

He reached out and laid his hand on the table, palm up. I eyed it for a long moment before placing my own hand in his. "Can I tell you what I'd like?"

Blue eyes implored me to listen, and I nodded, unable to speak. "I want us to do this." He gestured between us with his free hand. "I want to date you, learn everything about you, everything I missed."

He held up a hand when I opened my mouth to speak. "No more living in the past. Neither of us can change what happened. But we can change the future."

I swallowed hard, tears burning the backs of my eyes at his words. "Is that what you want?"

"I just want you, sweetheart. I want to come home to you and Alexia every night."

"But what if we don't make it?"

"What if we do?"

I bit my lip, my gaze fixed on our hands still joined on the table. Wasn't that exactly what I wanted? So why was I so afraid to take that last step?

"Lydia." He squeezed my fingers where they rested in his, and I lifted my eyes to his. "We're no different than anyone else. The journey was a little unconventional, but there's nothing that says we can't make this work. I like you. I care about you. And I think you care about me, too. Right?" I nodded solemnly, and he continued. "If we both work at this, I think we can be happy."

"I don't exactly have a great track record," I admitted. "I mean, look how my last relationship ended."

"Through no fault of your own," Xander cut in. "That had absolutely nothing to do with you."

"I should have seen the signs. I should have known."

Xander shook his head. "Why would you? You thought he loved you. And maybe he did—in his own way. But he couldn't love you the way you deserved. What happened to you sucks, and I wish I could take it back. You understand it had nothing to do with you, right?"

Deep down, I think I'd known it all along, but for some reason, hearing Xander say it aloud solidified it for me. I was still furious with Shawn—but I understood.

I nodded slowly, trying to absorb everything. I couldn't help but compare Xander to my ex-fiancé. Shawn had put on a façade, trying to be something he wasn't. While I think he was fond of me, his attraction to me was forced. He'd never been overly affectionate—not like Xander, who touched me and kissed me every chance he got. He made me feel… wanted. Desired. Loved.

"So… where do we go from here?" I asked.

Xander lifted a brow. "Bed?"

I let out a little laugh as I shook my head. I wasn't sure how he read me so well and knew how to lighten my mood. "Movie first. Then bed." I grinned, watching his eyes darken with lust.

"Deal." He pulled his wallet from his back pocket and tossed several bills on the table. Pushing his chair back, he held out his hand for mine. Looping my purse over my shoulder, I slipped my palm into his, leaning into the solid weight and comforting warmth of his big body.

The restaurant we'd selected was in a large plaza, and there was a cinema located across the street on the opposite corner. Stepping into the warm night air, we strolled down the sidewalk, dodging other pedestrians and couples outside enjoying the evening. We crossed over to the movie theater where Xander paid for our tickets—against my protests—and led me into the dark theater. Once settled in our seats, he wrapped an arm around my shoulders and dropped a kiss on my temple.

I tipped my chin up, studying his profile in the soft light. Things with Xander felt… different. Was I falling for him? My pulse kicked up, my blood thrumming through my body at the possibility. Maybe he was right. We could take this one day at a time. What was the worst that would happen? People divorced every day, even after years of marriage with someone they'd once loved.

My heart felt a little lighter as I settled in and rested my head on Xander's shoulder. I felt his head turn, and I smiled as I imagined the surprised look on his face. It was the first time I'd initiated anything—and it felt good. Warm lips brushed the crown of my head, and I tipped my face up to him. One hand cupped my jaw, and intense blue eyes studied me for a long moment. As if sensing the change between us, he lowered his forehead to mine and closed his eyes.

The moment was broken as the theater went dark and the previews started rolling. A silly smile on my face, I focused on the screen. I was so wrapped up in the movie—and the man next to me—that the buzzing of my phone half an hour later barely registered.

Xander tipped his head. "Do you want to check that?"

The vibrations stopped then immediately started again. Opening my bag, I peeked at my phone, then returned my gaze to Xander. "It's just Jolene. I'll call her back later."

Setting my bag to the side, I focused once more on the movie, only to be interrupted by buzzing once more. A text popped up on my screen.

Jolene: Why aren't you answering your phone?

I held the phone down to control the bright glare of light from the screen as I typed out my response.

Me: I'm in the middle of a movie

Before I could ask what she needed, three little dots popped up and another message came through.

Jolene: Need you to come over

Xander watched over my shoulder as I typed. "Do you want to go?"

"I'm not sure." Anxiety raced through me, and my fingers flew over the screen.

Me: Is everything ok?

Her next message came only seconds later, brief and chilling.

Jolene: Hurry

My hand fluttered to my throat, the pressure on my chest suddenly making it hard to breathe. Shit. I imagined the worst, that she was hurt or something bad had happened.

"I—I need to go check on her," I whispered.

Without a word, Xander grabbed my hand, and we crept out of the theater. Once in the car, I pressed one hand to my stomach as the lights of the freeway flew by and bled into the distance. I wasn't sure why, but I had a bad feeling. Sure, my mother had a tendency to be overly dramatic, but her messages tonight were abrupt, holding a sense of urgency I didn't know how to interpret.

Xander reached over and placed a hand on my thigh. "It's okay, babe. I'm sure everything is just fine."

I nodded and forced a smile, though doubt reigned. Following my directions, Xander pulled up in front of my mother's house seventeen minutes later. I was out of the truck before the engine cut off, halfway up the stone walkway to the large brick home. Without bothering to knock, I turned the handle, thankful it was unlocked, and shoved the front door open.

"Jolene?" I paused. "Mother!"

"No need to yell, I'm coming."

The tap of heels across the parquet floor reached my ears and I breathed out a sigh of relief. As my racing heart began to calm,

I became aware of several things at once. The first was Xander's heat at my back. Placing one hand on my shoulder, he shifted me slightly to the side and closed the front door. The second thing I noticed was the luggage.

Two suitcases and an oversized tote bag stood just inside the entryway, and my brows drew together. My mother rounded the corner, her handbag draped over her forearm, looking like she was ready to stride into a party.

It was ten o'clock at night. What the hell was going on? Before I could speak, Jolene waved to the suitcases by her feet. "All right, I'm ready."

Shock rooted me to the floor. "For what?"

"I need to catch the red-eye to Miami."

"Did something happen?" Did we even know anyone in Miami?

She lifted an eyebrow and looked down her nose at me as if I was an idiot. "I'm going on a trip, and I need you to take me to the airport."

Disbelief temporarily rendered me speechless. For several seconds, I floundered before finally managing to choke out words. "A trip?" My mother stared at me but didn't speak. A low boil began in my stomach and curled upward. "You called me out of a movie because you decided to take a last-minute trip to the beach?"

She lifted a shoulder. "I didn't want to leave the Mercedes at the airport. Besides, the suitcases won't fit in—"

"Are you fucking kidding me?" The words ripped from my throat as I threw my arms wide.

"Language!" my mother admonished. "It isn't ladylike."

"Neither is treating your only child like shit," I shot back. "For years I've been nothing but a pawn for you to use. I'm your daughter, not your damn assistant."

"Really," Jolene huffed, propping one hand on her hip. "It's the least you can do."

"Really? Because you loaned me money that I should have gotten from the bank in the first place?" I seethed. "I'm done playing your games. And after Monday, I won't owe you shit."

"What does that mean?" A faint trace of alarm entered her eyes.

"It means I'm paying off every red cent that I borrowed so I don't have to deal with your ridiculous, selfish antics ever again." I pointed a finger at her. "And you can forget seeing Alexia again until you get your shit together. We don't need your toxic attitude in our life."

"But…" She looked lost, and for a moment, I almost felt bad. Then she ruined it. "How am I going to get to the airport?"

"Like everyone else," I snapped. "Call a fucking Uber."

Turning on my heel, I threw open the door and stomped down the sidewalk. I refused to look at Xander, but I felt him just a step behind the whole way. Before I could reach for the handle, Xander held the door, and I hopped up inside the cab.

My body shook with anger from the top of my head all the way down to my toes, and I crossed my arms over my chest. I was afraid if I let go, I would lose my shit. How the hell could one person be so damn selfish?

Wordlessly, Xander climbed into the driver seat and started the truck. I stared out the windshield until we turned onto the main road. Then I burst into tears.

CHAPTER THIRTY-SIX
Xander

Fuck.

I checked the review mirror for headlights then pulled the truck to the side of the road. Hopping out, I circled the truck and opened Lydia's door. Unclicking her seat belt, I turned her toward me and gathered her in my arms. Sobs wracked her body, and I held her tight, unsure of what to say. I could feel the heat from her tears seeping into my shirt, and I cupped the back of her head, stroking one hand over her hair.

I was pissed she was hurting—but I was proud as fuck that she'd finally stood up to Jolene. Lydia shocked the hell out of me this evening. I don't know what I'd expected, but it wasn't my sweet-tempered girl dropping the f-bomb twice in the space of five minutes. Not gonna lie. It kind of turned me on. I knew she was smart and independent, but to see that spine of steel come out was sexy as fuck.

She'd let Jolene walk all over her for far too long, and I was fucking thrilled that she'd given Jolene a dose of her own medicine. I'd met the woman twice but had taken an instant dislike to the way she'd treated Lydia. How a mother could treat her child like that blew my mind. Lydia deserved far better.

Lydia leaned away from me and dabbed beneath her eyes with her fingertips. "I'm so sorry for ruining our date."

"Sweetheart"—I brushed a thumb over her cheek—"we have a thousand dates ahead of us. I don't care about dinner or a movie. I care about you."

"I just… I can't believe she did that!"

I couldn't either. Jolene was so wrapped up in herself she didn't care who she hurt as long as she got exactly what she wanted. Deciding to keep my opinions to myself, I just let Lydia vent and get it all off her chest.

"Damn it, I'm just so mad at her." Lydia vacillated between anger and sadness as her tears welled again. "God, she's such a bitch. Why can't she just be a normal mother like anyone else?"

I didn't have an answer for that.

"I mean, who does that?" Her hands cut through the air in an aggravated arc. "Like I'm her personal freaking assistant instead of her daughter. She doesn't give a damn about anyone but herself, and I'm tired of it."

She let out a defeated sigh, her shoulders slumping forward. "Shit. What am I going to do?"

I rubbed small circles over her back. "About what?"

"I don't have the money to pay her back."

I lifted her face to mine. "We'll take care of it Monday, just like you said."

Eyes still shiny with tears met mine. "We?"

"I told you before, sweetheart." I slid my hand up to cup the side of her face. "I'll do whatever I can to help. If you want to pay off what you owe, I'm more than happy to help you."

I knew Lydia hated to rely on anyone which was why I'd proposed the original offer I had. I thought she'd be more likely to let me help if she knew the money would go into an account for Alexia.

"Are you sure? It's a lot of money."

"It's worth it." Lydia had thrown down the gauntlet, and there was a chance that Jolene would come to terms with what she'd done and apologize. But it was more likely that she'd continue to abuse Lydia's good graces and use her as long as Lydia allowed it. I wanted Lydia away from that situation. Alexia was too young to know better yet, but she deserved far more than a grandmother in her life who tried to buy her love because she had nothing better to offer.

"I'll need to look at my finances," she finally said. "The shop does well, but I don't know how quickly I'll be able to pay you back."

"First of all"—I held up a finger—"you're not paying me back. Everything goes to Alexia. You just start putting a little bit away each month, whatever you can afford. It makes no difference to me."

I wasn't rolling in money, but I'd saved up enough over the years to be able to afford this with no problems. And if it was better for Lydia's sanity, then I would gladly sacrifice the money.

Her glossy eyes welled once more. "I don't know how to thank you."

I'd do anything to take that look off her face. I wasn't sure where her head was at, but I decided to test the waters with a gentle tease. "I have a few ideas."

She rolled her eyes and sniffled, a tiny smile lifting the corners of her mouth. "Right. I'm sure I'm super appealing right now."

"Liddy." Her head tipped heavily against my hand as she gazed up at me, and I studied the pewter depths of her eyes. She put on a brave front, but I saw the insecurity lurking far below the surface, mingling with sadness and hurt. "I always want you—from the first moment you wake up in the morning until the second you fall asleep at night. You're the most beautiful woman I've ever met, inside and out. Laughing, smiling, crying, yelling—I want all of you every way, every day."

She dropped her chin but didn't move away from my hand still cradling her cheek. A soft snuffle left her, and I felt the moist heat of a tear trickle down my palm. Pressing a kiss to her forehead, I continued. "I just want to put a smile on your face and treat you the way you deserve. I won't ever take advantage of you, and I'll do my best not to hurt you. I can't guarantee we won't fight or have bad days, but I'll do my damnedest to make you happy."

I wanted to tell her how I felt—that I was falling for her. That maybe I'd fallen for her long ago. But I kept my mouth shut. She had enough burdens to bear tonight, and I refused to heap anything else on her shoulders. I needed to wait for her to come to me. I prayed that just being here for her would be enough to prove my intentions were true.

"Come on, babe." I patted her hip and settled her back in her seat. "Let's go."

Taking my time as I rounded the truck, I shot off a quick text to Darlene to ask if she could watch Alexia a bit longer. We'd driven about a mile down the road when my screen lit up with an incoming message. I glanced at Darlene's affirmation, then set my phone in the cupholder. In the passenger seat, Lydia sat quietly, back to her reserved self. When I pulled into a pub on the outskirts of town, she threw me a questioning glance.

"What are we doing here?"

I turned to face her and laid one arm over the back of the seat. "We don't have to go in if you don't want to, but I thought you could use it. You never have any time for yourself."

She stared at me hard for a moment, then redirected her gaze to the bar. "I shouldn't. Darlene's watching Alexia and—"

"I already asked her to stay a bit longer." Lydia's gaze jumped back to mine. "She said to take as long as we need."

She was always too busy taking care of everyone else—Alexia, the salon, Jolene. She deserved a little bit of time to unwind. "I'm going to guess rum."

Her brows drew together in confusion. "For what?"

I lifted a shoulder. "I could tell the other night that you weren't really into beer. So I'm guessing rum is more up your alley."

"Close." A tiny smile lifted the corners of her mouth. "Vodka. Specifically, martinis."

I brushed a lock of hair away from her face. "Then how about we get you a martini?" After the episode with Jolene, Lydia could probably use a martini—or three.

She sank her teeth into her lower lip before replying. "I guess so."

Pleased that she'd agreed, I slid from the truck and went around to help her out. She slipped her hand into the crook of my elbow as I led her toward the front door. It was such a wifely thing to do, and it felt so natural that my heart swelled in my chest. It was the first time she'd reached for me first. She'd rarely, if ever, instigated romance between the two of us. Almost always I went 90 percent of the way before she'd move in to meet me.

I was starting to realize that I hadn't even begun to scratch the surface of Lydia's complex personality. She was outwardly serene and sweet, compartmentalizing all of her fears and doubts and insecurities and shoving them down deep. But now, things had begun to shift. She was touching me for the first time ever, as if I was more to her than Alexia's father. Even when we'd made love last night, she hadn't exhibited this kind of comfort. She'd been passionate, yes, and eager—but this was different.

I held the door, and we made our way to a corner booth in the back of the dimly lit bar. The heavy air held the tangy scent of lemon cleaner and sweet liquor. Lydia slid into the booth and I followed. She shot me a shy smile as I looped my arm around her shoulders, my thigh pressed tightly to hers. I knew she hadn't figured it out yet, but I was determined to make her understand—I wasn't going anywhere.

A waitress came by and took our order, and I turned to look at Lydia. "Do you want to talk about it?"

She let out a mirthless laugh. "The fact that my mother is an evil bitch? No, I'm all good on that. I've wasted over two decades getting caught up in her bullshit, and I'm done with it. My threshold for crap only reaches so far, and she definitely crossed the line tonight. I meant what I said back there. I don't want anything to do with her—and I don't want her around—unless she gets her shit together."

Fair enough. The amount of swearing she'd done in those few sentences alone told me just how serious she was. I let the silence stretch between us for a moment while I searched for something else to say. Before I came up with anything, she beat me to the punch, her voice filled with a combination of exasperation and frustration.

"You know"—she turned to face me—"I don't mind helping her out. I really don't. In fact, I'd have been more than happy to do it. But it's the principle of the thing. The fact of the matter is, she didn't even bother to ask if I would take her to the airport. Hell, she never even said anything about going before tonight. I'm sure she was just bored and needed a change, so she decided to hop on a plane, because she's spoiled and thinks she can have whatever she wants."

She paused to take a breath, and I stretched my legs under the table, settling further into the booth. Her body was still tight with tension, but I let my hand linger lightly on her shoulder, a gentle touch letting her know I was there for her.

Lydia sighed heavily. "I'm so tired of being treated like crap because she feels entitled to do whatever the hell she wants whenever she wants. It's bullshit."

I waited a moment, but it seemed her tirade was over. "For what it's worth... I'm glad you finally stood up to her."

"Yeah?" Steely eyes met mine. "You don't think I overreacted?"

"Not at all." I shook my head. "Granted, I don't know her all that well, but your mother seems... difficult."

Lydia let out a half laugh. "You think?"

"She strikes me as being a very strong personality who bullies people into doing what she wants." Lydia nodded in agreement. "Sometimes the only way to get through to someone like that is to stand up to them just the way you did. If they feel like they can push you around, they'll continue to walk all over you."

A tiny smile quirked her mouth. "Sounds like you're familiar with this."

I shrugged. "Not personally, exactly. But I knew guys like that in the service. Thought they were better than everyone else." I took a moment. "Your mother is kind of like those guys. Everyone is deserving of respect, and it's damn time she starts showing it to you. You have a successful business and you're an awesome mom. Who wouldn't be proud of that?"

She dipped her head, presumably to hide the flash of moisture I'd glimpsed in her eyes. Her voice was whisper-soft when she spoke, and the rasp told me my hunch was correct. "Thank you."

I wanted to pull her close, tuck her in next to me, but I didn't want to push her too far. I was here if—when—she needed me. I allowed almost a full minute to pass, giving her time to gather herself before I spoke again. "How have things been at the salon?"

"You know." She lifted one shoulder in a tiny shrug. "Busy. There's always something to do, some issue that needs to be fixed."

I nodded. It was the perfect in for the subject I'd wanted to bring up for a couple days now. "Have you thought about hiring anyone else?"

"Not really." She bit her lower lip for a moment. "It would be kind of a stretch with trying to pay the mortgage, plus my own rent and my debt to Jolene, and I'm not sure I want to take that risk right now."

"Well, maybe this is a good time to make a change," I suggested. "Once we pay off your mother, things won't be so tight. You can put some money aside for Alexia as you're able."

"Maybe." She worried that lower lip again.

Our conversation paused as the waitress delivered our drinks to the table, and I thanked her.

I pressed on, undaunted. "I'm sure having Brenda as backup helps but having another pair of hands to help around the shop would allow you to spend more time with Alexia."

"It would be nice," she acknowledged. She traced the rim of her glass with one finger as she spoke. "Gwen told me the other day she was looking for something else. I hate to lose her—she does such a great job. Maybe I'll promote her and hire another salesgirl to help out."

"You deserve it," I said. "You've done so well, but you're killing yourself trying to keep up."

Anger flared in her eyes as she met my gaze. "I'm fine."

"I didn't say you weren't. But I see the circles under your eyes." She quickly averted her eyes, and I knew I'd hit the nail on the head. "You deserve to have some time off. You're the only one who doesn't get a day off."

I knew, because the only day the salon was closed was Sunday. She worked from nine in the morning until at least seven each night and barely took the time to eat lunch during the day. I'd found this out by talking with Brenda the other day while I waited for Lydia. She always looked exhausted, yet she gave one hundred percent both at the salon and at home. If she kept it up, she would get burnt out. I knew she loved what she did, but it was slowly killing her.

I watched as she drew a little design in the condensation that had gathered on her glass. "Maybe you're right," she finally admitted. "It would be nice to spend more time with her. Before we know it, she'll be in school and all grown up."

She'd been in my life for less than two weeks, but I understood perfectly where she was coming from. I was momentarily hung up on her statement about Alexia before the first part even registered. She'd said *we*. Hope flared in my chest. That meant she was planning, subconsciously at least, for me to be in Alexia's life. It was progress, more so than anything else. We'd been close physically, but Lydia still held so much of herself back, keeping everything bottled up inside. I was incredibly pleased that she was beginning to think of us as a couple.

I pulled her a tiny bit closer and ran my hand up and down her arm. "I'll help however I can and support whatever you want to do. I don't want you to think I'm trying to tell you how to run your business."

"No, no." She waved a hand. "I know what you're saying. And I appreciate it." She shot me a little smile over her shoulder. "You've done so much for me. I don't know how we'll ever be even."

"It's not about getting even, Liddy." I slipped a hand beneath her jaw. "Besides, as long as I have you and Alexia, I have everything I need."

Gray eyes turned liquid, like mercury. Her tongue darted out and swiped over her bottom lip. "The things you say..." She inhaled deeply and closed her eyes for a second before meeting my eyes again. "Make me think you're really in this."

"I am, sweetheart. I can promise you that I'll be here as long as you'll have me."

And I hoped that it would be a long damn time.

CHAPTER THIRTY-SEVEN
Lydia

Humming to myself, I floated through the salon, straightening and fixing as I went. As I swept up to the front desk, Brenda crossed her arms over her chest.

"Okay, spill."

My eyes jumped to hers. "What?"

She lifted one eyebrow as she studied me. "Mhmm."

I fought a tiny smile and infused my voice with as much innocence as possible. "I don't know what you're talking about."

"Ha." Brenda scoffed and turned to pick up an inventory report. "You think we're blind to whatever happened between you and your man over the weekend?"

Apparently, I hadn't done as good a job hiding my emotions as I thought. "You knew?"

"Please." She let out a little snort. "You were all out of sorts all day Saturday. At first I thought you broke up, but this makes more sense."

She looked me up and down, and I shifted under the scrutiny. "What makes sense?"

She stared into my eyes for a long moment. "You're in love with him."

I bit the inside of my lips to contain my smile. "I don't know what you're talking about."

"Please," Brenda scoffed. "You're singing."

"I'm not singing," I shot back, unable to hide my smile this time. Everyone knew that, despite my terrible voice, I sang when

I was happy. Brenda lifted a brow in my direction, and I finally caved. "Oh, all right. I'm… happy."

"Happy or… *happy*?" she asked, a wicked glint in her eyes.

I swatted her arm, unable to control the laughter bubbling up. It felt so good to be able to talk about it with someone. I'd kept my feelings toward Xander bottled up inside for too long—first the bad memories, now the good. "He just…" I trailed off, unsure of exactly how to describe the way he made me feel. "Everything feels perfect when I'm with him."

"I like this look on you," Brenda said with a soft smile. "You're glowing like a new bride. Unless…"

Her gaze dropped to my midsection, and my own eyes widened, my hands pressing against my tummy. "Oh, no. No," I said on a laugh. "None of that."

Brenda smirked. "Yet."

The bell over the door heralded a new customer, and I sighed with relief as Brenda left to greet them. I allowed my thoughts to drift inward for a moment as I caressed my stomach. After I had Alexia, I'd sworn she would be my only child. But now… What if Xander stayed? Would he want another baby?

"I'm headed to lunch."

I spun at the sound of Gwen's voice, my hands dropping to my sides. "Okay. Just be sure to be back for Andrea's fitting. She should be here at one."

"I know," she snapped. "I was the one who scheduled her."

I reared back, caught off guard by her tone. She'd never spoken to me like that before, and I wasn't even sure what to say for a moment. Gwen's face was set in an expression of displeasure, lips pressed into a thin line, refusing to make eye contact. "Is everything okay?"

"Fine."

She looked like she wanted to say more, but she remained quiet. Was she that unhappy here? She'd been a little crabby the last couple days, but she'd never been downright rude. When she'd given me her notice a couple weeks ago and told me she was looking for another job, I was fairly certain it had something to do with her boyfriend. Now I was positive. Only a man could drive a woman to the edge of madness.

"Have you found another job yet?"

Her gaze flicked to mine, then away again. "Not yet."

I nodded. "Okay. I have a couple interviews set up for later this week. Getting another body in here should help take some of the stress off your shoulders. I know you're dealing with a lot right now."

She shot me a begrudging look. "Thanks."

"Of course. I appreciate your help around here, but I won't tolerate disrespect, Gwen, even from my best employees."

She dropped her head. "Sorry," she grumbled.

"Enjoy your lunch, and I'll get Andrea settled when she gets here."

Gwen nodded, then took off. I shook my head as I watched her. I wanted to ask about her boyfriend, the one she hadn't mentioned until just recently. Worry niggled at me. I didn't want her to lose herself trying to make him happy. But Gwen was a grown woman, free to make her own choices. If she came to me, I'd offer my advice. Otherwise, I'd just keep my mouth shut and not interfere.

I gathered Andrea's dress from the back room and hung it in the fitting room. I smiled as I caught myself humming again, and I warmed from the inside as I thought of Xander and how much my life had changed in just a couple short weeks. I wasn't sure what the future held, but I found that the annulment he'd offered me no longer held any appeal. Maybe we could make this work, after all.

CHAPTER THIRTY-EIGHT
Xander

I steered into Mickelson's driveway and parked in front of the mammoth white mansion.

"Jesus," Cole muttered from the back seat. "I picked the wrong profession."

My thoughts mirrored Cole's words. Who the hell needed a house like this? Three stories high, the house had to be at least six thousand square feet, and I hadn't even seen the rest of it. We climbed out of the standard issue white van, which that very morning had been decaled with the cable company's logo.

We needed to get cameras inside the house and around the property before this week's auction. Mickelson had managed to secure an invite, and the plan was for him to bid up an item until he won, then secure delivery. Hopefully, if it went anything like the last time he made a purchase, they would deliver the item right to his door. Getting the license plates on video was mandatory, but it would be an added bonus to get glimpses of the men's faces. If we could identify one or more of them, get them out to the public, the house of cards will hopefully start to fall. Once one of them started talking, they were bound to roll on the person in charge.

We still hadn't seen anything suspicious over at Oliver's shop, and he hadn't contacted Kingsley. Richter had been calling Con on a daily basis checking in and generally giving him hell, and everyone was getting antsy. The police would handle the sting, but we had been commissioned to at least install the cameras.

They could do whatever they wanted with the information they obtained. Jason was still ass-deep in trying to trace the source of the auctions but wasn't having any success.

Dressed in navy blue jumpsuits similar to what the cable company employees wore, we made our way toward the house, and I knocked on the giant oak door. Mickelson opened it seconds later, his shifty eyes surveying the area before opening the door the whole way. I didn't trust the asshole as far as I could throw him, but he was our only source right now. If this fell through, I wasn't sure what our next move would be. I was leaving that shit up to the local officers, though.

We got to work under the guise of setting up new cable and internet service for Mickelson. After unhooking the ladder from the carrying rack on top of the van, Cole headed off, scouting the best place to hook up the cameras. Once we had our placements marked, it took less than an hour to attach the cameras and run the wiring to the feed.

Next, I located the computer in Mickelson's office and used the landline to call Jason.

"Ready for that IP address?"

"Go."

I rattled it off while Jason worked his magic in the background. This would allow him to access Mickelson's computer remotely during the auction so we could try to track down the source.

"All good."

I moved away from the desk. "How does the feed look?"

He paused for a moment. "Camera two needs to move left ten degrees."

I relayed the info to Cole, who made the adjustment, then spoke to Jason again. "Better?"

"All good on my side."

I hung up and gathered my things to go. All we needed was one good lead to work with, and we'd follow it until we found the origin point. The police were determined to nail the perps responsible, and I couldn't blame them. A lot of the wealthy members of the community who'd suffered from the recent burglaries were out for blood, screaming for justice. The locals were doing everything they could, but they didn't have the manpower or resources. But we did. Con had somehow worked out a deal with them—we'd pick up the slack in exchange for some leniency. After the incident with Blake's girlfriend last week, they seemed to hop on board pretty damn quick, knowing that QSG would uphold our end of the bargain and help in any way we could.

We secured the ladder to the rails on top of the van and loaded all of the extra wiring and accessories in the back, taking one last covert look around to make sure nothing—and no one—was out of place. We now had several high-powered cameras covering the exterior of the house, from the main point of entry, vantage points from both ends of the property, as well as another angled toward the side of the lot. The vantage points all crossed paths at some point, so there was no space left unseen. If someone showed up, we'd see him.

We drove the van back to the body shop and dropped it off, leaving the keys on the back tire. Tomorrow morning, the owner would strip all the lettering off, and no one would be the wiser. Grabbing the stuff from the back, I shoved it in the back of Cole's truck, and we headed back to QSG.

It'd been a hell of a week with not a whole hell of a lot of answers, but I was hopeful—in more ways than one. It might take a bit of doing to trace the person—either his face or license plate—but it was a start.

That wasn't the only thing I looked forward to. I'd been spending as much time as possible with Lydia and Alexia—and loving every minute of it. Each touch, each kiss we'd shared seemed to lower her defenses and lift her self-confidence. I would damn well show her how much I appreciated her and how fucking perfect she was for me.

CHAPTER THIRTY-NINE
Lydia

I spread out the train, the scalloped edging looking like tiny flowers against the pale blue carpet. It was a masterpiece, and a warmth infused my heart. The bride fairly glowed, gushing about how much she loved it.

I grinned at her. "I'm glad you like it."

I heard the jingle of the bell over the door, but I didn't bother to see who had just come in. Brenda was up front; I'd let her take care of it.

I gave Macy a quick hug. "Why don't you go take this off, and we'll steam it before you take it home."

She beamed at me, then headed into the dressing room to change. Brenda appeared at my shoulder, and I turned to her. "Did you see how well Macy's gown turned out?"

"Oh, um... yes."

The concern on Brenda's face finally registered, and I turned to fully face her. "What's wrong?"

She wrung her hands together. "There are two men here to see you."

"Oh?" I couldn't imagine who it could be. Every once in a great while, guys would wander in here looking for tuxedos or suits for special occasions. "Send them back."

"It's... they're..." She trailed off and threw a look over her shoulder toward the front of the salon. "They're officers."

I jerked back. "Like the police?"

She nodded shakily. "They want to speak with you."

DEVIL IN THE DETAILS | 215

"Okay." I floundered for a moment. Was this about the break-in last week? Or, worse, maybe Caryn? She'd contacted a lawyer about her contract, but I'd shut him down, explaining that it was a done deal. He'd agreed that there were no loopholes, and I thought we'd let it go. Was Caryn trying to force my hand on something? I let out a sigh. "Send them to my office, please, then take care of Macy."

Brenda bobbed her head, then hurried off. Macy strode out of the dressing room a moment later and handed over her gown. "Thank you so much," she gushed.

"Oh, it was my pleasure," I assured her. "I'm going to have Gwen steam your gown, and Brenda will settle your bill."

With a parting hug, I hauled the dress back to the alterations room and passed it to Gwen. "Could you do a quick steam on this? Macy's waiting, and she wants to take it with her."

"Sure." She slipped the dress from my fingers and hung it on the rack.

"If you could take it to her when you're done, I'd appreciate it. I have a meeting in my office."

"Of course."

I met Brenda and the two police officers as I exited the alterations room. "Hello, gentlemen. Follow me, if you would."

I entered the office and gestured for them to follow. Once the door was closed, I leaned a hip against my desk. "What can I help with?"

"Are you acquainted with a Mrs. Darlene Henderson?"

"I am. Is everything okay?"

"She sustained a head injury this afternoon and is currently being transported to the medical facility for further examination."

"Oh, God. Is she okay? I mean…" It hit me, then. "She has my daughter. Darlene watches her during the day and… What hospital did you say they were at? I need to get over there."

I immediately moved to grab my purse, but the officer stopped me with his next words. "Actually, miss, we'd like to speak with you about that."

"What's that?"

"You said you left your daughter in Mrs. Henderson's care?"

"That's right." Unease slithered down my spine. "She watches her during the day while I'm here. She's my next-door neighbor and landlord. She's become kind of a grandmother figure for Alexia—my daughter."

"Is there anyone you might know that would want to hurt Darlene or yourself?"

"Me?" My hand fluttered to my throat. "N-no, I don't think so. And I couldn't imagine anyone wanting to hurt Darlene intentionally. She's the sweetest person I've ever met. She'd give you the shirt off her back if you needed it."

The officer nodded. "There was a break-in here last week, is that right?"

I folded my hands to keep them from trembling. "Yes, but I don't believe they took anything. Everything we inventoried turned out to be correct."

"We believe you may have been the primary target. I'm sorry to tell you this, but your daughter was taken from the scene."

What the hell did that mean? Panic and fear crawled up my throat. "So they took her to the hospital, right?"

"No, ma'am." He shook his head hesitantly. "We believe she was abducted."

CHAPTER FORTY
Xander

I strode through the salon, focused on one thing: finding Lydia. The fear and sadness in her voice had nearly broken me. I'd been sitting at the conference table at QSG when the call came through, and she'd uttered those awful words that played on loop the whole way here. "Please come. It's…"

It's what?

She hadn't been able to finish, her sobs filtering through the line, breaking my heart. One of the officers on scene with her had introduced himself and asked me to come to the salon but refused to give me more information over the phone.

My feet carried me through the room, my head still foggy, my heart in my throat. I threw open the door to her office. Lydia was pacing the small room, her hands tangled in her hair. "We're wasting time! We need to do something!"

I took in her aggravated posture, the anger in her eyes—underlined by sheer terror. "Lydia?"

She met my gaze, turbulence swirling in the gray depths. Her eyes filled with tears and her face went slack as her legs gave out and she sank to the floor. "Oh, God… Xander."

I hit my knees in front of her, already pulling her into my arms. "What's wrong, sweetheart? Talk to me."

"It's… She's…" Her voice broke, and sobs racked her body as she let out a keening cry.

I threw a beseeching glance at one of the officers. He had a familiar face, but I didn't recognize the name. "Childress?"

His gaze dropped to the QSG logo embroidered on my sleeve and let out a beleaguered sigh. "We have reason to believe your daughter was abducted this morning."

If I wasn't already sitting on the floor with Lydia in my arms, his words would've knocked me flat on my ass. "What the hell are you talking about? She's at home with—"

Lydia's head shook frantically against my shoulder. "She's gone."

Cold seeped into my bones. "Who? And where the fuck did they take her? Someone had to have seen something!"

"We've issued an Amber Alert," the second officer, Grimes, piped up. "They're canvassing the neighborhood right now, looking for her and questioning the neighbors."

Rage swelled up inside me. "Start from the beginning."

The officers explained that Darlene had been in the backyard, and it seemed that she was attacked just as she was allegedly taking Alexia inside for her nap.

"When we arrived on the scene, Mr. Henderson told us he'd heard a commotion and went to investigate," Childress stated. "He found Mrs. Henderson, but there was no sign of Alexia."

A cold fury enveloped my body. I hated the detached-sounding words they were throwing around. This was just another case to them, not a person. However, I was relying on a professional courtesy since QSG worked so closely with the local precincts.

"Tell us what we can do. We'll print off some fliers, hit the streets."

The younger cop nodded. "Appeal to everyone. As Grimes stated earlier, we've issued an Amber Alert and notified all the surrounding counties. We've also posted on social media to try to get her name and face out there as much as possible. Someone is bound to see her and call in."

I felt heartsick, and I watched as Lydia straightened. "We need to do this now. Isn't this how it works? The first day is the most important?"

The younger cop hesitated, then nodded. "Yes, ma'am. If we don't—" He stopped himself abruptly and seemed to change his wording. "It's imperative we hit the ground running."

"Then let's go." Lydia peeled herself from my arms and stood. Gone was the pitiful mess she'd been just moments ago. In her place was a woman with a backbone of steel, determined to get her daughter back no matter what it took. A ferocity entered her features, determination to protect her child. Our child.

I wanted to scream, to yell and throw things—but that wouldn't bring Alexia back. We needed to start at the beginning and follow the trail. The cops were already investigating the neighbors. I was calling in everyone else I knew. We needed feet on the ground and Jason's eagle eye in the sky, checking every possible camera from the surrounding areas.

I stood and squeezed Lydia's hand. She flinched at my touch, her face an emotionless mask. "We'll find her."

She didn't meet my eyes. All I got was a slight shake of her head.

Pulling out my cell, I dialed Con. "Yeah?"

"We're coming in. Got a situation."

His voice was cautious. "Does this have anything to do with the Amber Alert that was just issued?"

I swallowed hard. "Yeah." Hearing Con say it aloud hit me hard, made it more real. I was glad news was spreading quickly, though—that was a good sign.

"Fuck. I'd hoped I was wrong, but when I heard the name…"

My fingers clenched around the phone. "Be there in twenty."

Lydia mechanically gathered her things, and I led her from the salon, her eyes focused straight ahead. I met Brenda's curious gaze and gave a slight shake of my head. I'd fill her in later. She seemed to understand, because her eyes widened a fraction and her hand moved over her chest.

Lydia remained quiet as I hustled her into the truck. Lost in our own thoughts, we remained silent the whole way to QSG. When we pulled into the parking lot behind the brick building, she finally spoke up. "Where are we?"

"QSG headquarters. This is where I work."

She didn't react; she just climbed out of the truck and strode determinedly toward the front door. I was barely a step behind, and Con met us as soon as we entered. "This way."

We filed into the large bullpen type area, where several faces glanced up at us, varying degrees of hesitation and pity in their expressions. Con's little sister, Abby, stood beside a commercial copy machine that was spewing out papers. She picked one up, then held it out to me, and I slipped it from her fingers.

Alexia's face stared back at me, QSG's number listed along the bottom of the flier with all of her personal information. Lydia gripped my forearm, her nails digging into my skin as she peered over at the flier. Her body swayed the tiniest bit, and I looped one arm around her waist to steady her. Her entire body went rigid, and she held herself away from me, turning to meet Con's dark gaze.

"What's your plan?"

He didn't dance around the subject, just cut straight to the chase. "As soon as these are done, I'm putting guys in each district, starting closest to your home and working our way outward. We're joining forces with the PD to interview anyone we can in the hopes that someone saw or heard something. In the middle of the day, there has to be something." Lydia nodded stiffly, and Con continued. "You may want to consider a press conference. I spoke with the captain, who said the PD can get that organized for you by tomorrow morning."

"I'll do it. Whatever you need, just tell me. I have to…" She clenched her fists, the words dying on her lips. She inhaled sharply, and I worried for a moment that she was going to lose it again. Honestly, I hadn't fully come to terms with it myself. This was something that happened to other people; stories I heard on the news but that never happened in my own hometown. And not to me—never to me. I'd survived four tours overseas and sustained a multitude of scars, both physical and mental. But nothing hurt like this. The pain of metal ripping through flesh couldn't compare to the fact that I'd failed my daughter. I'd only known her for a couple of weeks, but she was as much a part of me as the blood thrumming through my veins. I couldn't lose her now—not when I'd just found her. No matter the cost, we'd bring her home. There was no alternative.

CHAPTER FORTY-ONE
Lydia

I held out a hand and tried to form a smile. Judging from the look on the man's face, I failed miserably. "Thanks for coming."

"Of course." Xander's brother, Abel, eyed me critically. "We'll do anything we can to help."

My lips twitched, again falling just short of the polite smile I'd been aiming for. My entire body felt brittle, like I would splinter into pieces at the lightest touch. I waved a hand toward the group assembled nearby. "We're printing off another batch of fliers right now. We're trying to get her in front of as many people as possible to see if anyone remembers anything."

My voice cracked on the last couple words. I never imagined those words leaving my mouth. We'd spent the past twenty-four hours tearing the city apart, speaking with anyone who would listen. My eyes felt gritty and they burned every time I blinked. I looked like shit and felt worse. Dark circles ringed Xander's eyes, but he kept bringing us a steady stream of coffee. He'd tried to get me to sleep last night, even just for a few hours, but I couldn't. Each time I tried, I saw her big blue eyes. Was she scared? Was she hurt? My mind conjured the most horrific images, and I didn't dare close my eyes. I couldn't bear to sleep when my little girl was out there somewhere all alone. I could rest later; right now I needed to be in the middle of the action, doing something. Feeling useful.

Abel's wife, Emily, moved forward. I caught sight of her softly rounded belly, and tears pricked my eyes. All I could think of was Alexia when I'd carried her. Words jumbled in my throat, turning my voice raspy. "You don't need to be out here; you should be relaxing."

She offered me a small smile. "Have you eaten yet? I'm starving."

I knew what she was trying to do, but I couldn't even begin to think about food. Out of the corner of my eyes, I saw Con and Xander speaking with a couple of the police officers heading up the investigation. I opened my mouth to speak but couldn't. I shook my head instead. The severity of the situation was pressing in on me.

We were now just shy of the twenty-four-hour mark, and my heartrate kicked up. I knew from the way the cops spoke in low tones to Xander and Con that they were running out of leads. They'd advised us earlier that no one matching Alexia's description had been seen at any of the airports or bus stations. That didn't rule out a car, though. We were close enough to the border. If someone wanted to smuggle her across…

Bile rose in my throat, and I pressed a hand to the base of my neck as if I could physically keep it from coming up. Abel set a heavy hand on my shoulder. "Stay strong. If anyone can find her, it's Xander and his team."

I nodded, though I wasn't nearly as optimistic. So much time had passed, and we had nothing. No one had heard or seen anything. It was literally as if she'd disappeared into thin air. I knew I was supposed to stay positive, but it was so damn hard. I wanted to yell and scream and demand answers. Why? Why me? Why Alexia? I turned the question over in my mind again and again. Who could have done this? And why? Nothing about this seemed logical.

With every moment that passed without answers, my tension ratcheted up. I was drained, both mentally and physically, running purely on caffeine and hope. I knew Xander was no better. All day he'd been edgy and abrupt, and I knew it was because he was focusing all his energy on finding our daughter. It was as if a wedge had been driven between us. I felt more dependent on him than I ever had, yet he'd never seemed further out of reach.

A steel vise constricted my lungs. I needed the reassurance of his touch telling me that everything would be okay. I needed him—even for just a second. It seemed so incredibly selfish when my daughter was missing that I felt like crying. I hated myself even more for that weakness. As a mother, I was responsible for my baby's well-being. I was supposed to be there for her, to keep her safe. And I'd failed her.

I offered Abel another wobbly smile. "Thank you."

They moved away, and I glanced around the room. We were once again assembled at QSG headquarters as we determined what to do next. Several search party groups were still out combing the city, but I could tell from the looks on the cops' faces that they thought the effort was futile. I felt completely helpless, and I needed something to do.

A man they'd introduced as Jason sat at a computer, looking as haggard as the rest of us. I knew he'd been working hard. I didn't think he moved from that spot since I first met him yesterday. His head swiveled from side to side as he studied the four monitors spread over his desk. The monitor to his far right bore a generic desktop-type screen like a home computer. The two middle monitors showed video feeds, and the screen to the far left was filled with code that made my eyes blur. He paused for a moment to rub his eyes, then his fingers once more flew over the keyboard.

I approached silently and moved into his peripheral vision. "Is there anything I can do to help?"

He glanced up at me, his tension evident in the set of his shoulders. With a short jerk of his head, he nodded to a chair. "Grab a seat."

I rolled the chair over and sat beside him. He pointed toward the two screens in the middle that showed black-and-white video feed. "These are from traffic cams at the major intersections close to your house."

The duplex was located a few streets off the main thoroughfare, so there were few businesses in the area to pull information from. I knew the police had checked with all the residents in the surrounding area to see if anyone had seen Alexia or any strange people in the neighborhood.

"At this point," Jason said, "we're looking for anything. I've been checking each car that goes through the intersection to see if there's a child inside." He paused for a moment before continuing, his tone warning. "The perp may or may not have a car seat to transport her."

My breath caught. She was barely a year old. I'd seen horrific videos of what could happen if a child wasn't properly situated in a car seat, let alone without one completely. I swallowed hard and pushed the thought away, focusing on the screen in front of me and praying we would find something to help us. From the corner of my eye, I saw Xander flick a look in my direction. For the briefest of moments, we made eye contact before he seemingly dismissed me again and went back to talking with the police. I blinked back the sting of irrational tears. I knew he wasn't ignoring me on purpose, but the knowledge didn't stop it from hurting any less.

For the next two hours, Jason and I scoured the video feeds with no results. We weren't the only ones. I knew the police were doing the same thing on their end, checking cameras and speaking with people all over the city. One of the most surprising things to happen over the past few days was that my mother had stepped up and offered her services. Her current boyfriend had invested a ton of money into putting bulletins on the local radio and TV during primetime hours so that Alexia's face was plastered everywhere. Jolene had been quiet, reserved even. It was the first time in my life I'd seen her more concerned about someone other than herself. I refused to read too much into it, though. I appreciated her help, but I was stressed beyond comprehension. They offered a reward if she was found safe, but so far I hadn't heard of any of the leads panning out.

Jason turned his attention to the monitor on the far right again, which had been ignored while we'd sifted through video feeds.

Con appeared over Jason's shoulder. "It's almost time for the auction to start."

"We've got more important things to worry about," Jason said tersely.

Con gave a little nod. "I understand that. Why don't you take over the auction, and I'll help look at feeds."

Jason look like he wanted to argue, but instead gave in. Con dragged a chair around to the other side of me, then rearranged the monitors to give Jason some space.

"I'm sorry for taking time away from your other jobs," I said softly.

Con shot me a fierce glance. "There's nothing more important than taking care of our own."

A steel band constricted around my heart at the loyal declaration. My eyes burned, but I blinked it away and refocused my attention on the screens. Beside me, I heard Jason on the phone with someone, and I watched a sort of live auction feed pop up on his monitor. I turned a curious glance on Con. "What's he working on?"

"Have you heard about the thefts around town?" I nodded, and Con continued. "Seems they're holding auctions every Friday night and shipping the goods all over the world. We're trying to find the origin point and the person responsible."

My eyes widened as I gave an appreciative nod. "Sounds… complicated."

We lapsed back into silence and delved once more into the video feeds. After a bit, Xander moved to stand behind me, but he offered no reassurance. He didn't touch me, never even said a word. Again, that irrational anger flared to life and simmered in my stomach. My emotions were ready to bubble over. Suddenly, I was mad at everyone and everything.

None of this was fair. I wanted my daughter back, damn it, and I wanted to know why the hell she'd been taken in the first place.

CHAPTER FORTY-TWO
Xander

The automated voice announced that the auction was over, and the screen went blue with a message that read "Session will expire in ten minutes." Jason's fingers flew over the keyboard, and he watched the monitor to his left as code rolled across the screen, a bunch of numbers and letters that may as well have been a foreign language for all the sense it made to me. Suddenly, he froze. "What the fuck is that?"

In place of the disconnection message, a new window popped up. "Re-homing needed, local pickup only. Blonde, blue. Enter bid now."

A timer popped up and began the countdown from five minutes. My stomach contorted into knots as I watched the seconds tick away. "What the hell is that?"

Jason's face was bright red, his expression livid. "Well, it's not a fucking dog they're referring to."

Beside me, Lydia let out a soft cry as a picture popped up on the screen. I sucked in a breath, my chest feeling like someone had planted a fist right in my solar plexus. Alexia's tear-stained face stared back at me from the computer screen, and I fought to drag in air. *Oh, Jesus.* I watched the nightmare unfold right before my eyes.

The minutes counted down, and the first bid popped up. Five thousand dollars. The number hit me with the force of a brick wall. That was the value someone had placed on my daughter's life. Red exploded across my vision, and I whirled on Jason.

"What the fuck are you waiting for?"

Jason stared up at me. "Let's see how this plays out for a second, and—"

"Are you fucking kidding me?"

Con stepped up between us. "Hold up. Let's relax for one second. We still have several minutes. No sense in bidding it up unnecessarily." He turned his dark brown gaze on me. "Whatever the cost, we'll bring her home. But we need to be smart about it."

Knowing he was right didn't make it any easier. I clasped my hands together behind my neck and stared at the screen. The counter moved downward while the bids grew until the number turned my stomach.

"IP address is different," Jason muttered. "This definitely isn't the same person."

"What the hell does that mean? Someone hacked the auction?"

Jason stared at the code zipping across the screen on the left monitor. "Can't say for sure yet, but it's possible."

When it came within the thirty-second mark, Jason tapped his bid in and pushed it through. Relief mingled with dread as the clock ran out, our bid still the highest. Where the hell was I going to come up with that kind of money?

As soon as the thought crossed my mind, a second window popped up, requesting personal information. I threw a glance over my shoulder at Con. "What do you make of that?"

"They're running background on the winners," Jason murmured. "We need someone's name. Can't be one of us."

My heart dropped to the floor. Fuck. He was right. Mickelson had participated in the auction, but I had a feeling that using him would be the wrong way to go. We sure as hell couldn't use Lydia, since she was Alexia's mother. And we were all ex-military—there was no way in hell they'd work with any of us.

Blake's deep voice cut through the silence. "Use Victoria's."

I whipped toward him. "You sure?"

She'd been through hell recently, and, though I'd do anything—literally anything—to bring Alexia home, I felt like a dick for putting an unsuspecting woman at risk for a second time.

Blake just nodded. "I'll take care of it."

I shot him an appreciative look and he rattled off Victoria's information, Jason's fingers flying over the screen as he typed it in. We all stared in silence as he submitted the information, and a message popped up. "Final winner to be contacted for retrieval."

Jesus fuck. So even though we'd won, they could still choose someone else? Mother*fucker*.

Rage threatened to consume me, and I slammed my fist down on the desk. I swore to God—as soon as I found the person behind all this, I was going to rip him limb from limb. He was going to die a slow, painful death for everything he'd put us through.

"Keep looking. I need a name." My voice was harsh and raspy to my own ears. I needed to know who this was. We didn't have the time or resources to try to run voice analytics. I needed to see this fucker's face so I knew exactly who I was looking for. Too bad he'd stayed out of view of the camera the whole time.

The fucker had been brash enough to walk right up to Lydia's house, in sight of everyone. Bitterness filled my tone. "Son of a bitch. At least a day care would've had security footage."

For a moment, all was silent. Lydia stiffened, and her furious gaze cut through me. "You think I did this, that this was my fault?"

The hurt in her eyes damn near broke me. I opened my mouth to speak, but the steely depths turned hard, fire rearing up in the wake of the sadness. "What about all this stupid secret spy stuff?"

"What the hell are you talking about?"

Her fists slammed into my chest, momentarily taking my breath away. "My baby was just fine until you showed up!"

Ignoring her earlier statement, I latched on to the one word I heard. "*Your* baby? She's fucking *ours*, Lydia! And you know goddamn well that I'd do anything for her!"

"Really? Then where the hell were you for the past two years?"

Red blurred my vision and I snapped. Grabbing her wrists, I shoved her back a step. "Maybe I would've been here if you'd told me I had a goddamn kid!"

"I tried!" She screamed the words as she fought my hold, anger making her movements erratic and wild. "You never should have come back. We were all better off before."

Anger and hurt mingled in my chest and exploded outward as I lashed out. "Then how the hell am I responsible for someone kidnapping our baby from your house?" I took a step forward, forcing her to retreat. "Fucking explain that one!"

Tears welled in her eyes. "I don't know!"

A piercing howl left her throat, the brokenness of the sound slicing through me like a knife. Jason was at her back in the blink of an eye. He caught her around the waist as her legs gave out and she crumpled to the ground. Her body shook under the force of her sobs, and Jason scooped her into his arms. Shooting me an indecipherable look, he strode away.

Already reaching for her, my feet moving of their own volition to breach the gap, I was stopped cold by a strong hand on my shoulder. Con shook his head as I met his gaze over my shoulder. Up until now, the guys had been watching the shitshow unfold. Now everyone turned back to their screens, uncomfortable at witnessing our breakdown. I couldn't look at them—couldn't bear to see the accusation and pity in their eyes. I felt fucking impotent. What kind of man couldn't protect his own wife and kid?

Guilt and hurt slammed into me, along with a thought I didn't want to acknowledge—maybe Lydia was right. Maybe they were better without me after all.

I shrugged off Con's hand, then turned and pinned my gaze to the screen. "What's the plan?"

He hesitated for a long moment, then pulled out a chair and sat. He kicked out a second chair, inviting me to do the same, but I ignored the gesture. I couldn't sit. My body was too restless, ready to fly apart in a thousand different directions. Lacing my fingers together, I placed them on top of my head, willing my ire to cool and breathing to slow.

Across the room, I heard Jason speaking softly with Lydia, and I couldn't help but glance in their direction. Lydia perched on the edge of the couch in the common area, bent at the waist, head cradled in her hands. Her body still shook as she cried, and Jason's hand moved over her back in soothing circles. My hands dropped to my sides and clenched into tight fists at the sight. I wanted to stomp over there and break every fucking one of his fingers, one by one, for touching my wife.

Con's soft voice doused my ire. "Don't kill him, he's just trying to help."

I threw him an irritated glance. The knowledge didn't temper my anger. Out of the corner of my eyes, I watched Jason guide Lydia to her feet. One hand on her elbow, the other on the small of her back, he led her from the room. Where the hell were they going? My gaze narrowed as I took a step forward.

Blake moved in front of me just as I started to storm in their direction. "Don't take it personally. She's a mess right now."

I couldn't deny that, but what about me? Alexia was my little girl, too, and though I hadn't known her for more than a couple weeks, she was my flesh and blood. It was as if someone had ripped my heart out. My jaw ticked, but I refused to voice my fears. My baby was out there somewhere, alone and scared. I needed to find her—I *would* find her. I had to be strong for both of us. Especially Lydia. She'd already been through so much by herself. I refused to heap more stress on her already full plate. I'd overreacted earlier, and I needed to apologize. But now wasn't the time. Blake was right.

He held up one hand. "He's taking her to my office to rest. The couch is a pullout, so she'll be able to relax close by."

My shoulders relaxed at the news, and I dug the heels of my palms into my eyes. "Goddamn it."

Blake continued. "She refused to take any meds but at least agreed to lie down for a bit."

It had to kill her to agree to that. She'd probably been awake longer than I had. Since getting the news of Alexia's disappearance, she hadn't slept a wink. The circles beneath her eyes were dark, her face lined with worry and fear. I couldn't believe she'd lasted as long as she had. I was trained for situations like this; Lydia was running on pure adrenaline and maternal instinct. She wouldn't relax until our little girl was back in her arms. It was my job to make that happen.

CHAPTER FORTY-THREE
Lydia

My body felt heavy, my mind tired as I blinked my eyes open. Almost immediately, they slid closed again, exhaustion pulling at me. Slowly, my mind came alive and the events of the past few days rose to the surface. My eyes snapped open once again, landing on the plain white wall in front of me. My brows drew together as I realized I was lying down, and I pushed myself to a sitting position, looking around. The dark green couch had been folded flat into a bed, and a light blanket was draped over me. Light from a lamp on the corner of the desk spilled a soft glow over the room.

I could feel a pair of eyes on me, and I turned my head, scanning for the source. A small, dark-haired woman sat in the chair along the left wall, and it didn't take but a few seconds to place her. I recognized Victoria from the morning she had shown up at the salon after the break-in. She caught my movement and met my gaze with a soft smile. "Hey."

I cleared my throat to rid it of the sleepy rasp. "Hi."

"I brought your toothbrush and a change of clothes for you."

I shot her a grateful look. I was thankful she hadn't immediately jumped in to ask me how I was feeling. She seemed to intuitively know that I would want to get back out and start scouring the streets again. "Thanks."

I slid from the makeshift bed and reached for the bag she held out. "Any news yet?" I couldn't help the hopefulness in my voice.

Unfortunately, Victoria shook her head. "Not yet, but the guys are still chasing every lead. Last I heard, Jason is still trying to figure out who is behind the auction."

Guilt stopped me in my tracks, and I shot a wary look at Victoria. "I'm so sorry about having to use you…"

She waved away my concern. "I'm happy to do anything to help. These guys know what they're doing, and I know they'll bring her home safe."

Tears burned the back of my throat at the conviction I heard in her voice. I knew she'd been through something horrifically traumatic, though I wasn't sure of the details. For her to speak so plainly both hurt my heart and gave me a surge of hope. I wanted to ask if she was okay, but I saw the haunted look in her eyes. I knew she wasn't, and I extended her the same courtesy of not dredging up bad memories. Instead, I swallowed everything down and gave her a smile, as genuine as I could. "Thank you."

"Don't worry about the bed," Victoria said. "I'll have Blake take care of it later. I'll let you get changed, and I'll be right outside."

I waited until she left, the soft click of the door announcing her exit, and I sank down on the edge of the bed. I dropped my head into my hands, shame and guilt welling up inside me at the memory of my recent altercation with Xander. My insides felt as if they'd been shredded. I was still hurting over Alexia, but I'd let my anger get the best of me and said so many terrible things to him that I would never be able to take back. I had no idea how to begin to bridge the gap between us.

Pushing the thought away for the moment, I moved behind the door and quickly stripped down, changing into the clothes that Victoria had brought. She'd even had the foresight to throw in some deodorant, for which I was incredibly grateful. Two minutes later, I felt cleaner, more awake, and I pulled the door open.

Victoria hovered on just the other side like a sentinel. "Good?"

As good as I could be. "Yep."

In silence, we trudged to the bathroom, where I quickly washed my face and brushed my teeth. I passed a window and noticed that it was pitch-black outside, the only light a faint yellow glow from a streetlamp. "What time is it?"

Victoria checked her phone as I stifled a yawn. "A little after one in the morning."

So I'd slept for about six hours then. "And they still haven't heard anything?"

How damn long were they going to wait to announce the winner? My pulse doubled, my heart threatening to beat out of my chest. I couldn't live like this. I threw another look out the dark window. We'd checked the entire city over the past day and a half, it seemed, but I couldn't tamp down the urge to run right back out there and search every crevice. I had to find her.

"Come on." Victoria set a gentle hand between my shoulder blades and propelled me forward. "Let's check in with the guys."

I allowed myself to be herded along, down a short hallway toward the lobby. Victoria stopped beside the door to the bullpen area and knocked. Seconds later, it swung open, and a large blond man I'd never seen before filled the doorway. He stepped aside with a nod.

"Thanks, Clay."

Victoria moved inside first, and I followed a few steps behind. A few sets of eyes darted to me, then immediately moved away again. I felt my cheeks heat under their scrutiny. I was sure they were all watching me like a hawk from behind their screens, waiting for me to break down again.

Pulling my shoulders back and lifting my chin, I strode toward Con where he hovered next to Jason's desk. I didn't look around, though I knew Xander was close by; I could feel his presence as if he were an extension of me.

Jason didn't even look up as I approached, but Con nodded at me.

"McDonald's," Jason said loudly, making me jump. Everyone looked in his direction.

His fingers flew over the screen a few more times before he lifted his gaze. "I just sent you guys the info. I was able to trace the IP address from the auction back to a McDonald's off Miner Street. It looks like this one"—he pointed to the screen—"was definitely done by a completely different person."

I stared at him. "What does that mean?"

"It looks like someone piggybacked off the original auction website for ease. The perp knew he'd still have an audience, and it's obviously time sensitive. He wants to—" He stopped himself midsentence. "I would guess he's strapped for cash and needs this to happen quickly."

"Is that good or bad?"

Jason hesitated, and my heart sank. "It's good that we have an approximate location, but we don't have the time or resources to check all the cameras. By the time we get our hands on the footage, there's a good chance the exchange will already be underway."

"So what now?" I fought to control the tremor in my voice.

He rubbed his eyes. "I keep pulling threads. Eventually one of them will lead us to the right person."

Con spoke up. "We've got eyes everywhere. The PD has been in contact with border patrol to make sure nothing slips through."

"Good." I couldn't think of anything else to say.

Con stood and gestured with his chin. "Come with me?"

It was really more of an order than a request, and I fell into step behind him, intent on ignoring Xander's piercing gaze as long as possible. My stomach twisted into a knot as we exited the bullpen area and turned left, then headed into the office at the end of the hallway.

Con closed the door behind us partway, then took a seat in a chair in front of the desk. He motioned for me to take the other, and I reluctantly slid into it. I watched him uneasily as he stretched one hand across the desk and picked up a small rectangular piece of paper. He shielded the contents from my view as he set it in his lap, face down.

"I need a favor from you."

"Okay?" I bit my lip at his serious tone.

He stared at me, dark eyes assessing. "I wouldn't ask this if I didn't think you were strong enough to handle it." I didn't say a word—I couldn't. My breath caught in my chest as I waited for him to continue.

"You know Alexia better than anyone." I nodded at the rhetorical statement. "Would you be able to look at the photograph and tell me if anything looks familiar?"

The image of her tear-stained face was seared into my mind, and I momentarily closed my eyes against the pain it wrought.

Forcing the tears away, I met Con's gaze and nodded. "I…" I cleared my throat and steeled myself. "Of course."

He lifted the photograph he'd had concealed at his side and swallowed hard at the sight of it. Those dark eyes cut into me. "You good?"

I nodded, unable to speak, and took the photo from him with trembling hands. I cleared my throat. "What am I looking for?"

"Anything." He sat back in his seat, giving me space. "Tell me if anything seems familiar. The floors, the walls, any distinguishing characteristics."

Tears cutting tracks down her face, big gray eyes stared up at me imploringly. She was still wearing the same outfit I dressed her in on Thursday before I left for work. The sight brought tears to my eyes. Was she being cared for? Was she safe?

I slapped a hand over my mouth to stifle the sob that I couldn't hold back. Grief was a crushing weight, and my body folded in on itself. Bending at the waist, I let the pain pour out, dimly aware of a heavy palm on my back.

I hated whoever had done this. At that moment, I was ready to rip someone apart with my bare hands. Cold fury replaced the crippling hurt. Crying wouldn't bring my baby girl back. I needed to focus for her sake. I swore on everything holy that I would make sure the person responsible suffered when we found him.

Pulling myself together, I drew in a ragged breath and swiped the tears from my face with the sleeve of my sweater.

Con's hand dropped away. "If you don't—"

I held up a hand, cutting him off midsentence. It took me several moments to get my breathing under control and form words. Con waited patiently. "I'm… I'll be fine. Just give me a second."

Forcing my gaze away from Alexia's as she stared imploringly at the camera, I studied the background. My eyes skated over the generic tan carpet, shabby and worn with use. A plain white wall stood in the background, devoid of pictures or mementos.

I focused on Alexia and the person holding her. Alexia sat on the ground, and a person's hand clutched her shoulder—keeping her upright or in place, I wasn't sure. I studied every line of that hand resting on Alexia's shoulder, fingers curled into the fabric of her shirt.

I shook my head helplessly. "I just don't know."

"It's okay. It was a long shot."

I nodded, my eyes still glued to the picture. I knew he'd been hoping for something, anything. There was nothing, literally nothing, of value in the photo. It could be anywhere in the world.

"We'll keep looking. We'll—"

A knock at the door cut him off. "Boss?" My head swiveled toward the huge man Victoria had called Clay. He glanced at me, then back to Con. "Confirmation came back."

"Good." My gaze was drawn back to Con, who wore an expression of guarded optimism. "Get everyone assembled. I'll be there in a minute."

Clay nodded and disappeared, leaving me alone with Con again, who turned to me. "Sounds like the offer for Victoria's bid was accepted."

My heart leaped with excitement. "So we're going to get her back?"

"We will." He held up a staying hand when I started to grin like a fool. "But we need to be extremely cautious. I want to make sure everything goes smoothly so your daughter isn't in any danger."

I nodded. "Absolutely. What do you need me to do?" My leg bounced restlessly, the idea of seeing her, holding her again ready to propel me out of my chair.

Con eyed me critically. "My team needs to be wholly focused on this. Can you let them do that?"

I blinked and went still. He was asking me to… what? Stay away? "But…"

"I can't imagine how hard this is for you," he said gently. "But the last thing I want to do is jeopardize this. I want you to be strong for Alexia. I want you to be there for her when we bring her home."

My face fell as his words sank in. "But I can't be there when you go get her."

"No. I'm sorry."

I understood—I did. But I hated it. I nodded, sniffing against the tears burning the bridge of my nose. It'd been too long since

I'd held her, and I didn't want to wait one more second.

"Lydia?" Con's voice was soft but firm, and I let out a little sigh.

"I understand. I won't interfere."

"Not interfering," he corrected. "But you're her mother. If the kidnapper sees you, all bets could be off. I'm not gonna lose this asshole just when we have him where we want him."

It was the first time he'd sworn in my presence, and his tone was fierce. I looked into the hard planes of his face and saw the commanding military man he must have once been. His eyes bespoke a power and assuredness I'd only seen rivaled by one other man—Xander. In that moment, I put my whole trust into them.

"Bring her back to me."

"We will." Con's expression softened just the tiniest bit as he stood. "Now, if you'll excuse me, I've gotta go get my guys prepped."

He was halfway to the door before I could formulate anything else. "Con?"

He paused and turned back to me. "Yeah?"

"Thank you."

He tipped his chin. "Thank me tomorrow."

With that, he was gone.

CHAPTER FORTY-FOUR
Xander

The book in my hands trembled as I gazed surreptitiously around the park. Everyone looked suspicious to me, and I sought out every person with a small child. So far, we hadn't seen anything. A handful of kids played on the jungle gym a hundred yards away, but none of them were the little blonde-haired girl I was looking for.

I'd been here for an hour already, and my nerves were shot. There were a dozen of us scattered throughout the park and the surrounding area, waiting on the perp to show. Victoria shifted again on the bench diagonal from me, crossing then re-crossing her legs as she checked her phone. I could read the anxiety in her features, and I knew it was genuine. She was just as worried about this as the rest of us—maybe more so. It hadn't been fair to pull her in, but she was holding up well under the circumstances. I prayed to God the suspect wouldn't find it suspicious at all.

Head down, I glanced around the park again, memorizing every face I saw. It would've been a hell of a lot easier if I knew exactly what—or who—we were looking for. I just had to hope that he would be true to his word and show up for the meet.

Phillips, one of the undercover officers, was dressed as a maintenance worker, and he made his way around the park picking up litter and other debris. Three other officers were also undercover as civilians. A patrolman waited in an unmarked car a block over, ready for our call. My knee jumped anxiously as time ticked away. I was ready to get this over with, and I fought to control my emotions. I couldn't afford to get worked up and blow this before he showed up. Really, I was lucky they let me in at all. Only Con's connections and personal assurances had gotten me a place here.

My thoughts momentarily drifted to Lydia, the despair on her face permanently burned into my brain. We would get her back. We had to. There was no other alternative. I refused to go back to my wife without our little girl. Come hell or high water, I would find her and bring her home.

I glanced over the edge of the book again, my attention drawn to a young male pushing a stroller down the sidewalk.

Phillips's voice cut through my calm in my ear. "Suspect, three o'clock." From his current position, Phillips had a good view of the child inside the stroller. My heart stuttered to a stop before kicking into high gear.

The man approached Victoria from the rear, so she didn't see him coming until he rounded the slight bend in the walkway. As soon as she saw him, her spine snapped straight, and a hopeful look entered her eyes. As if she'd caught herself, Victoria immediately redirected her attention to the phone in her hand in an attempt to play cool.

I forced my eyes back to the book as the man surveyed his surroundings. I could feel his gaze sweep over me, and I fought the urge to squirm. I wanted to face him head on, fist-to-fist, and settle this my way. With Alexia caught in the middle as potential collateral damage, I could do none of those things. It infuriated me, and the white-hot burn of rage took over. He was going to pay for this; I would make sure of it.

It took another agonizing ten seconds for him to reach her, each agonizing moment causing my pulse to ratchet anxiously. He sat on the bench, leaving several feet between himself and Victoria. They were at a forty-five degree angle from me, and I watched out the corner of my eyes. I watched as the man retrieved something from his pocket then nonchalantly placed his hand on the bench. Leaning forward as if to check inside the stroller, he slid his hand toward Victoria. She threw him a questioning glance before picking up the paper he passed her. Her eyes flicked around the park before returning to the note in her hands, and she cautiously unfolded it.

The low voices filtering through the com in my left ear faded to a muted din as I watched Victoria's reaction. Phillips angled himself away and ambled toward the park exit where the chain-link fence opened onto the sidewalk beyond. One of the other officers, dressed in gym clothes and watching a basketball game next to the park, slowly made his way to the opposite exit, effectively blocking it.

Following the man's apparent instructions, Victoria retrieved a nondescript white envelope from her purse and discreetly dropped it on the ground. Using her foot, she nudged it closer to him. He leaned over the stroller once again, fussing with the child inside. Fury welled up within me, and I was half a second from jumping to my feet, before Con's voice stopped me cold.

"Hold position."

Motherfucker. I closed my eyes and set the book on my lap. Tipping my head back, I drew in several deep breaths. I had to keep a cool head; God only knew what he would do if he got caught. I watched between lowered lids as the guy scooped the envelope off the ground, then, using the stroller as a shield, quickly opened it and counted the money inside. Apparently satisfied, he folded the envelope in half and stuck it in his back pocket as he stood. Victoria followed suit, and she fell into step beside him as he steered the stroller back onto the walkway. Outwardly they appeared like a normal couple out for a walk. But the truth was so much darker and more convoluted.

I watched as Victoria extracted the handle of the stroller from the man's grasp and fell a couple steps behind him. The plan was for her to break off so she and Alexia would be out of danger if anything happened. Instead of following the man toward the exit, she headed toward the playground where kids' happy cries pierced the air.

The man's back was now to me, and I couldn't stand it a moment longer. Throwing the book down, I jumped to my feet and hurriedly crossed the park toward Victoria. Relief flooded me as I drew level with the stroller and saw the big gray eyes peering up at me. Ripping the comm from my ear, I tossed it into the stroller as my hands went around Alexia's body and lifted her to me. Her tiny arms wound around my neck, and

I held her as tightly as I dared. I wanted to check every inch of her, make sure that she was okay, but right now at this very moment I just needed to hold her.

A scuffle broke out, and I turned to watch the suspect run toward the south exit. The undercover agents and policeman were in hot pursuit and had him contained in less than a minute. The other parents in the park pulled their own children close, shielding them as they watched the scene unfold.

Beside me, Victoria laid a hand on my arm and smiled gently up at me. "We should get her checked out, but she looks okay."

I nodded over the lump in my throat. I couldn't wait to tell Lydia, but I had sworn to the PD that I wouldn't say anything until they'd had a chance to speak with the suspect. We still had no idea how many people were involved, and we hadn't ruled out that someone close to her could be responsible. I didn't want to put Lydia in danger without having all the facts.

One of the guys had evidently already radioed EMS, because an ambulance pulled up near the east entrance to the park, and we made our way in that direction. Curious stares followed us, but I ignored them all, my attention focused firmly on my daughter. Alexia had been unusually quiet, and I shifted her in my arms so I could examine her more thoroughly. She looked exhausted, the dark circles under her eyes prominent, as if she hadn't slept at all while she'd been away from us. The sight broke my heart, and I promised in the future to do everything in my power to keep her safe. The only blessing in what had happened today was that she would never remember her ordeal.

I sat at the rear of the ambulance as they checked her vitals. She cried softly and turned her face into the crook of my neck as they poked and prodded at her. I spoke softly to her, rubbing her small back all the while, trying to soothe her. Two tiny hands latched on to my neck, sharp nails biting into the skin as she held on for dear life. She was probably terrified that she would be separated from me again, and my heart cracked. "It's okay, baby girl. I'm not going anywhere. You're safe now."

Blake stepped up and slipped an arm around Victoria. He directed his words toward me. "They're working on the guy right now."

I prayed that he would roll on everyone responsible so we

could wrap this up sooner rather than later. The medic finished up, and the three of us started back toward where the police had the suspect handcuffed on the sidewalk.

Though I couldn't risk telling Lydia just yet, I knew my brother wouldn't say anything. I snapped a selfie with Alexia tucked in close to my neck then texted it to Abel, unable to keep the smile off my face.

He'd said he wanted to know the second she was safe, so I didn't waste any time letting him know. Only a few seconds after I sent the message, my phone rang. I slid my thumb across the screen to answer it. "Hey, brother."

"Thank God," he replied on a relieved sigh. "I'm glad she's back."

"Me, too. Are you still with Lydia?" I asked.

"No, we headed out about ten minutes ago."

I couldn't wait to get Alexia home and see my two girls together again. I knew the stress had been killing her. "Was she holding up okay?"

"As well as can be expected," Abel replied. "I think having friends and family around helped to take her mind off it a little bit. Gwen was still there when I left."

Thank God for that. She'd been a lifesaver through this whole ordeal, practically glued to Lydia's side. I could breathe a little easier now, knowing that she wasn't alone. "Thanks again for staying with her. It means a lot."

"No problem, it was nothing. I—oh! Of course!" Abel said as if he'd just had a revelation.

"What?"

"I was just trying to remember how I knew Gwen. It's been driving me crazy."

My brows drew together. "How do you know her?"

"Seriously?" He laughed. "She had the biggest crush on you, remember? But it's been so long since I've seen her, and she looks totally different with that short, dark hair."

"I don't know what you're talking about."

Abel sounded confused. "I thought you were the one who got her the job at Lydia's place. I can't believe you don't remember her. Guinevere from down the street." He paused when I remained silent. "You know—Aaron's little sister."

I remembered who he was talking about. Aaron's sister was several years younger, and she'd always tried to tag along, much to his chagrin. But Guinevere had long, curly red hair. Or she had the last time I'd seen her, though it'd been several years ago. Was that really the same girl? "I can't believe she didn't say anything," I remarked. "And when the hell did she start going by Gwen?"

"I don't know," Abel replied. "I knew she looked familiar, I just couldn't place her. Anyway, I'll let you go. We'll stop over later once you guys are settled."

"Sounds good." I thanked him, then hung up, turning my attention back to Alexia. My attention was splintered as Cole came jogging toward us, waving a hand in the air.

My brows drew together. "What's up, man?"

His face was grim. "He's asking for you."

I couldn't conceal my surprise as I strode over to where the PD had a young man seated on the sidewalk, Cole on my heels. Con shot me an unreadable look as I approached, and dread congealed in my gut. The boy they'd apprehended looked fearfully up at me, and the officer beside him urged him on. "This is him. Tell us what you know."

He glanced between me and Alexia, his eyes filled with remorse. My arms tightened a fraction around my daughter's body. Mostly to feel her securely against me, but also in part so I wouldn't knock his teeth down his throat.

He shook his head. "I didn't want to do it," he whispered. "But she begged me. She said it would all be different once we got rid of her."

Chills ran down my spine at his words. "A woman did this?"

His expression turned hard, his tone bitter. "I would've done anything for her. I just wanted her to be happy, but it was never enough. It's you she wants."

CHAPTER FORTY-FIVE
Lydia

I nervously paced the room, unable to sit still. I couldn't help but wonder how everything was going. I raked my fingers through my hair, pulling on the ends. The pain shooting across my skull momentarily grounded me, detracting from the agony of not being able to do anything. I felt weak—absolutely helpless. I prayed to God that whatever plan Xander and his friends had in place worked. I felt like I was literally hanging on by a thread. Everyone tiptoed around me like they were walking on eggshells, as if the slightest noise would cause me to break.

It was killing me. I could feel it in the slow way that I moved, the sluggish way my brain reacted. Still, I couldn't give up. I forced myself to move on, to keep going. Alexia was depending on me, and I refused to let her down. I'd only slept yesterday out of sheer necessity before my body shut down completely. I'd gotten maybe three to four hours of sleep over the past couple days, catching little naps here and there. The past two days had slowly begun to drain the life from me.

Jason had managed to convince me to catch some rest where I could. I wasn't sure why, but I trusted him when he told me they were doing everything they could. All of the men at QSG seemed so competent, so sure of themselves. They came from various military and law enforcement backgrounds and were trained to handle any situation. It was reassuring, but I still couldn't fully relax.

The men had insisted I not breathe a word to anyone about

the sting the cops had set up today. If all went well—and I prayed it would—Alexia would be home soon. Con had gently explained that, until we knew who was responsible, we couldn't risk tipping anyone off. So here I sat, waiting for a single word that my baby was okay.

Mind spinning, emotionally drained, I sank onto the couch and dropped my head into my hands.

I would do anything if someone would just bring her back to me. Every part of my body hurt. My shoulders ached from carrying the tension of the past three days. My eyes burned from sleepless nights and endless tears.

Gwen's soft voice cut through the silence. "How are you holding up?"

Like shit. "Fine."

She'd insisted on being here with me today, if for no other reason than to lend silent support. I could feel her staring intently at me, but I refused to meet her gaze.

"How about some tea?"

I exhaled heavily through my nose and managed a small nod. "That'd be nice, thanks."

In my peripheral vision, I watched Gwen stand, her feet carrying her around the couch and into the kitchen. I heard her bustling around, heating the water to prepare the tea, but my mind was elsewhere. Each time I closed my eyes, I saw Alexia's pitiful face, stained with tears.

I'd stared at the picture for hours over the past two days, hoping something would come to me. I felt like I was missing something, and it was driving me crazy. Suddenly, it seemed vitally important that I figure it out. Pulling the worn photo out of the pocket of my cardigan, I fingered the edges of the shiny photo paper that had begun to fray.

As always, my eyes were immediately drawn to Alexia's face— huge gray eyes situated in her pale face, cheeks stained with tears. She didn't appear to be dirty or hurt—just terribly, awfully scared. Tears burned the back of my eyes, and I bit my tongue, using the pain as a distraction to keep from breaking down.

How could anyone be so cold and callous as to hurt a baby girl? Men like this were evil. I would have understood a ransom. But the fact that no one had reached out was hugely unsettling.

This was something that happened in other countries, to other people. This wasn't supposed to happen in the States, surrounded by members of law-enforcement and military. I couldn't begin to understand why this happened. I'd seen movies like this, read about it on the news. This was nothing but a business to the evil men controlling the darker parts of the world. My child was a transaction to line someone's pockets. I might be called naïve for praying for the best, but I wasn't stupid. If Alexia hadn't been taken to be ransomed, there were few other options—none of them were good. I prayed right now that she was safe in someone's home nearby instead of being transported across the border or even halfway across the world. Men were horrible, vile creatures.

As I looked at the photograph, something sparked in my mind. I stared at the hand gripping my daughter's shoulder, the fingers lean and small. The nails were bitten down to the quick, lending them an unkempt, masculine appearance. The longer I stared at them, the more sense it made. *A woman had done this.*

I stared harder, desperately trying to make sense of this new information. I'd accused Xander of bringing trouble to our doorstep when he'd arrived out of the blue, and now shame assailed me. This was directed at me. Why, I wasn't sure, but I couldn't deny that someone had been targeting me specifically. The rock that'd been tossed through the window. The break-in at the salon. And now this. Someone wanted to hurt me, someone with a grudge—but who?

Caryn was evil, but always well-manicured. She had the money to hire someone, but I couldn't see her stooping that low. She seemed to be the type of person to derive pleasure from verbally abusing others. I doubted she would let someone else take credit. Besides, to kidnap a child over a disagreement was a little extreme. I knew Megan was still unhappy that I'd fired her. Her words from that day came back to me. She'd insisted that someone was setting her up. Had she been right all along?

"Here you go." Gwen moved in front of me and held out a mug of tea, steam curling into the air. I started to reach for the mug clasped in her hands and stopped dead. My gaze snagged on her hands, the nails jagged and torn.

Like a puzzle, all of the pieces suddenly clicked into place.

Thoughts spun through my mind, recounting every moment: Gwen had closed with Megan most nights. She'd been at the salon the day the window was broken. She'd closed the shop the night of the break-in.

I dropped my hand back to my lap and lifted my gaze to hers. "Why?"

Gwen straightened, her shoulders pulling back tense and tight. "God, Lydia." The words left her mouth in an exasperated rush, dripping with condescension. "Are you really that stupid?"

My typically mousy assistant was gone. In her place stood a hard, terse woman. Her lips curled into a sneer as she stared down at me. "Do you really not recognize me?"

The question caught me off guard, and I skimmed her features. I took in her short, sleek black hair, noticing for the first time how unnatural it looked against her pale skin. A sprinkling of freckles dusted across her nose, cleverly concealed by a thin layer of makeup. Why had I never noticed those before? I tried to focus on the shape of her face, the honey-brown of her eyes. A memory slowly began to take shape. *The wedding*. All of a sudden, it made sense. I met her two years ago when I was in Vegas for Rose's bachelorette party. Except back then, Gwen had long red hair and freckles, and she'd been called Guinevere.

I kicked myself for not figuring it out sooner. She'd pleaded for a job, and I'd acquiesced just like she wanted. I even recalled with startling clarity why I never put two and two together—Brenda had taken care of all of the paperwork. She'd filed the application and run the background check on Gwen when we hired her.

Now I knew who Gwen really was. What I didn't know was why she'd lied. "How could you do this?"

Gwen let out a mirthless laugh. "Did you really think no one would find out?" The coldness of her tone sent chills creeping up my spine.

"What do you mean?"

Gwen glared at me. "He never should have married you. You lied to everyone about what happened. You made everyone believe that you and Xander married after some whirlwind love affair. But it was no more than a one-night stand. Isn't that right?"

My eyes widened in bewilderment. "How did you know that?"

Before she even answered, it hit me. She'd been in the lobby that morning when Xander and I had that awful fight.

She shook her head at me. "I heard everything. I couldn't believe he'd ever love someone like you, someone who spread her legs for him like a common whore. I knew he was honorable, but I never dreamed he'd go that far—especially when he didn't even know about the kid. I thought that once he found out you'd kept her from him, he'd be done with you for good. But no, not Xander," she said bitterly. "He always has to do what's right. God, do you know how good it felt to finally hear that he'd left you?" I cringed as Gwen threw the coffee mug against the wall, where it shattered with a crash. "Until I found out you lied about that, too, and you're not really divorced," she hissed.

I raised my hand in supplication. "I thought we were. I had no idea we were still married until Xander showed up."

"Exactly," Gwen snapped. "Then you threw yourself right back into his arms, knowing he would have to take you back."

My mouth gaped open. I couldn't believe she thought that. I was the one who kept pushing Xander away, not the other way around. "What is this really about?"

"It's about him!" she screamed. "It's always been about him."

For a moment, I was stunned speechless. I had no idea she'd even known Xander before he showed up the other week. A horrible thought occurred to me. "Were you ever… together?"

Almost immediately, I dismissed it. If Xander knew Gwen, he'd have said something.

Anger creased her face. "Of course not. I could never get close to him with sluts like you hanging around. But it should've been me. I've loved him since I was five years old."

"It was all you." I almost couldn't believe it. "The money, the break in. Everything."

She rolled her eyes. "You made it so easy, and you were too stupid to suspect a thing. Even Megan," she scoffed. "All I had to do was look over her shoulder a couple times while she was at the register to get her code."

"You hate me that much?"

Contempt curled her lip. "I wanted to make your life miserable any way I could. Getting Megan out of the way gave me the opportunity to get into the salon that night."

Suddenly, it made sense. Had Megan been there, Gwen would've had to leave with her. The security company said the alarm had been set at the normal time; Gwen would have set it without actually leaving the salon, giving her plenty of time to tear the place apart.

"But you helped—"

"That's right," she cut over me. "I helped. It was me in there that morning with Xander, *me* saving the day."

I jumped as a loud bang filled the air. Gwen's head snapped toward the kitchen, and she grasped my arm, pulling me to my feet just as Xander came into view. My breath stuttered to a stop as cold metal pressed to my temple.

CHAPTER FORTY-SIX
Xander

Cold fear mixed with fury snaked through my veins, and I held my hands up, my gaze fixed on Gwen. "Gwen, put the gun down."

Eyes filled with fire, she shook her head. The gun swung in my direction, and I sucked in a breath as she leveled a glare at me. "So you finally figured it out."

It was a statement, not a question, and I nodded. "I remember you." Now that I saw her—really saw her—all the pieces fell into place. I remembered the young girl who'd followed us around when she was younger, her flaming red hair and freckles nothing like the black bob she now sported. "I'm sorry I didn't recognize you at first. You look… different."

Her posture relaxed a bit, but she didn't lower the gun. "I had to do something to get your attention."

My attention? I fought to control my reaction. "I didn't realize…"

Gwen let out a soft snort. "Of course you wouldn't. I was never good enough for you. My hair was too red, I was too fat. I was just the ugly duckling that no one wanted around."

I shook my head. "That's not true." I remembered the chubby little girl who'd always been covered in dirt, trying to keep up with the neighborhood boys. And, apparently, me. "I'm sorry you got overlooked. Guys are dumb." I spread my hands wide, trying to come up with the words. "You know how it is. In high school, you think image is everything. We shouldn't have cast you aside, and I'm sorry. But please don't take it out on her," I pleaded. "This is my fault."

A sad expression entered her eyes. "It was supposed to be me. You were supposed to love me."

"Gwen…" I didn't know what to say. I didn't want to lie to her, but I couldn't risk her hurting Lydia. "Just… put the gun down so we can talk, all right?"

Her head tipped slightly to one side. "About what?"

"About us." I gestured between us. The gun in her hand never wavered. As long as it was pointed at me, though, Lydia was safe.

She closed her eyes briefly before meeting my gaze again. "I wanted you for so long." Her voice was quiet, full of emotion. "I hoped when you came back, you'd finally see me. But you just wanted her." Lydia let out a soft gasp as Gwen gave her a little shake. "I did everything I could to make you see her for the liar she is. That's why I told you she was on a date. I put Alexia right in front of your nose, for God's sake!" Gwen let out an aggravated sigh. "You should hate her for lying to you. Why do you care about her so much?"

"She's the mother of my child."

"That's bullshit!" Gwen seethed. Her hand shook, and I prayed to God she wouldn't accidentally squeeze the trigger. "The person I should be mad at is you. I should be your wife. Alexia should be mine!"

"Gwen…" Fuck. I scrambled to defuse the situation. "You're right."

She blinked at me. "What?"

"I made a mistake with Lydia. You were always there for me, and I should've seen it sooner." I had to keep her talking, had to get close enough that I could disarm her. I took a small step forward, my hands still at my sides, unthreatening. "I'm sorry. I want to… start over."

Her head canted slightly to the side as she weighed my words. "You do?"

"Yes." Another tiny step. "Lydia might be the mother of my child, but she's not the love of my life, Gwen."

Something flickered in those light brown depths. "She's not?"

I shook my head, hoping to hell that she wouldn't see right through me. "No, Gwen. It's not her I want."

I watched a myriad of expressions flash across her face. "Let's find out."

The ground seemed to drop from beneath my feet as the barrel of the gun swung away from me toward Lydia. I couldn't stop myself from reaching out despite the distance between us, and Gwen's face darkened. Her eyes never left mine as the sound of the front door opening reached our ears. I focused on her alone, terrified to even glance in Lydia's direction. I couldn't let my focus waver.

"You lied to me, Xander. So you know what I'm going to do?" Her tone sent a shiver of fear down my spine. "I'm going to take away the thing you love most."

Everything happened in slow motion. The barrel of the gun moved again as Gwen pressed it to her own temple and pulled Lydia close. I screamed as the report of the gun filled the air and a pink mist filled the room, splattering the walls and ceiling.

Launching myself over the back of the couch, I landed on my knees beside Lydia's crumpled form. "Lydia! Oh, God, no, no, no!"

One hand lifted listlessly toward her face, and I pushed it away. Blood slipped through my fingers, its coppery scent permeating the air as I pressed my hands to her head. I couldn't tell where she'd been hit or how bad it was; the thick red liquid coated and concealed everything.

"Lydia!" I screamed her name, and her eyes fluttered open. She met my gaze for a second before they shuttered once more. "Stay with me, baby. Everything's going to be okay."

The pounding of footsteps filled the air, but I didn't bother to see who it was. "Get help!" A radio crackled to life and Phillips's voice moved closer as he called for EMS, kneeling next to Gwen to feel for a pulse.

"Lydia! Stay with me, honey. Alexia needs you. I need you," I whispered. Her chest rose and fell in a shallow motion, the seconds between each breath growing longer and more labored. Blood soaked the carpet around us, covering her face and seeping into my pants. I didn't dare remove my hand from the wound. My heart crushed in on itself as my wife slowly bled out in my arms.

※

I shoved my fingers through my hair, tugging anxiously at the short strands, scraping my nails over the flesh, needing to feel the pain. I lowered my hands to my lap and stared at them. Though I'd washed them damn near a hundred times over the last couple days, I didn't think I would ever get the sight of Lydia's blood saturating them out of my mind.

I could still see the blood gushing from her head, the red liquid slipping between my fingers. I felt her pulse beneath my touch, life slowly draining from her. I would never forget that moment as long as I lived, never forget the fear coursing through me as I walked in on that scene straight from hell. I would never forget the look of pure malice in Gwen's eyes, wild and fierce. I had tried to stop her, but she was too far gone. I couldn't believe I'd missed all the signs right in front of me.

I swear my heart stopped when she pulled the trigger and I watched Lydia's body crumple to the ground, a sea of red splattering the walls and saturating the creamy carpet. Thank God Phillips had been right behind me. He'd radioed for EMS, and the medic I'd just visited with Alexia arrived at Lydia's house mere moments later.

I wasn't ashamed to say that I hadn't asked after Gwen. She'd made her choice, and I didn't bother to spare a thought to try to save her. My priority was saving my wife and keeping her from bleeding out in my arms.

The door to Lydia's room opened and closed softly. Expecting to see a doctor or nurse, my eyes widened in surprise when they landed on Con. He gave a slight nod as he moved toward me to sink into the extra chair. His gaze skated over Lydia's form, so small and fragile-looking in the huge white bed, before jumping back to mine. "How is she doing?"

The soft, steady beeps from the machines pierced the silence, relentless in their persistence. Numbers flashed on the screens as they constantly monitored her vitals. I watched Lydia's chest rise and fall rhythmically, aided by the endotracheal tube they had installed in her airway two days ago. The first day at the hospital was touch and go, but they finally had gotten her stabilized. Now they were keeping her medically sedated until the swelling in her brain went down.

The bullet had passed through Gwen's head and into Lydia. Thank God Gwen had misjudged the angle. By some miracle, the bullet had ricocheted off Lydia's skull when it penetrated, forcing the trajectory upward instead of directly into her brain. It had still done some damage, but not nearly what it could have. It was no real consolation—head wounds were tricky. Lydia still hadn't woken, and we wouldn't know just how bad it was until she was awake and coherent.

"She's hanging in there."

Lydia's mother had stopped in this morning to check on her, as well as Blake and Victoria. Each had insisted I go home to rest, but I couldn't bring myself to leave her here alone. Darlene had been invaluable over the last few days. I went home each evening to spend time with Alexia and put her to bed, then grab whatever little amount of sleep I could. Around five a.m., Darlene took over and I made my way back to the hospital. Thankfully the ICU didn't have restricted hours, because I couldn't bear to leave Lydia for more than a few hours at a time.

Con slid a look at me from the corner of his eyes. "How are you holding up?"

I sat silently for a moment, unable to answer. I couldn't begin to put into words the emotions the past several days had wrought—the fear, the anger at both myself and Gwen, but mostly the helplessness. Guilt assailed me. I should have seen the signs, should've stopped this before it got this far. That no one else had recognized them either wasn't reassuring in the least. Abel had tried to reassure me, as did Emily when they came to visit yesterday. Gwen was deranged, willing to go to any length to get what she wanted. Never had I imagined this whole thing revolved around me. I was single-handedly responsible for bringing Gwen into Lydia and Alexia's lives. Their entire world had been turned upside down because of me. Lydia was now fighting for her life because I hadn't seen the truth until it was too late.

Seeming to sense my conflict, Con spoke again. "Kingsley is taking care of the house. They were pulling up carpet and prepping to paint when I left."

"Thank you," I managed to choke out. He'd mentioned yesterday that he planned to have Bennett Kingsley come in and fix the damage. The same man who'd assisted in the case with Oliver Eldredge, Kingsley's company had done some of the work on QSG headquarters when they'd been remodeled. I was grateful to both him and Con for the offer. I didn't want to leave Lydia's side, and renovating the house was the last thing I wanted her to deal with after everything that had happened. I knew Darlene and George would have helped out, but I felt it was my responsibility. Lydia was my wife, and I should have protected her. She never should have been in that position in the first place.

I would never be able to pay Con back for the things he'd done over the past week. His connections had enabled us to find my daughter and the person responsible for the recent upheaval in our lives. I shuddered as the memory of that night washed over me. I was incredibly grateful that Lydia would never have to see that gory scene, the creamy carpet saturated in blood, tissue splattered over the walls and ceiling. I didn't know what it would cost to have somebody replace all those things on such short notice, but it was worth it. I wanted Lydia to be able to walk into her house and not be uncomfortable. I had a feeling, however, that that night would haunt both of us for the rest of our lives.

Con stayed for a few more moments and made small talk, telling me about Gwen's boyfriend, Justin. Unable to make bail, he was still sitting down at the jail waiting for his arraignment. As it turned out, Eldredge had been behind the auctions all along. Justin and two other young men had broken into the residences and shops, then transferred the items to Eldredge to auction off. Justin had some informal training in computer science, so he'd been able to easily access the auction platform he'd set up for Eldredge. He'd also had the foresight to record their conversations, and the police had arrested Eldredge yesterday on multiple charges.

Justin himself was facing several charges for kidnapping and human trafficking, though in exchange for his confession, the charges for larceny had been dropped. According to Justin, Gwen had asked him to get rid of Alexia however possible—permanently. Gwen had been willing to eliminate anything in her way to get to me, but Justin insisted he couldn't do it. Instead, he suggested they set up the auction, enticing her with the money they could make. It also allowed him to run background checks to ensure Alexia went to a good home.

The thought made me see red. Gwen had stalked, then attacked Lydia because of me, because of her jealousy over a childhood crush that hadn't been returned. I wish I could go back in time and change everything, but it was too late. I never even suspected a thing. Gwen had seemed so nice, so helpful—but it was all a ruse. Everything she had done was out of spite. Justin had confirmed what we'd all suspected.

Megan—the young woman Lydia had fired a few weeks back—had claimed she hadn't stolen the money. Ironically, Gwen had closed with her each night it happened. It would have been simple for her to reopen the register using Megan's code and take the cash. When she had supposedly been in the back working, she had plenty of time to go around the front of the building and throw the rock through the front window. Even the night that the salon had been broken into and trashed—Gwen had closed that night, and Justin admitted that Gwen had been out until the wee hours of the morning. Instead of going home after clocking out, she had taken her time pulling dresses from the racks and making a mess in the salon. It made sense now why nothing had been stolen and nothing truly destroyed. It burned me to think that she had come in and offered to help the next morning knowing that she was the one behind everything. All she had to do with the dresses was make a few minor fixes here and there, and they were good as new.

Con made a quiet exit, and I scooted closer to the bed. Lydia's hand was cool and limp in mine when I picked it up and pressed it to my lips. I cradled her hand against my cheek and whispered against her soft skin. "Fight for me, sweetheart. I need you to be strong."

I squeezed her hand a little bit tighter, hoping that she could feel me, could hear me. "Our daughter needs you, Liddy."

I need you.

CHAPTER FORTY-SEVEN
Lydia

My throat ached, and the bright white light blinded me as I blinked my eyes open. I looked around the unfamiliar room, a low beep cutting through the silence every few seconds. It didn't take long to recognize the medical-grade machines and the IV attached to the inside of my arm. I turned my head to the right. Had I been able to, I would have smiled at the sight that greeted me. Xander slept in a chair beside my bed, his head propped up on one fist.

I thought I'd been dreaming before when I'd woken up for a few seconds and seen a handful of people, their faces hidden behind masks. At the time, it'd seemed like a nightmare, some alien-type movie that I'd seen years ago. All I'd been able to make out was the people's shapes, backlit by bright lights. Their words were unfamiliar, barely registering over the buzzing in my ears.

My entire body felt heavy with fatigue. I licked my lips and tried to speak, but all that came out was a soft croak. Next to me, Xander stirred. I watched as his eyes fluttered open and darted toward the door. A smile tugged at the corners of my lips. He was always alert, on guard. Awake barely a second, he was ready to react to anything life threw at him.

Noticing that it was still closed, his gaze swept the room, over the bed and up to my face. His eyes alighted on mine and widened with surprise. He jerked upright and leaned toward me, already reaching for my hand.

"Hey, babe. How are you feeling?"

I swallowed, but the soreness of my throat made it almost unbearable. I lifted one hand toward my throat, and Xander nodded.

"Hold on one second." Reaching over my head, he hit the call button on the remote sitting next to me on the pillow. He pulled the chair closer to the bed and resumed his sitting position. His eyes never left mine as he grasped my hand tightly in his. "Does your throat hurt?"

I nodded, my eyebrows drawing together in question. My mind still felt fuzzy and sluggish, as though I couldn't quite wake up.

Xander grimaced. "I'm sorry. I'm just glad you're okay."

His words triggered a memory, and I bolted upright as Alexia immediately came to mind. *Oh, God.* My baby was missing. I reached frantically for him, my eyes searching his, pleading for answers. My mouth tried to form words, but nothing came out. He seemed to know exactly what I was asking, because he gripped my hand tightly, his voice low and soothing.

"Alexia is fine. She's at home where she's safe."

I relaxed and fell back against the pillow. Those had been some of the worst days of my life, and I wanted to never repeat them again. I was thankful that Xander and his friends had brought her home where she belonged. I started to ask him how he found her, but we were interrupted as the door opened. A nurse strolled through, a smile on her face as she approached.

"Hey, glad to see you awake."

Xander squeezed my hand and spoke up for me. "Her throat hurts. Is there anything you can give her?"

The nurse, whose name tag read Amanda, affected a sympathetic expression as she ventured closer and stopped next to my bed. "That's from the breathing tube we just pulled yesterday. It will probably be tender for a couple days." She smiled. "I can grab you some ice chips, though. Help hydrate you and soothe the ache."

I nodded and she reached for a blood pressure cuff. It constricted around my upper arm, and she made a couple notations on the iPad. "Vitals are looking good."

She removed the cuff and replaced it, then patted my arm. "I'll be right back. Need anything else?"

I shook my head, and she left the room in search of ice chips. I turned back to Xander to find him studying me intently. "What?" I mouthed.

His mouth opened and closed, his gaze darting away for a second before meeting mine again. "Do you remember what happened?"

I closed my eyes for a second and thought about the past few days. I remembered the helplessness I'd felt when the police showed up at the salon to tell me Alexia had been taken. I remembered two days of searching and appealing to the public, hanging fliers, handing them to every person I met on the street, and conducting the press conference. I remembered staring at Alexia's picture, wondering where she was and if she was safe, praying that she'd be found soon.

The picture.

Oh, God. Gwen. Xander. The gun. Images flashed before my eyes in rapid succession as it all came flooding back. I had to know. Somehow I managed to croak out the words. "Is she…"

"You don't have to worry about her anymore."

My eyes drifted closed again as Xander grasped my hand tightly. Exhaustion clung to me, pulling me under, and I finally gave in.

*

I pulled Alexia into my arms again, needing to feel her slight weight against me. Even though barely fifteen minutes had passed since I'd last held her, it had been too long. I hugged her tight, and she squirmed in my hold, wriggling to get down and play. Reluctantly, I set her on her feet and watched as she ran away. Part of me wanted to haul her back to me and never let her go again. But I couldn't hold her back because of my own insecurities.

She seemed to have no memory of what happened. And thank God for that. Kids were so resilient—much more so than adults. She would never remember the events that had transpired over the past few days. I, on the other hand, would never forget. Every time I saw her precious little face, I'd see that photograph of her tear-stained cheeks, eyes filled with misery.

My heart tugged, and I vowed to destroy that photograph. I didn't want any physical reminders of what had happened. From now on, I'd make sure she was safe at all times so nothing like that ever happened to her again. I would never let her out of my sight.

As I watched Alexia play with her toys, I couldn't help but feel that something was missing. And I knew exactly what it was. Or, rather, *who* it was.

Xander had been fairly distant the past few days since I'd awoken in the hospital. He'd encouraged me to come spend some time with Alexia alone, and he'd left immediately after dropping me off this morning. He hadn't said much, and he hadn't touched me except when absolutely necessary.

I knew he was struggling to come to terms with everything. He blamed himself for allowing this to happen, I knew that much. Somewhere between consciousness and dreams, I'd heard him quietly berating himself as he kept vigil by my bedside.

I wanted to reassure him that it wasn't his fault and tell him I needed him here by my side. I couldn't quite shake my unease. Even though my house looked normal, it still wasn't the same. It didn't feel the same without him here. The carpet had been replaced, but I'd noticed it was just a shade darker. The walls had been cleaned, possibly even repainted. I knew because the small scuff I'd left when moving the couch was no longer visible.

I couldn't remember the exact details no matter how hard I tried. I figured that was for the best. Gwen had hurt all of us. Now she was gone. There was no more justice to be exacted. She'd lost her mind over a guy. It wasn't the first time something like that had happened. People did crazy things for love—or obsession.

For the rest of the afternoon, I idly watched Alexia. We made dinner together, then I got her ready for bed. With each hour that passed, my heart sank a little more. Xander hadn't called or texted. I'd gone so far as to invite him for dinner, but he hadn't bothered to respond.

Was he done with me already? Had he realized I wasn't worth the trouble? That we weren't worth the trouble? Once more I thanked God that Alexia wouldn't remember the time she'd spent with him. My heart would take a little longer to reconcile the loss, but that didn't matter. I'd always put Alexia first.

CHAPTER FORTY-EIGHT
Xander

I slipped in the front door and cocked an ear, listening. A floorboard creaked upstairs from the vicinity of Alexia's room, and I ached to go to them. Somehow I refrained and made my way to the kitchen. Taking a seat at the table, I tossed down the manila envelope I'd agonized over bringing with me. But it was the right thing to do.

I heard her footsteps come closer, but I couldn't bring myself to meet her eyes—not yet. I didn't want to see the anger, the condemnation, the reproachful glare I knew would be there.

Her footsteps faltered, then drew closer. The chair across from me pulled away from the table, and she moved fully into view as she sank into it.

I closed my eyes, envisioning a scene from two years ago. This was so like the morning we'd spent in the coffee shop in Vegas. It was as if life was forcing me to replay the biggest mistake of my life all over again. Only this time it was so much worse. It was like déjà vu as I glanced up and met her steely eyes.

"You came."

Her voice was soft, but I couldn't deny the faint thread of accusation beneath, and I cringed. I should've manned up and responded to her text message earlier. But I hadn't been able to. For both of us, I had to do the right thing.

Her face was unreadable as I studied her, and my eyes flitted to the space just above her temple. A small patch of hair had been shaved away, and a one-inch square of gauze had been taped over the wound. Though I'd seen it every day for the past week, it still made my stomach clench. I wanted to pull her into my arms, bury my face into that sweet spot between her neck and shoulder and hold her close, never let her go. I swallowed down my need and straightened in my chair. I reached out and spun the manila envelope until it faced her, then slid it across the table.

She eyed me warily but didn't say a word. Finally, she broke our gaze and dropped hers to the envelope. With a trembling hand, she reached for it and extracted the sheaf of papers within. Her pretty eyes skimmed them, but she never said a word. Her expression never changed. It made me want to scream that she was so controlled.

She flipped to the back, and her gaze lingered for a long time on the page. I knew exactly what she was seeing, and I could see the weight of it in her eyes. I wouldn't keep her tied to me, not anymore. If she still wanted the annulment, I would give it to her.

Her face contorted in pain, and my heart twisted. If it killed me, I would do what was right for her. Guilt from the past few days ate away at me, exacerbated by the look of disappointment on Lydia's pretty face. She should be happy. She should want a husband better than me, someone who could protect her and our little girl. I had let Lydia down, let Alexia down. They had both depended on me to protect them and keep them safe, but I had failed. Not only that, I had brought this whole situation down on them. If it weren't for me, this never would've happened.

With a shudder, I turned my mind to the situation at hand. Lydia looked fragile and lost sitting across from me. There was an undefinable emotion in her voice, one that damn near broke me. "Is this what you want?"

Hell, no. I shook my head. "No. But I won't blame you if you do."

Her head tipped to one side as she contemplated me. "What if I don't?"

Hope curled through me, immediately followed by regret and self-loathing. Didn't she know she was too good for me?

"Don't you understand?" I seethed. "You deserve better than me. I was supposed to keep you safe—keep both of you safe.

Instead, I brought that crazy bitch right to your door. She came after you because of me." I jabbed my chest with my index finger. "*Me.* I should have known, should have seen it coming. But I didn't, and I couldn't do a damn thing to stop her until it was almost too late."

I pushed out of the chair and ran both hands through my hair as I spun away from her, refusing to acknowledge the disappointment I knew I'd find in her eyes. Goddamn it.

I flinched as a hand landed softly on my back. "Xander, look at me."

Her voice was firm, insistent, but I couldn't… I just couldn't do it. If I did, I would break. I didn't deserve her. I shook my head. "No, Lydia."

"Xander." More forceful this time, I shook my head, trying to drown her out. But she wouldn't be ignored. Her hand trailed along my side, as if she couldn't bear to lose contact with me for even a moment as she ducked beneath my arm and stepped in front of me. Curling her tiny hands into the fabric of my shirt, she began to speak.

"You didn't bring this into our lives—Gwen did. She devised this horrible scheme by herself—not you. None of this was your fault. You can't be responsible for everything that happens around you. And you especially can't rationalize someone like her." She tightened her fists, pulling my shirt more tightly across my body. "She had everyone fooled—you, me, the police—every single one of us. I worked with her every day and I never would have guessed she was behind it."

The entire time she spoke, I kept my gaze fixed to the wall above her head. I couldn't let her see the guilt I felt swirling inside me. But somehow, hearing her try to justify it helped. She had forgiven me when I hadn't been able to forgive myself.

Dropping my gaze, I lowered my hands to my sides. I ached to pull her into my arms, but I couldn't bring myself to do it. Not yet. "Liddy…"

"Xander. Listen to me." Gray eyes peered up at me, a fierceness in their depths. "You were amazing. Even when I lost my mind, you stayed calm and did what needed to be done. I'll never be able to thank you for that."

I swallowed hard. "You never should have had to go through

that."

"But you're missing the important part, Xander. I didn't go through it alone. You were there—the whole time, you were there supporting me when I couldn't do it myself."

This time, I couldn't tamp down the urge. I grasped her hips and pulled her against me with a gentle tug. Her hands unfurled from my shirt and slipped around my lower back, holding me tight. Needing her even closer, I looped one arm around her back. The other went to her temple, careful to avoid her injury, and I pressed her head to my chest. "I never want to let you go, Liddy. I did it once… I don't think I can do it again."

"Then don't." Her words rumbled against my heart, and I slid my fingers into her hair, using a gentle pressure to ease her head back.

I stared down into those gorgeous gray eyes. "What does that mean?"

"It means I want you to stay. I resisted initially because…" She trailed off and bit her lip, "I resisted it because I knew no one else would ever compare to you."

Her confession brought a smile to my lips. "Are you telling me you love me, Lydia?"

Her cheeks flamed bright red, and she dipped her head, but I wasn't letting her hide anymore. Sliding my left hand beneath her chin, I lifted her face to mine. I waited a beat to make sure she was looking at me—really looking at me—before speaking.

"I hope that's what you're saying. Because I love you. I've been crazy about you since the moment we met, and being with you these past few weeks has only made me love you more."

Joy lit her face as a smile spread over her mouth. "I love you, too."

Not wasting another second, I bent and pressed my lips to hers. It was hard and fierce, me claiming her mouth so she'd never want anyone else.

Her gaze darted back to the counter, and worry flickered in her eyes. "So, what do we do about…"

I set her away from me and grabbed the papers off the table. Why had I ever tried to walk away from this woman? I held them up to her. "Last chance, beautiful. Say the word and you're mine forever."

She bit her lip, looking unsure as hell. "I just want you."

As she watched, I ripped the papers down the middle and tossed them in the trash. I turned back to her and pulled her into my arms. "Now you've got me."

She snuggled into my chest, her arms a tight band around my waist. "Forever."

A smile lifted the corners of my mouth at her possessive tone. "Yeah, babe. Forever."

EPILOGUE
Lydia

My mother's friends milled around the impeccably manicured lawn behind her home, the heels of their hideously expensive shoes sinking into the thick grass. A smattering of applause broke out, followed by a few happy cries. I assumed my mother had Alexia entertaining people again, because I had left her with Xander and Jolene several minutes ago before coming into the kitchen to get the cake.

Glancing out the window, I gave a little shake of my head. I didn't know a single one of these people, yet Jolene had insisted they be here to celebrate Alexia's first birthday with us. I pushed away my irritation. I should be glad that she at least wanted to do something for Alexia, but deep down I knew most of it was still for show.

Xander came up behind me just as I put the single candle in place. I admired the intricately decorated cake for a moment. No homemade cakes for Jolene. In her usual fashion, she'd gone over the top and ordered a three-tiered cake from one of the city's most prestigious bakeries. It was beautiful, but I was terrified to know what it had cost.

I shivered as Xander dropped a kiss on the side of my neck. He spoke quietly next to my ear. "Do you want the good news first or the bad news?"

My heart sank as I turned to face him. Alexia was cuddled high up on his chest, her head nestled in the crook of his shoulder. As long as Alexia was safe, I didn't really care about anything else. Still, today wasn't a day for bad news. "Give me the good news."

He tipped his head toward the backyard. "The caterer said everything was going well, and she's packing up for the day. Everyone loved the food and sends their thanks."

At least that had gone well. "And the bad news?"

"Your mother's boyfriend showed up."

My eyebrows drew together in confusion. "Um… Okay?"

"Well…" He drew out the word, a tiny smirk lifting the corners of his mouth. "He may or may not have just proposed to her in front of everyone."

I blinked up at him. "He proposed to her? Here?" I couldn't keep the disbelief out of my voice. "At our daughter's birthday party?"

I knew I sounded like an idiot, but I couldn't help it. Who did that?

"On the bright side," Xander continued, "you didn't miss much. And if it's any consolation, with her track record, it'll probably happen again in another three years or so."

And just like that, my irritation was gone. His dry sense of humor never failed to lift my spirits, and I was incredibly thankful he'd come back into my life. I couldn't help but grin at Xander's wry comment, and I delivered a little slap to his upper arm. "You're terrible."

He shrugged one shoulder. "Just honest." His gaze darted toward the elaborate cake, then back to Alexia. "There's something I want to talk to you about later."

I swallowed, suddenly nervous. "What is it?"

"Now's not the time or place." He leaned in and kissed my forehead. "Just something that's been on my mind a lot lately."

Over the next few hours, worry and doubt plagued me. By the time I put Alexia to bed, I was ready to rip my hair out. I went in search of Xander to get some answers and found him in our bedroom. He sat on the edge of the bed, and his gaze lifted to mine when I entered the room. I paused in the doorway as I took in his expression. There was worry in his eyes, a vulnerability I'd never seen before.

"Come here, darlin'."

He opened his arms to me, and I went to him, simultaneously wanting to get this over with and avoid the conversation altogether. He enfolded me in a tight hug, his face pressed to my chest. In moments like these, I swore I would do anything for him if he would just hold me like this forever. Angling his head up at me, he framed my face in his hands and pulled me down for a kiss, stealing my breath and my sense. He tipped us backward so we were sprawled on the bed, his mouth never leaving mine. He propped himself up on one elbow and stared down at me.

"Are you happy?"

I froze, swallowing hard. Was this a trick question? "Yes?"

It was more a question than a statement, hoping it was the answer he was looking for. It was also true. I'd never been more content in life than I was right now. Though I'd fought it so hard in the beginning, Xander was everything I needed and more. He was an amazing lover, a fantastic husband, and a wonderful dad. I couldn't ask for more. But the deep line between his brows worried me.

Xander nodded, his fingers trailing lightly up and down my arm.

Worry tightened my stomach. Did he not feel the same? "Why?"

His hand moved to my belly, teasing the skin above my waistband, then moving upward toward my navel. "I've been thinking," he said as he splayed his hand over my stomach. "How would you feel about… you know… another one?"

It took a moment for my mind to make the connection. Another baby? I automatically pressed one hand to my midsection, right over his, as if I could feel the phantom life growing inside me. Xander's huge hand slipped from beneath mine and wrapped around the back of my neck, directing my gaze to his.

"If it's too soon, or if you don't want to, I understand." He took a deep breath. "I know we haven't really talked about it, but… I promise I won't let you down this time. I want to be here for you, for Alexia and any other kids we might have."

My heart raced. "Are you sure?"

He placed my hand over his heart. "I love you so much it fucking hurts. Nearly losing you scared the hell out of me, but it also made me realize how quickly shit can go sideways." He swept his hand over my stomach again. "I want to see my baby grow inside you. I want to be by your side every day. I want to grow old and gray together and die by your side."

My smile started small then grew until my cheeks hurt. "I want that, too. All of it."

He tumbled me to the bed, his mouth hard on mine. When we finally broke apart, he smiled wolfishly down at me. "First, let's work on getting you pregnant."

※

Xander

TWO WEEKS LATER

The soft rustle of sheets and the gentle shifting of Lydia's body next to mine brought me fully awake. I blinked my eyes open, immediately alert and ready to start the day, conditioned from years of military training. The dim light seeping through the bedroom window told me that it was still early, and a glance at the clock on the nightstand confirmed the fact. I listened intently for any indication that Alexia had begun to stir, but the house remained quiet. I didn't have to be at work for another two hours, and with a beautiful woman cuddled up next to me, there was no reason to get up yet.

Twisting my head, I glanced over at Lydia to see if she was still asleep. She was. One hand curled under the pillow, the other draped over her waist, her lips were parted slightly as her chest rose and fell on deep, even breaths. She looked so peaceful, so angelic, and a fierce protectiveness washed over me. For so long, she had tried to take on everything all by herself: parenting, her business, every single thing life threw at her. Though I'd told her nearly a month ago that I was here for the long-haul, she gave me that little half smile of hers, like she didn't quite believe me.

Lydia struggled with love and trust, and I knew I'd have a hell of a time overcoming what she'd experienced in the past. Over the last few weeks, I'd done my damnedest to prove to her that I was different, that *we* were different. We would never have a marriage like her parents' respective relationships, jumping from one partner to the next, selfishly viewing their unions only in terms of financial stability and social status. But I'd never been one to turn down a challenge, and I wasn't about to start now. So I'd terminated the lease on my apartment, moved into the duplex with her and Alexia, and set about proving to her just how serious I was.

Each day had been better than the last. Lydia had gradually begun to shed the doubt and insecurity that had plagued her for so long. She seemed more relaxed, more free. Now that she finally trusted me, she was less reserved, offering her smiles and affection in abundance. I planned to spend every day of the rest of my life loving her and Alexia, and what better way to start the day than doing just that?

Lydia shivered as I lifted the covers, briefly allowing our body heat to escape. I tugged them over our heads, then gently rolled her to her back and maneuvered between her legs. Her muscles tensed and twitched as I skimmed my hands over the sleek curves of her waist and hips, then hooked my thumbs in the fabric of her panties and tugged them down. She slipped one foot free, then the other, and she let out a sleepy little sigh as I spread her thighs and settled in.

Slender fingers delved into my hair as I dipped my head to kiss her. Her sweetness filled my mouth, and I leisurely explored her pretty pink folds until she was writhing beneath me, soft, sexy little pleas falling from her lips. She trembled and quaked as I brought her to the edge of orgasm, her teeth digging into her lower lip to contain her cries of ecstasy.

I flicked the tiny bundle of nerves with my tongue, and her hips jerked as she hovered on the precipice, ready to explode. I pulled away with a little grin and glanced up her, her head pressing into the pillow, bracing herself for the sensation. It took her little more than a second to realize it wasn't coming, and her nails dug into my shoulders.

"Damn it, Xan!"

A rough chuckle left my throat, and I kissed her inner thigh before levering myself over her. "No need for threats."

My dick leaped as I dropped to my elbows, bringing every inch of skin against hers from nose to toes. I loved the feel of her, soft and silky smooth, so different from my own hardened muscle. No matter how often I made love to her, it wasn't enough. I wanted to sink inside her and stay there forever.

Long, lean legs curled around the backs of my thighs, urging me on, and I gently pushed forward. The sensation of her hot flesh yielding to mine stilted my breath for a second, and Lydia wrapped her arms around my shoulders, pulling me closer. Sliding one hand under her bottom, I angled her hips upward the slightest bit as I sank all the way to the hilt. Slowly, in deep, measured, strokes, I began to move. Cocooned in our own little world, I made love to her slow and unhurried, tender and sweet. I teased her lips with soft kisses, drawing out her pleasure as she finally came on a gasping breath. The tightening of her flesh set off my own orgasm, and I came hard, emptying myself inside her with a ragged groan.

I slowly withdrew, then turned onto my side, pulling Lydia against me. Instinctively, she found that sweet spot right between my neck and shoulder and burrowed in, tangling her legs with mine. Her chest brushed mine as our lungs fought to draw in air, and our pulses gradually returned to normal. For several long minutes, only the sound of our combined breaths filled the air. Then Lydia spoke.

"Xan?"

I could barely make out the word as she spoke against my chest. "Yeah, babe?"

She drew a deep breath. "I have to tell you something."

Instantly on guard, I stiffened. "What's wrong?"

She lifted her head and peered up at me, insecurity and worry swimming in the gray depths. "We haven't... It's been..." She trailed off, then started again. "I mean, I know you said..."

She looked so lost that I took pity on her and stopped her rambling by brushing my thumb over her lower lip. "Liddy, what's going on?"

She bit her lip, and her gaze darted away for a moment before returning to mine. "I'm late."

My brows drew together. "Late for what?"

"*Late* late." She paused. "Like, two weeks late."

Understanding slammed into me with the force of a freight train. "You're sure?"

She shook her head. "I haven't taken a test yet, but…"

I slipped my hand between us and rested it on her stomach as a smile slowly bloomed over my face. "You're pregnant."

"Maybe." She lifted her shoulders a tiny fraction. "I think so, yeah."

I dipped my head and kissed her hard, my tongue sliding against her own. It was full of love, passion, gratitude and everything in between. It was something we both wanted, and nothing made me happier than the idea of having a big family with Lydia.

Alexia's happy cry from the next room ripped us apart, and I grinned at my wife. "Your turn or mine?"

She smiled and pressed one hand against my chest. "I'll get her. Take your time."

After one last lingering kiss she peeled herself away from me, and I let my hand trail over her back as she climbed from the bed. She pulled on her robe and, with a parting smile, disappeared out the door to collect our daughter.

I collapsed to my back and stared at the ceiling for a minute before launching from the bed and heading into the bathroom. I couldn't curb the stupid grin that took up residence on my face as I showered and shaved. Lydia was pregnant; we were having a baby.

"Holy shit." I caught my reflection in the mirror, stunned but ecstatic nonetheless. I still couldn't believe it. My grin grew. "A baby."

Saying the words aloud made it seem all the more real. I thought of her changing every day, growing round with my baby. I barely held back a whoop of joy. I couldn't fucking wait.

I threw on clothes then bounded down the stairs and into the kitchen. Tossing a glance toward the living room, I saw Alexia playing on the floor, babbling quietly to the stuffed elephant she was strapping into a doll-sized stroller. I grinned at the sight, then turned my attention back to Lydia. My wife.

She stood at the stove, her back to me, and I stepped up behind her, then wound my arms around her waist. She tipped her head to one side, and I kissed the side of her neck. My lips brushed the sensitive skin when I spoke. "Have I told you how happy you've made me?"

"In the ten minutes since I last saw you?" She let out a little laugh, then turned to face me and looped her arms around my neck. "I don't think so."

One handed tightened around her waist while the other slipped up to cup the back of her neck. "I feel like the luckiest man in the world."

Her teasing smile slipped away, and moisture gathered in her pretty gray eyes, rife with guilt. "I love you so much. You mean everything to me."

"No tears, babe." I dipped my head and leaned my forehead against hers. The past was the past; not a damn thing mattered but this moment right here. "We've got a beautiful little girl and another little one on the way. Nothin' better that that."

Her chest lifted on a half-laugh, and I dropped to my knees in front of her, then placed my hands along the curve of her waist. My thumbs traced the still-flat plane of her stomach that housed the tiny form of our baby. "Do you think this one will look like me, too?"

I couldn't help teasing her, and she gently smacked my shoulder. "I'd better get at least one that looks like me."

I glanced up at her, a wide smile on my face. "Sounds like a challenge. We'll just have to keep trying until we get it right."

The sweetest smile curved her mouth, and I was so absorbed that I never heard the patter of tiny feet approaching.

"Da-da!"

Those two syllables slayed me, and I thanked God I was already on my knees because I was sure I'd have hit the floor otherwise. Every muscle in my body froze, unable to respond to the sound of my beautiful little girl saying those words for the first time ever. I was dimly aware of Lydia clutching at me, her fingers curling into my flesh. Slowly, I swiveled my head toward Alexia.

"Who am I?" I said it quietly, encouragingly, desperately holding back the holler of elation that was bubbling up my throat.

For a second, she hesitated as if she wasn't quite sure what to do. Then she said it again, almost like a question. "Da-da?"

I shifted to face her fully, an elated grin forming on my face. "Who am I?"

She tipped her head to one side, a mischievous little smile curling her lips as she regarded me for a long moment. I knew she was making me work for it, but I didn't even care. I would wait a fucking lifetime to hear that sweet baby's voice call me her daddy again.

The word came out with more conviction this time. "Da-da!"

"Damn right, baby girl." My heart swelled with pride and unadulterated joy as I lifted her to my chest and hugged her tight. Lydia slid to her knees next to us, and I slipped an arm around her shoulders. I closed my eyes, my heart threating to explode out of my chest as I clutched them both to me.

I dropped a kiss on Alexia's head and released her as she squirmed to get down. Over her head, Lydia's tear-filled eyes met mine. Reaching for my wife, I cupped the back of her head and took her mouth in a single hard kiss. I pulled back and met her gaze again, sincerity drenching my tone. "Thank you."

My girls, the loves of my life. This—this was everything worth living for.

Also by Morgan James

QUENTIN SECURITY SERIES
The Devil You Know – Blake and Victoria
Devil in the Details – Xander and Lydia
Devil in Disguise – Gavin and Kate
Heart of a Devil – Vince and Jana
*Each book is a standalone within the series

FROZEN IN TIME TRILOGY
Unrequited Love – Jack and Mia #1
Undeniable Love – Jack and Mia #2
Unbreakable Love – Jack and Mia #3
Frozen in Time – The Complete Trilogy

BAD BILLIONAIRES
(Novella Series)
Depraved
Ravished
Consumed
*Each book is a standalone within the series

DECEPTION DUET
Pretty Little Lies – Eric and Jules #1
Beautiful Deception – Eric and Jules #2
*Each book can be read as a standalone but are best read in order for maximum reading pleasure

SINFUL DUET
Sinful Illusions – Fox and Eva #1 (Summer 2021)
Sinful Sacrament – Fox and Eva #2 (Summer 2021)
*Books are best read in order for maximum reading pleasure

STANDALONES
Death Do Us Part
Escape

About the Author

Morgan James is the bestselling author of contemporary and romantic suspense novels. She spent most of her childhood with her nose buried in a book, and she loves all things romantic, dark, and dirty.

She met her own husband when he crashed a friend's wedding (Just kidding. Kind of...) and they've been together ever since. They currently live in Ohio with their two kids and an adopted mutt that sheds like crazy.

Here are a few fun facts: She can swear like a sailor. She loves to bake but hates to cook. She loves a man in uniform. She pulls inspiration for her stories from real life. Her husband is the absolute best, supplying her with infinite one-liners. Like her characters' dialogue? There's a good chance that those conversations have really happened!

This book is a work of fiction. Places, events, and situations in this story are purely fictional. Any resemblance to actual persons, living or dead, is coincidental.

© 2004 by Ron Aigotti. All rights reserved.

No part of this book may be reproduced, stored in a retrieval system, or transmitted by any means, electronic, mechanical, photocopying, recording, or otherwise, without written permission from the author.

First published by AuthorHouse 06/10/04

ISBN: 1-4184-7342-1 (e-book)
ISBN: 1-4184-3879-0 (Paperback)

Printed in the United States of America
Bloomington, IN

This book is printed on acid free paper.

THE WOLVES OF BROOKLYN

by

Ron Aigotti

Dedication: Dedicated to all the family, friends and neighbors who made my years 1933 through 1952 so memorable.

CHAPTER ONE
The First Straw

Francisco Mastrangelo, otherwise known as Chico, was clearly uncomfortable in his new blue serge suit with its tight fitting vest. But he thought the black silk shirt, white tie and navy blue hat with the white band set off the contrast very nicely. The new patent leather, narrow nosed shoes were also a little snug fitting but definitely suave. Maybe it was just that he was not used to wearing such fine Fifth Ave. clothes. What would a construction foreman need with clothes like these on an everyday basis?

But this was no ordinary occasion. He was going to visit his little brother, Mario Mastrangelo, the District Attorney for the Borough of Manhattan. This was no little fish in a big pond. He's a "real big-a shot", as Chico would put it. "After all," he had told his friends, "it's not every kid from the tenements of Brooklyn who can make himself a big-a shot lawyer in New York. And District Attorney, they no come no bigger than that-a."

He had ridden the Independent Eight Avenue subway line up town to 34th Street and then walked over to the Empire State Building where Mario had one of his offices. The long walk in the hot August sun had not done very much for the press in his suit. He silk shirt now stuck to

The Wolves Of Brooklyn

him like a wet sheet and the perspiration had come through the armpits of the jacket.

At five foot six and 210 pounds with his jet black hair Chico was at least 50 pounds overweight and his labored breathing reflected this. In spite of his pot belly he was very strong and his arm and chest muscles bulged through his clothes quite visibly. After 35 years of working hard construction labor and then as a mason one didn't become a foreman without considerable physical and emotional strength. They had both served him well enough to help his widowed mother raise his four brothers and sisters and put three of them through college. Then he raised a family of four kids of his own with the help of his wife.

The fact that he had not taken a taxicab over to the office building was a reflection of the kind of frugality he had learned in order to accomplish these goals. Although he was now fairly well off at a comfortable salary of $45,000 a year, a tidy sum for 1956, the lifelong habits of thrift were not discarded readily. He would frequently remind his brothers and sisters, " you 'member what Papa used to always say, don't waste nothing. This a great country, this America, but too much waste." And now that they were all grown up and on their own he still taught the same lesson to his children. He took a great deal of pride in his family and their accomplishments but never asked anything in return except respect. He felt he had earned at least that much. They gave it too him gladly. All except his second son who was becoming a difficult behavior problem in high school. But a little stern discipline would correct that problem Chico was sure.

The perspiration was really beginning to roll off him as he approached the main lobby to the office building. One of the pieces of toilet tissue he had placed over a razor nick on his face was beginning to run and the small dab of blood was running onto his shirt collar. He dabbed at it with his white handkerchief which appeared now red poker dotted. He moved quickly into the lobby looking for the directory to find the office number of the district attorney.

Then he darted about searching for the elevator to the 78th floor.

Half a dozen other people were waiting for the elevator. They eyed him and his gaudy outfit with some dismay. He appeared very much out of place among all the gray, pin-stripped suits, homburg hats, and black patent leather high heeled shoes. But he was totally oblivious to their apparent disapproval of his appearance. He was to self-confident and secure to feel ill at ease.

"Buon giorno," he said as he bowed slightly at the waist and tipped his hat to all of the waiting passengers. His warm congenial smile and pleasant manner could melt the coldest of hearts. All of the women and many of the man smiled back at him and answered, "good morning". When the elevator car arrived he stepped aside, held the door open while pressing on the safety boot, bowed, and with a sweeping motion of his arm let all the others step into the car first. The elevator operator looked at him also with obvious disapproval. "Good morning," said Chico with his sparkling smile as the elevator started its ascent.

"Your job must-a be very exciting," he said patting the operator on the back. "Riding up to the high floors everyday way up above all these people. And all the nice business people in their fancy suits, and the ladies in those pretty hats. I bet you love your work, heh?"

The operator did not answer immediately. He was not used to conversing with the passengers who, more or less, considered him as just another fixture in their everyday routine.

"A. . . yeah. I guess so," he answered.

"Just think, some people living right in this-a city never been inside the Empire State building. The tallest

The Wolves Of Brooklyn

building in the whole, wide-a world. And you work in it everyday and ride up close to the clouds. You get to look out over the whole, big city where all-a them work. And they gotta look up to you to see where you work. It's a nice-a feeling, no?"

"Yeah," he said with little conviction. Then after a few moments he threw back his shoulders, stuck out his chin and said with much pride, "Yeah, that's right. They have to look up to me. I never thought of it that way."

"And look at all these important people. Lawyers, doctors, politicians, engineers, even the district attorney, they all depend on-a you to get them safely to their offices every morning and on time. You must feel very important."

Of course, the poor wretch never had felt any of this but Chico had this way of making everyone feel important and indispensable. And he was sincere in his convictions about this. It wasn't any put-on to make friends and influence people. He just liked people, all people. And most, if not all, liked him for this pleasant character trait. It was his main weapon of defense against the snobs of the world. It took only a few minutes of his charm to make anyone forget his not very debonair appearance and to warm up to him as a sincere, friendly man.

The operator turned to him and cheerfully asked, "what floor did you want, sir?"

"Oh, thank you too much. I'd like the 78th floor, please. That's the district attorney's office. That's-a my little brother, Mario."

"Here you are, Sir," said the operator," 78th floor. The office you want is 7806. Here, let me take you to it." He placed the elevator on the off position with his key and left the other passengers waiting in the silent elevator. But no one complained about the waiting. Several of the passengers said, "goodbye, Chico. Nice to meet you. And good luck with your brother and your problem."

Chico sauntered up to the double glass doors of the district attorney's office with his bulky arms sticking out at a forty-five degree angle from his massive shoulders. He approached slowly then stopped and backed up several feet. The lettering on the door read, Mario Mastrangelo, L.L.D. District Attorney of Manhattan.

"Well, well, well. Look-a here. Big beautiful words for my baby brother. He puts our family name in a high place of respect. If Papa were here he would be very proud."

He stepped softly on his toes up to the receptionist's desk, bowed gently at the waist, tipped his hat and said, "Scuzzi, beautiful senorina, I would like to speak to the District Attorney, Mr. Mastrangelo, if you please."

The doting, middle-aged spinster maiden stood up and stepped from behind the desk to examine the full length and breadth of this repulsive individual in a most condescending manner.

"I beg your pardon. . .sir. But you just can't barge in hear and expect to see the district attorney without an appointment. Not that I'd give you one. Now go along your way. . ."

"Begging your pardon. . . lady. I think Mr. Mastrangelo will see me when you tell him I am here, and who I am."

"Oh, really. And whom should I say is calling that his so important he would recognize your name immediately?"

"Whom? Whom? I'm not a whom, I'm a who", Chico mumbled to himself.

"You can tell him Mr. Francesco Mastrangelo his oldest brother is here to speak to him about a big family problem, that's-a whom."

"His brother?" she asked skeptically. "I didn't know he had any brothers or family for that matter".

"I guess he was just to busy to talk about us but he's got them, you can bet."

The Wolves Of Brooklyn

"Well, I'll just check first." She leaned over, switched on the office intercom and said,"Mr. Mastrangelo I'm sorry to disturb but there is a . . .a gentlemen here who says he is your brother. . .Frances."

"Not Frances, Francesco" Chico interrupted.

"Who is he?" returned the attorney voice through the intercom.

When Chico heard the voice of his little brother he was astounded and immediately excited. He picked up the box off the desk, held it directly before his face and said, "Hey Mario, Mario is that you in that box. It's me Chico, your big brother. What's a matter you too big a shot to tell this lady about your family? I gonna box your ears when I get you out of this box".

"Chico, Chico is that you? Wait there. Don't break the box I'll be right out", said Mario with real enthusiasm.

Mario soon emerged from behind two large mahogany office doors with his arms outstretched to Chico. Tall, slender, dark and handsome one would hardly suspect his was related to Chico.

"Chico, Chico it's so good to see you. You look wonderful and not a day older than the last time I saw you. Come in."

"Hey, hey mister big shot lawyer don't give me that bull. Save it for your high class friends. This is your brother Chico, remember. I helped raise you from a little snotty-nosed kid in the Brooklyn tenements. Don't try to snow me, heh, please."

"Yeah, yeah, Chico. You're right forget that stuff. Come on in to my office. We have a lot to talk over."

"I'm afraid this ain't gonna be no social call, Mario. We got some big trouble, family trouble, to talk about. And we gotta fix 'em if we can do it," he said glumly.

Mario felt that sinking feeling in the middle of his chest that always signaled deep concern and foreboding.

Something was seriously wrong but the stress of his office responsibilities had almost brought him to the breaking point as it was. He didn't need any additional problems at this time. 'This comes at a bad time,' he thought to himself. 'I don't need this. I don't need this now.'

"So what's the big problem, Chico? It's not mama is it? Is she sick? Does she need money? It's that trouble-making son of yours again, isn't it? Is he bothering you again?"

"No, no. It's not mama and it's not my Angelo." Chico hesitated momentarily knowing full well he was bringing some very painful skeletons out of the closet of Mario's past.

"It's. . . it's your brother Vito."

"Vito, Vito? I don't have a brother named Vito. I once had a good-for-nothing bum who lived with us called Vito. He almost killed my father and mother. A Vito almost destroyed my baby sisters life and disgraced our family name and all Italian-Americans. But he wasn't my brother. He was just a leech, the rotten apple that almost spoiled the whole barrel. I don't want to hear anything about. . ."

"Wait a minute, wait a minute. Mama sent me here to get your help and he hurt her the most. So you know it's gotta be important to her."

"Okay, for mama's sake I'll listen. But I'm not making any promises that I'll help that bum."

"Well, we may already be to late. I don't know."

"Too late for what, Chico?"

"Vito's been missing for almost two weeks. We're afraid. . . that . . .he's been killed, murdered by Louie Lupo."

Mario's face turned ashen. "What? What are saying? It can't be. It can't be." Tears welled up in his eyes and as much as he tried he couldn't hide the deep feeling he had for Vito. And now he was dead.

The Wolves Of Brooklyn

CHAPTER TWO
BEGINNINGS

The two eight-year-olds had played hooky from school and were wandering around the neighborhood's empty lots, the abandon houses and the docks looking for entertainment. They eventually wandered toward the small, dark secluded areas under the Manhattan bridge where the derelicts usually slept off their night of excess booze and drunken stupor.

"Hey, Mario. Ya got any matches?"

"What'a ya want matches for? Vito".

"You see those bums sleepin' under the bridge? I thought it would be fun to give them a hot-foot".

"What's a hot-foot?"

"You know. You put some matches in the crease between the sole and top of the shoe with the red head in first. Then you light the wooden end of the match and when it burns down to the head it flares and burns their foot."

Mario hesitated uncertain whether he wanted to engage in this form of entertainment.

"But, don't it hurt them. I mean can't they get a bad burn from it?"

"Nah. They're to drunk to feel it anyway. And, who cares anyway they're just a bunch of bums."

The Wolves Of Brooklyn

"Yeah, I know but Mama and Papa would sure get mad if they found out."

"Don't worry. They won't find out. You're such a chicken. You never wanna do nothin'."

"I'm not a chicken", said Mario with anger seething and the veins in his neck bulging. "I can do anything you can do and I'm not afraid of nothin' and don't you ever say different." Tears were beginning to well up in his eyes but he fought them back so Vito wouldn't see he was emotionally shaken.

"Oh, yeah. Let's see how tough you really are."

They proceeded to place several matches in the shoes of the four derelicts they found sleeping under the bridge and lit them. Standing back behind a concrete wall they waited for a good belly laugh when the bums started waking up, dancing around holding their foot and screaming in pain. But not one of them even rolled over after the matches had burned down and gone out.

"Hey they didn't feel nothin'. They must really be out cold from all that 'sneaky Pete' they drink", said Vito.

"Yeah, that stuff is as strong as turpentine."

"How do you know? Did you ever drink it?"

"Sure I did. Me and some of the guys bought some once and tried it."

"Well, that didn't make for any fun. Let's find something else to do."

"Naw, wait a minute Mario I got another idea. You go get some of that packing crate wood layin' around and we'll make a fire."

"What for?"

"Never mind. You'll see. Just go get the wood like I told you. And get a whole lot of it. I wanna make a real big, hot fire. And while you're at it see if you can find some iron washers layin' around."

"What size washers?"

"You know, the ones that are about as big as a quarter."

Mario and Vito began scavenging the area and found plenty of the fast burning wood and a half-dozen of the washers.

"Okay, now pile all the wood up here and get the fire really goin'."

"What are you figuring on doing, anyway?"

"You'll see. It's somethin' to see how much guts you really have."

"I got as much as guts as you", said Mario with the quiver and emotion returning to his voice.

When the fire had burned down to a mass of glowing ashes they dug the washers out of their pockets.

"Okay now throw all the washers on those red hot coals in the middle of the fire. Leave them in there until they get a red glow."

Once the washers were glowing red hot Vito picked them up by slipping a piece of bailing wire through the holes in the middle. He then carried them over to where the derelicts lay anesthetized from alcohol.

Mario watched as he approached the sleeping men. Vito then proceeded to place one of the hot washers on the top of the toe of the shoe of each of them.

"Come on let's get behind the wall again and watch the fun."

Several seconds transpired as the boys could hear the sizzling of the hot washers and then they could smell the odors of burning shoe leather and then burning flesh. Soon the men were up dancing around and screaming in pain. They lunged desperately at their foot trying to dislodge the source of the searing pain. Each time they reached down into the hole made by the washer they would burn their fingers and withdraw immediately.

The Wolves Of Brooklyn

"Hah, hah, hah." Vito laughed out loud unafraid of the suffering men.

Mario stood back, silently. Eyes transfixed at the horrible scene.

Eventually in desperation one of the derelicts began urinating on his foot to extinguish the agonizing heat. The others got the idea and soon followed.

The site of the men endeavoring to evacuate their bladders' contents onto to their foot made Vito laugh all the louder and harder.

"Hey, you damned rotten, stinking kids. I'll kill you for this," yelled one of the men. But as he tried to run after the boys he was hampered by the fiery pain in his foot. He fell to ground holding his injured appendage.

"Oh, yeh. you lousy bum, you gotta catch us first," Vito shouted back and taunted them to try to run after him. But none of them were able to stand, let alone walk or run.

"Come on, Vito", said Mario tugging at his sleeve. "Let's get out of here before somebody sees us."

"Naw, naw. They can't get us anyway and ain't nobody gonna see us neither." He picked up some stones and began throwing them at the crippled men lying on the ground. Inevitably a large stone struck one man on the side of the temple and he toppled over, unconscious.

"Come on, Vito. Stop it. Let's get out of here." Mario almost pleaded with him as he slowly drifted away from the revolting scene.

"If I get home without you Mama and Papa are gonna know somethin' is wrong. I'm leavin' without you."

Vito realized the accuracy of his statement and drifted away. He continued looking back at the men pausing every few yards to throw, "just one more stone". The man who had been struck on the head lay completely motionless on the ground. Mario was stunned but Vito was ecstatic.

"See, I told you that you were a chicken," Vito baited Mario.

"What are you talkin' about? I helped you, didn't I?"

"Yeah, but then you wanted to go and miss all the fun. You're a chicken. Mario is a chicken. Mario is a chicken."

They wrestled for a few moments as Mario lost his temper and went into a rage as he tried to punch Vito in the face. But as usual Vito dodged the blow. He wrestled Mario to the ground and immobilized him for several minutes.

"Okay, you give up now? Well, do you give up or do I give you a bloody nose?" Mario relented and Vito walked slowly away leaving him lying on the ground.

Mario lay sobbing on the ground for some time. He was experiencing a mixture of emotions in response to the entire episode. He felt some guilt for being involved in the terrible ordeal and for not trying harder to stop Vito. There was anger because he had lost another fight to Vito. Then there was that same old feeling of worthlessness and self deprication.

"Ah, what's the use. Vito's better than me at everything, anyway." He slowly lifted himself from the ground, brushed the dirty snow off his clothes and walked slowly home dejected with head hung low.

It was the summer of 1941 when the world was just beginning to recover from the great depression. The recovery was fueled by the need for arms production spurred on by the war in Europe. The United States had not yet entered World War II and was still to experience the devastating blow that Japan would deliver at Pearl Harbor in December of this same year.

Vito's and Mario's lives together had actual begun in 1933, the year of their births, in a New York City maternity clinic shortly after their parents had immigrated from Italy.

The Wolves Of Brooklyn

CHAPTER THREE
First Generation Americans

The waiting room of the city free-clinic was crowded, noisy and unclean. Dozens of expectant mothers sit around on the rickety, wooden white chairs which had long since turned yellow and had enough chips to give them a salt and pepper effect. But most of the woman were standing, and obviously quite weary, with their huge bellies sagging under the burden of seven and eight month pregnancies. The odors of body sweat, vaginal discharge, and antiseptic washing compound simply added to the already precarious status of their 'morning sickness'. This usually served to add the odor of vomitus before the day was over.

"Amelia, I'm not sure I can stand this place 'til October when the bambino's expected to come."

"Yeah, I know, Annunciata. I'm gettin' sick of this-a place too. But what else can we do? Until our men find-a work we gotta use the free clinic to have healthy babies."

"Ma shuse, I guess-a you right. Anyway, I remember my aunt, in the old country, no have no doctor 'til the baby was ready to come. The mid-wife come to the house to help but it was no good. My aunt and the baby died. I no want that to happen to me and my bambino."

The Wolves Of Brooklyn

So they swallowed their pride and tried to accept their fate for the safety of their unborn children.

Finally, after nine months and many unpleasant hours in the smelly waiting room, Annunciata and Amelia had their babies in October of 1933. They were each delivered at the home within ten days of each other. There were no complications and both were very healthy, robust boys. Amelia named her boy Ferdinando after her father and Annunciata named hers Mario after her grandfather.

As the boys grew up, the first generation Americans for either family, they developed into their own distinct personalities and characters even though they were constant companions.

Ferdinando developed into a vibrant, lively, fun loving youngster. His vitality was so outstanding that his friends and family gave him the nickname "Vito". It just seemed to fit his personality and blended well with his family name. He was also physically larger than Mario. Vito was two inches taller, ten pounds heavier and very handsome-- even at age five this was apparent to all. He was outgoing, intelligent, and just fun to be with. All the mothers, aunts and cousins just loved to cuddle and kiss him. His hair was jet-black, wavy and very thick which complimented his olive complexion very well. His eyes, however, were a bright, sparkling blue, unusual for an Italian unless there was some ancestry routed in the north. Vito's great-grandfather was from Piedmont--a northern province.

Mario was Vito's opposite in many ways. He was slight of build, brown sandy hair, deep dark brown eyes, fair skinned and somewhat withdrawn and shy. Not a handsome face like Vito's but not an unpleasant face either. He outshone Vito in only one striking way; he had a brilliant mind. Some felt it bordered close to genius. Diligence and hard work were natural off-shoots of these traits.

Their families had been close friends back in Italy and the close ties continued in America. They even lived in the same tenement apartment in the slum section of Brooklyn, a short distance from the Sand Street gate of the U. S Naval shipyard. Their fathers and uncles worked as unskilled laborers in the navy yard.

Their tenements were considered depraved slums and fire traps because they were constructed of wood frame and tar paper. On the street where Vito and Mario lived, High Street, there were none of the stately, celebrated brownstone houses and very few brick dwellings. But the boys never considered their homes as 'slums' or ghettos. Their entire lives and world revolved around their neighborhood, school, church, families and friends. They were secure and content in their closely knit Italian-American 'village' in the midst of a giant city. At the time the population of Brooklyn was the fourth largest in the world boasting over 4.5 million inhabitants.

The tenement consisted of three floors above ground and one basement apartment. Vito and his family lived on the third floor, Mario and his family the second, an aunt and uncle without children and Mario's grandmother co-occupied the first floor and basement apartment. The nest seemed very secure, safe and permanent.

"Hey, Mario. If you help me carry a couple of gallons of kerosene up to my house I'll help you carry yours."

"Okay, Vito, that seems fair. Hey, wait, your apartment is one more flight up from the basement than mine. So I'll be doin' more work then you."

"Ah, how come you always have to think and figure so much. You're gonna wear your brain out. Just help me, will ya?

The apartments were heated by burning kerosene in black, coal burning stoves that had been converted. The stove was located in the kitchen and provided the energy for

The Wolves Of Brooklyn

cooking, heating and hot water for bathing. The kerosene had to be poured carefully into a metal reservoir tank which was then inverted into a stand where gravity fed the fuel to the burning wicks. The boys filled the reservoir tanks about every 48 hours depending on the outside temperatures. Their was no duct work or fans to carry the heat to the other rooms. Whatever heat the other rooms received was by air convection which was very inefficient. But no on suffered frostbite or pneumonia. The greatest disadvantages were the odor of the burning fuel, the fire hazard and the work required to fill the tank.

"Vito, you hold the funnel while I fill up the tank. Hold it steady so none spills on the floor. My mom would brain me if I messed up her clean floor."

"There ya go thinking again. Just pour, will ya?" They finished filling the tank in Mario's usually meticulous, careful way. Then they carried the one gallon glass jugs up to Vito's apartment. All the apartments, except the basement, were exactly the same floor plan. The black stove stood in front of what was once a wood burning fireplace which had been sealed closed except for the black metal chimney pipe that now led from the stove to the old chimney stack. The reservoir tank stood on a narrow metal stand off to the left of the stove and copper tubing carried the fuel to the wicks inside. More than once we had knocked the tank out of the stand or actually bent the stand during some of our wild play.

The black stove had four circular openings on the top surface. The covers were lifted off with a small curved device that fit into a groove in the lid. One of the lids was composed of four concentric circles which could be lifted out individually to accommodate a pot or other cooking vessels placed over the opening. Directly below each lid were three concentric, progressively smaller circular kerosene wicks which glowed red hot when the kerosene burned. Off to the right side about one-third of the area of the stove accommodated an oven for baking. Temperature control was virtually impossible so the contents required constant attention, turning and basting. Mama and Nonna (grandma) spent countless hours laboring over these black monstrosities, especially in preparing large holiday meals for twenty to thirty people.

Vito uncapped the jug while Mario held the tank.

"Wait a minute. Don't you think you oughta use the funnel so you don't spill none," warned Mario.

"Ah, never mind that, I ain't clumsy like you. I can pour without spillin' none."

"Whatever you say, Vito."

But he did spill a considerable amount of the smelly, flammable liquid.

"Not clumsy, heh. You must 'ave spilt a half-gallon on the floor, you jerk."

"Shut up and hand me that dish towel. I'll just clean it up."

The two boys worked feverishly to clean up the spill when they heard Vito's mama climbing the long two flights of stairs up to the apartment. The climb was especially difficult for Amelia who had gained a great deal of weight after she delivered her only child, Vito.

"Hurry up, here comes my mama. She'll kill me."

Just as she entered the apartment the boys had finished cleaning the spill but Vito couldn't find a place to hide the kerosene soaked dish cloth. Immediately before she stepped into the kitchen he threw it behind the black stove in a dark corner.

"Did you boys fill the kerosene tank?"

"Yes, Mama. We just finished."

"Yes, I can tell. The kitchen stinks of kerosene."

"Did you spill some?"

The Wolves Of Brooklyn

"Yes, Mama but we cleaned it up. The smell will disappear in a little while."

"Just the same I'm gonna open a window at the top and bottom a little more to let the fumes out."

One of the windows in the kitchen was always left open a small amount to let noxious gases out. She pulled down hard on the top window but the old wooden frames were swollen with age and dozens of coats of paint.

"Mama, mia. It's stuck."

She tried a trick that usually worked. By closing the window first, very forcefully, and then opening it again quickly you could usually get an extra inch or two of opening. But as soon as she had closed the window, and before she could open it again, she heard a loud knock on the wall from the apartment next store. The thin wood frame walls afforded little insulation against the passage of sound. She could hear her neighbor Rosa calling, "Amelia come quick my baby swallowed some roach paste." She dropped everything, ran down the two flights of stairs, out into the street then back up the stoop and the two flights to Rosa's apartment.

When she entered the apartment the ten-month old child was lying on the floor gagging and Rosa was frozen and screaming in panic. Amelia moved quickly, picked the child up by the feet, and with the child's head hanging down, she struck her hard on the back. Finally after two or three blows the child dislodged a large piece of raw potato and coughed it out.

The boys had followed Amelia to the scene.

"Mario, you run quick to Louie Lupo's shop and tell him we need him to come right away and take the bambino to the hospital."

Louie Lupo, the local 'bookie' and Mafia man was one of the few people that could afford to own an automobile. She knew he would come to help even it was only to maintain his hold over the neighborhood and not because of his humanitarian concerns for the child.

"I'm-a don't understand you women. Why you no put the roach paste where the bambinos no can get. It seems like once a month I gotta take somebody to the hospital for eatin' that junk."

Cockroaches, like rats, were just considered a normal part of life for the tenement district residents. It seemed no matter how much you cleaned your apartment there were always roaches. The first one out of bed in the morning could expect dozens of them to go scurrying back into the woodwork. It was simply routine after cleaning house each Saturday to apply some fresh roach poison to some leftover piece of food and hope you could kill some of them.

"Well, Mr. Lupo you see we no got lots of money like you to buy a nice big house and hire the exterminator to come in an' spray for the cockroaches. Excuse-a me for troubling you," said Annunciata sarcastically. She had no use for gamblers and Mafia men. She also had no fear of them.

Lupo did not answer since he had encountered her wrath before and knew there was no way he could best her in a verbal confrontation.

"Oh, madonna mia," sobbed Rosa. "The baby's throwin' up so much. What I'm gonna do."

" No worry. Turn the baby on her side and her head down. It's good she vomits out all the poison. Just be sure she no suck it into her lungs," they assured her.

The child was rushed into the emergency room where the doctors and nurses went to work immediately to pump out the baby's stomach. After what seemed like an interminable wait the doctor came out and assured them that the child would be fine. But he decided to keep her in the hospital for observation for a day or two.

The Wolves Of Brooklyn

By the time they arrived back at the tenement it was long after supper hour. Tony Vitale had returned home from work to find no supper waiting which displeased him very much. Louie's barber shop had long been closed up for the night by his helper and bodyguard, Salvatore Abruzzo. He was sure that Sal had locked all the policy slips, racing bets and cash in the safe.

"Ay, how come-a no supper?" asked Tony when Amelia and the boys returned home.

"Oh, Antonio, cara mia. We had a terrible thing happen today. We just-a now come back from the hospital with Rosa and the baby."

"Why, what happened? The baby, she's gonna be okay?"

"Yeah, the doctor says she be all right. She swallowed some roach poison. Don Louie Lupo and me, we take her to the hospital emergency room. They pump her stomach and just-a gonna keep her a few days. I'm-a sorry, no supper ready for you. I make some-a-thing right away."

She removed some left-over spaghetti and meatballs from the ice box and prepared one of Tony's favorite dishes. The entire conglomeration was placed in a frying pan and mixed with beaten eggs to hold it together. The end result was a pie shaped, omelet-like affair fried to a crispy, golden brown on the surface with the fragments of meatballs scattered throughout the semi-solid mass. It was Vito's favorite also.

"Papa, can I sleep at Mario's house tonight?" said Vito.

"Ask you mama. If she say okay, it's okay with me."

"Is it okay, mama. Can I please? What do ya' say. Heh?"

"Wait-a minoot. Let me have a chance to think, will you? Yeah, I guess it's okay. You no make no trouble for "Nunciata and Carlo."

"No, mama. I won't make no trouble."

"That's-a my good boy," she said and kissed him on the cheek.

"Ah, ma. Why do you have to get so mushy."

"Go on, you love it and you know it. You no fool me."

Vito changed into his 'hand-me-down' pajamas which were originally red and white stripes but now were all faded. The sleeves and legs were at least two inches too short for him and the pocket over the left breast was long gone. He grabbed an assortment of toys including his Tom Mix six shooter, his collection of major league baseball cards and some lead soldiers. He particularly liked to play war, and cowboys and Indians. He started for the door and called, "good night, mama and papa. I'll see you tomorrow morning."

"Just a minute, my Texas bad man. Let's see what you bringing downstairs to Mario's. That's what I was afraid of. Where's your toothbrush and toothpaste."

"Ah, Ma, I don't wanna brush my teeth. Mario's mother don't make him brush."

"Oh, yes, she does. I know that for sure."

She put the things in his paper bag, swatted him gently on the bottom and lead him to the door. Mario's apartment was one floor below theirs. The hall and stairway were very cold and very dark. It was not heated and just one stark, uncovered light bulb hung from a socket and wire suspended from the ceiling. In the cold months the entire tenement had a strong stench of kerosene and smoke but all the tenants were so used to it they hardly noticed.

The only two toilets in the building were located at the ends of the halls on the first and second stories. Therefore, they were, of course, not heated so that a cold toilet seat was even more shocking than usual. During exceptionally cold winters the water in the toilet bowls and the wooden

The Wolves Of Brooklyn

flush tanks suspended high on the wall would freeze and crack. This had to be anticipated by the tenants so they could add either kerosene or rubbing alcohol to the water in the toilet and tank to act as anti-freeze. This only added to the mixture of odors pervading the building. The greatest hazard came if the smokers in the building didn't remember these precautions and tossed the lighted cigarette butts into the toilet.

They both sat silently and waited to hear the door to the second floor apartment close and for the lock to be turned.

"Amelia you make a good idea when you have 'Nunciata and Carlo take Vito one weekend and we take their kids one weekend. Now at least we get some time alone."

She glided over to Tony's side of the table and sat on his lap. "And now we gonna used the time alone." She kissed him passionately and he carried her to the bedroom.

"I think it's time Vito had a little brother or sister."

They proceeded to do their best to increase the size of their family and then fell off to a contented sleep.

***

Down in the second floor flat Mario and Vito were conducting a different kind of play under the covers on the sofa in the parlor.

"Okay, Mario put the sheet over the back of the sofa like a tent. And remember be quiet, everybody is sleepin'."

Ordinarily Mario slept in a double bed with his two brothers Chico and Carmine. Although it was crowded he didn't mind it too much since it lent itself to a lot a play and fun when the lights went out. But he still welcomed the times Vito stayed over and they could share the comparatively spacious sofa in the parlor. They played well past midnight and then finally fell asleep, also very contented.

It was now 3 a.m. and the entire tenement was quiet except for the sound of snoring and the occasional gust of brisk winter wind through the alleys and down the old chimney stacks. The kerosene soaked rag still lay behind the stove in the Vitale's flat. The liquid in the cloth had slowly seeped out and ran down the slant of the kitchen floor, under the linoleum and into the bedroom where Tony and Amelia slept. The area rug on the floor of the bedroom acted like a sponge and absorbed much of the combustible fluid.

The Mastrangelo's also slept soundly in a bedroom directly below the Vitale's since all the flats were exactly alike.

"Carlo, Carlo wake up. I smell smoke. Don't you smell it?" said Annunciata.

"Yeah, but this place always smells that way."

"No, I mean it's really strong this time. I think there's a fire somewhere, somewhere real close."

He awoke reluctantly, and slowly, still half asleep. Sitting on the edge of the bed a few seconds, he tried to clear his head. Now he opened his eyes widely and felt a bit of panic as realized that the smoke was very strong and close at hand.

"Quick, Amelia wake everybody up and get them out of the flat. I think it's in our building."

He switched on the light and then he could feel the heat emanating from the ceiling above his head. Some of the smoke was also visible seeping through the cracks in the ceiling of the poorly constructed structure.

Annunciata screamed, "Carlo, look it's coming from Tony's flat. Oh, my God."

Carlo bounded up the stairs, still in his underwear and slippers. He rushed down the hall and grabbed the door knob to the Vitale's flat but quickly pulled his hand away. The old brass door-knob was scalding hot. The door was locked and bolted from the inside. "Tony, Amelia", he yelled

The Wolves Of Brooklyn

and pounded on the door which was also very hot. "It's a fire. Get up, get up. Get out of there."

No one answered. All that he could hear was the crackling of the flames and the hissing of the hot gases trapped in the rooms.

He ran to the bathroom, soaked some toilet paper in the water in the overhead tank and tried to cool off the door knob enough to grasp it. This did help for a few seconds but not enough. Then he pulled off his T-shirt and soaked that in the tank water and put his bare shoulder to the door and crashed it in after several blows. He could feel the searing heat scalding the skin of his shoulder and the palm of his hand.

But total panic had seized him now and he seemed oblivious to the pain. The only thing he could think of was trying to get his friends out of the flat. When the door finally gave way the roaring flames leaped out into the hall and into Carlo's face. He put the wet T-shirt over his head and lay flat on the floor. He tried to enter the kitchen but couldn't.

"Tony, Amelia," he cried out in desperation with tears running down his blistered and burned cheeks. But no reply was forthcoming. The sirens of the fire engines were now barely audible over the roar of the fire.

The fire at first had raged in the kitchen engulfing the black stove and the reservoir tank of kerosene. Since Amelia had left the kitchen window closed earlier in the excitement the flat quickly filled with the acrid smoke and the couple were never aroused enough to be alerted. The flames spread quickly to the kerosene soaked rug under their bed and they died motionless in their bed.

Luckily all of the other tenants had gotten out of the building in time. The firehouse was only three blocks away and there was a fire hydrant only twenty feet from the building. Since the fire had started on the top floor the remainder of the building was saved but the entire third floor had been gutted very quickly.

"Oh, poor Vito. What has God done to you. Mama and papa now gone so quick," said Amelia as she held Vito against her. All the neighbors also tried to console the boy who seemed frozen with disbelief. He was not sobbing or hysterical only gentle tears rolled down his dirt and soot covered face. He was in emotional shock and didn't utter a sound but simply stared into the smoke and flames.

"How come they didn't smell the smoke or hear the fire and run outside?" asked one of the other tenants of the building.

"The firemen said that all the windows were closed tight. Maybe they get knocked out first by the gas in the room. If they were unconscious they couldn't get up anyway."

"There will most likely be an autopsy done. That should tell them if they died from asphyxiation before they were killed by the flames. Poor little Vito. I wonder what will happen to him?" asked a neighbor.

Carlo and 'Nunciata answered the question, immediately and simultaneously.

"No worry. Vito, he come to live with us. He'll be in my family now. We take good care of him, just-a like he's my own son."

Vito turned his head at hearing these words. He was still in a daze but managed a slight smile to indicate his appreciation to his new foster parents.

Only Vito and Mario were aware of the kerosene soaked rag that was tossed behind the black stove. They could only guess what effect it had had on the extent and origins of the fire. They could only speculate. What effect this knowledge would have on the boys future and development only time would tell.

The Wolves Of Brooklyn

CHAPTER FOUR
The Chinks

"Carlo where will Vito sleep?" asked 'Nunciata.

"Chico will have to sleep on the sofa in the parlor and Vito will share the double bed with Mario and Carmine."

Vito resented not having his own bed as he had had before the fire but he never complained or divulged this to anyone. He simply made the best of a cramped situation. But he vowed that he would some day have all the money he needed to have his own house, a car, a motorcycle and all the things he had ever wanted.

"Vito, it's gonna be great. Now we can be together all the time. We can even play in bed every night before Carmine comes to bed. It's gonna be so much fun."

***

The following December 7, 1941 Japan bombed Pearl Harbor and America found itself involved in World War II. Shortly after the U.S. declared war on Nazi Germany and the worldwide struggle escalated. Mario's two older brothers, Chico and Carmine, were drafted and shipped overseas. This solved a space problem that had developed when Vito moved in with the Mastrangelos.

The Wolves Of Brooklyn

The two boys now had the double bed to themselves, much to their delight. The previous limits on their bedtime play were extended.

"Hey, Mario. Let's take our BB guns to bed with us tonight."

"What for? What are we gonna shoot at?"

"You'll see. I'll think of something."

After school they went out into the back yard to play. The window of the bedroom they slept in looked out over the long narrow back yard area.

"I got it, Mario. Go get all the glass jars you can find in the kitchen. I'll go into the alley and find some empty tin cans."

"What for? What are you gonna do?"

"We'll turn them upside down on the stakes in Nonna's garden that she left last summer for the tomato plants. Then later tonight when everybody's asleep we can shoot at them with our Daisy Air rifles."

"Hey, that's a great idea. Vito you think of everything. How come I never think of those things?"

Later that night, as everyone else slept, the boys had their fun.

"Look Mario there's a nice bright moon out tonight. See how it makes the shiny glass jars and tin cans sparkle. Now we can see them easier."

"Yeah. Look at all those targets gleaming out in the yard."

They pumped their air rifles and added plenty of BB's into the magazines. The soft puffing sound of the guns was not enough to disturb anyone's sleep.

"What about the noise of the breaking glass and the clinking sound of the cans, do you think it'll wake anybody up? I don't wanna get in no trouble," asked Mario

"Ah, don't worry, you chicken. We ain't gonna get in no trouble. Just start shootin' at those targets."

They stuck the barrels of the rifles out the window, which they had raised only a few inches, and rested them on the sills. The foot of the bed was forced right up against the window sill since the double bed just did fit into the small room. It actually touched three of the four walls. There was one chest of drawers in the room which butted right up to the side of the bed. As a result only the top two, and the fourth drawer at the bottom could be opened. The third drawer was useless since it couldn't be opened.

Plink, plink came the sound each time one of the tin cans was hit. The glass jars shattered with a slightly louder but muted crash of glass. The sounds of the rifles were barely audible with the barrels outside the window. At least no one in their flat was disturbed, but the Chinese family on the other side of the yard could hear the noises.

"Hey, Vito look. The chinaman across the yard must've heard the noise. His lights just went on in his bedroom."

"Yeah, yeah . . . that's perfect," said Vito.

"What ya mean perfect. Now we'll get in trouble."

"No, we won't. But now the light in his window is a perfect target."

"What? you ain't gonna shoot at his window, are ya?"

"I sure am. He'll never know where its coming from. It's too dark for him to see us. Come on start shooting and we'll knock out that dirty chink's whole window."

Vito took careful aim and made every effort to hit the window. He noticed that Mario wasn't shooting.

"What's a matter? you ain't shooting. Are you chicken? Afraid you're gonna get caught?"

"No, I ain't afraid." He raised his rifle and began firing at the window. But he deliberately aimed low and to the right so that he came close without actually hitting the glass.

"I see you're still the lousy shot you always was," said Vito.

Small holes began to appear in the glass but the pane was too large to be shattered by the air rifles. Soon the chinaman heard the sounds of the pellets against the glass, ran to the window and opened it wide.

"Hey, who shoot my window," he yelled blindly out the window, looking around wildly trying to determine the source of the pellets.

"You stop that, you hear. You stop or I call the cops on you," he shouted with increasing fury in his voice.

"Vito, get away from the window. Stop shootin'. That chink is gonna wake up the whole neighborhood."

"Nah, nah. What do I care? He still can't tell where it's comin' from. Let him yell his head off."

"Come on, Vito, close the window. We gotta stop his screamin'."

"Yeah, you're right. But there's one sure way to do that." Vito raised his air rifle and began firing at the old man's face. The old man abruptly stopped yelling and raised his hands to his face to protect it from the pellets. He let out one final screech and put both hands over one eye. Stepping back, he quickly closed the window and turned out the light. As he did so the glint of the moonlight threw a beam of brilliance on the boy's bedroom window and reflected off the rifle barrels.

"Ah, so," said the chinaman. "Those two little 'Wop' hoodlums make trouble for Wong Fat, do they? I fix them good."

The next afternoon the boys were returning home from school when they saw the police squad car, the familiar green and white Plymouth, two- door coupe, parked in front of their tenement.

"Oh, oh, Mario. Looks like were in for big trouble now. There's a cop's car parked in front of our house."

A huge knot began to tie up Mario's gut and tears welled up in his eyes.

"Oh, boy. Papa's gonna kill us now," said Mario.

"Nah. Just play dumb. That 'chink' can't prove nothin'. It's our word against his. And who's Carlo gonna believe, us or some slanty eyed, old coolie washerman," said Vito.

"He ain't a washerman. He owns that little Chinese restaurant on Sand Street."

"I know. But what's the difference. He's still a coolie, ain't he?"

"There they are, officer Flynn, that's them. That's the hoodlums who shot my window full of holes and almost knocked my eye out"

"Okay, okay, Mr. Fat, just calm down. I'll handle this", said the policeman.

Carlo and 'Nunciata had joined the policeman and the Chinese at the door of their flat. They then stepped inside the apartment to discuss the situation.

"Now, Mr. Fat, did you actually see these two boys shooting the air rifles at your window?"

"No, it was night time and it was dark. But me saw two gun barrels sticking out bottom of the bedroom window. The moon shine on them very bright. It very clear night and I see the guns for sure."

"See, Mario what'd I tell ya, he can't prove nothin'. It his word against ours. Ain't that right Carlo?"

"Papa, you call me 'Papa' now. I adopt you since your parents left this world and you call me Papa. You understand? And you call Annunciata mama or I break-a you neck. Now, you stand over there and keep-a you mouth shut while I decide who to believe."

"Mario, you come over here, please. Now, you tell-a me. Did you and Vito shoot at Mr. Fat's window and at him

The Wolves Of Brooklyn

too? Remember what I'm-a tell you. You no lie to me and your mama or you get somethin' worse. You understand."

He had a firm hold of Mario's arm and turned him around so that he could not look at Vito's eyes."

"Yes, Papa", said Mario. He hesitated, then he heard Vito murmuring, "ah Jeese, you jerk."

Carlo let loose of Mario's arm and walked over to Vito, pulled him by the ear and turned his face to the wall.

"Now, you be quiet like I tell you ,if you no want more than I plan to give you."

"We did it, Papa. We shot the chink's window. . .", said Mario.

"Excusa please. What-a you say?" said Papa.

Mario apologized to the Chinese and proceeded. "I mean, we shot at Mr. Fat's window and at him, too."

"Well, Carlo that settles it. What do you want me to do?"asked the officer.

"Well, officer first you take the BB guns and bring 'em to the station house. Then you do whatever you do with other weapons."

"We usually destroy them."

"Very well, then you destroy them."

"Hey, you can't do that. That's not your gun, it's mine. My real papa gave it to me for Christmas. . . ", said Vito.

'Crack', suddenly Carlo whirled around and with the palm of his hand, dealt Vito a sharp blow across the face which sent him hurtling backwards against the wall.

"Along as I put food in your mouth and clothes on your back, I am your papa and you no answer me back."

Vito held one hand over his red hot cheek, seething with anger and hate but he would not allow himself to cry.

"Now you go to the bedroom and stay there. I deal with you later. Mario you go to."

"Excusa me Mr. Fat for my boys. I pay for the broken window and for anything you pay to fix-a you eye. You just send me the bill. I mean to say the boys will pay. You tell me if you need them to work at your restaurant to wash dishes, sweep the floor. Whatever you want."

"Ah, so, that very good, Carlo."

"You wanna press any charges Mr. Fat," asked the policeman.

"No, no. Mr. Mastrangelo pay for everything. I no press charges."

"Okay, Mr. Fat that's fine. . . ."

"Thank-a you Mr. Fat but I want 'em to have a good lesson. Officer Flynn you think you can lock them in jail for a little while to scare them good?"

"Yeah, I guess I can arrange it. Are you sure you wanna do that? We got some pretty tough characters in that jail?"

"As long as you can watch them and keep the 'homos' away from them. But not for over night, just for a few hours."

Annunciata interrupted, "No, Carlo, that's-a too much. They just bambinos."

With a stern look and a scowl he led her back to the corner of the room. "You leave-a this to me 'Nunciata. I make the discipline in this-a house." She lowered her face and eyes, stepped back into the fringes of the scene, and said, "Yes, Carlo."

The boys were brought from the bedroom. Mario was visibly shaken and frightened. Vito remained arrogant and unrepentant.

"You have handcuffs, officer?"

"Yes, I do Mr. Mastrangelo."

"Good! You will please put them on the boys before you take 'em outside. And have your partner turn on the red light on top of the patrol car, please."

"But what for, Carlo?"asked the policeman.

The Wolves Of Brooklyn

"I'm-a want all the neighbors to see these two hoodlums goin' to jail."

"Whatever you say."

The other officer went ahead and turned on the swirling red light and within a few minutes dozens of neighbors lined the short path from the stoop of the tenement to the patrol car. The boys were led out handcuffed to each other at the wrists. Vito thrust his chin out defiantly and Mario hung his head to hide the tears trickling down his face.

"Hey, Vito, what'd ya do, rob a bank or somethin'?" someone called from the crowd.

"Nah, we just broke the chink's window", he called back almost with pride.

A split second later, Carlo struck Vito another blow with his cuffed hand to the back of his head. Again, no tears or remorse from Vito. Everyone knew the blow inflicted pain because of Carlo's strength. Although he only stood 5 foot 6 or 7 inches tall, he was very muscular. Wielding a heavy pneumatic paint chipper in the Navy Yard all day long produced strong, powerful arms which were quite visible through his black, long sleeved turtle neck shirt. His face was one of righteous power and total command. Squared chin, dark black beard-stubble, heavy black eyebrows, noble Roman nose, and straight combed back, wavy hair lent themselves to his air of authority. There was no doubt he was in charge of this family and of any situation he cared to control.

Even now, everyone knew he was orchestrating the entire incident with the policemen playing a minor role and following Carlo's instructions.

"Okay, officers. You take them to jail and you call me when the judge finishes with them. I pay any fines or any bail money they need."

***

Four hours later Carlo picked the boys up at the station house where they had been locked in a cell by themselves after going through the mock formalities of booking, finger printing and having their photos taken.

"Well-a, how you tough guys like being locked up in jail?"

"I don't like it Papa," answered Mario. "I ain't never gonna do nothin' to go to jail again."

For the moment Vito was silent. "What about you? Vito, you like 'em?"

"Ah, it wasn't too bad. They didn't beat us with rubber hoses or nothin' like that." Defiance and arrogance were still apparent in his voice and gestures.

"No? They no beat you? I guess they forget about that. Well, 'at's all right. I take care of that myself when we get home."

Now both boys turned white with fear and anticipation. They had tasted the broad end of Carlo's leather strap before.

"Vito you go get the leather strap. Take it, and yourselves, out to the kerosene shed. I be out in a minute."

Carlo always had one of the boys handle the thick, leather razor strap to magnify their dread. He used the strap to sharpen his straight razor before shaving. It was three inches wide and an half-inch thick and very stiff. Perfect for sharpening razors and dealing with disobedience. As usual, he left the boys waiting in the shed for about ten minutes to contemplate their fate.

The boys sat on empty wine barrels in the dimly lighted wooden shed in the back yard. The shed leaned perceptibly to the left side. The foul odor of dust, sour grapes and kerosene lent to the discomfort of the entire experience they now faced. The only light available inside the shed passed through the spaces in the clapboards which were dry and cracking. One board had a strategically placed knot hole so that they could see Carlo approaching when the time was right. They heard the back door of the house slam shut and waited while Carlo walked slowly, deliberately, almost ceremoniously the fifty feet of path through the garden to the shed.

"Okay, who's gonna be first?"

They recognized this statement as a test of their courage. They also knew that whoever volunteered was usually shown some mercy and his punishment was diminished. At first no one spoke. Mario waited for Vito to have the opportunity to speak first. But as usual, he refused to volunteer.

"I will, Papa. I'll go first. But I deserve as much as Vito does. We were in this together and . . . "

"No, that ain't true. It was all my idea. I thought it all up myself. And Mario didn't shoot at the old chink but I aimed right for him."

"I see," said Carlo. He was obviously angered and distressed by Vito's lack of penitence.

"Okay, then, Mario, you first."

The boy wrapped both arms around a wooden beam in the center of the shed that held up its dilapidated roof, lowered his pants and undershorts, and protruded his buttocks outward.

Carlo brought his arm back mid-way and administered ten strokes across his buttocks. After the fifth or sixth the boy began to sob softly knowing this would soon bring his sentence to an end. Carlo stopped at ten and the boy stood back by the door with tears running down his face.

Vito's facial expression reflected his thoughts--'Ah, what a sissy.'

"Okay, Mr. Ringleader, you're next."

Vito assumed the same position near the post but hung on in a nonchalant, cavalier manner. The first five or six blows were of moderate force but as it became apparent that Vito wasn't going to show any reaction to the pain the force of the remaining blows became stronger.

Carlo stopped and walked around to where he could see Vito's face. There were no tears, not even a grimace of discomfort.

"You had enough yet?"

Vito didn't answer or even acknowledge the question. He simply raised his chin high and gritted his teeth.

"All right, big shot. If that's the way you want 'em. That's the way it's gonna be."

Carlo took a deep breath and delivered ten more strokes. Still no reaction was forthcoming from Vito.

Carlo was about to deliver more punishment when Mario said, "No, Papa. No more, please. Look," he said pointing to the seat of Vito's trousers where two linear streaks of blood were visible. Carlo relented.

"Now, you both go get your bath and get ready for bed. Tonight you get no supper."

'Nunziata was giving the boys their bath in the large slate double sink in the kitchen. Vito squirmed in discomfort.

"Ouch, that Kirkman's brown soap burns my bottom when in gets in those cuts."

"I know, filio mio, but I know can help it. Here, stand up an' get you backside out of the soapy water. I try to rinse you off with the plain, clean water."

"But then there won't be enough hot water for Mario.," said Vito.

"Oh, he won't mind this one time. Will you Mario?" she asked.

"No, mama, it's okay," said Mario half-heartedly. He kept his real feelings hidden in his thoughts--'Yeah, sure, Vito gets everything. You'd think he was the real son around here instead of me.'

She dried Vito's body with the soft, smooth towel being very careful to pat his buttocks gently to dry them. Mario dried himself with the hard, coarse thin towel with the still barely visible words 'St. George Hotel' on it.

The boys were put to bed without supper as Carlo had ordered. But when he was at the kitchen sink washing up Mama sneaked some Provolone cheese and Italian bread into their bedroom.

Vito took it upon himself to divide the food between them.

"Hey, my pieces are smaller then yours," complained Mario.

"So? Who got the worse beatin'? You or me? So I need it more 'an you. Now shut up before I don't give you any."

They both ate it voraciously.

"Boy, I ain't never gonna make our papa mad as that, not never again. Our butts are gonna hurt for a week.," said Mario.

"Yeah. I ain't never gonna get 'Papa' that made neither," said Vito.

"Hey, you called him Papa. He's gonna like that."

"Yeah, I know. I'm gonna do and say whatever he wants from now on. . . at least when he's around to see and hear. But he still ain't my real papa."

He sat up in bed and grabbed Mario tightly by both shoulders and squeezed hard. "But you better not tell him I said that unless you want to me to break both your arms."

"Don't worry, I won't say nothin'. Let go of my arms you're hurtin' me."

"Just remember that."

They soon dozed off into a deep sleep. Vito vowed to himself to always stay on the good side of his foster parents even if he had to use deception.

"Yeah, I'm gonna be the 'good boy' of this family and I'll get whatever I want."

The Wolves Of Brooklyn

CHAPTER FIVE
The Black Jack

The United States and the rest of the free world was still struggling to hold there own against the superior forces of the Axis consisting of Nazi Germany, Imperial Japan and fascist Italy. The Japanese had recently succeeded, in late February 1942, in pulling off a daring feat when a submarine shelled an oil refinery off the coast of Santa Barbara, California. The populace was becoming more demoralized every day. A moral victory, even if strategically insignificant, was needed to bolster the spirit of the people and F. D. Roosevelt and Winston S. Churchill knew it. Their only task remaining was to find one such act, and to achieve it.

Vito in the meantime began to develop his skills as a diplomat and people-pleaser. The sisters of St. Joseph were the easiest to mislead with the right kind of behavior and Vito had been using this device at school for quite some time.

All eight grades of the parochial catholic schools were still taught by the nuns because religious vocations were still plentiful at the time. St. James' school was considered one of the finest in the borough of Brooklyn and the city of New York. Although the parish was poor, it was favored by the bishop as one of his pro-cathedrals and he

The Wolves Of Brooklyn

made certain enough funds were provided to keep it going. It stood as a symbol of what could be accomplished even with the poor, ignorant immigrants of society with the proper dedication, hard work, and strict discipline of the nuns.

The student body was predominantly Italian-American and Irish-American with a smattering of Poles, Hungarians, and Puerto Ricans. Serious discipline problems were non-existent at the school. And yet, just three blocks away at the the public school, P. S. 5, it was a different world. Zip guns, switch blade knives, straight razors, gang fights and truancy were the order of the day. A public park was located between the two schools which was, therefore, shared by the students of both schools. The nuns didn't like the idea that the two groups of students could mingle after school was out for the day but they had no control over the arrangement. However, during the school day the kids at St. James' School were not permitted out of the school grounds for lunch or for recess period.

"Hey you, punk, come 'ere," said one of the twelve year old bullies from P.S. 5 to Mario.

The young hoolagan-look of the day was characteristic. His long, black hair was greased down with a pompadour in front and the duck's back in the rear. He wore the ominous black leather jacket with the many zipper pockets in the sleeves and the metal snaps on the collar; the black pegged pants with the bright blue stitching in the seams and along the edges of the pockets.

"Who me?" Mario answered.

"Yeah you," he said as he grabbed Mario by the scruff of his neck and squeezed hard.

"What'd ya want?"

"What's your name?"

"My name is Mario Mastrangelo."

"Oh, a wop kid, heh? Well, my name is Butch Brady and I own this park. If you wanna play in here you gotta pay protection."

"Hey you're hurtin' my neck."

"Shut up or I'll hurt more than your neck. You got any money on ya'?"

"No I don't got nothin'."

"What about lunch money. You get lunch money don't ya'?"

"No, I make my own lunch everyday."

"How about milk money? You get milk money don't ya'?"

"Yeah, I get milk money," he said, immediately wishing he had lied.

"Well, I want it. Besides you don't need no milk. Don't you know milk ain't no good for you. It curdles in your stomach". He gave the bully the two nickels for the milk. "Good. I'll meet you outside of school every morning to get that milk money. You better not try to run away or sneak into school or your name will be 'scar face' when I get through with you."

Butch reached into the back pocket of his pants and produced a glistening pearl handled switch blade knife. The snap of the button releasing the six inch, sharp pointed blade added to the fright of the threat, as Butch added, "Remember, tomorrow mornin' in front of the school and you better have the money."

Vito stood to the side observing the incident carefully but without moving or making any comment.

"Hey, you, weasel. Are you with him?" Butch asked Vito.

"Yeah, I'm with him. His my brother. What of it?"

He pulled Vito close to him by the lapels of his coat and shouted into his face, "well, I want your milk money, too. You be there in the morning too, or else."

The Wolves Of Brooklyn

Although Vito was three years younger than the bully he was well built and muscular for his age. But he was still four inches shorter and 20 pounds lighter. Nevertheless, there was no fear in his demeanor and he simply stood face to face with the hood. Butch closed his switch blade knife with a loud metallic click and strode confidently away.

"What are we gonna do Vito? Mama don't always have the money to give us for milk and he said he wants it everyday. If he don't get it that creep means to hurt us, bad."

"Don't worry about it, I'll take care of that bum. He ain't gonna get my milk money or anybody else's. There ain't no way I'll let any Irish Mick get the best of two Italian kids no matter how big he is. One WOP is worth any five shanty Irishmen, any day."

"I don't know, Vito, he's pretty big and he looks real tough. Did you see that stiletto he was carrying'?"

"Yeah, I saw it. But there are ways to bring those big guys down to your size. All you need to do is catch him when he ain't ready and before he can use that switch blade. All we need is some weapon that's faster, and then beat him to the punch. Let's get home and work on it."

They ran home from school in their usual fashion, jumping over the 'Johnny' pumps--otherwise known as fire-hydrants. Vito was always able to jump them without using his hands and could jump the tallest ones that Mario couldn't.

"The adventures of Boston Blackie is on the radio. Let's turn it on while we do our home work," said Vito.

They clicked on the small, table-model, RCA radio in the kitchen and sat at the kitchen table to work their arithmetic problems.

". . . . . after the burglar disarmed Boston Blackie he felt safe in continuing to rifle the bank vault. But when he had his back turned Blackie took off his fedora hat where he had hidden a small blackjack. Quick as a cat he struck the burglar from behind and. . . ." said the commentator.

"Hey, did you hear that? Boston Blackie had a hidden blackjack. That's our answer to Mr. Butch and our milk money," said Vito.

"Oh, yeah. Where're we gonna get a blackjack? smart Alex."

"We'll make one. It ain't nothin' but some lead weight covered with some black stuff."

"And where are we gonna find that kind of stuff?" asked Mario.

"We got it all right here in our house. Quick, let's get the stuff and make it before mama and papa get home from work. Now let's think. Where can we get some heavy weights?"

"I know," replied Mario. "Papa's fishing tackle box. He's got some big lead sinkers in it and he don't use it no more."

"Yeah, that's good. You go get them and I'll find some kind of tube to put them in."

They separated as Vito went into the basement and Mario looked in the junk closet for the tackle box. Several minutes later they met again in the kitchen with their makeshift components. Vito had found some old rubber garden hose and some black friction tape. Mario had a collection of lead fishing sinkers in a variety of sizes.

"Now," said Vito, "first we'll stick all the weights we can into the garden hose."

"Wait. You better cut it into a shorter piece first," said Mario.

"Okay. What, about this long?" Vito said, and cut an eight inch section of the hose with a sharp kitchen knife.

"Yeah, that's good. Just big enough to get a good grip on, and small enough to hide in a coat pocket. It's perfect," said Mario.

The Wolves Of Brooklyn

"Let's put that biggest weight into one end and the smaller weights above it. That way one end'll be smaller and easier to hold on to."

They placed the large, tear-drop shaped 10 ounce weight on one end and the smaller weights toward the other end.

"Wait, this ain't gonna work. The sinkers flop around inside too much," noted Mario.

"Yeah, you're right. Hey, I got an idea. Go get all the BB's that we didn't use in our air rifles."

"Gotcha, Vito. That oughta work."

Mario brought back the pellets and started to pour them into the piece of hose but they fell between the sinkers and out the bottom.

"Wait. Let's take this tape and wrap it over the big end first."

This trick worked perfectly. After the end was sealed with the tape they filled the spaces between the sinkers with the pellets and packed them tightly together by tapping the closed end on the table. The problem of loose weights now solved, they proceeded to wrap the full length of the hose with several layers of the black tape. When it was completed it made a perfect home-made blackjack which fit snugly into the pocket of Vito's Mackinaw jacket.

"Now, let's work out a plan to meet Mr. Butch Brady outside school in the morning.," said Vito.

The following morning Vito and Mario left for school earlier than usual. They were so confident their scheme would work they were anxious to put it into effect. As they approached the school on Jay St., they could see Butch standing across the street, in front of the church, waiting for them. He had one hand in his right, back pocket, caressing his switch blade knife no doubt, with his other hand he was swinging a long key-chain in a vertical circle in front of him. The other end of the chain was fastened to his black leather marine belt. He also seemed confident and fearless, like an Apache Indian Chief looking out over a butte and surveying his domain. His arrogance gave Vito and Mario second thoughts. Beads of perspiration began to appear on their brows and rivulets were trickling down their backs.

"I don't know, Vito. He looks awful scary to me. If he gets out that knife before we can . . . ."

"Shut up and cool it. He won't get the knife out first. You just follow the plan like we talked about and we'll beat this hood at his own game. Just don't chicken out on me."

"Okay, okay. I won't chicken out."

They approached Butch cautiously and hesitatingly. They walked a few feet apart so they could maneuver better. Butch turned to face them, square on.

"Well, well, well, if it ain't the two wop punks. It's a good thing you ain't late or I might have to charge you interest on your protection. Did ya bring the money like I told ya'?'

"Yeah, we got it right here."

"Okay, well let's have it before I fillet you like a flounder."

Mario put his hand in his pockets pretending to be unable to find the coins. As he did so Vito began drifting over to Butch's right side. Then Mario located the money and said, "Oh, here it is. I forget where I put it."

"Just, hurry up and give it here, you stupid wop."

As Mario removed his hand from his pocket he let the coins fall to the sidewalk making every effort to let them fall to the right of the bully so that he'd have to use his right hand to pick them up.

"Ah, you clumsy, greasy daygo. Get out of the way, I'll get 'em."

When Butch bent over to retrieve his booty Mario quickly grabbed his right arm and twisted it up behind Butch's back. He let out a scream of pain. "You no good guinea son-

The Wolves Of Brooklyn

of-bitch. . . " But before he could complete the phrase Vito wielded the blackjack and struck him a savage blow just behind his right ear. Butch fell to the pavement landing on all fours. He started to try to regain his equilibrium and get to his feet. His right hand instinctively and reflexly moved toward the knife in his back pocket.

"Oh, no you don't, you dumb, Irish Mick," yelled Vito as he swung the homemade blackjack in a large arc over his head and dealt a harder blow to Butch's skull. You could hear the bone crack, see the blood and flesh splash under the impact. He fell again to the pavement face down groaning and rolling from side to side holding his head.

"Come on, Vito, pick up the money and let's get out of here before the Sisters see us."

"No, wait, you pick up the money, Mario. I got one more job to finish here."

Vito rolled Butch over on his back, stretched his right hand on the pavement and stepped on his wrist with his foot. He then delivered three vicious blows to the palm of Butch's hand. The cracking sound of the fracturing bones made Mario vomit.

"Now," said Vito. " it'll be a long time before an Irish crumb like you picks on two stronger and smarter Italian kids again."

"You'd better through away that blackjack now. We don't want no body to catch us with it."

"Naw", answered Vito, "this is our equalizer now. It's gonna keep us one step ahead of the hoods. I ain't gonna lose this baby."

Vito wiped the blood off the weapon on Butch's leather jacket then he put it back into his coat pocket until they reached the lockers in the school basement. Then he hid it among his books, sneakers and other assorted junk in the bottom of his locker.

They still had fifteen minutes before classes began so they went to the cafeteria to recover from their ordeal. Mario's stomach still felt a little queasy. They found a remote corner to sit down and Vito got Mario a glass of cold water.

"Here, you better drink this. You look as white as a ghost. Boy wasn't that somethin' the way Butch went down after the first shot to his head. I could feel his skull cave in under the end of the 'jack, and he ain't never gonna used that hand again."

Vito's vivid recollection of the incident was making Mario nauseated again.

"Hey, will ya quit talkin' about it so much. It's over and done with. Let's just try to forget it, will ya." His hands began to shake, the sweat reappeared on his face and his head was pounding like a drum. Vito could see that Mario was disturbed by the reliving of the scene, so he goaded him further.

"Yeah, did ya see the blood and hair on the end of the 'jack," he taunted Mario by dramatizing and saying the descriptive words directly into his face.

"Hey, cut it out will ya. You're just tryin' to make me get sick again."

"What's a matter? can't ya take it."

"But, you hurt him real bad. You could have killed that guy. Don't you know that? Then we'd really be in trouble."

"Who cares. He was just an Irish bum anyway. The world could do with one less of those Mick slobs. And besides, he started it. He picked on us first. If we'd let him get away with that once he would have never stopped."

"Yeah, I know, but he's still a human *bean*. It ain't right to kill nobody, except maybe during a war."

"Oh, yeah. Well if he tries that again I'll hurt him worse 'an that. Next time I'll crush his balls with that blackjack."

Mario began to wretch. He placed one hand over his mouth and the other over his abdomen and ran to the boy's bathroom to throw up. Vito followed him, laughing and taunting him. After a couple of minutes of vomiting Mario felt better, washed his hands and face with cold water and they went to class.

***

Sister Regina stood up on the platform next to the podium waiting for all the children to take their seats. She was a tall, stately looking young woman in her late twenties. She was still slim and robust and had not taken on the portly appearance most of the nuns acquired after a few hard years working with the tough immigrant families. Her face was very pretty with smooth white, slightly glossy skin but with just the right amount of pink color in her cheeks. The large, square shaped headpiece of her habit outlined her face in a rectangle like a picture in a frame. The huge white, oval, stiffly starched front collar reflected the light onto her face which illuminated her beauty. Her figure was fine, trim and full breasted.

When she stood on the platform and spoke all the children stopped and listened. There was no doubt as to who was in charge in this fifth grade classroom.

"All right, children. Everyone will take their seats now. And I mean, right now." With a class of forty-eight, unruly ten-year-olds that was a large order but they complied immediately. Although all the children liked Sister Regina they respected her authority since they had all experienced her wrath when she was angered.

Vito and Mario sat at desks directly in front of the platform, and Sister Regina's desk, instead of the usual arrangement which placed the tallest children in the back rows and the shortest in the front. Mario had engineered the change so he could be closer to the blackboard and could see and hear well. He was the studious one with a real thirst for knowledge. Vito went along with the change to be with Mario.

"Now class, we'll go over the spelling test you had last week. I'll return your test papers and you may take a few minutes to discuss it with your classmate nearest you." She asked Vito and Mario, obviously her favorites, to pass out the papers.

Mario had a grade of 96% with a gold star pasted next to the grade mark. Vito had a 100% with two gold stars pasted next to it.

"Hey, Mario. How'd you do? I got a 100% and two gold stars."

"I got a 96 and one gold star," he answered with that look of disgust with himself for being bested by Vito, again.

"Nice goin'. And stop looking like that. I only beat you by four points and it's no big deal anyway," said Vito, gloating over another triumph.

"Yeah, you always say that but you always beat me."

Mario found this especially irksome since Vito hardly ever studied but always got the best grades while he had to work twice as hard for everything he earned. He would take his books into the bathroom with him and sit on the stool reading and studying for long periods of time. More than once Vito would be awakened by Mario reading with the aid of a flashlight under the blankets long after everyone else was asleep. It seemed everything came so easily and naturally to Vito and with very little effort. Mario also knew Vito sometimes cheated by writing some answers on his hands, wrists or used crib sheets.

"I'll get you next time, though. Our next test is in geography and I'm better than you at that," said Mario, as he smiled trying to hide his disappointment.

The Wolves Of Brooklyn

Sister Regina was walking up and down the aisles of school desks congratulating the good students and consoling the poor ones in an effort to encourage everyone.

"Well, how did my two little geniuses do on their tests?"

Vito immediately stood up in a obsequious show of respect and also because he knew she liked this kind of young gentlemanly behavior.

"We done real good, Sister."

"You mean you did very well, don't you Vito?"

"Yeah. . . . I mean, yes. We did very well, Sister."

"Mario got a ninety-six percent and a gold star."

"Well, that's very good Mario. Now be sure and study the words you missed when you get home so you'll get them right next time."

"And what grade did you get, Vito?" she asked.

"Oh, I did okay too, I guess." The demonstration of false modesty he knew would impress her a great deal, and indeed it did.

"Come on now. What was your grade, exactly?"

"Well, I got a hundred and two gold stars," he mumbled softly.

"Please speak up so the class can hear, also."

He repeated it loudly enough for everyone to hear. The class applauded the accomplishment for what was considered a very difficult test. It was apparent that Vito was a class favorite and a leader. Mario slid down a few inches in his seat and frowned. 'Yeah, sure. Make everybody think you not lovin' every minute of it. Some day I gonna beat you, Vito. I'll beat you at everything and show you up for the phony that you are,' he vowed to himself.

"Now, class, it's recess time. Please proceed to the coat room. It's a bit cool today. Boys through first and when they're all out the girls will follow."

The so called coat room was actually on long narrow closet just wide enough for the children to file through in a single line. Both side walls had coat hooks. It was not lighted inside. When the heavy winter coats occupied the hooks the walking space was quite narrow. Also, the bulk of the coats made it possible for some of the boys to hide under them waiting for the girls when they came through. This was one of Vito's favorite tricks.

"Okay, Mario, this is my chance. I'll go in first and you stay out here. When the girls start through you make some trouble so sister won't notice that I ain't come out yet. Make sure you wait 'til Consuelo gets inside, though."

Consuelo Martinez was a very attractive Puerto Rican girl who was also very well endowed for her age with large, shapely breasts. Vito had had his eye on her for some time.

"Okay, Mario you get in the front of the line. I'll go in last."

"I don't know Vito. What if we get caught?"

"We won't get caught. The plan is perfect."

Mario hesitated.

"And remember," said Vito, "next time will be your turn to get her."

Mario's hidden, smoldering desire began to surface especially since the girls never noticed him nor were they attracted to him as they were to Vito.

"Oh, all right," he agreed, reluctantly.

The boys filed through taking their coats or jackets with them and then returned to their seats waiting for the girls to file through. Vito had hidden himself in a mass of coats about half-way through the closet. When it appeared all the boys had come out the girls began to file through. Mario waited until Consuelo Martinez entered the far end of the closet.

The Wolves Of Brooklyn

"Oh, oh, my stomach," Mario yelled and threw himself to the floor.

Sister Regina immediately came to his aid. "What's the matter, Mario, are you sick?"

Vito could hear the noise and distraction going on outside and waited for Consuelo. When she passed by he emerged from under the coats and grabbed her and kissed her hard while fondling her breasts. At first she feigned resistance, "Don't, Vito. You stop that and leave me alone." But then she responded by letting Vito run his hands over both her breasts inside her bra. After a minute or so they both exited from the closet very flushed and elated. Mario noticed them coming out of the closet.

"Wait, Sister, wait. I think it's over now. Yeah, I'm feeling better now," said Mario, suddenly recovering.

"Are you sure, Mario? Maybe, you'd better go down to see the nurse. You feel awfully hot. You might have a fever."

"Nah, Sister. I'm okay. The pain is all gone now. Really, I feel good now. Look, I can walk around with no pain. It must have just been a gas pain. No foolin' I feel fine."

"Very well then, children, let's put on our coats and proceed to the playground."

Sister Regina began to put on her heavy, black coat and woolen shawl. Vito ran over to help her by holding the coat for her and smiling. He looked over at Consuelo with a satisfied expression. She looked back and smiled. They would have many such interludes in the coat closet in the future before they graduated from the eight grade. Oddly enough Mario's turn at hidding under the coats to wait for Consuelo never came.

Thus began Vito's long, adventurous romantic career. After word got around the school about his little closet trick many of the more aggressive and precocious girls arranged to meet him under the coats.

***

The remainder of the school year passed for Vito and Mario as spring approached and they were looking forward to summer break.

"Oh, boy, only three more days of school until the summer, Vito."

"Yeah, then it's baseball, fistball, Coney Island and wrestling with the girls inside the blankets under the boardwalk."

"Don't you never think of nothin' else?" said Mario.

"Sure, I think of hanging out with the guys and having all the fun we have every summer."

The last three days of the school year were spent cleaning up the school before closing for the summer. All the children and the nuns rolled up their sleeves and scrubbed the building and grounds from top to bottom, inside and out. Even the priests came over from the rectory to help out.

"Hey, Sister, how come we have do all this cleaning? It ain't got nothing to do with teachin' and learnin'," said Mario.

"Mario. . . you mean it has nothing to do with education, don't you?"

"Yes, Sister, that's what I meant."

"Well, it saves the school and the parish thousands of dollars each year. It also shows God that we appreciate his providing us with a nice school and a catholic education with no tuition for your parents to pay, doesn't it?"

"Yeah, I guess so."

"Good. Now that that's settled let's get busy. You boys can start on the windows. I want them sparkling clean inside and outside."

The Wolves Of Brooklyn

The school building was a sturdily built, all brick structure made with durable materials used to withstand the stresses of children of all ages. The classroom windows were large with multiple small panes of glass in each of two panels that slid up and down on pulley chain mechanisms. Each double set of panels reached a height of twelve feet. Each classroom had a row of eight windows on one sidewall to let in all the natural light possible. This construction did cause a small problem when cleaning the glass.

"Please, children, I want you to be very careful when cleaning these windows even though the roof of the gymnasium is only one story down. I don't want anyone leaning outside the windows. And you will clean the upper panel by sitting on the sill and pulling the upper panel down. One of you will hold the legs of the person sitting on the sill as he cleans. And there will be no standing on the window sills. . . . under no circumstances. Do you all understand?"

"Yes, Sister," the class answered in unison.

They all understood, except Harvey Doyle. Harvey was two years older than his classmates and physically the largest in the class. He was a slow learner or 'learning impaired' in modern terminology. But the sisters were helping him through since special classes were unheard of in the 1940's. Harvey always had a far-away, starry-eyed expression on his face. But all the children liked and protected Harvey because, despite his size, he was very gentle and kind. He was also very protective of those he liked.

"Harvey, I want you to watch over the little ones in the class," sister instructed him in gentle tones. "Don't let them carry anything too heavy or strain themselves."

"Yeah, okay Sister. Sure, sure, Sister, I'll watch them. I won't let nothin' happen and not nobody get hurt."

"Thank you, Harvey."

"How come she never corrects the way he talks? She's always doin' that to us," Vito asked.

"Because he's a dummy, you jerk," responded one of the other boys.

"Talk low, will ya?" said Mario. "Do you want him to hear you. And he ain't. . . isn't a dummy. He's just a little. . . slow. Don't ever let me hear you call him a dummy again or I'll bloody your nose," he warned in a rare show of anger.

"Yeah," said Vito, "you better be careful what you say about Mario's special bosom buddy. Harvey keeps him safe from all the tough guys and he don't want none of you pickin' on Harvey. You might hurt his feelings. . .if he had any."

"What'd ya mean? He's got feelings just like anybody else," said Mario.

"No he ain't. Didn't you ever hear that old saying?-- 'no sense, no feeling."

All the kids laughed, mocking Mario and Harvey. But Harvey had missed the jist of the entire conversation and simply smiled, then laughed because everyone else did.

"Come on Harvey. You come with me. We'll work together on these windows by ourselves. We don't need these dummies."

"Yeah, Mario, yeah. We don't need them there dummies, do we?"

The entire class laughed all the louder.

Mario leaned over and reached for the full bucket of soapy water.

"No, Mario, you let me take that. It's too heavy for you to carry."

"It's okay, Harvey, it's not that heavy. I can carry it."

"Oh, no. Oh, no. Sister said I gotta protect you little guys. Yeah, you heard her. She said that. Didn't she Mario? Didn't she say that. . .or did I get it wrong again? I think she said that. Didn't she Mario? Didn't she? Mario." Harvey hung his head in shame and confusion.

The Wolves Of Brooklyn

"Yes, Harvey, that's what she said. You didn't get it wrong. We all heard her say it," said Mario trying to cheer Harvey up. "We all heard Sister Regina say; 'remember class, Harvey is the strongest and bravest one in the whole school. You let him carry the heavy things and let him take care of you.' We all heard her say that, Harvey, really."

Harvey raised his head and smiled with a renewed gleam of pride in his eyes. "Yeah, you're right. She did say that. I heard her, I heard her say that. Didn't I?"

"Yes, Harvey. Yes, you did. We all did."

They then proceeded to wash the windows. Washing first the inside panels standing on a small ladder, when necessary, to reach the higher panes.

"Now, wait, I'm bigger 'an you Mario. Let me stand on the ladder. I don't want you gettin' hurt. Sister'll be mad at me if you got hurt or somethin'," said Harvey.

Harvey went up the ladder to get the upper panels while Mario held the ladder steady for him. The windows were washed with a sponge soaked with soapy water. Then they were wiped dry with newspapers collected by the children from home.

"Okay, Harvey, now we have to clean the outsides. You sit on the sill and I'll slide the window down to your lap. Then I'll hold you by the legs so you can't fall."

"Why, Mario. Why can't I just stand on the sill outside? I can reach it good that way. Why, can't I, Mario. Huh, why?"

"No, Harvey. Didn't you hear what Sister said? Nobody is to stand on the windowsills. It's too dangerous and somebody might fall and get hurt."

"Did Sister Regina say that? Okay. Whatever she said, I'll do. 'Cause I don't want Sister gettin' mad at me. No, sir, I don't."

"You boys are doing a very nice job on those windows," said Sister Regina. "Mario we are going to need more soap. Would you please go over to convent and get some for us. It's under the kitchen sink in the cabinet."

"Who's going to help Harvey and hold his legs?"

"I'll get one of the other boys to help. Here, Michael," she called out, "come here and hold Harvey's legs while Mario runs an errand for me. Thank you."

She then left the room to make her rounds and check on the other classrooms and the progress the children were making.

Vito waited until she had gone and then went over to where Harvey was working.

"Hey, Mike, let's have some fun with the moron."

"Okay, Vito. What'd ya have in mind?"

"You just follow my lead and agree with everything I tell him."

"Hey, Harvey", said Vito, knocking his knuckle on the glass. "What are you doin' it the hard way for?"

"What'd ya mean? Vito."

"It'd be a lot easier to clean the glass if you stood up on the windowsill. And I'll bet you could do a better job. Sister would like that. She would really like it if you made those windows sparkle."

"Yeah, I'll bet you're right. Gee, thanks Vito. I think I'll do that."

"Here, let me help you. I'll raise the window and then you can stand up on the sill." All the children gathered around to watch and giggle at Harvey's blind obedience to Vito's mischievous antics.

Harvey stood up on the sill precariously balanced on the narrow ledge.

"But how, am I gonna hold on, Vito?"

"I tell you what. I'll leave both the panels open a little and then you can hold on by putting your fingers in the space between the two, up there near the lock."

The Wolves Of Brooklyn

"Oh, yeah, okay. I get it Vito. Gee, you're smart. I'm gonna really do a good job and Sister's sure gonna like me, then. Won't she Vito? Heh, won't she?"

"She sure will, Harvey. She'll love you for it."

All the class was laughing softly at Harvey teetering on the ledge. Harvey saw them, smiled back at them and waved with his free hand containing the sponge while his other hand gripped the edge between the two panels.

"Hey, I just thought of somethin'," said Vito. "Watch this. I'm gonna close the bottom panel down on his fingers and he'll have to let go."

"But if you do that he might fall off the ledge," said Michael.

"Naw, he won't fall. Even if he does it's only one floor down to the roof of the gym. He's too big and tough to get hurt anyway."

Mario was just returning from the convent and entering the classroom when Vito began to close the window.

"Wait, Vito. Don't do that. Harvey's holdin' on by the . . . ."

Vito ignored him and began to slowly lower the window as Mario ran and tried to pull him away. But Vito pushed him to the floor and lowered the panel.

"Watch out, Harvey," Mario yelled. "Hold on, hold on."

"High ya, Mario. Look what I'm doin. . .," yelled Harvey just before he fell backward off the sill.

All the girls screamed as they saw him disappear out of sight below the window sill. Vito and Michael laughed loudly but the others suddenly realized the possible consequences of their little prank. Sister Regina reentered the room just as she saw Harvey's head drop out of sight. "Oh, my God, Harvey," she yelled, quickly making the sign of the cross.

Everyone ran to the window as Sister opened it. They looked down to see Harvey sprawled on the roof of the gym. He was not moving and his eyes were closed. His left arm was twisted back under his torso.

"Mario, quick go get Father Reilly and tell him to call an ambulance," she said as she ran toward the stairs.

Everyone was sitting at their desks now frightened about what would follow. Some of the girls were crying and all the boys were solemn, even Vito was afraid. "Gee, I hope he's not hurt. I didn't mean to hurt him. I was just havin' a little fun," he said defending his actions.

"Yeah, sure," said one of the girls, "some way to have fun."

Several minutes passed, although it seemed like hours, as they waited for some word of Harvey's injuries. The classroom door opened and Sister came in . . .with Harvey walking right behind her with his left arm in a sling. All the class stood up and cheered.

"Oh, thank God, you're safe Harvey."

The jubilation of the class astounded him.

"Yeah, high everybody. It's me Harvey. I'm all right. I think I broke my arm but I'm okay. It don't hurt too much. Naw, it don't hurt none at all." The children cheered and applauded.

Vito leaned over toward Mario's desk and commented, "the big jerk is to dumb to even know when he's hurt."

"You just better pray that Papa don't hear what you've done."

"Oh, yeah. Who's gonna tell him, you?"

"You don't scare me, Vito. I know you can beat me up but you still don't scare me none."

"Oh, so now you're a little snitch, too."

"No, I won't snitch on you. But if he asks me if you did it I'll tell him. I won't lie to cover up for you."

The Wolves Of Brooklyn

"Ah, go soak your head in the East River and all the turds and scumbags'll shut you up for good."

When Mario and Vito got back to the tenement Carlo and 'Nunciata were excitedly listening to a news-flash on the radio.

"Come here, boys. Listen to this report. We're showing them Japs somethin'."

CHAPTER SIX
THE HOT SHINE

The allies finally did find and carry out the morale boosting action needed to create some light at the end of the proverbial tunnel, although, the attack had very little, if any, strategic benefit toward winning the war. In a daring bomber raid Major General Jimmy Doolittle bombed the Japanese capital of Tokyo.

But the Japanese, at the time of this bomber attack in 1942, already occupied Corregidor, Mandalay and Bataan. Thousands of American and Phillipino prisoners perished on a forced "Death March" brutally conducted by the Imperial Japanese troops.

***

Spring passed into the usual long, hot summer in the Brooklyn tenements. But the boys utilized the out-of-school-time enjoying themselves in the streets, sand lots and back alleys of the city.

"Now, I don't want you boys wasting your whole summer foolin' around. I expect you to earn some money for yourselves. I no can give you no allowance because all the prices are up and everything is scarce and rationed by the government," said Papa Carlo.

The Wolves Of Brooklyn

"What does rationed mean, Papa?" asked Vito.

"Well, we get a book of coupons each month for the whole family to buy things like butter, eggs, sugar, cigarettes, coffee and that kind of stuff. When the coupons run out you can't buy no more until you get next month's ration book. That makes the prices of all them things go very high. So money's tight."

"Gee, how are we gonna go to Coney Island when its hot if we ain't got the subway fare?"

"Like I say, you gotta earn some money for yourselves."

"But how? We're too young to get any jobs."

"Maybe so. But you can do something else, like. . .like-a shine shoes."

"Where could we do that?" asked Vito.

"That we gotta think about."

"I know where, Papa. How about outside the Navy Yard main gate on Sand Street?" said Mario.

"Yeah, that's-a good thinkin'. There's even more sailors now that the 'Yard' is working three shifts a day and lots of them come out on weekends for liberty. You-a very smart with the ideas, Mario."

"Yeah, sure, he's a real genius," mumbled Vito. Carlo ignored the wise crack as he was learning to do. The less he noticed these remarks the less secondary gain Vito got from them.

"But what about a shine box and supplies. We need shoe polish, shoe cleaner, some rags, brushes and stuff like that. And that takes money," added Vito, who wasn't too keen on having to earn his own money.

"No problem," said Carlo. "Tomorrow we make some shoe-shine- boxes out of the scrap lumber I got and I lend you the money to get your supplies to start with. But you both gotta pay me back when you start making a profit. Agreed boys? What-a you say?"

"Agreed," said Mario. "Yeah, I guess so,"said Vito. "What choice do we have, anyway?"

"Hokay, I go to the cellar and start making the shine boxes and you make a list of the things you need. We have you both all fixed up and ready to start this weekend. I hear a lot a big ships are in. Should be good business with all the sailors on liberty."

Carlo left and went to the cellar to start working and the boys sat at the kitchen table with pencil and paper to prepare their list.

"Gee, this is gonna work out real good. We'll be able to make a lot of money. Maybe I can make enough to buy that new red Schwinn bike I saw in Davega's front window," said Mario.

"Yeah, terrific. What a way to spend a summer. Shinin' shoes for some drunken swabbies from hillbilly country who probably never owned a pair of shoes before they got drafted. It ain't my idea of spending a fun summer. When are we gonna have some fun? What about goin' to the beach, playin' fistball and baseball, and chasin' the girls?" said Vito.

"We'll have time for those things. It'll only be on weekends and holidays that we'll have to shine shoes. And some times it's gonna be slow when their ain't no U. S. Navy ships in the Yard and when the sailors ain't got their monthly pay yet."

"Yeah, I never thought about that. There wallets will be really fat once every month. Yeah, I'll have to talk to 'Little Sallie' about that."

'Little Sallie' Abruzzo was the son of Louie Lupo's bodyguard, 'Big Sallie', and of the same moral character. A real "chip off the old block" in every way.

"Why would you want to talk to him about that?" asked Mario.

The Wolves Of Brooklyn

"That ain't none of your business. Besides you won't understand and I know you won't go along with it."

"Why won't I?"

"Because you're a big chicken, that's why."

Mario let the subject drop since he was sure Vito was up to no good again.

"Let's get these lists of supplies done," he said.

Carlo came up from the cellar with the beginnings of two shine boxes made from old shipping crates from the docks. Each box had a hinged door on the side to put the supplies under a platform. The platform held two wooden blocks so arranged as accommodate a shoed foot with a notch for the heel. He even planned to construct a false bottom inside to hide the days receipts to protect them from any attempts at theft.

"All right, the boxes are started. Now, here is a dollar each for you to buy the things you need. It's not much but it'll have to do. Only buy what you gotta have. The rest you can buy when you start to make money. But--and remember this--you both must pay me back in one month."

"Gee, ain't you gonna charge us no interest?" Vito wise-cracked.

Carlo cuffed him across the side of his head.

"Ow, what'd you do that for?"

"I only take so much guff from you, Mister Smart Alec. Then, enough is too much. You capicé?"

Vito didn't answer. Carlo cuffed him again. "You understand, yes or no?" He raised his hand again waiting for a response.

"Yeah, yeah. Okay I understand."

"I understand. . . what?"

"Yes, . . . Papa. I understand."

"That's-a more like it."

"Now, take the money and go to the hardware store and buy what you need. I gonna work on the boxes. When you get home you do your homework and we make more plans for the business."

"Let's go to Heimie's store," said Vito.

"Why? It's a good five blocks further away than Goldstein's," said Mario.

"Just let's do it. I think I know a way we can get the stuff we need for less money. Then, we can use the rest of it for some fun."

"Okay, if you think we can save money, it's all right with me."

Heimie Abramowitz's hardware store was located on an out-of-the way side street and, thus, the flow of customers was slow and small. Heimie tried to conserve money and keep expenses down as much as possible. Consequently, the store was poorly lighted with only one single bare light bulb of about 40 watts burning just above the ancient hand-cranked cash register. It was so old and used that the raised lettering which once clearly spelled out 'National Cash Register', was now barely visible.

The shelving throughout the store was constructed by Heimie out of scrap lumber from the docks and painted once in what probably was white paint but now had turned to a dull, dirty, dingy gray. The shelves reached almost completely to the ceiling making the lighting even less effective. A customer could easily loose himself in the maze of bins of pipe fittings, electrical supplies, nails and general hardware supplies. But Heimie was keenly aware of this fact and kept a sharp eye out for shoplifters unless, of course, he was distracted by someone.

The boys arrived at the store and Mario started to go in the door.

"Wait, will ya. Wait a minute," said Vito grabbing him by the arm.

"Wait for what?"

"We gotta make a plan first."

The Wolves Of Brooklyn

"What plan? What are ya talkin' about?"

"You wanna save some of the money don't ya?"

"Yeah, but. . . "

"Just shut up and listen. Here's how we'll do it. You go in first and that will ring the little bell on top of the door. But before Heimie comes out of the back I'll crawl in way down low on the floor on my hands and knees."

"Why?"

"So he can't see me, stupid. Then I crawl back behind the shelves to where he keeps the shoe shine stuff and I'll take what we need, except for one can of black shoe polish. You keep him busy for a few minutes 'til I get everything. Then you make him take you back to show you where the polish is kept. Play dumb like you don't know where it is. That shouldn't be too tough for you."

"Listen, Vito. Stop callin' me stupid or I'll leave right now and you'll have to buy everything."

"Okay, okay. I was only kiddin' ya."

Mario opened the door and walked in. The bell suspended from a coiled spring hanging on the door immediately rang. It was a dull, rusty sounding tinkle but enough for Heimie to emerge quickly from the back of the store. Mario stood momentarily holding the door open a few extra seconds to let Vito crawl in.

"Vell, vhat are you standing there for?" asked Heimie in his Russian-Jewish accent.

"Oh, sorry Heimie. I just wasn't sure if you were opened up yet."

"How could I not be open if the door is unlocked and you walked in, already. Such a shlept."

"Yeah, yeah. I guess you're right."

"So what is it you needed?"

"I need some shoe polish, black shoe polish. You know the hard wax kind not the liquid stuff."

"Sure we have that it's right back here," said Heimie and he started to walk from behind the counter.

"But . . . what brands do you have. I think I need a special kind," he said trying to stall as long as possible.

"What brand? We have Griffin and Kiwi."

"Are they very good brands? I want the good stuff."

"Yes, they are very fine brands. Kiwi is a little better and slightly more expensive but it's worth the money."

"Oh, but I don't wanna pay too much. How much is it for each?"

"Well let see," he removed a price list from under the counter and searched for the listings of shoe polish. "The Griffin is twenty-two cents and the Kiwi is thirty-one cents a can."

In the meantime Vito quietly found the articles they needed and began to slip them into his opened shirt front. He took two cans each of brown and black shoe wax, four polish rags, four shine brushes, four bottles of liquid shoe cleaner and four small brushes to apply the cleaner. He could hear Mario and Heimie talking and occasionally peaked around the corner to make sure they weren't yet coming back toward the shelves.

As he started to move he realized that the bottles and cans inside his shirt were hitting each other making a muffled clinking sound. Heimie stopped talking mid-sentence and looked back in that direction. Vito froze.

"What was that noise?" he asked Mario.

"Noise, I didn't hear no noise."

"What were those prices again?"

"Now look here young man. . ."

"Well, I need to know if those are large or small cans. That's all. I ain't buyin' nothin' until I know what I'm gettin'."

"All right, all right. That was the price for the small cans. The large cans are ten cents more each. Such a goy," he mumbled under his breath.

The Wolves Of Brooklyn

"I don't know. . ."

In the interim Vito had removed the cans and bottles from his shirt and wrapped each in the shoe rags to quiet the noise. He again moved but as quietly as possible. No sounds emitted from inside his shirt and he felt more secure.

"Look, you little WOP. I haven't got all day to . . ." then Heimie realized he could loose the first and perhaps the only sale of the day so he tried to calm himself.

"Look, young man. I'll take you back to the shelves. If you like the size and price of the polish you buy it and I'll take two cents off the price. Okay?"

"Okay, let's have a look."

Heimie walked with a slow limping gate back toward the bins. Almost simultaneously, Vito circled around the shelves toward the door making sure he was not in the direct line of sight of them. He slithered slowly and quietly behind a pyramid-stack of paint cans on display near the door. Mario delayed another minute or two debating with Heimie about the cans of polish and finally chose a small can of black shoe polish. They walked back toward the counter which held the ancient cash register.

The real trick was to get out of the door without Vito being seen and without opening the door a second time. Mario thanked Mr. Abramowitz and started to leave. At that same moment Heimie started toward the back room. Mario opened the door slowly and held it open to let Vito crawl out first. But Heimie was so used to the same fixed time interval between the door opening and closing he automatically looked back over his shoulder toward the door just as Vito emerged from behind the paint cans, his shirt bulging with the booty.

"Hey, you little hoodlums. Stop. Come back here!" yelled Heimie.

Vito jumped up to run and deliberately knocked over the stack of paint cans with his leg.

"Come on, Mario, let's get outa here."

Heimie limped toward the door and fell over the paint cans strewn across the threshold.

"Come back, you little 'daygo' crooks. Help, help police," he yelled as he struggled to his feet and hobbled down the sidewalk after the boys. He slipped and fell to the concrete holding an obviously painful leg.

Vito stopped and turned around on the sidewalk to taunt the old man. "Hey, Kike, look what I got," he said as he opened his shirt to reveal all the items he had stolen. "This is one sale you don't make any big profit off poor hardworking people."

"Come on, Vito, let's get out of here. What do you want to aggravate the old man for. We got the stuff. Let's go," he said pulling Vito's shirt sleeve.

"Naw, I just want to rub the old Hebs nose in it."

Just then two pedestrians dressed in the traditional garb of the orthodox Jewish faith turned the corner, saw Heimie on the pavement and ran to his aid.

"Come let's get out of here before they call the cops," said Mario.

"Aw, let 'em. We'll be home before the flat-feet can get here, anyway."

The boys turned up and alley, headed away from their neighborhood for a few blocks then doubled back behind the hardware store to deceive the witnesses.

"Look at all this stuff. We got enough for our shine boxes and still got most of the two dollars left to spend. Now that's what I call the right way to shop." They laughed and strolled calmly home.

***

The Wolves Of Brooklyn

The following weekend the boys were ready for their first adventure into the the world of business. It was payday for the sailors on liberty and many ships were in port, including the huge air craft carrier Hornet and the battleship Missouri. Carlo had completed the shoe boxes painted in red, white and blue except for the words "10¢ a shine; Spit Shine 20¢; Hot Shine 25¢" painted in black letters on the side.

"Hey Vito, where do ya think we oughta set up shop?" said Mario.

"Ah, I guess anyplace will be as good as any other."

"Naw, I think we need to be as close the main gate as possible and where most of the sailors come out."

"Then there's only one place. That'd be next to the cathouse run by the gypsies, two blocks up the street."

"No, you know we can't do that. Papa said we had to stay away from those bad places like that and the saloons."

"Yeah, I know he said that but he wouldn't have to know anything. He'd just notice how much money we brought home," said Vito.

"Well, you can go their if you want. I goin' in front of Max Cohn's tailor shop. The sailors are always stopping there to get their uniforms cleaned and their ties pressed."

"You go where you want. I'm goin' to the front of the whorehouse. Who knows, maybe one of the ladies will give me a free sample," said Vito with a mischievous chuckle.

"You better not. Mama says those girls carry a lot of diseases. Bad diseases."

"Ah, go on. We better go home together, though. I'll meet you at Nick the Greek's restaurant around 6 o'clock. And don't take any wooden nickels. Hah, hah."

Mario walked quickly and with great anticipation toward the tailor shop. Max was just opening up the front door and letting down the green and white stripped awning over the large front window.

"Good morning Mr. Cohn," said Mario.

"Good morning, young man. What brings you out so early in the morning?"

"Oh, I gonna catch the sailors coming out of the main gate early to sell them a shoe shine."

"So, I see. That's a very patriotic shine box you have their."

"Yeah, thanks. My papa made it. He thought it would make the sailors and marines take notice easier."

"That makes very good business sense. Your papa's a *shmart* man. And what do you plan to do with all the money you're going to make in this thriving business?"

"Well, Papa says we need it for living expenses. But I heard him talking to Mama the other night when they thought we were asleep. He's goin' to save and maybe invest it to use for college tuition for me and my brother Vito."

"Ah, ha. Very wise man is your papa, also."

"A. . . A, Mr. Cohn. . ."

"Yes, what's your name, anyway?"

"Mario, Mario Mastrangelo, sir."

"Ah, a good Italian name. From the old world like me. What did you want to ask me? Don't be shy, young man. That will never do in business."

"Yes, sir. Well. . . I was wondering if it would be all right if I set up my shoe shine spot in front of your store. I won't bother nobody, I promise. And, I'll give you. . . ten percent of what I make."

"You have a very good business head, too. Sure, it's okay. You can set up in front of the store. And stay under the awning out of the sun. The customers will like that. We'll talk later about that commission."

"Why, isn't ten percent enough? I could raise it, a little bit anyway."

The Wolves Of Brooklyn

"Don't worry about that now. You start making some money. We'll discuss it later, Mario."

"Yes, sir."

***

Three blocks away, on the upper part of Sand Street, Vito had set up his spot in front of the store-front building the gypsies and their pimp used to show their wares. The girls sat just inside the store in front of the large display window with spot lights on them. Some sat with their legs crossed and their skirts high above their knees. Others sat in profile if they were well endowed with large breasts. Still others danced in a slow, tantalizing, hip-swinging dance to imaginary music.

"Yeah, oh yeah. I got me the best spot in the whole Navy Yard district. Ain't no sailor or marine gonna miss stoppin' here. That's when we get them. First the shine then the roll," Vito said to himself.

Janos Corvinus, the gypsy pimp, known on Sand Street as 'King Janos', noticed Vito setting up his shoe box in front of his store. His first inclination was to chase him away.

"Hey, kid what da ya think you're doing in front of my place?" he said in his thick Hungarian accent.

"What's a matter, are you blind? I gonna shine shoes here."

"Oh, yeah, who said you could?"

"Well, seeing how this here is a public sidewalk and city property, who's gonna stop me."

He grabbed Vito by the scruff of the neck, turned him around and held him by the lapels of his coat close to his face at eye level . "I'm gonna stop you, smart ass."

"Oh, yeah. Then I guess I'll have to call the cops and show them your little cathouse set up here."

"It ain't no cathouse. It's a. . . , it's a dating service."

"Okay, if you wanna call it that. Then where's your city license. Every business's gotta have a license. That's if it's legit."

He slowly lowered Vito back down to the pavement. "You're a pretty smart kid. And you got moxie, too. I like that. Tell ya what. I'm gonna let you set up your shoeshine spot here. Who knows, it might be good for business. Speakin' of which, do you have a license to run your legit business?"

Vito began to sweat. "It's . . . it's pending. I applied for it last week."

"Yeah, yeah, sure you did. Tell ya what. You forget about my license and I'll forget about yours. But you give me twenty percent of your take."

"Not on your life. I'll give you five percent."

"Fifteen percent, kid. Take it or leave it. If you don't take it you can find another spot."

"I'll go twelve and a half, and that's it."

"Okay, you got yourself a deal, partner. Let's shake on it."

They shook hands and Vito stationed himself just to the right of the large plate glass window, next to the front door. It was Friday night and the sailors were beginning to exit the Sand Street gate in ever increasing numbers. The shoe shine business was good for both Mario and Vito. But Vito was getting bored with the slow action and the small intake of money.

"Hey there, sailors. How about a shine? The best shine in the borough of Brooklyn. No, best shine in the whole city of New York. Guaranteed to make the girls come runnin' after ya' when they see ya'." Vito called, as three ordinary seamen walked by the gypsy store.

"Sure kid, why not? How much is it for this great shoeshine of yours?"

"Well, it depends on the kind of shine you want. I got this 'regular shine' for a dime. Then there's my special 'spit shine' for fifteen cents. Then I got this stupendous, super colossal, flaming "hot shine" for a quarter. None of them prices include tip, though."

"Yeah. Well, I just got in from the South Pacific and I almost got my head blown off. But I'm back, and I got a fat paycheck, and I'm lookin' to have a hot time," he said in his southern drawl. "I'll take that hot shine of yours."

Vito was all wound up and raring to go especially when he saw the wad of twenty dollar bills bulging out of the sailors wallet. The navy men had a habit of carrying their wallets in the waist of their trousers. They didn't have much choice since the traditional thirteen button, bell bottom trousers didn't have any pockets. Half of the wallet was stuck into the waist band and the other half hung down over the outside. It made for real easy snatching by the many pick-pockets who knew the sailors habits well. Vito was well versed in their habits, vices and weakness. He intended to put his knowledge to profitable use.

Janos came out of his establishment to sell his wares to the sailors as they had their shoes shined.

"Ah, Captain, you look like a fun loving gentlemen. Why don't you come inside when you're done with the guinea-kid and I'll introduce you to some fine ladies I think you'll like."

"Oh, yeah, do you think I want to get a case of the 'clap'?"

"No, no clap. My girls are real clean. The doctor checks them every week."

"You don't have to worry, sailor," Vito chimed in. "This here is the cleanest cathouse in the whole Navy Yard district. I swear. My father even uses it once in a while. I mean it."

The seaman was convinced. He and his companions went right into Janos' house after the shoeshines.

"Hey, little guinea kid. You're okay. I like the way you help my business. You can set up your shine stand here anytime. And you can forget about my cut of your take. Just keep pitching my house to the swabbies."

"Terrific," Vito shouted. "I just saved myself twelve and a half percent of my take with a little cheap advertising.

***

"Where is that 'Little Sallie'? I asked him to meet me here an hour ago," Vito muttered to himself. "There are a lotta swabbies here with real fat wallets."

"Hey, little paesano," he heard Little Sallie's raspy voice calling out from a half block away.

Little Sallie Abruzzo was by no means small of stature. He was built very much like his father, Big Sallie. Big Sallie was the personal chief bodyguard of the local bookie and Mafia captain, Louie Lupo-the Wolf.

'Big Sallie' was grooming his son to follow in his footsteps as Lupo's chief bodyguard. Although Little Sallie was only fifteen years old, his father had made him work on the docks as a longshoreman after school and during the summer until Sallie Jr. was able to legally quit school at age sixteen. He also taught him all the tricks of street fighting and mugging. He considered it an art to disable a man bigger than himself without leaving any tell-tale visible marks. At the same time, he had to learn the technique of going just far enough without killing his adversary.

At age fifteen Little Sallie was only five foot, six inches tall but weighed a solid, muscular two hundred pounds. His head, somewhat squared, was covered with thick, black curly hair. He had a beard as dense and dark as a man who had been shaving for twenty years. Even right after shaving with his father's straight-razor he looked like he had 'five o'clock shadow'. Tufts of thick black, curly hair were visible protruding above his shirt collar and from under his shirt cuffs. Everyone said he was the spitting image of his papa, Big Sallie, and twice as mean.

"It's about time. Where ya' been? I've been waitin' for ya' for an hour," said Vito.

"So what's ya big hurry? These swabbies ain't runnin' away. There's plenty of time to roll 'em and get their dough."

"Keep it down will ya'. I don't want Janos to hear our angle. He'll wanna get his cut. He's a greedy one."

"How do ya' wanna work this thing, Sallie?"

"It's real easy. You gotta wait till a sailor or marine comes along by himself. If there's more than one it's tougher to handle them both at once. You ask him if he wants a shine and when he pays you for it you check out his wallet. If it's real fat and it's got some big bills like fifties or even 'C' notes you just give me the high sign--just take off your cap and put it on the sidewalk. I'll stand across the street in front of that 'Army and Navy' store like I'm minding my own business."

"But where are ya gonna jump him?"

"I'm comin' to that, hold your horses. After I get the sign you tell him there's some nice clean whores, white girls, he can get for free. Then you send him up the alley behind the saloon and I'll be waitin' for him. He won't know what hit him. Then later we'll split up the take."

"Yeah, sounds okay. It'll work. By the way what's my cut gonna be of the roll?"

"Ah, let's see. Twenty-five percent for you and the rest for me."

"No deal. I set up this whole thing. It was all my idea. I want fifty percent."

"Now wait a minute, punk. I'm doin' all the hard work and takin' all the risks beating up these sailors and marines. Some of them is pretty tough and mean. I'll let ya have thirty percent and that's my last offer."

"No good, I want forty five percent."

"Forty percent, and that's it."

"Okay, it's a deal. A sixty - forty split sounds good."

"Done. I'll go across the street and act like I'm readin' the newspaper."

"Yeah, okay."

'Who's he think he's kidding. He can't read his own name,' Vito thought to himself.

"Oh, boy, here comes the first sucker. A sailor all by himself just beggin' to be plucked. Hey, sailor how about a shine.?

"Sure, little mate. Why not?"

***

In the meantime Mario had set up his shine box under Max Cohn's tailor shop awning. He had borrowed a chair from Mr. Cohn so the customers could sit comfortably while having their shoes shined. When he saw a prospective customer coming he moved up the sidewalk to meet him.

"Hi, sailor. How are ya' today? What about a nice shine for your shoes. It'll make a good impression on your C. O. And, and it helps protect the leather, real good. Please, mate. What'd ya say?"

Most often he would charm them into accepting. Although he was slight of build, even skinny, there was a glint in his eye and a sparkle of honesty that made people trust him immediately.

"Where're you from, mister? Oh, California. Hey, I hear that's a swell state. Lots of sun and the ocean and the beaches. I'll bet you miss home a lot." He could engage anyone in conversion and showed keen interest in their backgrounds and their need to feel welcomed in a strange city. Mario gave them a run down on the local sites and highlights of Brooklyn and the city of New York. His manner was so engaging and endearing he always got a big tip.

The Wolves Of Brooklyn

Max Cohn watch with sincere interest in Mario's business-like acumen and demeanor.

"Young man, Mario, come here a minute. You have a good way with people. They like you right away. That's good. You're going to very successful someday. That's a prediction from Rabbi Max Cohn. Mark my words. . . some day."

"Thanks Mr. Cohn."

"Call me, Max. Please."

"Okay, Max, sir." Cohn smiled in recognition of the automatic respect Mario paid his elders.

"I was just wonderin', how much do you charge to press, say, a sailors neck tie?" asked Mario.

"Oh, usually just twenty-five cents to press, without dry cleaning. Fifty cents with dry cleaning. Why?"

"Well, I thought you might like some business, too. If I could talk the sailors into letting you press their neckties and maybe you'd give me, say, a nickel for each. Is that fair?"

"It is more than fair. As a matter of fact it is too fair. I'll give you a dime for each tie. And if you can talk them into having their entire uniform dry cleaned and pressed while they wait I'll give you. . . ten percent. That costs them two-dollars and fifty cents. You get twenty-five cents for each. What'd ya say? A deal."

"You betcha. It's a deal," said Mario.

As the day progressed Vito and Janos, Mario and Max Cohn were very busy. Two more warships had docked and the sailors and marines poured through the Sand Street gate by the hundreds. The gate itself reminded Mario of the entrance to a castle like those he had read about in books. The archway of the gate was constructed of the same dull gray granite stone that formed a wall around the entire Brooklyn Navy Yard. Jagged pieces of glass standing on edge were embedded into a thin layer of concrete on the top of the wall to discourage any would-be climbers and spies. The gate had a large entrance for vehicles, and two smaller revolving entrances for pedestrians. The vehicle gate was made of tough black wrought iron bars two inches in diameter. At the top and bottom, each bar was forged into a flat point like a spear and the edges were honed razor sharp.

The pedestrian entrances were intricate affairs also made of wrought iron bars. The bars were placed horizontally and revolved around a central point and through the spaces between another set of stationary bars of the same size. It extended to within six inches of the top of the wall and four inches above the sidewalk at the bottom. It reminded Mario of the exit gates at some of the subway stations except they were much more sturdy.

There were two armed Marine M.P's at the vehicle gate which remained closed at all times unless a vehicle passed through. Each pedestrian gate also had two armed guards on duty at all times. One guard was stationed on the inside and one on the outside. Four other guards stood station on the top of the wall just above the gate armed with the powerful M-1 rifle, a 45-caliber side arm, and a night stick. Two hand grenades hung from the garrison belt of each guard. A water cooled machine gun mounted on a tripod and surrounded by several tiers of sandbags stood unattended over the center of the gate. The bandoleer of 50 caliber rounds could be seen hanging from the magazine ready for action with a single pull of the lever.

The entire atmosphere with the secrecy, security, and weapons, frightened Mario a little bit. It made him realize the possible dangers of living so close to a military instillation which might attract spies, saboteurs or even enemy bombers.

Vito, on the other hand, was fascinated by the whole affair. Especially the guns and other armaments. He enjoyed

The Wolves Of Brooklyn

the air of superiority and power which the weapons seemed to give their bearers. He vowed that someday he would own a 45-caliber automatic pistol or maybe even a Thompson submachine gun.

"Hey, squirt. How'd you do today? Did you make any money?" asked Vito as he strolled toward Mario's spot in front of the tailor shop.

"I told you a million times, Vito, don't call me *squirt*."

"Yeah, yeah, don't get excited. Hold your water will ya'. I was only kiddin', you know."

"So, how much gilt did you make, you and the Heb tailor?"

Mario reached into his pocket and proudly produced eighteen dollars and seventy-five cents.

"You made all that dough just from shinin' shoes?"

"No, Mr. Cohen and me had a little deal goin'. If I got the sailors to have their clothes or ties cleaned and pressed he gave me a cut of the take. Pretty good scheme, heh?"

"Yeah, you bet. Not a bad scheme."

"How'd you do, Vito?"

"Well, I did pretty good too", he said and started to walk off toward home. He just knew Mario would have to ask to show him how much money he had earned.

"What'd ya mean pretty good? How much? Heh, how much? Come on Vito don't play games with me. You made more than I did, didn't ya?"

"Maybe, yes. Maybe, no."

"Come on now, Vito. Don't torment me like that", said Mario as he felt the anger and frustration well up inside him. He rushed Vito from behind and wrapped one arm around his neck, reached his other hand into Vito's pocket to remove the money. He had Vito at a rare but distinct disadvantage and was ready to press it.

"Let go of my neck, punk, or so help me I'll kill ya", Vito muttered in strangled tones. Mario could see the real surge of anger in his face and eyes. "I mean it, Mario. Let go, or else."

Mario relaxed his grip and took his hand out of Vito's pocket. He was astonished at that amount of strength he could arouse through his anger and frustration. He could have forced Vito to yield, he thought, but he backed off to savor and digest this unusual show of power.

Vito straightened himself up and said, smugly, "If ya' really gotta know I made this much." He held out his hand full a bills including an obvious twenty dollar bill and at least two fives.

"Holy cow! How much is there?"

"Why don't you count it for me and found out?"

Mario started to reach for the cash but hesitated, "I don't wanna count your money. Count it yourself. What do I look like, your bookkeeper?"

"Twenty, twenty-five, thirty, thirty-six, thirty eight", Vito counted aloud and very deliberately, "and seventy-five cents. Thirty-eight dollars and seventy-five cents. Not a bad day, heh?" he concluded, beaming with triumphant.

"You made all that loot on shining shoes? I don't believe ya," said Mario.

"Course not, you dummy. Shining shoes is for niggers. Not for Vito Vitale."

"Then where'd the rest come from? Did you steal it? I hope not, 'cause if you did Papa's gonna kill ya'."

"Nah, I didn't steal it. Me and Janos had a deal going too. If I steered some suckers into his whorehouse he'd give me a cut of his take. It was a real busy evenin' with all the ships comin' in, and all." Of course, he didn't show Mario the fifty dollars hidden in his shoe as part of the take from the sailors 'Little Sallie' had mugged.

"We'd better get home now. It's gettin' late. I can't wait to show Papa and Mama all the money we made. There gonna be real proud of us. Heh, Vito, what'd ya think?"

The Wolves Of Brooklyn

"Yeah, well, I don't want 'em to be too proud."

"What'd ya mean?"

"I think I'll keep a few bucks for myself. They won't never know no difference. I think I'll keep . . . ten bucks for myself to spend. Twenty-eight, seventy-five ain't bad for a take-home bundle. I wish I could keep it all. I earned it and I should."

"Did you forget we had to pay Papa back for the supplies he lent us the money for? We have to give him that much, you know."

"Yeah, I know. But I want the rest of my dough put in a bank account in my name. I don't want nobody to take my money. Least of all, Papa."

"What are ya' gonna do with that extra ten bucks you kept."

"Well, wouldn't you like to know so you could tell Papa."

"Nah, you jerk. I don't really care what you do with it. Stick it up your nose, if you want. I don't tell Papa everything, you know."

"Oh, no, but almost everything."

"We better get home now. You know how mad Mama gets if we come late for supper."

"No, you go ahead without me, Mario. I gotta run an errand before I come home."

"What errand?"

"It ain't none of your business. Do you gotta know everything. Just go home. I'll be there in a little while."

Mario turned left at the corner of Gold and Sand Streets and headed toward their tenement. Vito continued up Sand Street toward the YMCA but his primary destination was the Army-Navy store. He had seen a nice set of rosary beads in the window that he knew his Mama would like. By coincidence he had also noticed a brand new, shiny switchblade knife with a pearl handle with a silver inlaid anchor set in it.

The so called 'Army-Navy' store was supposed to carry surplus, government military goods, such as clothes, tents, and other camping equipment. And it did have its assortment of these items but it also carried some souvenir and tourist type articles for the servicemen to bring home to family and friends. It was strategically located right next door to the YMCA building where many of the sailors and marines congregated for social events. It also contained many hotel rooms they could rent by the night, week or month.

The large plate glass, storefront windows of the store were dimly lighted, even at night, which lent a certain mystique of secrecy to the shop. The display contained the usual collection of second hand uniforms, military brass and water canteens. But right up front, catching the infrequent sunlight that fell on them, were displayed the pocket knives, gaudy jewelry, silk scarves decorated with Japanese dragons, identification wrist and ankle bracelets, and other eye catching wares to lure in the customers.

Vito went into the shop even though it appeared to be closed because of the poor lighting. But the sign hanging the door said, 'Open 24 Hrs.' As he entered a battery powered electric buzzer sounded announcing his admittance. The back of the shop was not visible through the wall of navy blue and khaki colored uniforms hanging from the ceiling as well as from racks cluttering every square inch of floor space. Even the walls were entirely covered with the dark uniforms except for an occasional white, ordinary seaman's blouse or officer's jacket. He wondered why there were so few white uniforms displayed even in the summer time.

The front ten feet of space, however, was occupied by two large glass display cases with sliding glass doors which were sealed by lock and key. These contained

The Wolves Of Brooklyn

more of the eye catching merchandise, like in the front window, except the selection and numbers of items was much greater. One long, naked incandescent lamp with its yellow wire filament visible spewed concentrated light on these items with their highly polished brass, bronze, silver, and even occasionally real gold, surfaces. The glinting, sparkling reflections dazzled the eyes of young men, and boys like Vito.

Like most businesses near the Navy Yard—except for the restaurants run by the Greeks and the whorehouses run by the Gypsies—it was run by a small, elderly Jew dressed in his orthodox black suit and large black hat. Very little of his face was visible because of the large gray beard, mustache, bushy eyebrows and dark rimmed spectacles. He did wear a black tie and a white shirt. It reminded Vito of the occasional white uniform among all the dark ones.

Only the young Jews seemed to be clean shaven. They even sometimes wore contemporary clothes like a plead shirt, or an argyle sweater, or a pair of blue or brown slacks. But they never wore any blue jeans--commonly called dungarees. Always, however, with the black skullcap--the yarmulke. And the yarmulkes were always black, except for when worn during wedding ceremonies. Vito couldn't understand these people anyway. He just knew he shouldn't trust them. At least that's what his dead, biological father used to tell him. His adopted parents, however, never preached this to him.

"What can I do for you, young man?" said the storekeeper.

"I wanna buy some of those silver rosary beads you have in the window. They're for my mama. . . my foster mother." 'A Christ-killer selling rosary beads, ha. It just proves you can't trust none of them.' thought Vito.

"Certainly, certainly, young man. We have several nice ones. Some with black beads, white beads or colored beads. Even some with silver beads but, of course, they are more expensive."

"Let me see one of the ones with white beads. I don't really like black. . . ones, too much. Beads, I mean." Vito looked away from the old man's eyes and bent over to look into the glass display case.

"I see, as you wish," said the proprietor without flinching.

"Ah, yes. These are very nice. The chain and cross are silver plated. And notice the authentic details of the nail heads in the hands and feet." Again he didn't waver or flatten out his best salesman's smile.

'Yeah, I'll bet you think that's real nice. Don't you. Almost like the real thing, huh,' Vito thought to himself.

"Don't ya have no real, solid silver ones instead of silver plated?"

"No, I'm afraid not. We don't get much call for them. They are too expensive for most. . .Catholics."

'Almost said wops, or daygos, or guineas or somethin', didn't ya?' thought Vito.

"How much are you askin' for them and how much are they really worth?"

"Now, young man, I have to make a small profit to stay in business. Don't I?"

"Never mind that crap, just tell me how much you want for them."

"Ordinarily, we get five dollars and ninety-five cents. Plus tax."

'Yeah, you mean six bucks. Why do they do that? Drop it down one cent to make it seem less than six bucks. More of their Kike tricks. It don't fool me none.'

"But since they are for your mama I'll let you have them for. . . say. . . five, forty-nine." Vito stepped back and winced as if repelled by a suddenly, strong pungent odor.

The Wolves Of Brooklyn

"Whoa, that's pretty steep ain't it. I don't imagine you sell too many of these. I'll bet you don't get one . . . catholic a month comes in here to buy anything, let alone rosary beads."

"Now that's where you are wrong. I have many . . .catholic neighbors and friends. And they come in my shop very frequently."

"Okay, I'll tell what I'll do. I'll buy them for that price if you sell me a switch blade knife, too."

"For the price that it's marked?" said the proprietor.

"Yeah, for the price that's on it."

The old shopkeeper stopped for a moment of thought. Then he came out from behind the counter and went out the front door of the shop. He leaned out the door from the top step of the entrance and looked up and down the block. Then he glanced over to the alley across the street. He stepped out to the edge of the curb where he could see into the large main entrance to the YMCA, a dozen yards away. Strolling casually back to the store he checked up and down the street again looking for the familiar green and white New York city police patrol cars. Seeing nothing suspicious he strolled back inside.

While the old man was outside checking the streets Vito thought of a way he could possibly get everything for nothing. The sliding glass door to the display case was left unlocked and opened. If he could only go around and reach in to get one of the switch blade knives before the old man came back. Then he could open the blade and put under the man's chin and threaten to cut his throat if he shouted or resisted. While the old man was still startled and frightened Vito could run out the door with the loot. As he began to move to the other side of the counter he heard a noise from behind the rows of coats and uniforms hanging in the back of the shop.

At first he couldn't see anyone. Then, running his eyes along the floor under the long trench coats his gaze suddenly stopped at a barely visible pair of dark brown shoes, blue argyle socks and the cuffs of a pair of dark brown slacks. Just as he raised his glance upward to search the dark shadows a younger, about seventeen years old, Jewish boy stepped out from behind the parted coats. His face was clean shaven, his crew cut hair had the black yarmulke in the center. A moderately obese belly could be readily seen under his green plead shirt and the navy blue sweater over it. The shirt collar was buttoned up snugly under his double chin but he wore no tie. The cuffs of his slacks were at least six inches above his shoe tops.

"Is someone taking care of you? kid."

"Yeah . . . yeah. Your grandpa. . . he is. I think he just stepped outside for a minute. Here he comes now. He's comin' back in now. Thanks."

"He's my papa, not my grandpa. He may look old and feeble and helpless. But I'm not. . . helpless, I mean."

Vito slowly backed up the two steps around to the front of the display case. The old proprietor came back inside.

"Sammy, what are you doing out in front? Is something wrong?"

"No, Papa, Nothing's wrong. I just came out to help with this . . . customer while you were outside."

"Oh, thank you, but I can finish this up now. You may go back inside. Go, go. Go back to your studies." The young man stepped back and disappeared into the sea of garments.

"All right young man. As we agreed, the rosary and the switch blade knife for the list price."

Vito took the roll of bills out of his back pocket and peeled off the twenty dollar bill as the man's eyes opened

The Wolves Of Brooklyn

wide glaring at the large amount of money he was sure was not legally obtained by so young a . . . guinea hoodlum.

As Vito left the Army-Navy store he glanced back as the door closed and he saw the sign flipped over to the other side which said, "CLOSED. BE BACK SOON."

CHAPTER SEVEN
THE GREAT CAT HUNT

The year of our lord, 1943, produced a series of conflicting milestones for Americans, Brooklynites and the rest of the free world. After smashingly successful victories on the eastern front, the German Weirmacht began its slow, but steady, retreat from Russia surrendering in Rostov, Kharkov, and Stalingrad.

More seeds of immortality were sewn for the borough of Brooklyn when Betty Smith's classic novel, *A Tree Grows in Brooklyn*, was published. Brooklyn at this time boasted having the fourth largest urban population in the world with four and one-half million souls. Many of them Italian-Americans.

Italy surrendered to General Eisenhower's forces on September 8. Beneto Mussolini deposed political leader of Italy and the new government in Rome declares war on Germany.

Thousands of American servicemen died defending the stars and stripes, and in recapturing Guadalcanal; sinking a 22-Japanese warship convoy in the Battle of the Bismarck Sea; landing in New Guinea; and recapturing the Aleutian islands.

The Wolves Of Brooklyn

The U.S. Supreme Court rules that school children need not salute the American flag in schools if it is against their religion.

October 16,1943, Mario and Vito celebrate their tenth birthday.

Carlo gave each of them a metal lapel pin replica of the American flag he bought at the American Legion post.

"Hey, Vito you know Papa's birthday is coming up soon. What'd ya think we oughta get him for a gift? I'd like to make it somethin' really special. What'd ya say?"

"Well, since it's Halloween, too, maybe we could get him a new broom to fly on and when he lands we can throw a bucket of water on him. Ha, ha, ha. Hey, that's a good one, ain't it. You know, like Dorothy in the Wizard of Oz."

"Yeh, yeh. Very funny. If it wasn't for him you might be livin' in an orphanage right now. Or maybe you woulda been sent back to Italy to live under Mussolini. You coulda seen the whole World War, if you lived through all the bombs and everything." Vito clenched his fist and gritted his teeth but didn't otherwise react.

Halloween night and Carlo's birthday arrived with very little fanfare. Nancy, as Annunciata now called herself to be more Americanized, planned a small party for the family and close friends. She served espresso coffee and rum soaked cake for the adults, coke for the kids.

Mario bought Carlo a carton of 'Lucky Strike' cigarettes, Carlo's favorite brand. He had to beg, borrow and buy a lot a ration stamps from everybody so he could purchase them on the black market. Carmine and Chico, his older brothers, had helped since Mario had no access to the black market himself. He signed the birthday card, from 'Your loving sons, Mario and Vito.'

But Vito was angry when he read it because he didn't give Mario any money for the gift and didn't want his name on the card. But, what was done, was done.

"Come on Mario, it's Halloween. Let's go out and do some trick or treat. But mostly trick, if you know what I mean."

"Is it okay? Papa. After all it is your birthday?" asked Mario.

"If-a you Mama say it's okay, it's okay with me. Kids shoulda have fun on Halloween . No be out too late and no make no trouble. You capicé?"

"Yes, Papa." Mario answered but Vito stood silent and pretended not to hear.

"You capicé?" he repeated again in a louder, harsher tone."Vito. . . ?

Vito hesitated, then he said, "Yeah. . . I understand."

"Come on, let's find the gang and make some trouble," said Vito.

"I thought you wanted to go trick or treat?" Mario replied.

"Sure that's what all the sissy kids do. Anybody can get candy and junk on Halloween. The real fun comes from ringing doorbells, soaping up windows and kickin' over garbage cans. Besides, if we want candy we can always steal it from the store. Come on, let's meet up with the gang."

'The gang', so called, was started by Vito and organized as an athletic club for their summer baseball and fist-ball teams. They were called the High Street 'Wolves', at Vito's insistence. His strong will dominated the eight members of the club. The name was the English translation of the sir name of the local bookie and Mafia boss, Louie Lupo. This two-bit-mobster was Vito's idol, his role model.

The other members of the club were Pattie Flanagan, Joey and Dommie (Dominic) Torelli, Tony Carlucci, Juan Santiago, Iggie (Ignatio) Fortunata and Harvey Doyle who functioned as bat boy, scorekeeper, mascot and water

The Wolves Of Brooklyn

boy since his mental impairment made him incapable of following the game.

"Where are we gonna meet them?" said Mario.

"I called a meeting for 8 o'clock tonight in front of Mr. Lupo's barber shop. I told everybody to bring a bar of Kirkman's brown soap, a lot of chalk, a lady's silk stocking, a bag of flour, and a broomstick sawed in half."

"That's the usual Halloween stuff Vito, except for the broomstick. What's that for?"

"You'll see. Just wait and you'll see."

"I told them not to wear their team uniforms, neither."

"How come?"

"So nobody would know who we are, you dope."

The team uniforms, which consisted of a black jersey with yellow lettering and yellow trim, short yellow sleeves, and black jeans with yellow trim, were well known in the neighborhood. The name 'Wolves' was written out in cursive on the front and a large team number was sewn on the back. Also, on the front over the left breast pocket, was written in small letters a nick name which corresponded with the member's favorite player on the then Brooklyn Dodgers National League baseball team.

Pattie Flanagan was the quiet, respected one and the best hitter on the team. Tall, lanky and very thin he didn't look at all athletic but was clearly the best athlete in the group. Right field was his domain. He was a boy of few words.

The Torelli brothers, Louie and Joey, were second in leadership qualities only to Vito, but they lead by fear and force rather than finesse as Vito did. Their athletic abilities were modest but they were good organizers and planners. They were constantly devising schemes and solving problems.

Carlo Carlucci was the comedian and clown of the group. Practical jokes, teasing and taunting were his stock in trade. But he was liked by everyone with his perpetual bright smile, twinkling eyes and playful personality. The group was slow to accept him in the gang initially because of his mixed ethnic origins. His father was an Italian-American but his mother was Puerto Rican, an ethnic group not socially acceptable by their parents in the 1940's. He was a better than average athlete and a great swimmer so the other boys cared less about who his mother was.

Ignatio (Iggy) Fortunata was the best with the girls but still second best to Vito. The boys all knew that Iggy would be the first to marry or get some girl pregnant. He was even more obsessed by sex than Vito. Every place and any place the team happened to be playing, Iggy could always be expected to find the sociable girls in the area. Even at the age of ten he carried pinup-girl photos in his pocket and always was the first to spot the nude pinups in gas stations and repair shops. The others liked to be around Iggy and Vito hoping some of their female rejects would trickle down to them.

Juan Santiago was by far the most controversial member of the Junior Wolves. His parents were both Puerto Rican and his father was very dark. Some of the parents even insisted he was black. But Carlo Carlucci's mother and Juan's mother were first cousins. This connection led to Juan's slow acceptance into the group. He was also very dark skinned but not nearly as close to black as his father. However, when Vito and the others saw his athletic performance and physical strength they decided they had to have him on their fistball and baseball teams. So, he was in to stay much to the dismay of some of the parents.

Mario was the 'tolerated' member of the team and, because he was Vito's adopted brother, there was never any dispute about his joining the team. Athletic ability was

The Wolves Of Brooklyn

not one of Mario's attributes but he was a master of game management and strategy. It would take him no more than two innings of a game to decipher the weakness and strengths of any opponent team. If the opponent was engaged in games more than once each season Mario had all its attributes committed to memory. He kept written records of the players of each team including their estimated height, weight and age.

The large green ledger-like volume he carried to each game listed how each opponent performed under various climatic conditions, whether he could hit the ball far, or was a good defensive player, or if he choked under pressure. 'Mario's Green Bible' was the name given the book by everyone. The opponents mocked it and him for it but his teammates treasured and protected it with zeal.

The gang spent the early, twilight hours of Halloween with their usual pranks. The safer, benign tricks were used as long as visibility was good. Soaping the apartment windows, ringing doorbells, kicking over trash cans full of garbage were only levied on the neighbors considered unfriendly or undesirable by the 'Wolves'. Writing on the backs of the girls' coats with chalk and pelting them with old socks filled with wheat flour served as innocent distractions until dark descended. Then the real tricking would start.

As usual Vito was the ringleader of the vilest plots.

"Okay, guys gather 'round", he said, as they all sat in a circle under the street lamp. "Here's what we're gonna do different this year. That's why I told all of ya' to bring a sawed off broomstick."

"What is it, Vito?" asked the Torelli brothers anxious for his latest contrivance knowing full well it would be thrilling and risky. Vito hesitated just long enough to get their juices flowing.

"Yeah, come on Vito. Out with it. What's the deal?"

"Cats," said Vito, "Cats."

"Cats? What'd ya mean cats. You don't like 'em. Everybody knows that," said Mario.

"Right, Mario. So that's it. We're gonna have us a cat hunt. These alleys and airy-ways are full of stray cats out huntin' food in the garbage cans. We'll have all that we can handle."

"What'd ya mean . . . handle. What'll we do with them?"

"That's where the broomsticks come in. When we find one we'll chase him down and whack him with the sticks," said Vito.

Some of the boys were cool to the idea and they didn't react.

"Don't ya see", added Vito, "when you whack a cat he squeals and screams like a banshee. All the people will hear it and think the ghost and goblins are really runnin' wild on Halloween Night."

"Yeah, we get it", said all the Wolves, except Mario who was mute with fright.

"But . . . but you might kill them", Mario finally stammered out almost choking on the words. All eyes turned in his direction.

"So what if we do?", said Dommie Torelli. "Who's gonna care about some dirty, old alley cats?"

"No, no. We don't wanna kill 'em 'cause we wanna keep them sreamin' and squealin' to keep up the noise. Don't nobody hit them in the head. Just on the body and the legs. And just hard enough to make them howl", Vito said.

Mario broke out in a cold sweat and his stomach began to churn. Vito noticed his facial pallor, scowled and walked away shaking his head.

"Oh, guess what? 'Mr. Goody Two Shoes' don't like hurtin' nothin'. Right Mario? You're gonna chicken out again. Come on guys let's go find some cats and leave

The Wolves Of Brooklyn

the scarecrow alone so he can throw up. See you later, 'chicken', he called back over his shoulder.

The boys separated into pairs leaving Mario sitting under the street lamp alone like the central character under the spotlight on a stage for all to see.

Vito and Carlo crept into a dark alley squinting at some trash cans looking for prey.

"Look, Vito," Carlo whispered, there's one inside that garbage can."

"Where?"

"There, the one laying down on the ground with the lid off. See the cat's tail sticking out?"

"Oh, yeah. Let's get it. You stay at this end of the alley in case it tries to run out."

"Okay," answered Carlo, and then he stood in the center of the alley, feet spread widely apart, broomstick at the ready to strike at any fleeing prey.

Vito stalked the cat feeding in the trash can. When he came close, the cat, all black except for white splotches around his face, the ends of his paws and the end of the tail, heard his approach. It backed slowly out of the can and made a frantic dash toward Vito. Swinging his broomstick horizontally, six inches above the pavement, he struck the animal a vicious blow across the breast bone which sent it somersaulting back six feet. The feline regained its footing and dashed passed Vito toward the end of the alley. Carlo waited as the cat passed around his left side and he struck it with a broad sided blow which slammed it against the wall of the alley.

"Hey, that was great. Look at the dumb cat go."

"Yeah, Carlo, we got it good, didn't we?" said Vito.

They stood laughing at the cat running down the street, the left front leg dragging perceptibly behind the others. There was a small trail of blood on the sidewalk tracing the animals path of escape.

Joey and Dom Torelli had cornered an older, slower calico female in an airy-way a half block away from where Mario still sat on the curb.

Then Joey went down the steps into the airy-way while Dom stood on the top step of the stoop to block her escape route.

"Okay, Joey. Now! Get it."

Joey lunged with his broomstick but missed the animal.

"Get it, Dom. It's comin' your way," he yelled.

Dom jumped off the top step of the stoop on to the sidewalk and took a wide swing but the animal jumped over the stick and streaked up the street toward where Mario sat brooding.

"Hey, Mario, it's comin' toward you. Get it. Don't be such a chicken." That denigrating word, again, which seemed to haunt him, fired his ire.

"I'll show 'em I ain't no chicken, he muttered. Then he crouched behind the broad, lower end of the street lamp waiting for the unsuspecting quarry. He held the broomstick straight up over his head knowing that it remained hidden behind the lamppost. As the victim passed under the lamp Mario timed his swing perfectly and his weapon came crashing down on the center of its skull. The animal tumbled forward of few feet and the lay prostrate, motionless on the sidewalk.

"Eh, nice goin' Mario. Maybe you ain't no chicken after all," Joey congratulated him.

"Yeah, except I think you killed it," Dom added. "Vito didn't want us to kill none of 'em."

"Ah, what's the difference. He got it didn't he? He coulda just sat there whimperin' but he didn't," said Joey.

"Yeah, what's the difference. I got it didn't I," responded Mario trying to appear indifferent and unaffected.

The Wolves Of Brooklyn

Vito and the other boys came running down the street to where the others stood around the cat's carcass lying on its side.

"Who got this one?" Vito asked.

"Mario did. He hit it one good shot on the dome and down it went."

"No kiddin'. 'At's my brother Mario," he said throwing his arm over Mario's shoulder. "I don't want none of ya callin' him chicken no more. Do ya hear." Mario's face beamed with pride and the glory of real acceptance. He looked down at the immobile cat. His stomach did a flip-flop but he was determined not to vomit.

"But I think I killed it Vito. I didn't mean . . . I didn't realize I hit it so hard."

"No, you didn't kill it. Look you can see it still breathing."

The boys approached slowly, remembering the stories of how vicious wounded and trapped animals can be. Iggy nudged it gently with his foot. The victim stirred slightly but didn't regain consciousness.

"Watch it," yelled Juan. They all jumped back in alarm but the body settled back into coma.

"It ain't dead but its knocked out cold," said Pattie Flanagan.

"Joey, go get an empty bushel basket off your papa's truck. You know one of the ones what's got a lid on it. We'll keep it caged up until it wakes up. If it ever does."

"What for, Vito?" several of the gang asked in unison.

"Never mind. You'll see. Just leave it to the mastermind. Don't I always come up with some bright idea, heh?"

"Yeah, sure, Vito. Sure."

Joey returned with the makeshift enclosure. They scooped the cat into it, closed the lid over it and fastened it

with some wire. Then they went off to continue their hunting, or tricking or whatever suited them for the next hour. When they returned the captured victim was conscious but lethargic. She had clearly suffered some serious brain damage from Mario's blow but could still ambulate but with difficulty.

"So now what, guys? I'm getting tired of this cat hunting. It's getting boring," said Mario, inwardly wishing that the entire episode could come to an abrupt end. "Let's go home, now."

"Naw, wait a minute. I'll think of something." At that precise moment the wounded, caged calico let out a slow, painful, low pitched 'meow'.

"I got a great idea. Iggy, your the cigarette smoker in the gang. You got any lighter fluid at your house?'

"Yeah. Why?"

"Just go get it. Bring the whole can."

While Iggy made the trip to his tenement apartment and back again the rest of the boys had taken the injured cat out of the basket and fashioned a short leash out of some discarded clothesline rope they found in the street. The cat still moved very slowly and shakily but they didn't want to risk its running off or turning on them. After looping one end of the rope over the cats head and around its neck they secured the other end to the street lamp post.

"Don't make no tight knot. Make a slip knot so we can let it loose with one pull on the end," Vito said.

"Now, where the hell is Iggy with that lighter fluid?"

Iggy came running to the street lamp but he was empty handed.

"Well, where's the lighter fluid? you jerk."

"Just hold your horses, Vito. I had to hide it inside my shirt so my Ma wouldn't see it. Here it is. The whole can and its almost full."

"Good. Give it here."

The Wolves Of Brooklyn

Mario's eyes nearly popped out of his head. "Now wait a minute, Vito. What'd ya got in mind. You ain't gonna. . .?"

"Yeah, I see your plan," said Joey. "This oughta be good. Go ahead Vito do it."

All the others looked on in stunned amazement as Vito proceeded to soak the animal in the fluid.

"Okay, Carlo. You get ready to pull the knot loose when I give you the word. You other guys better stand back on the stoop in case it tries to attack. I'll throw a match on it, Tony'll pull the end of the rope then we'll run up on the stoop with you guys and watch the fun."

"I don't know, Vito," said Juan. "That cat's pretty near dead now. You don't have to make it suffer no more."

"That's right, Juanito. I'm gonna end its suffering. I'm gonna put it out of it's misery. Ha, ha."

Juan, Mario and Pattie started walking away.

"Where you guys going? You're gonna miss all the fun."

Mario's stomach started doing its flip-flops again.

"We ain't gonna watch none of this," said Pattie speaking for the others.

"Ah, go on you chickens. Go home to your mama's."

Vito inched as close to the calico as he dared risk. He took a wooden kitchen match from his pocket, struck it on the pavement and tossed at the tethered victim. It was shaking its head trying to remove the fluid from its eyes. Some of the fluid sprayed Vito and he jumped back just as he let fly the lighted match. It went out.

"You lousy rotten cat," said Mario wiping the fluid from his face and hands. He cocked his leg back and kicked the animal a hard blow to the abdomen. It collapsed to the pavement.

"Now, look what you done," yelled Dominic . "You went and killed it good now. It couldn't run now if it wanted to."

"Nah, look, its still moving. This match ain't gonna work, though. The breeze made by the throw will blow it out again. We gotta think of another way."

"I got a way," said Carlo Carlucci. He fetched some newspapers and twisted them tightly into a wick. "Here, we'll light this and throw under it. The wind ain't blowing this baby out."

"Yeah, good idea."

Vito lit the end of the paper wick and tossed it under the cat. After a second or two the lighter fluid caught fire. Vito yelled to Tony, "okay pull it now."

Tony pulled the end of the rope loose from the post. The cat burst into flames and suddenly gained new vigor as the searing heat burned away his coat. It thrashed about wildly at first, running in circles, swiping at her face and body with her paws trying to extinguish the flames.

The cat finally began to run wildly in all directions screeching and whining in a blood curdling howl. At top speed she slammed into the side of a tenement house wall and then into a parked car at the curb. As it turned and ran up the alley the flames went out but the flesh was still sizzling as she rolled over in the alley and let out her last shriek of life. The animal lay dead on the pavement as several people stuck their heads out of the tenement apartment windows to see what was causing all the commotion.

"Hey, what-a you kids doing down there? Go home now. Halloween's over. Go on, before I call-a the cops."

Mario and the others--even Vito--stared silently in awe of the terrible spectacle. No one showed any sign of having enjoyed the 'trick' as they had expected. They slowly, quietly walked home with heads bowed, the smell of burning flesh still permeating their nostrils.

The Wolves Of Brooklyn

CHAPTER EIGHT
THE TERRIBLE BOMB

The year 1945 was most tumultuous and included: the death of F.D. Roosevelt, who was succeeded by Harry S. Truman, his vice-president; Mussolini was killed in a most vicious manner by Italian partisans; Hitler committed suicide in his underground bunker, along with his new bride Eva Braun, on April 30; Berlin surrendered to the Russians on May 2nd and Germany capitulated on May 7 and the world celebrated 'V. E. Day'--victory in Europe--on May 8.

In the meantime, two other events which reshaped the future of mankind, passed almost unnoticed in the celebrating. Fleming and Florey received the Nobel Prize for medicine with the discovery of penicillin; and the first nuclear bomb was detonated in secrecy near Alamogordo, New Mexico on July 16.

The United States dropped a similar weapon on Hiroshima, Japan on August 6 and a second bomb decimated Nagasaki, Japan on August 9. Japan surrendered on August 10 ending World War II. It was estimated that 35 million died in the war itself and another 10 million in Nazi concentration camps.

The Wolves Of Brooklyn

"Did you hear about that bomb they dropped on Japan? They say it's more powerful then ten 'blockbusters'. That must be some monster bomb, heh, Vito?" said Mario.

Most Americans debated the extent of the power of this new weapon but its scope was beyond their wildest speculations until photos and newsreels of the devastation were shown to the public.

"Wow, Papa, look at this picture on the front page of the Daily News. This can't be right, can it? There ain't no bomb what could be that powerful. . . is there?" Vito's eyes bulged out of his skull and Mario's stomach began its all too familiar churning.

"Here, bring it to me, let me see. Oh, dio mio, this is really some-a-thing. Nunciata come here and look at this," Carlo called out to his wife.

The entire front page of the tabloid newspaper, except for the name and logo at the top, was covered by a huge aerial photo of New York city which included Manhattan, Brooklyn, and eastern Long Island. The range of damage of an atomic bomb equivalent to the one dropped on Hiroshima was depicted by several concentric rings overlaid on the map of the city. The center of explosion, now called the epicenter, was located precisely on the Brooklyn Navy Yard, just three city blocks from Vito and Mario's tenement apartment.

"It says here, 'the bomb can destroy buildings as far as two miles in every direction from the center of the explosion. But the deadly radiation can travel for many miles killing thousands of people for months after the explosion'. Papa, can this be true?" asked Mario astounded.

"It must be so, if it says so in the papers. They supposed to only print true things, no? Look at that picture. The rings go far out into Queens and up into Manhattan. It must be true," Carlo answered.

"Mama mia, Carlo, this is such a terrible thing that we make," said Nunziata.

"Why so terrible? Mama," asked Vito. "It helped end the war, didn't it? And it made those dirty Japs surrender, too. That ain't so bad."

"Yes, you right, Vito. But what happens if-a some other country who no likes us gets this. . .this 'atom bomb',too, like the Japanese or even the Russians. Such a weapon could make a very terrible war. Even worse than the one we just-a finished. Why, just a few bombs could wipe out all of New York city. And that means Brooklyn, too, you know."

"We must pray real hard that nobody else make-a this terrible kind of 'at. . .'"

"Atomic bomb, Mama, atomic bomb," Mario finished the phrase.

"Sh, sh, not so loud. Your sister Angela is sleeping in the next room. You no want to make her get scared. She's only nine years old and she no understand these things yet," their mama pointed out.

"I wonder if Chico and Carmine have seen this yet," said Carlo referring to his two older sons. Chico was twenty and married with a new baby girl of his own. A rheumatic heart problem had made him 4-F and ineligible for the draft. Carmine was sixteen and not quite old enough for the military draft. A concern his parents were relieved from now that the war was over. The youngest, Paulie age seven, slept with Carmine in a spare room on the first floor of the tenement.

"Papa, you said the Russian's might get the atom bomb and use it against us. Why would they do that? They're our allies, ain't they?" asked Mario a bit puzzled.

"Yeah, sure. They our friends now until we beat the Nazi's. But now the war is over they gonna try to eat up all of eastern Europe and they know we no can let them do this."

The Wolves Of Brooklyn

"But, why?" asked Vito.

"Well, they trying to make the whole world into communista."

"What's a communist?" said Vito.

"Let's see how do I explain this. The communist believes that the government should own and run everything. They no believe the people should own the land or the business. They no let no other kinds of political parties in the country. You know, democrats, republicans and like that. So, no need for elections by the people."

"Yes, and they no believe in God, or the church, or Jesus Christ," added Nunziata. "And they no let the people believe in these things either. They close down all the churches and drive away or kill all the priest and sisters. These are very bad people."

"And most of all they hate all the democratic countries like America, England and France. Yeah, I'm afraid some-a day we gonna have to fight the Russians in another war, World War III. But now this atom bomb make it all much more terrible. Maybe it be the last war, ever. I no like to think about it."

No one spoke for several minutes. They all pensively stared at the front page newspaper photo, gloomily imagining the worst. Nunziata gazed, instead, at her family, a tear slowly cascaded from each eye.

Vito and Mario were getting ready for bed much more quietly than was there usual habit. The image of the concentric circles of the atomic blast engulfing their tenement and their beloved Brooklyn burned into their memories, forever. Sleep would not come easily on this night and exploding dreams pervaded and disturbed their slumber.

Each of the boys dreamed about the 'Atomic Bomb' but each dream was in an entirely different context.

In Vito's dream, the sound of air raid sirens awakened the entire neighborhood. Vito, Mario and his entire family poured out of the tenement onto the street. Everyone was screaming and running in panic in different directions.

"Vito, come on this way," called Mario.

"No, this way. I'm gonna try to get to the subway station," said Vito.

"But that's six blocks away."

"So what? I know that but it's the only shelter that has a chance against the atom bomb."

"Well, I'm going to the basement under the city bath house. It's only two blocks from here."

Vito turned up an alley to take a shortcut and avoid the masses of people clogging the streets. Suddenly he found himself alone in the alley. It was very quiet. Even the air raid sirens had stopped and the air was still.

"Hey, what's that noise? That whistling sound?"

He looked skyward and saw the large bomb falling through the clouds heading directly for him.

"Oh, no. This can't be."

But the faster Vito ran and changed direction the closer the bomb came. It even changed direction when he did. He doubled back and retraced his path out of the alley. The bomb shifted directions, did an about-face and followed his new route out of the alley. He couldn't believe his eyes but he kept running while looking over his shoulder. The bomb was falling very fast, yet at the same time it seemed to move in slow motion. Slowly spinning through the clouds.

"It's a Russian bomb, I can see it. I can see the Hammer and Sickle on the side. It's spinning and spinning. Now I see the words 'Atomic Bomb' painted on the side of it. Oh, no. God, help me, please help me. Make it go away."

The bomb continued to fall rapidly and yet slowly enough the see the sides rotating slowly. First the words Atomic Bomb, then the Hammer and Sickle. Atomic Bomb. .

. Hammer and Sickle. . . Atomic Bomb, over and over again it rotated.

"I gotta keep moving." said Vito as he changed directions again and exited the alley but the bomb followed. "My legs are hurting and cramping. I can't run much more."

In desperation he turned into another alley. The bomb turned and followed him. Perspiration soaked through his clothes and the pajamas underneath. His head began to spin and his legs felt like rubber. He began to stumble to the pavement. He got up again and continued staggering toward the other end of the alley.

"Oh, my God. There's a high fence at the end of the alley. I can't get out. I gotta get out."

He reversed his direction and started to leave the alley. As he did he saw the bomb falling into the alley. It made a ninety degree turn and was now traveling four feet above the pavement and horizontally parallel to it. It was coming straight toward his head.

"No, please, God, no." He ran into the tall iron barred fence and tried to climb over it. But the bars were to slippery and he couldn't get hold. He looked up to see how high the fence was. There was no top that he could see.

"Oh, no. There ain't no top to this fence. What kind of a fence is this? I can't get over, I can't get over it." He wrapped his arms desperately around the iron bars shaking and screaming in panic. He looked over his shoulder as the bomb came spinning closer, and closer. Slowly rotating. Hammer and Sickle . . . 'Atomic Bomb'. . . Hammer and Sickle. Why was it taking so long to reach him? It seemed like he had clung to the fence for hours but the bomb never seemed to get there. It came slowly closer and closer. Now he could see the detonating pin in the nose, the stabilizer fins on the other end. But it never got to where he was.

Vito desperately squeezed himself against the bars so tightly that they were grinding into his body and head causing severe pain. Both his eyes were tightly closed, except for the occasional peak over his shoulder,through one open eye, to see the proximity of the bomb. He waited, and waited, hopelessly, for the loud explosion, the searing fire and heat. . .

"Hey, Vito. Wake up, wake up," said Carlo. But he could not loose him from his death-like grip on the bars of the bedstead as he shouted, "The bomb, the atomic bomb. It's coming right at me, right at me. . ."

"Vito, Vito, wake up," said Carlo again, shaking the boys shoulders violently. "It's only a dream, a nightmare. You're having a nightmare. Come on, wake up."

The boy at last, sweating profusely and shivering violently, awakened and loosened his grip. He gazed into Carlo's eyes, looked around the room for the bomb or the destruction and fire from its blast. The room was dark and quiet. Mario, miraculously, still lay asleep at the other end of the bed.

Vito started to collapse from exhaustion. Carlo grabbed him before he rolled off the bed and held the boy tightly to his chest. "It's okay, it's okay. It was just a dream. There was no atomic bomb coming. It's okay," said Carlo, as he stroked the boys head trying to allay his fear and calm his trembling body. Finally, totally spent, physically and emotionally, Vito fell back to sleep. Carlo carefully removed his perspiration soaked pajamas and replaced them with a clean, dry set. He pulled the cover back over his slumbering, adopted son, kissed his forehead and tucked Vito in. As he left the room he glanced over at Mario who stirred restlessly but remained asleep.

***

At least, it seemed that Mario slept. But Mario had aroused with Vito's shouting but pretended not to have awakened. But now Mario lied back in the dark, hands

The Wolves Of Brooklyn

folded behind his head, smiling. 'So the big, tough-guy is scared of somethin', after all. Well, what'd ya know.' He contentedly dosed off into his own dreamland episode.

Mario's dream also focused on the atomic bomb. The major difference was his reaction to the dropping of the bomb on the Brooklyn Navy Yard. The air raid sirens had not started sounding yet as Mario's fuzzy scene faded in.

"Hey Mario, did you hear?"

"Hear what, Vito?"

"The Russians have declared war on the U. S. Their planes are on their way here with atom bombs to blast the Navy Yard to bits. Come with me to the subway station, its the only real bomb shelter within miles."

"Yeah, but you go ahead, Vito. I'll catch up with you and everybody else in a few minutes."

"What for? we ain't got no time to mess around."

"I ain't gonna mess around. You go ahead. This is something real important that I just gotta do," said Mario.

Vito shrugged his shoulders and stretched out both arms, palms upward. "It's your neck. You can do what you want with it. I gonna get out of hear in a hurry."

As soon as Vito and the rest of the family were gone Mario ran up to the roof of the tenement house to see what was happening at the Navy Yard. On a clear, bright sunny day one could clearly see the warships, military vehicles, and uniformed men moving about the Yard.

"Just as I thought. The battle wagons and flat tops are moving out to sea but the destroyers and cruisers are staying behind to fight the Commies' planes. I gotta get into that Yard and get in on the action. But, how do I do it?"

"With all the excitement, maybe they won't notice a little kid like me. I hope they don't"

As Mario approached the Sand Street gate the streets were full of chaotic activity and confusion. People were running in all and any direction unsure of their destinations. Nevertheless, the heavy guard on the main gate had been doubled and the water cooled machine guns on the wall over the gate were constantly manned by marines ready for action.

"Boy, this is gonna be tougher than I thought," said Mario to himself.

An electric powered streetcar--more commonly known as a trolley car--ran down Sand Street to within twenty-five feet of the main gate. At this point the trolley-car usually made an abrupt right turn if it didn't stop at the gate. It was powered from an electric cable that ran overhead above the tracks. The long arm that rolled along the power line frequently slid off the cable if the car made the turn at too fast a speed, as it usually did. The car had to stop and the motor man had to get out and spend several angry minutes trying to place the pulley back onto the cable. Having seen this happen hundreds of times gave Mario an idea that might get him into the Yard. "Yeah, the trolley-car. That should work. I'll try it."

When the streetcar started down the top of the hill on Sand Street it always slowed to safely descend the incline. Mario, Vito and the other kids frequently jumped on the back of the car at this point to hitch a ride down the hill. It was, however, a dangerous ride. They had to catch the edges of the back windows and hold on just with the tips of their fingers, unless the windows were open. They never were open since they had been sealed by dozens of layers of paint over the years.

Around the bottom half of the car three narrow ledges ran horizontally around the outside walls. The ledges were just an inch wide but if the boys turned their body sidewards they could just get the edges of their sneakers on it to balance themselves for the short ride. If they had on leather shoes or were barefooted they were not able to get enough traction to hold on.

The Wolves Of Brooklyn

Eight years before, one of the neighborhood boys had been killed trying to hitch a ride to school because he didn't have the five cent carfare. He fell under the wheels of another street car following close behind. Mario thought of that fatal incident as he formulated his plan.

"Ah, I can do it. I done it a million times and never fell once. And I got on my new sneakers from Davega's store. The rubber is brand new."

He ran to the top of the hill and hid behind a garbage can to await the right moment. Shortly, a streetcar packed with frantic passengers trying to get some distance between themselves and the Yard, slowed at the top of the incline and began its slow descent.

"This is perfect. The trolley's filled with people. It's going real slow and it won't stop at the gate." 'Now, go', he instructed himself, ran up to the back of the streetcar in a crouched position. Then he jumped onto the back and simultaneously grabbed the edges of the windows with both hands, turned his body and hooked the edges of the soles of his sneakers on the narrow ledges. The first few seconds determined whether or not he had timed his leap just right. If he didn't hook on correctly, immediately, he would slip off instantly and fall to the cobble stoned road.

"Got it. A perfect jump. I'm hooked on real good," he congratulated himself.

The streetcar approached the Navy Yard gate and started into its right turn following the tracks. But it negotiated the turn too slowly.

"Oh, no, it ain't turnin' fast enough. The arm ain't gonna come off."

The large spool of rope which held the arm in place was wound around a pulley on the back of the car only three or four feet from Mario's left hand.

"If I can pull on that rope when he's in the turn, it'll come off. I'll have to let go my grip and pull it as I fall off.

That means I only got one chance. If it don't come off I'll have to start all over again and the Commie planes might be here by then. Well, here goes nothing."

Again he had timed his leap and his grab for the pulley rope perfectly. He held onto the rope until he hit the street and the electric arm flew off the trolley with a shower of sparks. The passengers screamed as the car rolled to a stop and the lights inside the compartment went out. In the confusion the nervous guards at the main Navy Yard gate abandoned their posts and ran to the streetcar expecting trouble. Mario ran around the other side of the car and slipped under the revolving gate. Even with his skeleton-like frame he just barely cleared the bottom bar. But he was inside.

The air raid sirens began to sound the alarm to warn of the approach of enemy planes. Officers and ordinary seamen were running to their action post as the Russian fighters began strafing the barracks and the decks of the ships. Men were falling like flies sprayed with insecticide.

Mario sucked in his belly to strengthen his courage and he ran aboard one of the nearest destroyers. Its machine guns were blazing and its anti-aircraft ack-ack guns were booming shots at the Russian fighters and bombers. He ran toward the sound and smoke of one of the more active ack-ack guns dodging bullets as he did. As in most dreams, remarkably impossible feats came easily.

As he approached the gun a shower of machine gun bullets rained down on the gun turret and all the men operating it were suddenly dead. The seaman operating the gun still hung from the harness that fastened him to the gun. Mario looked skyward and saw a single Russian bomber standing out in the center of all the other bombers and fighter planes. 'That must be the one carrying the atom bomb,' he assured himself. All the American guns were trained on that aircraft and poured every shot into its path but none were

The Wolves Of Brooklyn

able to hit their mark. Mario took the binoculars from the officer lying dead next to the gun and peered at the bomber. Its bomb bay doors were open and there hung suspended a single huge bomb. 'Its the atomic bomb,' he muttered, 'and nobody can seem to stop it.'

He unhooked the dead man from the harness of the ack-ack gun and placed him gently on the deck. Strapping himself into the harness was a bit difficult but he managed it after a few adjustments of the straps. Now he quickly familiarized himself with the operation of the gun. He located the cross-hairs of the sighting device, the triggers, the pulleys and wheels for changing the direction and elevation of the gun and the magazine filled with shells.

'I need to take a few practice shots without wasting too many shells,' he thought.

As he looked through the sights, a Russian fighter began strafing the deck and then concentrated his fire on Mario's gun. Mario swung the gun around just as the fighter approached him head on with all its guns blazing. Mario could see the piercing, blazing eyes, stubble faced, and jagged teeth of the Russian pilot, coming straight at him. ' I gotta make these first shots some good ones.'

Carefully, he squeezed the triggers on the ack-ack gun and allowed just two shots to scream from the muzzle. The first shell burst just inches above the cockpit without effect. But the second was a perfect hit that pierced the bullet proof glass of the cockpit, the fighter burst into flames and disintegrated just yards away from the deck of the cruiser. He now had confidence and was ready for the lone bomber carrying the atom bomb.

Dozens of American fighters launched from aircraft carriers were swarming all around the Russian bomber but none was able to bring down the giant. 'I gotta hit that bomber with every shot and make sure I don't hit any American fighters. I don't want to kill any of our guys.'

Ron Aigotti

Mario took careful aim, lead the bomber just enough to have it's flight path collide with the anti-aircraft projectiles, and waited for the right split second so that no American fighters could accidentally intercept the shots. His fists clenched slowly but firmly around the triggers as he slowly swung the guns along with the path of the bomber. In an instant he recognized that the time was right; he fired all the rounds of ammunition until the gun fell silent.

The missiles traversed the sky as if in slow motion as Mario coaxed and body-Englished them into the correct path. All the projectiles, about a dozen, struck the target, each penetrating the fuselage of the bomber in a straight line like a string of periods on a typewritten line. The bomber, and the atom bomb slung under it, disintegrated into a thousand pieces of harmless, metal fragments which fell into the waters of the East River.

As Mario's dream faded into a clouded, hazy mist he was being carried on the shoulders of two U. S. Marines surrounded by thousands of servicemen and civilians cheering, "Hurrah for Mario, the hero of the Brooklyn Navy Yard." But he didn't awaken in screams, like Vito but just rolled over into contented slumber with a broad grin on his face, whispering, "Mario Mastrangelo, the Hero of the Brooklyn Navy Yard and the World.

The Wolves Of Brooklyn

CHAPTER NINE
COURAGE IN A WINE BOTTLE

By 1947 the world was beginning to adjust to the end of the war and to peacetime living. The civilized world, however, was again divided, ideologically, by the "Iron Curtain", as it was dubbed by Winston Churchill in a speech in 1946. Communist Russia and the other totalitarian nations, called the "satellite nations", separated themselves from the western democracies. The world was plunged into a 'Cold War' characterized by an arms buildup, including nuclear weapons, the likes of which was unprecedented in the history of mankind's foolish quest to destroy itself.

Mario Mastrangelo said 'grace before meals' as the family sat around the oval, wooden table in the small kitchen. The table was unable to seat the entire family so Paulie and Angela, the two youngest and smallest of stature, ate meals off the black, kerosene stove covered with a board and a table cloth. The arrangement worked out fine in the summer time, when heat was not required, and mama cooked the food on the recently purchased gas range. During the cold weather the family had to eat in shifts, an arrangement Carlo did not like because he believed that family-eating- together-time was an important family function. Unbeknownst to 'Nunciata and the children, he harbored a deep sense of guilt and inadequacy over the inability to provide a better standard of living for his family.

". . .from thy bounty through Christ, Our Lord, Amen."

Vito stood up and reached across the length of the table to grab the serving bowl of Italian bread.

Carlo reacted immediately with a sharp smack across the back of Vito's hand with a one-half inch thick wooden stick he kept at his place for all meals.

"Ouch, what'd you do that for?"

"I'm-a tell you a thousand times, no reach across the table for the food. You ask somebody to pass 'em and then you give it to you mama first. You capicé? Now you get the food last, after everybody else, 'til you learn."

"Mario, you pass all the soup bowls to you mama and she'll fill 'em up with the pasta et fajoli (pasta and beans with a small ham bone for added flavor)."

"How come we don't get meat but twice a week?" asked Paulie who didn't realize how deeply these questions hurt his papa and mama.

"Well, filio mio, meat cost a lot more money to buy than pasta and beans. Anyway, this hot soup is very good for you. When I was a little girl in Italia my mama make hot-a soup everyday. Look how strong and healthy me and your papa turned out. Did you know that the Italian army lives and fights only on pasta and beans?"

"Yeah, that's why they couldn't run away fast enough from the allies during the war. They surrendered by the millions," Vito wise-cracked.

Carlo swiftly brought his stick down on Vito's shoulder. "Crack". The blow sounded worse than the small amount of pain it inflicted but Vito winced and fell silent for the rest of the meal. Carlo was profoundly ashamed of the performance of his countrymen during the war even though he was loyal to the allies and wanted them to win. He blamed Benito Mussolini for the mistakes of his homeland but he didn't like the image of cowardice branded on the Italians. The next several minutes passed in total silence until Carlo broke it.

"Next week, on Saturday, your mama and me are gonna be out all day until late in the evening. Your older brothers, Chico and Carmine, gotta work the late shift at the Yard. So, Mario and Vito, you stay home and take care of Paulie and Angela."

"How come, Papa? Where are you going?" asked Mario.

"Your great-aunt, Carmella, she just passed away. We gotta go to the wake and the funeral. She lives on Long Island and it's a very long ride on the bus, subway, and railroad. We gotta travel three hours each way since we no got no car." Alas, another source of humiliation for Carlo, although most of his neighbors could not afford an automobile either. But his brother-in-law had a brand new, shiny Studebaker.

"Why do we have to stay home and watch them? It's Saturday and we wanna play baseball," said Vito.

"You have to because I say you do," answered Carlo, trying to subdue his anger.

'Nunciata reached over and lay her hand on Carlo's to calm him.

"Now, Vito, and Mario, too, your papa and me need your help. We must go to Carmella's funeral out of respect for her memory. She help us very much when we come from the old country. She find us this nice flat to live in and helped your papa get his first job. We owe her this much since she would not accept any money from us. She was a very generous and independent lady. The kind that makes all Italians proud.

The Wolves Of Brooklyn

"Why don't you just take the kids with you to the funeral? Then me and Mario wouldn't have to be stuck in the house all day."

"Sh, sh, lower your voice, young man. I no want the little ones to hear about funerals and dying, and all that", said 'Nunciata.

"Why not, Mama?" asked Mario

"Because the little children must not know about these things yet. It might give them bad dreams and make them scared," she said.

"But that makes no sense, 'Nunziata. Everybody gotta die sooner or later. The children gotta learn these things, too," Carlo whispered. Then he realized he was getting no place with his reasoning, so he changed the topic.

"You boys are too young to understand. Just make sure you stay home Saturday. And no make-a no trouble. You understand?" he added.

***

The remainder of the week seemed to fly by since Vito and Mario hated the thought of that terrible Saturday arriving. But arrive it did.

"Now my little men. I got everything ready for you and Paulie and Angela. For breakfast you take that stale Italian bread from last week and you slice 'em nice and thin. Then you toast them over the gas range with that new bread toaster you put on the open flame. And please no burn yourself. When they still hot you melt some of that left over bacon fat I put in the icebox, and then some of that nice fig jam your Nonna makes. Then a nice big glass of cold milk. And you please drink all your milk. You no want to get rickets," said Mama.

"For lunch you make some nice spaghetti pie. Mario, you the cook in the family, you now how to make it. Take the left over spaghetti from Tuesday night and put 'im in the black frying pan and let 'im get nice and crispy. Vito you beat up two eggs with some water and some Parmesan cheese. Then you pour this over the spaghetti after you flatten it out with a fork. Then you cover 'im and let it cook until the bottom get almost black but not burned. Now you must be very careful when you turn it. Mario you see me do it many times."

"Yeah, Mama, I remember. You take the big platter and turn it over on top of the pan and then you turn the whole thing over real quick so all the grease goes in the platter. Then you slide the whole pie off the platter back into the pan and let it cook on the other side."

"That's-a right. You got 'im," she said smiling.

"Oh, ain't you the smart, little chef," said Vito, screwing up his face.

She ignored the remark. "And, Vito, since Mario is doing the cooking you and the others can clean up the dishes. That means you wash 'em nice and clean, you dry 'em very good, you put 'em away in the cupboard."

"But, why do I always get to do all the dirty work?"

"You do as I tell you or you do all the dishes for the rest of the week by yourself. You capicé?"

"Yes, Mama."

"What about supper? mama," asked Angela.

"Well, we got plenty of pasta and beans left over. I bought some fresh escarole. You need to get your green vegetables. You wash the leaves real good and put them in a small pot of water to steam them. When they done you put them in the pot with the pasta and beans and heat 'em up."

"Oh, terrific," said Vito. "Some more Italian army courage food."

She let the remark pass because Carlo was not in the room to hear it.

The Wolves Of Brooklyn

The couple reluctantly said 'goodbye' to the children, quite torn between their respect for the dead and their obligations to their family. Angela and Paulie tugged at their parents' coat sleeves as the Mastrangelos edged toward the front door calling out last minute instructions and warnings back to Mario and Vito.

"Now, you boys behave yourselves and watch the babies; don't leave them alone even for a second; don't open the door to any strangers, no matter what they say; if somebody try to come in you call the neighbors by knocking on the inside wall of the cupboard; don't play with matches; make sure you close the icebox door; if we no come back by dark you turn on all the lights in the house until we get home. You do a good job and Mama take you all out for ice cream later."

She kissed each of the children three or four times as she backed out the front door with Carlo gently pulling her by the hand.

"Come on, 'Nunciata. We're gonna miss the bus. And if we miss this one we never gonna make it to the Long Island railroad train. Come on, please. They gonna be okay," said Carlo.

The bus stop was directly up the street from the tenement. The children could just barely see the passengers waiting for the bus if they pressed their faces against the window pane and leaned as far back as they could against the corner of the window frame. Although the weather was warm Mama and Papa ordered them to keep all the windows closed and locked while they were out. They all strained their necks, except Vito, to catch last glimpses of their parents as they boarded the bus.

"Did they get on the bus, yet?" asked Vito.

"Yeah," said the others, dejectedly, in unison.

"Good. Now, Mario, that means that you and me are in charge of these kids. So you'd better mind what we tell you. You got that? you kids."

"Wait a minute, Vito, Mama and Papa said we are supposed to take care of them, not boss them around," said Mario.

"Yeah sure, sure, Mario, I know. But don't you start trying to give me no orders."

They fumbled through breakfast and lunch without too much trouble. Supper, however, was an entirely different matter.

"I ain't gonna eat none of the Italian army food you're planning to make for supper," said Vito.

"We ain't got much choice. The icebox ain't got no other food in it," said Paulie.

"Yeah. Well, if I gotta eat that garbage I need to get some courage first and then I need something to take the rotten taste out of my mouth."

"Oh, yeah. Where are you gonna get courage from, smart Alec?"

Vito didn't respond to the question. Instead, he went under papa's bed and found the tool box he kept there.

"Papa don't like nobody to touch his tools, Vito", said Angela.

"He'll never know unless you tell him. And you ain't gonna tell on your favorite brother, are you?"

Vito knew she had a soft spot in her heart for him and he took advantage of it as much as possible. She smiled a shy, coquettish smile and turned away.

Vito immediately headed for the front parlor after he secured the tools he thought he would need to get into the liquor cabinet.

"Vito, where are you going with those tools?" asked Mario.

The Wolves Of Brooklyn

Again Vito didn't respond. Mario followed him into the parlor where he found him kneeling in front of the locked bookcase Papa used as a liquor cabinet.

"Hey, Vito you better stay out of there. Papa'll kill if he ever finds out you been into his liquor."

"How's he gonna find out. . . unless you plan on telling him. And you wouldn't do that Mario. Not if you know what's good for you."

Slowly, carefully Vito tapped the hinge pins out of the cabinet door. He even covered the edge of the screwdriver with a cloth to avoid leaving telltale marks on the hinges. Once the doors were removed it was an easy matter to remove the contents.

"Ah, vino. Chianti, that's my favorite. It'll be perfect to wash down that pasta e fajoli. But first I'll need an appetizer to give me the courage to eat that junk. Now let's see here, some Grappa (strong brandy) ought to make a good appetizer."

"What's all this business about booze and wine all of a sudden, Vito?" asked Mario.

"Well, we're the men of the house, ain't we? And a real man can hold his liquor. Anybody who can't, ain't no real man. What'd you say Mario, are you a real man or ain't you?"

Vito removed two whiskey shot glasses from the liquor cabinet and filled them to the brim.

"Okay, Mario here goes nothing." He picked up the brimming-over glass of Grappa and threw it straight back into his wide open mouth as he had seen his elders do so many times. The potent liquid burned Vito's throat, all the way down the center of his chest and into his stomach. But he masked any obvious sign of the discomfort from Mario and the kids. Mario watched in awe, and apprehension of his impending challenge, as Vito swallowed and smiled.

"Okay, Mario. You're suppose to be the other man of the house, ain't you? There's a full glass waiting for you, unless you ain't grown up enough the act like a man."

Mario picked up the glass, moved it slowly toward his lips and took a sip of the burning brew. He visibly winced.

"No, no. You don't drink it that way. It ain't hot soup, you know," said Vito as his face flushed and his head began to spin as the potion began to take effect.

Mario took a deep breath and bolted the glassful of courage into his mouth. He held it in his mouth for a second and gasped at the sting. Mustering all his bravery he gulped the flaming liquid done and coughed slightly. It took all his determination to avoid grasping his throat and screaming in pain.

"So, you did it. Nice going. But you're beginning to look a little green. Want to try another?" asked Vito chuckling.

"Naw, maybe later," said Mario, trying to appear nonchalant. "I gotta get the supper finished now."

Vito poured himself another helping. But Mario wasn't watching so he only filled the glass about half full.

"Vito, I don't think Papa would like it if he knew you were drinking," said Angela.

"Now don't you worry none about that my little sweetheart," answered Vito with a noticeable slur in his speech. He stumbled into a kitchen chair and sipped the liquid out of the shot glass.

"Now you kids eat your food like Mama and Papa said you should," said Mario, whose speech was also becoming more slurred.

Angela and Paulie ate their supper while Mario and Vito sipped their large glasses of Chianti wine. They barely touched any of the food set before them.

The Wolves Of Brooklyn

"Mario...Vito...I getting scared", said Paulie. "You're both acting very funny. Please stop drinkin' that wine. It ain't no good for you and Papa's gonna be real mad at you."

"Don't you worry none, Paulie. You just finish eatin' and me and Mario'll put you to bed."

They poured themselves a second helping of the red wine.

"No, no. I don't wanna go to bed", cried Angela.

Very quickly she and Paulie were crying and sobbing uncontrollably.

"Now look what you done, Mario. They're screamin' their heads off and the neighbors are gonna hear them."

"It's okay, it's okay. I know how to calm them down", answered Vito.

"Wait a minute, kids, wait a minute. Don't cry, don't cry and . . . and I'll give you some of that Cream Soda that Mama saves just for special days."

The children began to ease off on their crying as they contemplated the much relished, sweet drink reserved just for Sundays and holidays.

"Yeah, yeah, you'd like that wouldn't you?", added Mario in support when he noticed how they were becoming appeased. "Sure you would, sure. You stop crying and me and Vito'll give some right now."

"First you gotta get ready for bed, though," added Vito as he winked his eye at Mario.

"Yeah, get your pajamas on first then we'll give you some cream soda."

Although everything was beginning to appear fuzzy Mario and Vito managed to find the children's night clothes. They undressed both the children and helped them into their nighties.

"Here, let me button the front of your pajamas", said Mario. But after fumbling with the buttons for a few minutes Angela could see he was unable to coordinate his movements. She proceeded to button herself up and then she helped Paulie.

"All right, you kids get under the covers and we'll get you some cream soda."

They went into the kitchen, took out some glasses and opened the bottle of cream soda hidden away in the back of the liquor cabinet. Mario began to pour a generous serving of the soda into each of the glasses.

"Wait a minute", interrupted Vito as he stayed Mario's hand. "I got an idea. We don't want them gettin' up and spoiling our fun. We gotta make sure they go to sleep fast and stay that way until morning."

He grabbed the bottle of Vodka from the shelf and began to pour a generous amount into the half-filled glasses of soda.

"What're you doing? Are you crazy? You can't give little kids like them no whiskey. It's liable to hurt them."

"Naw, it won't hurt them none. Besides, I'm only gonna give them a little bit. Just enough to make them go to sleep so they'll leave us alone. The men of the house can't be disturbed when they're conducting family business. Right?" Vito grasped Mario around the shoulder in a grip of comradeship and repeated, "right, paesano?"

After a few moments of hesitation Mario said, "Yeah, right."

Angela and Paulie each swallowed a large gulp of the liquid and realized, too late, that it had a harsh burning effect on their throats and stomachs.

"Mario, this soda taste terrible," said Paulie.

"Yeah, it's burning my mouth and my stomach", added Angela.

"Naw, it just a different brand than you're used to. Here, maybe you gotta drink more slower." He grabbed Angela's glass, placed it to her lips, and forcibly poured more of the mixture into her mouth. Mario did the same to

Paulie. By this time the first initial large portion had begun to take effect on the little ones. Their eyes glazed over and their speech became slurred as the alcohol took effect.

"Come on kids finish up your soda and get to bed", said Vito, as he continued tilting their glasses until all the soda and vodka mixture was drained. By the time Vito and Mario had put the kids into bed and tucked them in they were both sound asleep. At first their breathing was sonorous, later it became very shallow and barely perceptible. But the boys were off enjoying their manhood-play and didn't notice the change.

"Hey, Mario, look what I found."

"What, what, didja find?", Mario stammered through numb lips.

"Cigars, and Papa's pipe. Come on let's light up."

"I don't know, those DeNoble, Italian cigars are pretty strong. I saw my uncle turn green once from trying to smoke one of them."

"Yeah, but we're men now. We gotta learn how to handle these things if the other men are gonna respect us," said Vito.

"Here, if you're scared, you smoke the pipe and I'll smoke the cigar."

Reluctantly, Mario packed the pipe with Prince Albert rough cut tobacco and Vito unwrapped a DeNoble cigar from its cellophane envelope. He ran the cigar under his nose to savor the aroma as he had seen Papa do so many times.

"Now that's what I call a good smelling cigar," he said, trying to hide the mild nausea it actually produced.

Vito struck a wooden kitchen match on the sole of his shoe again mimicking his papa. He tried to steady his wavering hand as he brought the flame to the wavering end of the cigar.

"Come on, cigar. Hold still so I can get you going," he said giggling. Mario also giggled.

Then Vito passed the burning match to Mario. Instead of trying to hold it in his own fumbling fingers Mario simply leaned forward and let Vito hold it over the pipe bowl. After a few deep puffs the tobacco in the pipe began to glow bright red and Mario's face took on that green tint he had seen on his uncle. Vito laughed, took a long puff on his cigar and inhaled deeply. Immediately, vertigo set in and the room begin to spin but he sat back and closed his eyes to steady himself while pretending not to have been effected by the inhaled intoxicant.

Back in the bedroom Paulie and Angela lied in a stuporous state totally oblivious to the raucous noise the boys were making. Of course, the boys were also unaware of the deepening coma into which the children had lapsed. Angela cried softly, moaned and vomited. Since she was lying on her back she immediately aspirated some of the vomitus and coughed violently. The boys continued to frolic in the front room and never heard the convulsive, rasping cough. Angela rolled reflexively on to her side, vomited again and slipped back into a deep sleep.

Now Mario was experiencing the same vertigo. He slumped down in the sofa and laid back putting one hand on the floor in a vain attempt to stop the movement of the room.

"Wow, what a cool feeling. Everything is whirling around. You know like when you're on the merry-go-round and you lean way over backwards. Oh, oh. I think I'm gonna be sick," said Mario.

He tried with great difficulty to lift himself off the sofa to get to the bathroom in the hallway. But he slouched back into the chair and vomited on the sofa cushion.

Vito roared with laughter.

"Ha, I knew you wouldn't be able to handle it. Now wait 'til Papa comes home and sees the mess you made." Then he raised the uncorked bottle of Chianti wine to his

The Wolves Of Brooklyn

mouth and took a long swallow. While raising the bottle he said, "look, here's the way a real man does it."

After two or three gulps of the wine he began to regurgitate the fiery fluid. Burning, hot, red fluid mixed with acrid stomach juices poured from his nostrils and flowed down the front of his chest all over the parlor rug. Bits of undigested food and globs of mucus were visible after the rug soaked up the liquid. Vito's complexion quickly changed from a brilliant red to a pale white, and then to a dull green.

"So that's the way a 'real man' does it, heh, big shot," said Mario exploding into convulsive laughter.

Vito slumped to the floor still holding the bottle of wine which proceeded to slowly trickle from the tilted neck gradually spreading out into the rug. Mario fell over sideways, unconscious. His face squashing into the vomitus soaked cushion. The entire apartment was now quiet except for the deep, sonorous breathing of the intoxicated youngsters.

There were still several hours to transpire before Carlo and Annunciata were due to return. The children spent those hours in profound, undisturbed slumber. Except for Angela whose breathing was becoming labored, and as her body temperature climbed to 104 degrees. She tossed and turned fitfully intermittently moaning for "Mario, Vito, Paulie,. . . Papa, Mama" but no one was able to respond to her beckoning.

***

"Oh, mama mia, Carlo. I'm so worried about the children. The train was so late. It's already one o'clock in the morning and we're still an hour away from home. Please, let's call them on the telephone."

"You know the company only lets me call for business and emergencies."

"Yeah, I know. But they never check the bill anyway. No one will know. If they find out, we pay for the call."

"Do you know how much it costs to call from way out here on Long Island. It might be as much as a whole dollar. We no can afford that kind of money."

"Oh, please, cara mia," she whispered as she caressed his arm to her bosom. She knew that this tactic almost always had its desired effect.

"All right, all right. But we can no talk for more than one minute. Sixty seconds. You understand?"

Carlo dialed the operator and instructed her to make the collect call. One ring, two rings, three rings--Annunciata became apprehensive as a frown appeared on Carlo's face.

"What's the matter? How come they no answer the phone? Carlo, something is wrong. Something has happened to the children."

"Now, now don't get all excited. They're just probably so sound asleep they can't here the phone. They probably stayed up so late they were exhausted and are sleeping so deep they are dead. . . I mean lost to the world."

"Oh, my God, Carlo. Come, quick, we must get home right away. Let's take a taxi cab from here instead of the subway."

"I don't have enough money for a cab," Carlo said.

"It's okay. We pay him when we get home. I'll borrow it from one of the neighbors."

Carlo was obviously worried, also, since he agreed without argument. They flagged a cab and urgently encouraged the driver to drive as fast as he could. About forty five minutes later they pulled up in front of the tenement. Carlo bolted out of the cab door and ran up the stairs to the apartment. After she borrowed some money from a neighbor and paid the cab driver Annunciata was not

The Wolves Of Brooklyn

far behind. They rushed inside and were immediately taken aback by the foul, odoriferous mixture of alcohol and vomit.

"Carlo, it smells awful in here, like a bar room on skid row."

Carlo entered the front parlor to find the two boys sound asleep. Vito was on the over-stuffed chair with the empty wine bottle still in one hand and the now extinguished DeNoble cigar in the other. Mario lay on the sofa with his face still in the now drying, sticky vomit.

Carlo instinctively went to Vito first, grabbed him by the shoulders and shook him vigorously.

"Wake up, Vito. Wake up you good-for-nothing bum." He slapped him across the face several times and Vito struggled to open his eyes.

"Hey, hey, what's the matter? What are you so crazy about? I didn't do nothin'."

"Nothing, huh. Look at this parlor. Look at you. Stinking drunk and smoking cigars just like a hood."

Mario began to stir out of a stuporous sleep at Carlo's shouting and Vito shouting back.

"What's the trouble Papa," he stammered.

"What's-a the trouble. Look at the two of you." He slapped Mario across the face, also, but only once and not as violently as he had struck Vito.

"Carlo, Carlo, come quick," he heard his wife call from the bedroom.

"What? What is it?" He ran to the bedroom.

"Something's wrong with the bambinos. I no can wake them up."

He picked up Paulie and immediately detected the odor of alcohol on his breath. "He's drunk, too. Those little hoodlums gave the kids some booze, too. I'll beat them both to a pulp." He started toward the parlor in a wild rage.

"Just a minute, Carlo. Angela is worse than Paulie. She breathes very shallow and she's burning up with fever."

"What? Here let me see her." He picked her up in his arms and immediately knew she was in grave danger.

"Quick, go down the block and wake up your brother-in-law, Tom-the-plumber. Ask him, please, to drive us to the hospital. Never mind. I'll go myself with Angela so we can leave right away for the hospital. You stay with those two bums and don't let them out of your sight. I'll fix them when I come back from the hospital."

"Oh, please, Carlo. Hurry up. Get her to the hospital right away. Oh, dio mio, please, God, no let her die."

Carlo bolted through the door, down the two flights of stairs and out into the darkened street. It was beginning to rain heavily. He called up to the apartment window. "Nunciata, quick throw down a blanket to cover Angela."

In a few moments she had yanked the blanket off their bed, wadded it up and threw out the window to Carlo. He wrapped the little girl in it, carefully, covering her head and ran at great-neck speed the two hundred yards to Tom's house. His was one of the few families on the block who could afford to own a car.

"Tommie, Tommie," he yelled while pounding on the front door of the apartment house.

"Tommie, please, wake up. My baby is very sick. PLEASE," he shouted as tears ran down his cheeks.

Very soon the lights went on in Tom's apartment.

"Hey. Who is it? Are you crazy wakin' everybody up in the middle of the night. It must be two o'clock in the morning. Go away before I call the cops," he said, still half asleep and he began to close the window.

"No, wait. Tommie, it's me your brother-in-law, Carlo. Please, my Angela's very sick. She's burning up with fever and is in a coma. I gotta get her to the Brooklyn Hospital right away. Please," his tears were now accompanied by sobs.

"Okay, yeah sure, Carlo. I didn't know it was you. Wait just a minute, I'll get on some clothes and take you quick. Here's the keys," he said tossing them out the window. "You get the car warmed up. I'll just be a minute."

Carlo picked up the keys from the wet sidewalk. The rain poured off his bear head and into his eyes to mix with the flood of tears and sweat. The engine cranked over several times but didn't start."Oh, please you gotta start. Please." He continued to crank as Tommie came down the front steps.

"Wait, Carlo. Stop. You're gonna run down the battery. It's just a little wet. Here, slide over. Let me try it."

Tommie slipped in behind the wheel and crank it once with no response. "It just needs to be coaxed." He jumped out, lifted the hood on the Studebaker and wiped the wires and the inside of the distributor cap with his handkerchief.

"Now, we give it another try." He pulled out the choke, pumped the gas peddle twice and turned the ignition key. The engine roared to life. "Now listen to that. Smooth as silk, ain't it?"

"For God's sake, Tommie, never mind how smooth it is. Get moving," Carlo yelled in frustration.

"Yeah, okay, okay. Sorry."

The sleek four door sedan, with its bullet shaped hood ornament shining, zipped away from the curb spraying the water from all its four wheels like sea water thrown by the hull of a speeding boat. The Brooklyn Hospital was a twenty minute drive from the tenement at ordinary speeds. They arrived at the emergency room entrance slightly more than seven minutes after they pulled away from the curb. Carlo jumped from the passenger side door on the run before Tommie had even come to a complete stop.

"Hey, watch out. You want to kill yourself. I ain't got no insurance you know."

Carlo was in such a panic at this point he didn't hear a word the Tommie said. He staggered momentarily with Angela in his arms but quickly regained his balance and continued through the swinging doors into the emergency room.

"Please, doctor, nurse, somebody. Help my bambino. No let my little angel die."

A nurse grabbed the child out of Carlo's arms and placed her on a examining table.

"Please, sir. Let us handle this. You wait out in the waiting area."

"No, no," screamed Carlo. "I'm not gonna let her out of my sight until she's all right."

The young doctor-intern entered at that precise moment and ran to the little girl's side. "It's okay, nurse. Let him stay as long as he doesn't get in the way."

Carlo backed off about ten feet and leaned against a nearby wall. He was totally spent but the adrenaline pumping into his veins kept him upright, eyes bulging, heart pounding like a base drum.

"Her breath has the odor of alcohol. Vodka, I think," said the doctor.

Carlo was ashamed and embarrassed by what the doctor might think of him as a parent, so he feigned surprise and indignation.

"What are you talkin' about?" asked Carlo. "I don't let my kids drink nothing like that. Why, I even keep my liquor locked up. . . in a closet," he said realizing the revelation of his own words. "Those boys. That hoodlum, Vito. He did this to my little Angel."

Carlo dashed out of the emergency room shouting over his shoulder, "you take good care of her doctor. I'll be back soon. Please no let her die."

The Wolves Of Brooklyn

The Studebaker was still parked in the parking area but Tommie was standing near the end of the driveway smoking a cigarette. Carlo jumped in the car, started the engine and made a vicious U-turn in the lot and sped toward the gate. Tommie yelled, "Hey Carlo, where're you going? Wait for me."

Carlo slowed just enough to yell instructions out the window to him. "No. You wait here and watch my Angela. I come back to get you. I gotta teach some young hoodlums a lesson about liquor and bambinos."

Tommie stood at the gate, threw his hands in the air in confusion and walked back to the emergency room.

It took Carlo even less time to get back to his tenement than it took to get to the hospital. He came to a screeching stop at the curb in front of the apartment house and bounded out of the vehicle not even bothering to turn off the engine or close the car door. Bounding up the stairs two at a time he called out, "Vito, Mario, you little bums. Where are you hiding? You better come out or I give you twice the licking I want to give you."

The door to the flat flew open under his full weight and the door knob crunched into the plaster wall with a thud. The door bounced back in his face and he threw it back all the harder as the doorknob now stuck into the lathe wall. His wife came running from the boys bedroom.

"Carlo, what are you doing back home? How is Angela?"

"She's gonna be fine. Where's those two animal sons of yours?"

"They're asleep. They smell like vino and puke. I can't wake them all the way up. What's wrong with them."

"What's wrong with them? I show you what's wrong with them and with Angela, too." He went over to the liquor cabinet with its door hanging haphazardly from its hinges.

"This is what's the matter with them. They broke into my liquor cabinet and drank the vodka and vino."

"But Angela and Paulie would not do that."

"Those good-for-nothing boys must have tricked them or forced them to drink some. Well, I'm gonna find out right now what did happen."

Bursting into the bedroom he grabbed Vito and Mario by the scruff of their necks, dragged them out of bed. He slammed them both against the wall bouncing their foreheads off the hard plaster which aroused them immediately. Paulie barely stirred in his bed from the ruckus.

"Carlo, be careful, you're gonna hurt them. They are sick, too," said his wife.

"Sick, sick? I'm gonna make them wish they were dead before I'm through with them."

"Hey, what the hell is going on," said Vito in garbled tones.

"Watch your language little gangster or I give worse than I wanted," he said as he forced Vito's face more forcibly into the wall with a grinding motion.

"Ow, that hurts."

"It hurts, huh? Well you ain't seen nothing yet. What did you do to Angela and Paulie, huh?"

"We didn't do nothing to them."

"You lie to me and I break your neck," he said and applied more pressure to the back of Vito's neck.

"Is that right, Mario? You didn't do nothing to them, either."

Mario hesitated before answering. Carlo pushed harder on the back of his neck.

"Okay, Papa, okay. We just gave them a little vodka to make them go to sleep. They were so afraid because you and Mama weren't home."

"Why, you little creep. Now you're a stool pigeon, too."

Carlo pulled Vito's head back six inches from the wall and slammed it forward again.

"Shut up your face until I ask you to talk."

Blood began to trickle from above Vito's right eye and his nose.

"Carlo, please. You gonna hurt them real bad. Please, stop it."

"Be quiet, 'Nunciata. You stay out of this or I give you some of the same."

She ran from the apartment screaming for help from the neighbors.

"Now. Tell me again. How much Vodka and wine did you give the little ones?"

"Not much Papa. Honest," answered Mario. As quickly as his words finished leaving his lips his head also bounced back off the wall. He felt one of his front teeth loosen and blood trickled out of his mouth.

"Not much, huh? Not much. How much is not much?"

"Okay," said Vito with a smirk. "They wouldn't shut up and go to sleep so we helped them into slumber land. What's the big deal, anyway? You and your friends drink it by the gallon all the time. It ain't killing you, is it?"

A scene flashed across Carlo's mind of him and his friends staggering home in the small hours of the morning after a long weekend binge.

Without saying another word he dragged the two teenagers out to the kerosene shed for a large dose of disciplinary persuasion.

'Nunciata came running into the shed with three or four of her neighbors. "Please Carlo. Don't do this." She turned to her companions, "please do something to stop him. They are only boys."

When they saw the burning anger in his eyes, however, they slowly walked away and out of the shed.

"We're sorry but this is a family matter. It's not our place to interfere." But she could see their fear of Carlo in their faces. She, too, ran from the shed heading for the police station.

Carlo tied the boys hands over their heads to the posts of the shed and ripped their trousers and underwear from their back sides. Then he found his widest and thickest barber strap, wrapped it around his hand but this time the buckle end was hanging at the loose end.

"Now, now we see if that booze helps to ease the pain of my strap."

Bringing his strong right arm back behind his shoulder he dealt one vicious blow after another into each of the boys buttocks. The metal buckle cut into their flesh raising large, rectangular welts.

"You like to drink like the grown men, heh? Well, then you gonna have to remember when you do, then you get more then just a hangover."

Several of the blows missed their mark striking the boys on the back, thighs and arms. Mario screamed out in pain after the first few blows but Vito bit his lips to the point of bleeding rather than show any discomfort. This only made Carlo all the more angry and soon he was striking Vito only, as Mario hung from the post motionless but whimpering.

"So, my little tough guy. You not hurting enough yet? Well, I'll make you hurt, all right. I won't stop until you beg me to. Do you hear. You have to beg me to stop."

As Carlo continued to deliver blow after blow the anger and rage began to boil in Vito's gut. One of the last blows had driven the pin of the buckle deeply into the flesh of his thigh. He pulled and tugged at the dry, gray clothesline binding his hands and ruptured it.

The Wolves Of Brooklyn

Vito's weight-lifting workouts at the Boy's Club had proved their value. However, he was distinctly large, muscular and very strong for a boy of fifteen. His height had already surpassed Carlo's average five foot, four inches. Carlo, nevertheless, was also very strong , even though his muscles did not bulge and ripple like Vito's did. Mario, on the other hand, remained the scrawny, frail, intellectual type everyone knew him to be.

Vito spun around behind the post as Carlo's next blow struck it instead of his flesh. With a lightening-like move Vito grabbed the buckle of the strap and pulled it from Carlo's hand. Carlo fell forward to the ground, stunned. While Carlo was regaining his composure Vito untied Mario's hands from the post. Mario immediately ran from the shed seeking help.

"Now, you mean, crazy 'Il Duce'. Let's see what you can do without a weapon. Without my hands tied up like an animal," said Vito as he crouched in an attack position.

"So, the big shot hoodlum boy thinks he's now big enough to take on his Papa."

"You ain't my Papa. I've told you that a million times. You're. . . you're more like my warden."

"Okay, have it anyway you like. But now the warden gonna teach you a real lesson on how to be a man without no vino or booze."

Carlo raised both his fist in front of him in classical boxing style. Vito responded in assuming the same posture. They slowly shuffled around in a counterclockwise circling motion. Carlo fired out a vicious left jab into Vito's face and quickly followed with a looping, powerful right. Vito ducked and fired back a vicious blow into Carlo's abdomen. He buckled at the waist and threw both hands and arms up to cover his face. Two more of Vito's blows bounced harmlessly off Carlo's elbows. The senior man stepped back, clearly shaken by the blow to his soft, sagging, middle-aged midsection. Slowly restoring his oxygen supply Carlo, suddenly changed direction, moved in a clockwise circle and cleared his head. Vito flicked out two left jabs to Carlo's head. The first missed but the second glanced off Carlo's cheekbone and raised a small welt.

"Well, well, it looks like the little gangster is growing up. Maybe someday you could work for the Mafia. The way you been goin' that's-a where you're headed. A Mafia man in training. A 'Mafia Apprentice' just like a carpenter apprentice. So now I show you what it takes to make Master's grade."

Carlo faked with a left to the belly, Vito dropped both his hands to block the blow and Carlo countered with a vicious right to his nose. Blood immediately spurted from Vito's nose as he felt and heard the bones crunch under the force of the punch. Vito fell back into a pile of empty kerosene cans as Carlo lunged toward him. Vito raised his foot and drove the heel of his shoe into Carlo's groin. Now doubled over at the waist, Carlo recovered in time to catch Vito charging into to him. They fell to the dirt floor and rolled in the dust of the kerosene-shed exchanging punches several times before regaining their feet. Carlo was much more short-winded than Vito, but Vito was clearly staggering under the power of the blows he had received.

Both of Vito's eyes were partially closed from the swelling around his eyebrows. His lower lip was split and oozing blood. He tried to wipe the blood out of his eyes with his fists but his vision only blurred even more.

"So, what's a matter, tough guy? You had enough. You ready to see that your 'Papa' is still boss, or not?" Vito staggered from side to side and Carlo momentarily dropped his guard believing he was finished. In a mad flurry of wild punches he landed several more blows to Carlo's face and head. Now in a complete rage and responding like a caged animal Carlo was all over Vito punching him repeatedly to the eyes and nose. Vito fell to his knees but Carlo held his head up with one hand clenching his long hair as he continued to strike with the other hand.

"Stop, stop. Are you crazy, Carlo? You want to kill him?" said his wife Nunciata bursting into the shed with two policeman close behind.

As Carlo let go of Vito's hair and turned around Vito took advantage of the distraction and dealt him two vicious blows. The first, a left hook, bounced off his forehead but the second hit the button. Carlo staggered backward and fell to the ground very near unconsciousness. Vito got up some steam and started to lunge for him but his was grabbed by one of the policeman and subdued.

"Hold it right there, young fella," said the officer as he hooked Vito's arm behind his back. Vito struggled violently in spite of the pain to get to the prostrate Carlo.

"You stop it right now," yelled Nunciata. "You here me? You stop this crazy fighting. You want to kill each other? What's the matter with you two?"

"I don't know what his problem is but I'll tell you one thing, if he ever lays a hand on me again I'll. . . I'll kill him. I mean it, I'll kill him with my bear hands," stammered Vito through swollen lips and cheeks.

Carlo had regained consciousness just enough to understand Vito's words. He stared in astonishment, and with a perceptible amount of fear, at his statement. Blood trickled from the corner of his mouth and gushed from his forehead. The other policeman pressed on the forehead laceration with a handkerchief.

"No say things like that," said his foster-mother. "It's not right for a son and his papa to fight . . . to hate."

"He ain't my real father. I told you that a thousand times."

"Oh, is that so? And what about me? I ain't your real mama either."

"No, that's different. . . you're different."

At her insistence the police took Vito to the Brooklyn Hospital emergency room to have his injures attended. Carlo, however, refused to go and insisted on having his wife care for his wounds at home.

"I'm-a tell you, 'Nunciata. I don't want that bum in my house no more. When he comes home I gonna throw him out on the street. He's no good, he's a little gangster."

"But, Carlo, he's only a boy. Where can he go? Where can he live? You promised on his mama's and papa's graves that you would take care of him until he was a man. What about that promise? You gonna break your word?"

Carlo sat quietly, pensive for several long moments. His word and his bond were more important to him than his self-respect.

Their thoughts were interrupted by the ringing of the telephone. 'Nunciata picked it up. "Carlo it's the hospital. They're calling about Angela. Carlo bolted out of the chair and ran to the phone and pulled the receiver from his wife's hand in mid-sentence.

"Hello, doctor? Yes, this is her papa. Is she okay? Will she be all right? When she gonna come home?" All the questions were asked too rapidly to be answered.

The doctor took several moments to calm Carlo down. "Now just slow down, Mr. Mastrangelo. She's fine but she's still unconscious from the alcohol. However, I think she'll come out of that very soon. There is one complication that will bear some watching and vigorous treatment. She has pneumonia from sucking the vomit into her lungs. But she is young and strong. I believe she'll survive but she'll be in the hospital for about six weeks. You may come and see her at anytime. Goodbye."

"Oh, thank you doctor. Thank you so much." Carlo replaced the receiver of the phone in its cradle with a deep sigh of relief.

"Oh, dio mio," he said as he blessed himself with the sign of the cross. " Thank you so much for saving my little Angel."

Annunciata was kneeling in silent prayer in front of the statue of the Virgin Mary on the mantle. Carlo knelt at her side, bowed his head and they prayed together for a long time.

"Carlo, what about Vito? It would not be right to put him out after the Blessed Mother saved our Angela. I'm sure the Holy Mother wants us to take care of him like we promised."

"Okay, okay. He stays. . . for now. But one more thing like this and out he goes. OUT! You understand?" he shouted. Then he rested his head gently on his folded arms on the kitchen table and sobbed quietly hoping his wife could not perceive his grief.

CHAPTER TEN
QUEER BASHING

'SOVIETS TEST FIRST ATOMIC BOMB', read the headlines in the New York Daily News and the Brooklyn Eagle in 1949. Several other events of the year further underscored the "Cold War" as a fact of life to be reckoned with and to have an influence on American life and politics. The Chinese People's Republic formally proclaimed the communist party's control of that country on October 7. The German Democratic Republic officially established communist control over East German on that same date. The North Atlantic Treaty Organization (NATO) became the cornerstone of Western military policy as a deterrent to the military might of the communist world.

The Junior 'Wolves' --with Vito as its newly elected president by acclamation--met regularly in a small, unoccupied store owned by Louie Lupo. He is the local 'bookie' and small-time crime boss. He had offered the vacant store, rent free, to Vito and his gang when he had heard of Vito's reputation. Carlo and 'Nunciata didn't care for the influence the hood might have on the boys and they forbad the boys from frequenting the club. Pragmatically, however, there was little they could do to enforce their ban.

The Wolves Of Brooklyn

    The eight members of the gang, plus Harvey Doyle who acted as mascot and bat boy for their athletics, gathered around the pot-bellied kerosene-burning stove used to heat the premises on those still cool, early spring evenings.

    Tall, slender, round-shouldered Pattie Flanagan leaned against the far wall of the club room. He didn't look to have the physical strength to walk let alone stand. But his spindly limbs contained great power when it came to hitting a baseball. His was appropriately nicknamed after Dixie Walker, a powerful right fielder for the Brooklyn Dodgers. Each of the members took the name of major league player as his own nick name.

    Seated in the front of the room was the Torelli brothers, Joey and Dominic. They looked no more like brothers than the cartoon characters Mutt and Jeff. They differed in age only but fifteen months. Joey was short, wide and a little flabby. He couldn't run very fast but he was a good infielder. Eddy Stanky, the Dodgers' second baseman, was his team name. His older brother, Dommie or Dom, was almost as tall and slender as Pattie Flanagan but he didn't possess the same hitting power. Duke Snyder, the center fielder, was his team name but not because he played ball as well. He did have a remarkable resemblance to the Duke in his playing style.

    Tony Carlucci with his short, wiry build and curly black hair earned him the name Billy Cox, the Dodgers' third baseman. He couldn't hit the ball at all but was an excellent glove man, like Billy.

    Juan Santiago was very strong and powerful but quiet and subdued. He received the name of Jackie Robinson because of his dark brown skin. Juan's half-Puerto Rican ancestry gave him this skin quality but he couldn't play outstanding ball, like Jackie could.

Iggy Fortunata, alias Carl Furillo, had no qualities at all resembling the Dodgers' outfielder but he took his name because there were no others that remained.

Vito acquired the name of Gil Hodges and Mario's was Bruce Edwards the, off-again-on-again Dodgers' catcher.

Harvey Doyle was given the bat boy job because of his slow mental capacities as evidenced by the fact that he never figured out that it was Vito who closed the school window on his fingers and caused him to fall off the ledge into the school yard a few years back. But everyone else knew the culprit. Harvey's I.Q. never progressed beyond the ten year old level even though he was three years older than the other gang members.

The most conspicuous characteristic of the Junior Wolves is that all but two of the members, Pattie Flanagan and Juan Santiago, had Italian family names. But they were accepted as the 'half-breed element' only because each of their mothers were Italian-Americans who married non-Italians. Of course, in addition, there was Harvey Doyle who was also a half-breed but since he was only the mascot and not a member it didn't matter.

"All right everybody," said Vito stamping his foot on the uncovered wooden floor. "This meeting of the Junior Wolves is called to order by me your new elected president."

"The first thing we gotta do is talk about monthly dues. Mario is the treasurer and he'll collect the dues the first of every month. The dues for each member--except Harvey who's our beloved mascot--will be ten cents a month." A slight but audible groan arose from the group of members.

"Now, wait a minute. What's all the moaning about? One thin dime ain't a lot to ask to be in on all this clubs

The Wolves Of Brooklyn

activities that I got planned. Anybody that don't pay up on time don't get to do none of these activities."

"That ain't it, Vito. It ain't the money but a lot of us don't get no allowance from our parents. Where are we gonna get ten cents a month?"

"Oh, is that all your worried about? Well, don't worry. I got that all figured out, too. I have got some neat ideas for ways this club can make some money of its own. You won't need no parents' allowance. We won't need nobody."

"Oh, yeah? Like what?" said Pattie Flanagan.

"Don't you worry your make-believe brains about that. I'll tell you all about it later."

"Tony Carlucci, you're the secretary. So you can take the minutes of each meeting and save them for later."

"What minutes? I ain't got no watch. How am I gonna take any minutes? And where would I take them anyway?"answered a bewildered Tony.

"No, you dummy. You take notes. Taking the minutes means to take notes about the rules passed in the meetings and you write them down. What an ignorant WOP you are."

Tony blushed. "Oh, yeah, I get what you mean now."

"Harvey, you're gonna be the sergeant-at-arms."

"Ah, gee, Vito. I thought you said I was gonna be an officer in the gang. Maybe a general, or something like that."

"Yeah, Harvey, yeah. You are an officer it's just called sergeant-at-arms. You're like. . . like the bouncer at a nightclub. Yeah, that's it. You're the bouncer. Anybody gets out of hand you get to throw them out just like the bouncer does. You see?"

"Okay, Vito, okay. I like that. I'm the bouncer. If anybody don't behave I get to throw them out. I get it. I get it," he said as he turned to face the other members, smiling. "You get that you guys? No messin' around or I get to bounce yoose out." All the members chuckled and slapped him good naturedly on the back.

"All right. Next order of business is, kerosene for the stove. Every memeber's gotta bring one Coke bottle full of kerosene from home each week. At least until it gets warmer. You just pour the kerosene in that five-gallon can we stole from Angelo's kerosene truck. Then you take the bottle home and save it for next time."

"What about you, Vito?" asked Joey Torelli who was fully aware of Vito's aversion to fire, in general, and kerosene, in particular. Of course, only Mario and Vito knew the reason for these phobias.

"I'll get two bottles a week," shouted Mario. "That'll take care of my share and Vito's, too."

"How come you don't bring it yourself, Vito? What's this thing you got about kerosene, anyway?" asked Pattie Flanagan.

Vito hesitated in answering. Admitting to fears of any kind to anyone was not something he relished. He tried very hard to hide them.

"Ah,. . .well. You see. . ."

"He's allergic to kerosene," said Mario. "The doctor says he can't touch it without getting a bad skin rash."

"Yeah, sure, I'll bet," said Iggy Fortunata.

Mario stood up quickly, assuming a challenging posture and said, "Yeah, that's right. The doc said he could even die from it. He doesn't even have to handle it at home. I do all of that work. Anybody want to make something of it? Let's just step outside, if you do." No one took up the challenge, although, no one in the club had any doubt that they could best the skinny, timid Mario in a showdown.

Luckily no one noticed the beads of cold sweat gathering on Vito's forehead and back as he relived the flashback vision of his tenement flat blazing with his parents trapped inside. He felt a deep sense of gratitude toward his foster-brother, Mario, whom he was certain had hated him for a long time. But expressing gratitude to anyone for any reason was something Vito found very difficult, if not impossible. He considered it a sign a weakness to admit needing anyone's help. And, the words, 'thank you', were just not in his vocabulary. He quickly changed the subject.

"Okay, let's talk about some ways the club can earn some money then we won't need no allowance from nobody. We'll carry our own weight."

"Hey, I know what," cried Harvey from the back of the room. "We can run a raffle, and sell lemonade in the summer time, and. . ."

"Nah, nah, Harvey," said Vito. "I'm talking about real money. You know twenty, fifty, maybe even a hundred bucks a night. That's real dough."

"And where do you think we can get that kind of money? Are we gonna rob some banks?" asked Juan Santiago, the muscular, athletic, Hispanic member of the group. A low chuckling laugh emitted from the group.

"No, no," shouted Vito, in all seriousness. "We ain't gonna rob no banks but we're gonna. . . roll some queers."

"What are you talking about, Vito?"

"You know queers, fags, queenies, homos. What's the matter with you guys? Were you born yesterday?" said Vito, shaking his head.

"But, why them?" asked Mario in puzzlement.

"Why? Lots of reasons. First, they can't fight back so they'd be a push over. Second, they usually got lots of cash on them so they can buy drinks for the John's they pick up. And third, and most important, the cops ain't about to do nothing to us for rolling them."

"Why won't they do nothin'?" called someone from the membership.

"Because they hate the faggettes as much as we do. Why, I even seen them beatin' up on them myself a couple of times. So their ain't nobody's gonna stop to help them or turn us in. It's a perfect set up."

Several of the boys, including Mario, harbored some doubts about their courage in such an encounter. But Vito had anticipated these doubts and had already made contingency plans to bolster their intestinal fortitude.

"Now I know a lot of you ain't quite up to such a big-time move so I arranged a way to get up your courage. I know exactly how to give you guys courage."

"What do you mean Vito?" asked Tony Carlucci.

"Hold your horses and you'll see in a minute. Mario, here, hand out these I.D. cards. Everybody take just the one with your name on it."

Mario asked, "What I.D. cards? Where did you get these, anyway? Hey these are Social Security cards and there's one for each of us. There's even one for Harvey. But, the birth dates ain't right."

"That's right. And if you'll look real close you'll see that the month and day is right but the years been fixed so we are all legal drinking age. Now we can buy beer or booze in any bar in Brooklyn. Neat, huh?"

"You know these are all illegal forgeries, don't you?" said Mario. "In fact, it's a federal offense to fake government papers. How did you get these?"

"Never mind how. I got 'em and now you all got one, too. As simple as that and, presto, you're no longer a minor. Let's say I got connections in high places," said Vito, thrusting out his chest with pride.

However, he had no intention of revealing to them that his new, powerful connection was---Louie Lupo. As part of his plan to groom the boys for taking part in his petty crime activities Louie used some of the officials in the postal service to provide the bogus cards. A combination of bribes and personal blackmail are stock and trade in Louie's business. He used them often and effectively.

The Wolves Of Brooklyn

"All right, this is how the scam works," said Vito. "This Saturday night we'll all get dressed up in our best suits and stuff. Then we'll go to a bar outside the neighborhood and put away some drinks for courage."

"Why does it gotta be a bar outside the neighborhood?" asked Pattie Flanagan.

"So that we don't run into nobody who could recognize us and call our folks, you jerk. What a stupid Irish Mick you are."

"Hey, watch your mouth, Vito," said Pattie . But there was no anger in his tone since all the boys jibed each other about their ethnic origins all the time just as their families did. Vito ignored the remark.

"Yeah, Vito, watch out what you say about the Irish," added Harvey. "I'm Irish, too, you know."

"Yeah, I know, Harvey. That's why I said it," answered Vito. All the boys laughed. . . except Harvey, who added, "huh, what d'ya mean?"

"Never mind, never mind, Harvey. It's too deep for you," added Mario. Another raucous laugh followed.

"What'll we tell our mama's and papa's when they ask why we are all dressed up on a Saturday? It ain't church day or nothin'," asked Juan Santiago with an Hispanic accent.

"Yeah, what about that Vito?" asked several from the membership.

"Let's see," said Vito thinking for a moment. "Wait, I got it. Just tell them you're goin' to a dance at school."

"They ain't gonna believe that bull. They know we don't never go to no sissy stuff like dances. That ain't gonna fool them none," said Joey Torelli.

"Just tell them you turned over a new leaf. And, now you're gonna be a good, clean cut kid. Maybe you'll even go to college, and become a doctor, or a lawyer, or a priest, or somethin'." Everyone giggled at the absurdity of the statement.

"What d'you care what they believe. Just get dressed and go. Sneak out if you have to. I know you done that before," said one of the others.

***

The special Saturday night arrived and all the members met at the club house in their special, grown up attire. Their shoes were shined, their shirts pressed, and their hair was slicked back in the classical pompadour and 'duck's ass' style which was most popular among the 'greasers' of the day. It was simply known as a 'Tony Curtis' cut after the popular movie actor at the time.

"Well, well, don't you cats look cool in your fancy duds," said Vito.

"Yeah, I feel like I'm goin' to a wedding or a wake or somethin," answered Harvey obviously quite uncomfortable in his fancy clothes. Harvey almost always wore blue jeans and sneakers, even when he went to church.

"Well, you ain't. We're going 'queer bashing' and we're gonna make some money so this gang can carry its own weight. There ain't gonna be no welfare or home relief for us like some of those good-for-nothin' slobs in the unemployment lines," said Vito.

They started out to walk the fifteen blocks to a small, second rate bar near the Brooklyn Borough Hall on Court Street, intending to conserve every dime for beer. Everyone checked to be sure he had his illegal ID card in his pocket.

Finally, after a thirty minute brisk walk they reached their destination: "Finnigan's Rainbow Bar & Grill". The tavern was a converted store front building built next to an alley. Its main entrance went through an unlit door ten feet into the alley and was well out of site of the large, plate glass covered front of the establishment. The large window which

The Wolves Of Brooklyn

stretches from six inches above the pavement to ten feet over the sidewalk and across the entire front, approximately twenty feet in length, was badly in need of washing. The words 'Finnigan's Rainbow' were spread across the upper half in a semi-circular, rainbow fashion in a faded, gold leaf, three dimensional design.

The inside of the window was dappled with a variety of dust covered signs: red neon letters saying 'Schaefer Beer'; green letters on frosted glass lighted from behind by two light bulbs boasting the attributes of 'Fox Head Ale'; a diversity of sun faded, cardboard signs with barely visible words such as—'Ladies' Night, Wednesday'; 'Knights of Columbus Meeting', followed by a series of illegible dates and times; another very small, inconspicuously placed square of construction paper with the Crayoned words--'No Minors allowed'.

In between the multitude of announcements, the dust, and grease smudges gave the impression the glass was tinted, which it was not. One could barely see inside even with the shielded eyes and face pressed against the formerly transparent material. Mixed with, and adherent to the grime was a multitude of dead insects, dried remnants of human vomitus, sputum, food fragments and dehydrated globs of liquids which were probably residues of beer, wine and other spirits. In all four corners of the window frame were located several large formations of triangular cobwebs with their entrapments of dead flies, mosquitoes, bumble bees, and faded bits of confetti from several previous years New Year's Eve celebrations.

Vito, Mario and the others peered through the opened alleyway-door but the dimly lighted interior gave no clues of the type of welcome that awaited them.

"Come on in, fellas," reverberated a deep, husky voice from behind the barely visible, dark, wooden bar. "Don't worry. You're always welcomed here as long as you got some money and a passable ID. Come on in boys, I mean young men."

Vito, Joey and Dom Torelli strode in confidently. Mario and the others slinked cautiously into the dimly lighted interior.

"How did you find my little establishment?" asked Mr. Finnigan.

"Louie Lupo sent us," Vito said quickly, certain the name would evoke the proper response.

"Oh, yeah, sure. Well, any friends of Mr. Lupo is friends of mine."

"Step right up here to the bar, gents. What'll ya have. Just name your poison and it's yours," said the gruff looking bartender-owner.

Some of the boys hesitated and looked around the bar to check for friends, neighbors or relatives who might recognize them. Vito, Dom and Joey had no such reservations.

"Yeah, we'll have a beer for everybody, that's nine beers, said Joey.

"Do you want Schaefer's in bottles or on tap?" asked Mr. Finnigan.

"No, we'll take the house beer. . . on tap," said Mario knowing full well that it was cheaper.

"Short or long?" Finnigan asked again.

"Short," Mario fired back quickly before anyone else could respond.

"No, no. Wait a minute," said Vito. "Hold that order, barkeep. We'll have boilermakers all around for my gang, the Wolves"

"What's a *berlermaker?*" asked Harvey as the barkeep poured the nine shots of a cheap, no-name, rye whiskey and short glasses of pale, yellow, watered down beer.

The Wolves Of Brooklyn

"That's a shot a rye with a beer chaser, you nitwit," said Pattie. "Don't you know nothin'. That's what all the big, tough guys drink."

"Don't say that, Pattie. That ain't nice. I know lots of things."

"Oh, yeah, like what, Harvey?"

"Never mind, never mind you guys," said Vito. "We came here to drink, not to argue. Drink up. It'll make you feel good, real quick like."

After three hours, and six boilermakers the boys were really feeling loose and frisky. In fact, their behavior become so wild and uncontrollable that Mr. Finnigan forcibly ejected them from his establishment. Now their confidence in their machoism was confirmed. They had been kicked out of their first gin-mill for rowdy behavior. Now they went hunting for 'big game'.

"Come on, guys. . . I mean, men. Let's go over to the cocktail lounge at the St. George Hotel," said Vito.

"What for? That's a queer bar," said Tony Carlucci.

"Exactly. Don't you remember our plan, stupid? We're gonna make some real dough rollin' some of them queen's."

"Oh, yeah, I forgot about that. Let's go get 'em," said Mario. There was now an alien, new enthusiasm in his speech that had not existed before for such a potentially violent venture. . . except during the episode of the cat hunt.

The St. George Hotel was a plush hostelry, even by today's standards . And, relative to the slum surroundings of the 1949, it was comparable to the Taj Mahal. Millionaires and million-heiresses not only stopped there on business visits but many even used it as their permanent residence. Movie actors, radio personalities, politicians and even the non-resident members of the famed Brooklyn Dodgers baseball team stayed there during home-game-series. As a result, all the boys in Brooklyn, especially the members of the Wolves' Social and Athletic Club, knew the environs of the hotel very well.

Vito and the others managed to slip by the doorman in his red coat with its brass buttons, and braids, since he would have known immediately they didn't belong. They eased passed the heated, mirrored, luxurious indoor swimming pool to the cocktail lounge on the mezzanine level.

Vito entered first since he had a fleeting acquaintance with the chief bartender or Maitre de, who called himself Adrian Primrosa which he alternated with the female form Adrienne Primrose as suited his current role and mood.

He was a slender, bleached blonde, effeminate man in his mid-thirties. His face was lightly powdered to cover up any semblance of a shaved, stubbly five-o'clock-shadow. A dull red, thin layer of lip color gently highlighted his lips. On the left side of his chin, a half-inch below and one inch diagonally away from the corner of his mouth was painted a large, black birth mark, more aptly called a 'beauty mark'. His soft, white delicate hands were perfectly manicured, but sharply pointed, fingernails covered with a clear, colorless but glossy nail polish. With his shoulders pinned back his posture appeared so perfect as to make one certain it was artificial and forced. His brassy blonde head of hair was perfectly groomed with each and every strand in place with a pompadour in front and the back sculptured to a geometrically precise square at the neckline. His eyes betrayed a faint touch of eye-shadow, eye-liner and the eyebrows were distinctly artificially darkened to a jet black.

The white diner jacket he wore had a distinctly feminine cut with a tightness about the waist and a slight flare to the bottom of the coat. His glossy silk slacks were tightly fitted around the buttocks and gently tapered to the ankles without cuffs. The entire ensemble was neatly complemented by a pair of black patent leather shoes with pointed toes and tasseled laces.

Adrian glided, more than actually walked, across the room with a definite swing and swivel of the hips. In his right hand he held a long, thin cigarette between his index and ring fingers. The arm was cocked at the elbow, and the hand-held-cigarette was just inches from his painted lips. The left arm swung at his side with the wrist flexed so that the fingers were horizontally placed but slightly flexed at all the knuckle joints. He approached Vito and the others as discreetly as possible.

"Excuse me, gentlemen," he said with a slight but clear lisp to his s's. Can I help you?" Are you sure you are in the correct establishment?"

"Well, well, well, look what we got us here," stammered Vito with his numbed lips still under the influence of the alcohol. "This here must be the head waitress of this joint. Ain't she lovely, guys?" Mario and all the others responded with a raucous laugh.

"Yeah. She's really beautiful. I wonder if she's spoken for," said Mario in an unusual show of assertiveness and aggressiveness.

"Hey, be careful, Mario. She might be the bouncer and might throw you out of this a. . . establishment," said Pattie Flanagan chuckling.

"I ain't worried because she's a 'she', not a 'he'. I mean, he's a she, not a . . .ah, you know what I mean."

"Now, now we don't want any trouble, do we? You look like nice young men. So, why don't you just leave quietly and try not to disturb our customers. If you please, the door is this way," said the maitre de diplomatically trying to avoid a confrontation.

"Naw, naw," said Vito and the others as loudly as possible. "We ain't leaving here 'til we get a drink and meet some of your other 'lady' customers." He knew full well that there were no real ladies in the gathering.

They glanced around the dimly lighted room and easily picked out some other gay men and some transvestites sitting at the bar or in couples at the tables.

Mario went up to a table where two transvestites were sipping drinks. He sat himself on the lap of a plump, red-headed 'lady' wearing a clashing red dress and with exaggerated, uplifted, false breasts.

"How you doin', honey?" said Mario, reaching his hand down into the front of the dress between the extravagant cleavage.

Vito and the others could not believe the boldness with which Mario behaved. In response, they all followed suit and began to harass some of the other homosexuals.

"Hey," shouted Mario. "There's something funny about these bosoms. They don't feel real. They feel kind of . . . you know, spongy."

The redhead tried to throw Mario off his lap and pulled at his hand sticking down the front of the dress. He did manage to remove Mario's hand and pushed him off his slap into Vito and Joey who caught him and held him upright.

"Hey, Mario don't you think you goin' a little to far this time?" warned Joey. "Even though they're queers some of these guys look pretty big and strong."

"Naw, I ain't scared of no fairies. Besides, everybody knows they don't fight back. That's why they ain't real men and they turn queer. They gotta act like girls 'cause they never learned how to be guys."

Mario lunged back at the redhead, pulled off his red wig and, while the transvestite was distracted, put his hand underneath the his skirt.

"Hey, what'd you know. This ain't no girl, after all. She's a guy, or should I say 'a gay', dressed up like a dame."

The Wolves Of Brooklyn

All the boys began to laugh at and heckle all the patrons in the cocktail lounge.

Just as it appeared that things were getting out of hand and might lead to violence Adrian appeared with two security men from the hotel security force. The two uniformed officers were carrying night sticks and wearing revolvers. They sauntered over to where Vito stood since he had all the appearances and attitudes of the leader.

"Well, punk, guess what? This here parties over for you and your hoodlum friends. So, round them all up and get the hell out of here. Now!"

Vito stepped back a few feet until he had his back to the wall and began to reach into his back pocket where he still carried the home made 'blackjack' he and Mario had made years ago to handle the school bully.

Adrian Primrosa came rushing forward interdicting himself between Vito and the officers. "Now, just a minute officers, let's not cause an unnecessary scene. I'm sure I can convince this attractive young man and his. . . companions to leave quietly. Just give me a moment alone with him." He escorted Vito into the nearby men's restroom after making sure it was unoccupied.

"I believe Mr. . . what is your name again? I know we've met before but I can't recall."

"Vito Vitale. What's it to you?"

"Well, its obvious you and your friends have been drinking and are a little out of control. I don't want to make any trouble for all of you, especially with your fine face and physique. If you promise to leave quietly I'll call off those goons and we won't have to get the police involved to press charges and all the sort of messy court stuff. What do you say Vito? Is it a deal?"

He reached out to shake Vito's hand to seal the agreement. Vito hesitated but finally placed his right hand in Adrian's. Adrian immediately flexed the index finger of his right hand and stroked the palm of Vito's hand as they touched. This was a crude but well known expression of sexual overture with which Vito was quite familiar. He returned the affirmative response of stroking Adrian's palm in the same manner.

Adrian smiled. "Good, then it's settled. I'll send the officers away and you leave quietly with your companion's. Okay, Vito?"

"Okay, its a deal."

"Wonderful. Goodbye then and I'll see you soon. By the way I get off work at 2 a.m. If you have no plans we can . . . get together, as it were, at that time."

"Yeah, sure."

Adrian slinked out of the men's room with an even more than usual swagger to his hips. He stopped at the door, looked back over his shoulder at Vito, slowly stuck out his tongue and blew him a kiss.

After the door closed behind Adrian Vito said, 'Yuck'. I think I'm gonna puke. I hate fags. But this just might be an opportunity to pick up some easy money." He immediately began formulating his plans for 2 am.

Swaggering jauntily out of the restroom Vito called out in a triumphant, face saving tone to his fellow Wolves, "Come on you guys. Let's blow this joint, if you'll excuse the expression, ladies . . .and gentlemen." Many of the patrons moaned or swooned as the boys left the cocktail lounge.

"Hey, Vito, what's wrong with you? Why did you give up so easy? There was only two of the house cops. We could've taken them," said Mario with an uncharacteristic show of bravery.

"Yeah, I know that, dummy. But that won't help us get what we came for in the first place."

"What was that?" asked Iggy.

The Wolves Of Brooklyn

"Money, dough, mazzula, remember? Can't you idiots keep anything straight in those thick heads of yours?"

"Oh, yeah. But how's quittin' gonna get us any dough? Tell me that would ya? smart ass," said Iggy.

Vito did not answer the challenge until they were outside of the St. George Hotel and lounging in a vest-pocket-park across the street.

"Now that nobody can hear our plans, I'll tell you guys what I have in mind." They gathered in a tight circle as Vito whispered his scheme.

"When we were in the head that queer waiter, Adrian, made a pass at me." None of the boys were surprised since they were aware of Vito's many heterosexual exploits and wide sex appeal.

"Anyway, I'm gonna meet 'her' at 2 a.m. when he gets off work."

"Then what are you gonna do? Make him give you two bucks for makin' love to him? That ain't no real dough," said Juan with a look of derision.

"No, you jerk. Besides, I'm worth a lot more than that. No, this guy's in charge of this joint and I'll bet that he takes the nights receipts to a night depository or something like that at the end of the day. Now you add that to the cash he carries to buy guys like me and I'll bet he's got a couple a grand in his pocket. And that, my brainless friends, is real dough."

"You mean it Vito? You really think he's got two thousand dollars on him? That's a lot of loot," said Mario.

"Yeah, that's more than your old man brings home in half a year salary," added Vito.

"So, what do we do at 2 a.m.?" asked Pattie.

"I'll be sittin' hear on the park bench trying to look as sexy as possible, which ain't too tough for me, when he comes out of the hotel. At about 1:30 a.m. you guys will go back in the bushes and hide, real good. And you have to be real quiet."

"Why hide so long?"asked Tony.

"In case the queer gets wise, smells a rat, and comes out early, that's why."

"Oh, I got ya."

"Then, he'll probably try to hold my hand, or something else, if you get my drift. Then when he ain't lookin' I'll give you the signal and you all come out and jump on him. Now we can't let him yell so one of you has gotta cover his mouth. Tony you're strong, almost as strong as me, you grab him around the neck to choke off his wind and then cover his mouth with your hand and drag him to the ground. The rest of you hold his arms and legs and drag him back into the bushes where nobody can see us."

"What if he puts up a fight?" asked Joey.

"Go on, fairies don't fight," said Mario.

"That's what you think. Some of them is pretty strong," said Dommie.

"They may be strong but they ain't got no guts," said Mario.

"So what?" said Vito. "He's only one queer and there's nine of us. No problem."

"Okay, now everybody into them bushes. And don't make no noise, don't even breath," said Vito.

"But, Vito, we can't live if we don't breath," said Harvey.

"Never mind, Harvey, just come with me and do what I do," said Mario as he tugged at Harvey's arm pulling him into the cover.

***

An hour passed with Vito sitting on the bench and the rest of the Wolves hiding in the brush. After a short time they became impatient but passed the time by smoking

The Wolves Of Brooklyn

cigarettes, telling dirty jokes and arm wrestling. All the time Vito was admonishing them for making too much noise and revealing their cover. Finally, Adrian came out the back door of the hotel. The echo of the hotel back door slamming was magnified by the cool, quiet but vibrant night air to the level of a shot fired from a starting-gun .

"All right, you guys, be quiet here he comes. Now get ready and watch for my signal," said Vito.

Adrian pranced as delicately and seductively as he could toward Vito sitting on the park bench. As he reached the halfway point to the bench he stopped, turned to profile a silhouette for Vito and lit a cigarette. Then he proceeded to glide toward the bench.

"Hello there, Vito. How are you? I hope you're in the mood for some excitement. I feel very. . . very, how should I put it. . . adventurous I guess is the right word, my dear, young Italian stallion." He followed the statement with a giggle in his best soprano voice.

"Yeah, yeah, Adrian. I feel good, too. Only I wouldn't call it feeling like a stallion. I feel more like the bank robber riding the stallion away from the bank with the bags of loot in his hand."

"Why, whatever do you mean, dear lad?"

Before Adrian could complete his question Vito give the signal to the others in the brush. In a split second they were all strolling casually toward Adrian as he smoked his cigarette. They slowly formed a circle around the victim. His hand dropped to his side and the cigarette slowly slipped from between his fingers to the pavement. As he turned around slowly looking at the assailants approaching, his cheeks sagged from his coquettish grin to a frightened frown.

"Now, just a minute. What's going on here? I hope you are not thinking of doing something very foolish, dear boys," he stammered trying to sound humorous and unafraid.

"Well, I guess that depends on who the fool is," said Mario.

Pattie Flanagan was the first to make contact with Adrian. He threw a right hook at the bleached-blonde head but he ducked and kicked Pattie in the groin. Pattie fell to the pavement groaning. All the others were shocked at first and stepped back one step.

"What are ya waitin' for," shouted Vito, "Let's get him."

With that they all rushed Adrian, grabbed all four of his extremities while Mario threw his arms around his neck in a choke hold. They wrestled him to the pavement punching and kicking him in the body and head. Vito, in the meantime, reached inside his pockets searching for his wallet, cash, car keys, and pulled any and all jewelry from the half-conscious, bleeding body. A soft, quiet sobbing sound seeped up from Adrian's throat.

"Listened to that, will ya," said Mario laughing mockingly. "Sounds just a like a woman cryin'. Don't it?"

Pattie Flanagan was being helped up by some of his companions when he realized what had happened. He approached Adrian in a fit of rage and began kicking him viciously in the groin.

"Ain't no queer gonna get the best of me," he muttered through clenched teeth. "Kick me in the balls will ya? Well, since you ain't got no real use for yours I think I'll kick 'em 'til they're crushed." After several kicks Adrian vomited and rolled over face down on the concrete walk and fell unconscious.

Mario sauntered over very brazenly, grabbed a hand full of the blonde hair and lifted Adrian's head to hold it steady. He then delivered several punches to the face and head of the senseless victim.

The Wolves Of Brooklyn

As the gang walked away from their wounded prey counting up their loot Vito and Mario drifted back away from the main group.

"Say, you were pretty brave there tonight, Mario. A real tough cookie when it comes to queers and cats, ain't ya?" he said and laughed again.

Mario didn't answer. Instead, he ran ahead with the other gang members to celebrate their new found wealth and to split up the shares.

Vito and the other Junior Wolves roamed around the Brooklyn Heights for a couple of more hours trying to find some more mischief to get into but all was fairly quiet by 4:00 a.m. Having decided they had accomplished enough and taken enough money for their first night's work, they scattered back to their respective tenements.

"Hey, Vito, did you see what time it is? We are gonna be in big trouble. You now how strong Papa feels about our curfew of eleven o'clock."

"Don't you worry none about it, Mario. I'll make up a good story to cover us and get the other guys to back it up. Then, we'll back up their alibi's with their folks, too. They're ain't no way that old man can out smart us any more. Besides, what can he do about it? He ain't gonna beat us no more since that last time. Come on, let's get home and get some sleep."

As they walked east past the Manhattan Bridge, the Sperry Bombsight plant, and the Howard Clothes factory toward the High street tenement, they were feeling quite victorious in their first encounter with the forces of the street and their quest for easy money.

CHAPTER ELEVEN
BIG GAME

Unquestionably, baseball, and the Brooklyn Dodgers, was the most loved professional sport in Brooklyn. But playing baseball was difficult for kids living in the Navy Yard district for two major reasons. First, there were no baseball diamonds or even empty lots that could be used as playing fields. Second, most families could not afford to purchase bats, baseballs, and baseball gloves for the boys.

The most popular sport the Wolves and all other gangs in their neighborhood engaged in was called--fistball, otherwise known as--punch ball.

It was an improvised variant of baseball just as was the more widely known variety called stick ball. The construction of the tenements in the Brooklyn Navy Yard district, however, made stick ball impractical. In the Bronx and lower Manhattan the tenements were much taller and the streets were much wider.

As a result of this difference too many of the 'Spaldeen' (Spalding) balls they used were lost over the roof tops in the Brooklyn tenement district. The local youths adapted to these environmental differences by devising their off-shoot of fistball. Instead of using the pink, harder rubber 'Spaldeen' they used a softer, pimpled, and cheaper white rubber ball called, appropriately, a 'pimple ball'.

The four bases--first, second, third and home plate--were painted on the sidewalks and street pavement just as they were in stick ball. These always included the major league adornments--the coaching boxes, the batters box, the on-deck-batter's circle, a scoreboard, two dugouts and the team name, 'The Wolves', painted on a large brick wall behind the home dugout. Since their was no pitcher, as there is in stick ball, their is no pitcher's mound. They try to emulate the major league ball parks, as much as possible, with a cheap can of house paint and paint brush usually left over from home apartment painting.

Instead of using a bat or broom-stick to hit the ball, the ball was tossed up over the head by the batter and he struck it with his fist before it hit the ground. The batter had only one strike at the ball and, of course, there are no bases on balls, passed balls or wild pitches since there is no pitcher.

The boys organized their own fistball leagues according to neighborhoods and the ethnicity of the players. The 'Wolves'--comprised of predominantly Italians--played against; the 'Rainbows', mostly Polish; the 'Danny Boys', primarily Irish; the 'Tiger Sharks', mostly Puerto Ricans, and the 'Vikings', comprised exclusively of Sweeds. The blacks also had organized teams but they only played against other blacks. The white parents would not allow any mixture and co-mingling of the races on any level--not even sports.

Mario, with his penchant for organizing and bookkeeping, had arranged the league playing schedule with one game played on Saturday and Sunday each weekend, at least after school was out for the summer. On special occasions like Memorial Day, Fourth of July, and Labor Day double headers were even scheduled. He kept very meticulous records including league standings, batting averages, home runs hit, fielding errors and the like. At the end of the season there was a final 'championship' game between the first and second place teams which had some significance for the boys.

However, the major event of the season, at least for the boys and their families on High Street, was the contest between the Junior Wolves and the Senior Wolves. The team of the Seniors was made up of former alumni players of the Juniors who continued to play in their own seniors' league. The annual contest, held on Columbus day, which was a legal holiday in New York City, had gained enough attention and prominence to make all the friends, neighbors, relatives and parents--both mama's and papa's-- attend the game and at which large sums of money were bet on the outcome. All of the bets were covered, with appropriate odds, by Louie Lupo, the local gambling kingpin.

The 'Big Game' was almost equivalent to the Baseball World Series in their corner of the world. All the neighborhood people for blocks around came to the game, It was a major area event of the summer. Since most families only dreamt of going on a real vacation for the holiday, most would be home anyway and needed some way to break the monotony of city life.

Instead, all the families and friends gathered at the tenement apartment of the senior surviving matriarch or patriarch for a huge, four hour long dinner that began in mid-afternoon. The meal was followed by an all night poker game for penny-ante stakes and some serious drinking of home made Chianti wine. But come Labor Day Sunday, after all the women and children had returned from church, everyone gathered at the upper one-third of the street, which was marked off for the playing field, and painted afresh for the the big event--The annual 'Junior-Senior Wolves' fistball game.

The Wolves Of Brooklyn

The entire street was barricaded at each end with large, galvanized-metal garbage cans with planks or lead pipes laid across their tops. The barricades were guarded, in shifts, by the huskiest and toughest men available. However, strangely enough, the police never seemed to challenge this minor violation of the law. On the contrary, most of them helped to maintain the road blocks to keep out the auto and truck traffic. Of course, they also came to watch, and bet on, the fistball game.

All the tenement buildings bordering the "playing field" had their windows opened to allow all the spectators as good a vantage point from which to watch the game. All the fire-escapes were occupied, all the front windows were filled with people, all the front stoops were covered with enthusiastic fans sitting on the steps. Even the roof-tops were utilized by the more courageous neighbors.

Only one tenement building, just behind third base, could afford a real front porch. It was the home of Louie Lupo, alias 'Louie-the-Wolf'. There were several folding chairs, borrowed from the local funeral parlor, lined up in rows on the porch for Louie, his bodyguards, his family and one or two honored guests--usually a lower echelon Mafia member or two.

Louie was actually a small-time hood but he wielded considerable influence since it was known that he often recruited new prospects for the local Mafia from the neighborhood gangs and clubs.

Although the game was not scheduled to begin until 2:00 pm. many of the spectators gathered early for the placing of small wagers on the outcome of the game. No one but Louie was permitted to cover all the bets.

"Hey, Louie, comé sta? I like to bet a dollar and fifty cents on the seniors. You can cover this huge-a bet?" said one man from the crowd, smiling.

"Si, but of course, Armando, anything for my favorite barber. I'm a gonna give you three to one odds, just-a-because I'm-a like you so much," said Louie.

"T'ank-a you, so much. You're too kind."

For this years big game their was something unusual about Louie's front porch spectators. There were, as usual, two other gamblers sitting on the chairs but there were also three Mafia men present. All of the Mafia men appeared to be from higher up in the chain of command, judging from their expensive clothes and individual bodyguards. Even one of the police sergeants from the local precinct put in a rare appearance on the porch. The array of special visitors had immediately started rumors flying among the spectators.

"Good-a day, Sgt. Clancy, my good friend. You come to watch the big game, heh?" said Louie.

"Not exactly, Mr. Lupo, not exactly."

Louie and the policeman walked over into one of the remote corners of the porch, turned their backs to the others and began whispering. After several minutes had passed, the sergeant left the porch smiling after shaking Louie's hand vigorously.

"What did he want Louie?, asked Joey Feets (Giuseppe Piedi), one of the Mafia men, is he trying to make trouble for us?"

"No, my friend, no trouble. What does the polizia usually come around for when he knows we are making book, huh? Some pay-off dollaro. So I make a nice big bet for him on the big game. Now, he's happy. No trouble."

"I'm sure you fix 'em so that he wins some money no matter which team wins the game, right?" said Joey.

"Ma shuse, my paesano, you just gotta do it to keep the 'bulls' on your side and off your back."

There was more excitement and anticipation than usual regarding the outcome of the game this year, the

The Wolves Of Brooklyn

reason for which no one could really put their finger on . . . yet. Perhaps it was the presence of the Mafia men; or maybe it was because there were more bookies present than usual; or, perhaps, it was because everyone could sense that more money was being bet on the game than in previous years. Then, of course, there was the arrival of the precinct sergeant which just heightened everyone's anticipation and confirmed their suspicions that "some-a-thing big" was riding on this game.

"Hey, Louie," asked one of the lady spectators, "who do you think gonna win the game today?"

"Ah, ha, Madelina, bella mia, I don't know for sure but the Senior Wolves got some nice strong hitters this year."

Although this was true, to a certain extent, everyone knew that all the real hitting talent was on the Junior team, as was all the speed, and the best defensive abilities. And most of all, everyone believed in Vito's skill and leadership. He was the major advantage they had over the Seniors. Everyone just surmised that Louie had said this to influence the betting for his own gains. Like most sports fans, the Italian-Americans bet primarily in accordance with their emotions, perhaps they even more than other ethnic groups. And all their hearts were with their local Italian hero, Vito Vitale . . . all the way.

As in most years the game was a high scoring contest, but still very close. The lead changed hands almost every inning of the nine-inning battle. The temperature and humidity were both in the mid-90s which was typical for Brooklyn and New York City at this time of year. The torrid weather conditions, clearly, were beginning to take their toll on all the players but especially so on the seniors. The effective difference was not only related to the age difference, itself, but the older boys were now regular cigarette smokers; they were more heavily into alcohol intake; and they were up most of the night before the big game engaged in the all night poker playing.

In addition, the greater stamina and better physical condition of the 'Juniors' was beginning to increase their edge. They were hitting the ball farther, more accurately and the defensive fielding was very sharp. It seemed certain to everyone that victory would belong to them, just as the majority of the neighborhood people were betting. . . except, of course, for Louie-the-Wolf.

It was the top of the ninth inning and the Seniors--a very hot, tired lot, indeed--were at bat. The score was tied 12 to 12. Somehow, they gathered enough strength to score 3 more runs and go ahead 15 to 12. The play that scored the three runs came when there were two men out and two runners on base. An easy fly ball was hit to Vito in left field. It took a high, easy bounce off the front of a building--still a catchable out--making it even easier to catch for a player with Vito's abilities.

However, he misjudged the carom off the building, an error he almost never made on a high bouncer. The ball bounded away from him and far enough down the street for all the runners and the batter to score. The Seniors lead 15 to 12.

"That's okay, Vito, don't worry about it.," said all his teammates and fans as they applauded and cheered him on. "You gonna get 'em back."

Then the third out was made. It was now the Junior's turn at bat in the bottom of the ninth inning. They needed three runs to tie and go into extra innings or four runs to win it. Through several scattered hits and defensive errors by the Seniors, the Juniors now had two men out but with the bases loaded--and Vito, the best home run hitter on the team, was at bat. It was the perfect opportunity for him to redeem himself for his defensive mistake, win the game, and be the hero--as he usually was. His skills this day had

The Wolves Of Brooklyn

already produced five hits, two of them home runs, and six runs batted in. The entire outcome was in his hands.

Mario was on third base, taking a big lead off and cheering Vito on.

"Come on Vito, my paesano, you can do it. Hit one into the big oak tree in left field and we can all come home winners."

"Come on, Vito, smack a big-a home run," yelled one spectator. "I'm-a got a lots of dollari bet on this one," called another.

All the spectators sitting on Louie's porch were on the edge of their seats awaiting the outcome. Except Louie Lupo, he just leaned back in his chair, smiling and very confident of the outcome.

Everyone knew Vito could hit a home-run almost at will and clear the bases to win the game. They had all seen him do it many times before. He finally stepped into the batters box, tossed the ball up high, as is best to hit it far, and swung a powerful swing. The crowd was on its feet yelling when the saw the ball sailing high and far. It was deep enough to be a home run but he hit it straight up the middle of the street instead of hitting it into the large oak tree way down the block. The centerfielder camped under it leisurely and made an easy catch for the third out. The game was over and the Juniors had lost.

But the disappointed crowd and his team members did not blame Vito nor did they chastise him. Instead, they applauded him loudly and called words of consolation.

"That's all right, Vito. It's not your fault. You did the best you could."

"We'll get them next year, Vito. Don't worry about it," said his teammates, patting him on the back.

As the crowd cleared the street, the tenements, and the roof-tops Mario tried to find Vito in the mass of people to try to console him. He knew Vito would be too hard on himself and take all the blame for the defeat. Standing on his toes to see over the crowd, Mario could barely see Vito running into an alley apparently running from his shame.

"Vito, Vito, wait," he yelled.

But Vito hadn't heard him and he kept running. It took Mario another five minutes to push his way through the crowd to get to the alley. A bit short-winded afterward, Mario stopped at the entrance to the alley to catch his breath. As he leaned against the building he looked around the corner into the alley searching for Vito. He slowly walked into the alley, puzzled.

"Hey, Vito, Vito where are you?" he shouted.

The alley was quiet, Mario could hear some voices, one of which he thought was Vito's but he couldn't be sure. He listened at several of the closed back doors to the buildings until he came to the door to their club house. The voice of Vito and another person was audible.

Mario opened the door and walked in to find Vito and Louie Lupo. Louie was handing Vito a fistful of twenty-dollar bills.

"What are you doing in here. . .Vito?" then he hesitated after realizing he had interrupted something he shouldn't have.

"It's okay, Mario," said Louie. "Come on in."

"Yeah, Mario, it's all right as long as you keep your mouth shut about this."

"Very good, Vito, my young paesano," said Louie. "You keep doing this kind of work for me and you'll go far in my organization. There's plenty more money where that came. Arrivederci."

Louie left through the back door.

Vito was counting the bills.

"You threw the game, didn't you?" asked Mario.

Vito didn't answer. He just smiled and went on counting.

The Wolves Of Brooklyn

"You hit that last ball straight up the middle on purpose, didn't you? And that easy fly ball off the apartment to score them three runs, you muffed that one on purpose, too, didn't you?"

"So what if I did? Look at all the loot I got for it."

"You and Louie fixed the game, he bets some dough for you, and you throw the game, right?"

"Right, right. So what? Now I got two hundred bucks to spend and I'll probably be on Louie's payroll for good. Now I can really make some big bucks."

"Well, yeah, I guess so. But I think you counted wrong, you only got a hundred bucks."

"What are ya talking about. There's two hundred smackers here. You wanna count it?"

"No, Never mind, I believe you. But I think I'm entitled to half of the take so we both got a hundred bucks," said Mario.

"You're crazy. I ain't giving you none of this. Why should I?"

"Well, what do you think Papa would say if he knew you threw the game for money and . . ."

Before Mario could finish Vito had punched him in the eye, which immediately raised a welt, and then he had Mario by the throat.

"You say anything to anybody and I'll break you neck, you creep."

Gasping and struggling to speak under the grip of Vito's fingers Mario said, "then you're gonna have to kill me to stop me."

Vito slowly relaxed his grip on Mario's throat.

"Go ahead, go ahead, kill me. 'Cause that's what you'll have to do to keep me quiet."

Vito could see he meant it. He grudgingly handed Mario five of the twenty dollar bills.

"Good, good, my brother, now we're partners on everything. Everything we do for Louie."

The Wolves Of Brooklyn

CHAPTER TWELVE
THE PETTY THIEF

"U.S troops halted their advance just north of the 38th parallel in Korea and peace talks begin," Carlo was reading aloud the column from the New York Daily News to his wife and family.

"Oh, magnifico", said 'Nunciata. "Now maybe Mario and Vito no have to be drafted in the army if this terrible war is really over."

"Well, it would be no problem, if they go to college. They can get a deferment to continue their education," Carlo pointed out.

"Yeah, that's right, Papa," said Mario. "I never thought of that. Does the deferment apply even to students in pre-law? That's what I want to be, a lawyer."

"Ah, so, very good, Mario. A lawyer, heh. That's a good profession as long as you're honest," said Carlo.

"And what about you, Vito?" asked 'Nunciata. "What are you going to study in college?"

"Nothing." Vito answered. "I ain't gonna study nothing."

"What do you mean, nothing. You can't go to college and not study something," scowled Carlo.

"That's an easy one. I ain't going to college," Vito said.

"Why not, Vito?" asked his foster sister, Angela.

"Because I don't want to be no college boy. I want to get into some big money, fast."

"That's what you think, young man," interrupted Carlo. "You gonna go to college and make something of yourself. No son of mine is going to work like a horse for peanuts all his life, if I have anything to say about it."

"First of all, I ain't your real son. I told you that a million times. And, second of all, you ain't got nothin' to say about it. I'll do what I want to do. Not what you want me to do."

Carlo's face flared bright red with anger as he reached across the kitchen table to take a slap at Vito. Vito sprang to his feet, grabbed Carlo's wrist, stopping it in mid-air. He then started to squeeze the wrist tightly until Carlo's hand turned white and he yelled in pain. Carlo stumbled back into his chair after the abrupt reminder he was no longer as young or as strong as he once was.

"Now, Carlo, Vito is old enough to make his own decisions about his future. It doesn't work to force him into anything he doesn't want to do," said 'Nunciata in defense of Vito's choice.

"Okay, okay, he don't have to go to college. But he can't stay in my house if he doesn't get a decent job and pay me for room and board," answered Carlo. "He's going to earn his own keep. If he's old enough to make his own choices, he's old enough to support himself. It's either that way or he gets out."

Carlo never passed up the opportunity to try to get Vito out of his house, if he could.

"That's fine with me, old man. I don't need nobody to support me. I'll make my own way. And as soon as I hit the big money I'll move out anyway. I ain't gonna live in a dump like this all my life."

"Now, now, Vito, don't be foolish. You can stay here until you earn enough for you own place. But, your papa's right. You should help to support yourself, learn to be independent and not live off of others. It's the only way to be a real man."

"Okay, these are the rules," said Carlo. "You got two weeks to find an honest, decent job. If you don't, you move out."

His wife looked at him gently shaking her head indicating that he should give Vito more time. Carlo relented.

"All right, all right, four weeks then. I give you four weeks and not another single day. You gotta pay me twenty dollars a month to live in my house. You buy your own clothes and you use your own money for everything else except for food. You understand?"

'Nunciata tried to give Carlo another sign to influence him to lower Vito's monthly room and board charge. Carlo did not relent on this point.

"Yeah, I got you, old man. I gotcha."

"And, Mario, since you are going to college we will provide everything you need including a twenty dollar a month allowance until you graduate. Except for the summer time, you gotta work in the summer and make your own spending money."

"Okay, papa. Whatever you say."

***

The following day Vito visited his benefactor, Louie Lupo.

"Eh, my young paesano, Vito. Come in," he said as he welcomed him into his well guarded, private office in the back of the barber shop.

The Wolves Of Brooklyn

"Now, what is it I can go for you, paesano?"

"I need a steady job, Louie. You've been good to me with odd stuff on weekends but now that I'm finished high school I need something full time. I'm gonna live in my mama's place for awhile. But I wanna get my own place and I need to make some real money, fast."

"Sure, sure, Vito. I give you a job but you're still to green for the big stuff just yet. First you gotta prove yourself to the big bosses. I mean, I think you're great, you proved that at the fistball game. But the big guys, they demand more proof and more tests of your courage. I can start you with, say twenty bucks a month. Then when you work you're way up I give you more, if the chief says it's okay."

"But, Louie, that ain't enough dough. That'll just cover my room and board. I won't have no spending money."

"For starters, you don't call me Louie no more. You address me as boss, or chief, or Capo, or Mr. Lupo, but not Louie. Next, the low salary for starters is part of the test of your brains and your guts. If you need more money you show us how you can get it without our help. It's part of proving yourself. Now, do you want the job or not?"

"Oh, I get it. You want to see if I can work any schemes or gimmicks on my own. Okay, okay Louie. . . I mean boss. You're on. I'll take the job and the challenge."

"Good, good. You report here every day at six o'clock."

"You mean six o'clock in the morning or at night?"

"I mean six a.m. And that's every morning including Saturday and Sunday. You come and clean up the barber shop. Then you clean up the betting room in the back. Sweep up and burn all the policy and betting slips. You erase the previous days numbers off the chalkboard. Any cash you find in the trash you turn in to me. You stay here all day running errands for me, all customers and anybody else that's asks you to, no questions asked. No ifs, ands, or buts. No job is too small or insignificant for you. You just do it and fast. You capicé?"

Vito was frowning at this point as his visions of starting with big money making assignments vanished. "Yeah, boss, I capicé. I'll be here at six sharp every morning."

'This ain't gonna work out. I gotta find another way to make some dough. I can't live on twenty bucks. I need spending money, and lots of it,' Vito thought to himself.

His scheming mind immediately began to search for bits of recollections of where he knew money was hidden among the places and people he knew.

'I need some seed money to start with. I gotta buy some tools, and a weapon. Yeah, I'm gonna need a weapon to defend myself.'

A week went by with Vito toeing the mark as Louie Lupo had ordered him to do. He always arrived a few minutes before six and was waiting at the curb to open the door of the black limousine for his new boss. No task was too menial or too difficult for him to accomplish. Louie began to rely and depend on him more each day.

***

Then another week passed with some very tight financial moments for Vito. He worked everyday until well after midnight. After a few short hours of sleep he was back at the barber shop to start over again. But he was getting used to the late hours and was learning to get by with less sleep. Carlo tried to enforce a curfew but his wife convinced him not to try to curtail Vito's free-wheeling life-style. Instead of coming home after work Vito started hanging out in all the cheap 'gin meals' and whore houses in the area. However, the lack of adequate funds was clearly restricting his social life. Vito was determined to change that permanently.

The Wolves Of Brooklyn

It was a little after 2 a.m. one night, as Vito quietly entered the flat. He had taken off his shoes to try to avoid waking Mario, mama, Angela and Carlo. As he passed through the kitchen, going toward the bedroom he shared with Mario, he glanced over at the kitchen cabinet. The red and green 'Stella D'oro' espresso coffee can immediately caught his eye. In a flash he remembered seeing 'Nunciata put part of her food allowance into the can every Saturday when Carlo brought home his pay envelope.

"Oh yeah," he whispered as he softly opened the can being careful not to rattle the coins within.

"Only six bucks," he whispered. "But it's better than nothing. And nobody'll know about it until next Saturday. By that time I can replace it and nobody will be the wiser." He stuffed the money into his wallet and stole off to bed.

The following Saturday came faster than Vito had expected and he didn't find a way to get the money to replace what he had taken from the coffee can.

"Here you are, cara mia. The pay envelope for this week. It's pretty good with the extra overtime I worked," said Carlo.

"Oh, bené, bené. Now maybe I can put some extra in the espresso can to buy some clothes for Mario when he starts college."

She instinctively reached for the can but immediately noticed its lighter weight and the absence of the clanking of the coins. She frantically opened the lid of the can and cut her finger on its sharp edge.

A small trickle of blood dropped from her finger which she ignored completely.

"Hey, 'Nunciata, what's a matter with you? You cut your finger on the . . ." said Carlo as he tried to put pressure on the laceration.

"Never mind that, Carlo. The money's gone."

"What? What do you mean gone? How could it be gone? Here, let me look at it."

Carlo took the can and also noticed the silence and lightness of it.

"It is gone. It's empty. Maybe you took it out to hide it someplace else? Maybe you bought something with it and forgot about it?"

"No, Carlo, I no buy nothing and I no hide it some place else. Somebody steal it. We have a thief in our house."

"Yeah, yeah. And I know exactly who it is. It's that good-for-nothing Vito. When he gets home I'm gonna squeeze that money out of his hide. I kill that little. . ."

"Now, now, Carlo, don't blame Vito right away. You don't know that he took it. You always ready to condemn him without any proof. Give the boy a chance to explain. He maybe know nothing about it."

"Oh, really. Then who else could've took it? Mario, or Angela, or maybe it was me. Maybe I took that money. No, no, it's got to be Vito. There ain't nobody else outside this house who knows you keep the money in that coffee can."

Carlo raged and fumed all evening waiting for Vito to get home so he could confront him. But Vito worked late into the night as usual. Carlo stretched out on his bed when his wife went to bed. But he couldn't sleep. He slowly simmered to the boiling point. Finally, a little after 2 a.m. Carlo heard Vito's stocking feet climbing the stairs to the second story flat. He waited quietly in his bedroom until Vito was well into the kitchen. As Carlo expected Vito headed straight for the cabinet with the coffee-can in it. Vito reached into the cabinet. Carlo suddenly flicked on the kitchen lights. Vito spun around, startled and momentarily blinded by the bright light after the darkness of the stairs.

"So, my little gangster is now a petty thief who steals from his mama, even though she ain't his 'real' mama. Like

The Wolves Of Brooklyn

I ain't his real papa. But our money is real enough to spend on women and drink."

"No, you're wrong, I didn't steal nothin'. I . . . ah, I just borrowed it. That's what I did. And I was just putting it back. . . with interest." He took out a crisp ten dollar bill he had just won playing poker and put it in the coffee-can."

"You lie to me, you punk? Out you go, out. Get out of my house. . ."

"No, Carlo, wait. It's true, I remember now. Vito asked me last week if he could borrow the six dollars. Me a stupido," she said, as she characteristically gestured by slapping her palm to her forehead. "I forget all about it. Thank you, Vito. Thank you so much for paying it back so soon, and with interest, too."

"I don't believe you, 'Nunciata. You lie to me to save this thief, this disgratiata animale (disgraceful animal)."

"No, no, Carlo. I swear to you, he didn't steal it. I swear to you on my mother's and my father's graves. I let him borrow it, I swear to Santa Giuseppe. Don't throw him out. He didn't do it."

"That's right, old man. I borrowed it. Me and mama, swear it."

"Stop, stop. Don't lie to me no more. Out of my house you go tonight, right now," he raged on.

"Carlo, you can't do this. You promised on his father's grave you would take care of him."

Carlo was firm in his decision. It appeared he would not relent this time. But his mind was made up. "NO, NO. . .OUT."

But his wife also stood her ground. She threw back her shoulders, stuck out her sharp chin and shook her head vigorously screaming. "NO, I cannot let you do this terrible thing. If Vito goes out. . . I, I go with him. And that is my final word."

Carlo was stunned. He had never heard his genteel wife raise her voice in anger at him or anyone else. Again, he hesitated. He knew he could not live without his beloved Annunciata. He was nothing without her and he knew it. But he was beginning to wonder about her loyalties. Was Vito more important to her than him, or Mario or Angela, and the rest of the family? The doubts wrenched at his heart. And again he yielded to her wishes. Without saying a word he walked into his bedroom and closed the door. Vito smiled quite pleased with yet another victory over Carlo. 'Nunciata smiled, turned to him and said, "now you go to bed like a good boy and get some sleep. Mama will fix everything up tomorrow."

"Yeah, mama. Yeah sure. Good night."

The Wolves Of Brooklyn

CHAPTER THIRTEEN
THE FINAL STRAW

"Heh, Vito, how's your love life?" asked Louie Lupo.

"Oh, sometimes good and sometimes not so good. But, if I look hard there's always some lady around willing to share her bed."

"What about that beautiful young sister of yours? What's her name. . . Angelina or something like that."

"No, it's Angela but we all call her Angel because she has a face like an angel. She's not going with anybody right now, if that's what you mean, Louie."

"No, that ain't what I mean. You know like you just said. Does she share her bed with you or anybody else."

Vito's face turned blazing, beet red. The hackles stood up on the back of his neck and he clenched his fist ready to attack. Then he realized that he was talking to the big boss and didn't want to jeopardize his new found goose which lays golden eggs. So he swallowed his anger and vowed to get even at a more opportune time.

"Now wait a minute, Louie, she is my sister, you know."

"No she ain't your real sister. You said so yourself. Your papa ain't your real papa, your mama ain't your real mama and the Angel ain't your real sister. As matter of fact you ain't related at all. Not even cousins. And so what? even if you were related, a good lay is a good lay, relative or not," Louie concluded laughing loudly as he and one of his bodyguards left the barber shop. The other body guard, Georgio, remained behind to mind the store.

"Hah, hah, hah," Georgio laughed, "that Louie is a real rip, ain't he?", he said. "A good lay is a good lay. And your almost sister would be a good lay."

Vito could no longer control the anger within himself. He sprang from his chair like a puma attacking a deer. His hands were around Georgio's throat like a vice within a half second.

"I'll kill you, you stinking, muscle bound ape. Nobody talks that way about my. . . about my Angel and lives to repeat it. Nobody."

Georgio, caught off guard by the assault at first, fell to the floor helplessly. But then his natural animal instincts, which had earned him a position as Louie's bodyguard, kicked in automatically. He immediately began throwing fierce blows to Vito's body and head. Blood spurted from Vito's lip and nose, and the first body blow was so severe he vomited into Georgio's face. But he did not loose his grip on Georgio's throat. Vito was like a wild man possessed with super human strength.

"Let go of my throat, you little punk, or I'll rip your liver out," gasped Georgio as his breath ran out.

Both men fell to the floor, crashed into furniture and fixtures but Vito's grip held fast as Georgio's face slowly turned more blue with each anoxic second. Georgio had at least a thirty pound weight advantage on Vito, as well as ten years experience as a street fighter and torpedo man for Louie.

Slowly but surely Georgio's thrashing and struggling began to diminish. First his arms became limp, then his torso and lastly his legs. His skin color tended toward an ashen blue-gray shade just as his lips and ears had done seconds before. Vito, his eyes bulging and his neck veins throbbing, stared as his victim's face virtually unaware of the proximity of Georgio's impending death.

"Stop! What are you doing? You're killing him you maniac."

Louie and his second bodyguard, Salvatore, were on Vito trying to rip his hands from Georgio's throat. When brute strength and verbal appeals failed to break Vito's grip Salvatore removed his 45-caliber automatic from his shoulder holster and was about to shoot Vito in the back of the neck.

"No, no, don't kill him, you stupido. Hit him, hit him hard with the gun," said Louie.

Salvatore raised the heavy weapon and struck Vito just behind his right ear. Vito flinched momentarily but did not relax his hold on Georgio's throat.

"Again, again, Sal," shouted Louie. "Harder, harder"

Salvatore brought the hand gun back again and struck Vito a vicious blow to the base of his skull, which emitted a crunching sound. Vito stiffened, then loosed his clutch, and fell flaccidly to the floor. Sal quickly ran to assist Georgio. He ripped open his shirt collar, rolled him on his belly and began administering pressure to his rib cage for artificial respiration and first aid. Louie watched passively and quite disinterested in the outcome of the life-saving effort.

"Hey, boss, call for an ambulance," yelled Sal.

"No, no ambulance."

"Why not? He's gonna die. He needs oxygen."

"No ambulance 'cause that always brings the cops, too. No ambulance and no cops. If he dies, so what? he dies."

Sal continued to compress Georgio's chest but raised his eyebrows and wrinkled his forehead wondering if

The Wolves Of Brooklyn

Louie would feel the same if he, Sal, were lying on the floor slowly asphyxiating.

"Okay, boss. Whatever you say."

But after two or three minutes Georgio's skin color began to show some signs of a return to a normal pink hue.

"Hey, he's comin' around, boss. I think he'll be okay."

"Good, good," said Louie. "At least we won't have to worry about getting rid of a stiff in the East River."

"You mean two stiffs don't you? You're not gonna let Vito live after this here, are you?"

"Live? Live? Sure I let him live. Don't you see. Vito has now proved himself worthy of being in the family. Do you know how much guts and power it took to get the better of a man like Georgio. Live, oh yeah. Vito's gonna be my third bodyguard now. How long he lives depends on how good he takes care of me and the family. If he crosses me, he dies. . . just the same as anybody else who works for me. Capicé?"

"Yeah, I get you, boss," answered Sal, getting the hint quickly.

Vito moaned softly and turned over on his back shaking his head in an attempt to revive himself but then he slipped back into unconsciousness. Georgio was still lying on his back breathing irregularly but deeply. After several minutes he was sitting on the floor leaning against a table, obviously still dazed and disorientated.

"What . . .what happened?" he said, shaking his head, rubbing his eyes and examining the bruises on his neck. Then he remembered when he saw Vito sprawled out unconscious ten feet away.

Georgio staggered slowly to his feet steadying himself on the corner of the table.

"Georgio, are you okay?" asked Sal.

Louie walked over to Georgio and helped him steady himself. Georgio's eyes were transfixed on Vito's motionless body. The rage within him bursting forth through his now red face and wide protruding eyes. He slowly reached inside his coat for his .357 Magnum, pointed it at Vito and cocked the hammer back. Sal and Louie heard the click and lunged at Georgio just as he was about to squeeze the trigger. They managed to reach him and his gun hand before the cartridge discharged. The large, powerful projectile tore a huge hole in the decorative sheet-metal covered ceiling.

"Are you crazy?" yelled Sal. "You can't kill him here."

"Wrong. You can't kill him at all," shouted Louie.

"Let me go. Nobody does this to Georgio Esposito and lives to tell about it. I'll splatter his brains all over the floor," he said as he tried to lower his revolver again toward Vito.

"No," yelled Louie who had taken Sal's 45 caliber automatic and pointed it at Georgio."That's an order. You don't snuff out nobody unless I give you the order. Nobody, Capicé?"

Recognizing the finality and commanding quality of Louie's 'Capicé' Georgio slowly replaced his weapon into its holster.

"But Boss that punk almost killed me. What is everybody gonna think when they hear about this? Everybody's gonna try to call me down and challenge me to test me and. . ."

"It's no matter what everybody else thinks. It's only what I think that counts. Besides, Vito ain't gonna tell no body about this anyway. I'll see to that. I give you my word of honor."

Louie was holding Georgio by the arm and gently slapping his cheek.

The Wolves Of Brooklyn

"You Capicé?" he spoke gently, reassuringly. "Heh? Did I ever break my word of honor to you? Did I?"

"Well, no boss, you ain't . . ."

"And you got my word on something else. If Vito ever needs to be. . . . eliminated you get the first crack at him."

"You swear to that boss?"

"I swear it, Georgio, on my sainted mother's grave. Now, sit, sit. Relax. Then get yourself cleaned up. We got business." Georgio left the barber shop calmed, appeased. . . for the time being, at least.

Vito stirred again, and then finally sat up on the floor holding the back of his head.

"So, Vito, you must really feel something strong for this sister . . .I mean this Angela."

"No, she's just . . . important to me, almost like a real sister."

"Sure, sure, Vito. You almost kill my best bodyguard with your bare hands. And then it takes two hard blows to your thick, Italian skull to get you off him. All of that just for an almost-sister."

Vito just stared at Louie without speaking but the anger within him again began to well up. Louie now recognized that anger, immediately, from recent experience. It was a special body language he would memorize for future reference. He changed the subject abruptly.

"But never mind that now. I like your style, Vito. I am very impressed by the way you took Georgio out--and with no weapons."

Vito's rising anger abated and was replaced with a sense of pride, accomplishment and flattery. Louie memorized this reaction also.

"How would you like to be my new bodyguard? like Sal and Georgio except you'll be number three. The pay's good--$300 a week and a small percentage of the receipts of the gambling operations. And you can make some extra cash by taking out one of my competitors every once in a while. You Capicé?"

"Yeah, I get you, boss. But what about Georgio? Will he work with me after what I just did to him?"

"You no worry about Georgio. He will do whatever I tell him to do. And you gotta be ready to do the same."

Louie was no fool, however. He knew he would have to deal with a stronger will and a greater intellect in Vito.

"Okay, Louie, it's a deal. Three hundred a week and. . . gratuities, you might say."

"That's cute. I like that, gratuities. But you still call me Mr. Lupo or Boss. I'll tell when you can call me Louie. That privilege you have to earn with loyalty, obedience and seniority. Capicé?"

"Yeah, Boss. Whatever you say, goes."

"Good. Now that's settled. Get cleaned up in my private rooms up stairs, and then go home. Take the rest of the day off. But be back here bright and early tomorrow morning."

Vito left the barber shop, after cleaning up, feeling elated over this unplanned turn in his good fortunes. He had always known he knew he would eventually move to the top but this was unexpectedly fast. The need to celebrate his good luck with someone overcame him. Mario and Angel were the only people who came to mind. Mama might join in but not Carlo, his foster father. No, Carlo would make a big stink about it. But Vito knew that Carlo would be at work although Mama, Angel and Mario should be home. After cleaning up in the apartment above the barber shop he headed straight for the tenement flat to share his good news.

"Hey," he yelled up the stairway, "Is anybody home? It's me Vito, the prodigal son, the bad penny that always comes back."

Vito bounded up the flight of stairs scaling two steps at a time. He knocked at the door to the flat, which was unusual for him but he was on his best behavior, but no one answered. After turning the knob and he barged inside in his usual fashion. Seeing no one in the kitchen, he strode in casually looking into each room. Almost ready to leave since no one was home, he heard a gentle moaning sound which he recognized as Angel. Glancing toward the converted sun porch, now Angel's make-do bedroom, he saw her stockinged feet on the bed. Her shapely ankles and calves were just two of her beautiful attributes. Slowly, Vito approached the doorway--unsure of himself-- a warm, impassioned sensation rose inside him which he had not experienced before with the sight of Angel.

As he gazed down at her lovely face, indeed the face of an angel, he became aware of her round, shapely breasts, and hips. He had never looked at his foster sister in quite this way before. He whispered softly to himself, 'only sixteen years old and already you are a gorgeous, desirable, mature women,' he sighed. Vito felt a lustful longing which he was ashamed of. Quietly, he turned to leave but then Angel slowly opened her eyes and sat up in the bed.

"Vito, is that you? What are you doing home in the middle of the day? And where are you going?"

"Oh, I had some good news today and I was just bursting to tell somebody about it. Where's Mama and Mario?"

"Mama went to visit Mrs. Carlucci. You know, Mario's friend's mother. She just had a serious operation. Mama went to prepare dinner for their family so Mrs. Carlucci wouldn't have to do it. And Mario, you know how Mario is, he went to the library to do some research on law schools or something."

It was the first time Vito and Angel had been alone since she was a little girl. And now she was a mature, lovely woman. This made him perceptibly uneasy.

"Come here, sit on the bed and tell me all about your good news. We'll celebrate together, just you and I," she said and sighed softly.

Vito moved hesitatingly toward her lying on the bed and sat at Angel's feet.

"No, silly, not way down there. Come closer to me."

She and Vito had always been close but as brother and sister. She always ran to him for protection when the boys tried to pull her pigtails, or when they threw snowballs at her. And he had always acted like her personal guardian angel staving off all the petty annoyances a little girl faced. But now he was feeling something different. And so was Angel, he could just tell that she was feeling it, too. But he remained seated at her feet. She moved closer to him on the edge of the bed.

"Now, my dear, big brother, you can tell me about this good news you had today."

"Okay, but you gotta promise not to tell Mama. I want to tell her myself. And you must not tell your Papa, ever."

"All right ," she said as she kissed him gently on the cheek. "I promise not to tell."

Vito flushed but not the flush of shyness or embarrassment. It was a flush of passion, and they both knew it.

"What about Mario? I can tell Mario, can't I? You trust Mario don't you?" She coquettishly slipped her arm inside his.

"Yes. I guess that'd be okay. But make him promise not to say anything about it either."

Vito then related the episode which had occurred between him and Georgio. Although he was trying to

The Wolves Of Brooklyn

emphasize the fact of his promotion, he still gave every detail including the remarks which precipitated the confrontation.

"You mean you risked your life fighting with that ape, Georgio, to protect my honor?"

"Well . . . yeah, I guess I did. But don't you see what this means to my prestige in the 'family'. A big raise in pay . . ."

She threw her arms around his neck, placed her head on his shoulder and began to cry gently.

"Oh, my dear, sweet Vito you did this wonderful thing for me. You do love me," she said, exhaling slowly.

"Sure, I love you. You're my . . . sister. Well, my half sister anyway."

"We're not really, you know, related I mean. Not really," she said.

Vito noticed the warmth of her sweet breath on his neck, smelled the delicate fragrance of her perfume, and felt the soft pressure of her round breast against his arm. Instinctively, almost reflexly, he lowered his head and kissed her on the neck.

Angel's flesh quivered. "Oh, Vito," she murmured, grasped the hair on the back of his head with one hand and pulled his open mouth to hers in a deep, sensuous kiss. Vito could not help but respond and respond he did. Soon they were lying side by side on the bed in a fond embrace.

At that precise moment Mama began to slowly climb the two flights of stairs to their flat. And Mario had, just a moment before, turned the corner and spied his mother entering the front doors of the tenement with both her arms full of packages. He trotted up the street to catch up with her to help her with the packages.

"Hey, Mama, wait for me. I'll help you," he shouted. But he was too late. She entered without hearing his call. By the time he got to the front door Mama had already ascended the stairs and stood at the door of the apartment ready to open it.

Vito and Angel were still locked in the embrace on the bed. Angela had removed her stockings, her blouse front was unbuttoned and, Vito was bare-chested but his blue jeans were still on but they were unfastened.

Mama entered the apartment as Mario simultaneously called to her again, "Wait Mama, it's me Mario. I'll help you with your packages."

But 'Nunciata's attention had been diverted from Mario's call when she spied Vito and Angel lying on the bed together.

"No, no," she screamed, "you filthy animal, you disgusting pig. How could you do this to your own sister?"

Mario rushed into the apartment when he heard all the screaming and scuffling.

"Mama, Vito? What's the matter? What's going on?"

"That good-for-nothing-bum, Vito, he try to seduce your sister, that's what's the matter."

"It wasn't his fault, Mama. And, anyway I'm not really his sister. . . not by blood relation. Besides, I love Vito and I think he loves me."

"Shut up your mouth, Angela. You're only a child, what do you know about love? Today's kids only now how to make babies, and there's much more to true love."

Then she slapped Angel viciously across the face with the palm of her hand and was about to come back again with the back of her hand. Vito stepped forward and grabbed her hand tightly at the wrist. Suddenly, Mario lunged at Vito but Mama and Angel subdued him.

"You animale," said 'Nunciata, "all these years I stand up for you against my Carlo. He always said you were no good. I always defended you when you steal my money, run around with those hoodlums and whores. I tell him, 'No, Carlo, he's a good boy. You just gotta give him a chance.'

The Wolves Of Brooklyn

But he was right you're just no good," she said with her lips quivering as she tried to fight back the tears.

"Now wait a minute, Mama, this is not what it looks like. I mean we didn't do anything . . . I was just . . ." stammered Vito.

Now Mama slapped Vito across the face, and this time Vito hung his head in shame for having offended the only mother he had ever really known.

"Don't you dare call me 'Mama'. I'm not your mother no more. Your real mama died in that fire that you started with your own carelessness."

Vito looked at Mario with deep hatred in his eyes knowing that Mario was the only other person on earth who knew how that fire had started.

"Now you get out of my house and don't ever come back. And I forbid you to speak to or see anyone in this family again, especially my Angela."

"Mama. . . I mean 'Nunciata, please listen to reason," pleaded Vito.

"No, no, I don't listen to nothing. Mario, you go and get all his things and throw them out the front window into the street. I want everybody in the neighborhood to see that we are getting rid of the black sheep in this house. I want to see nothing around me to remind me of this . . . this beast."

"Yes, Mama," answered Mario.

"And, if I were you, Vito, I'd go far away and hide. Because when Papa hears about this he will kill you, if he ever finds you," said Mario.

Vito slowly, dejectedly, edged toward the door pausing momentarily to look around the flat where he had spent most of his life, and then he looked back at Angel.

"Vito, Vito," called Angel, tears filling her eyes. Mama drew back her hand to hit her again but Angel threw herself on her bed sobbing.

"Goodbye, Angel," said Vito. "I . . . I do love you. You know that don't you? Always remember that I do love you. Please wait for me. I'll be back."

Mario shoved Vito with both hands toward the door. And for the first time in his life Vito did not retaliate against him. Vito left the flat vowing to return some day only to win Angel's heart.

The Wolves Of Brooklyn

CHAPTER FOURTEEN
IT'S ALL THE SAME BLOOD

Ostracized by his adopted family Vito moved into a plush bachelor apartment in the exclusive Brooklyn Heights section near the swank St. George Hotel. Now deprived of the affection of his true love, Angel, he began a hectic campaign of sexual exploitations. The only women he considered off limits, for the moment at least, were those who belong to any of the men of the Mafia.

But starving for real family ties, he decided to visit his older brother, Chico, who was now a very successful construction contractor. He hesitatingly stood in the vestibule of Chico's home reluctant to press the doorbell. Finally, he did so.

"Who is it? Who's there?" called out a female voice which he recognized as that of Candida, his sister-in-law and Chico's wife.

"It's me . . . Vito," he said, with a feeling of dread.

"Who?, Who did you say?"

"It's me, Vito Vitale, your brother-in-law," he said more loudly.

Over the sound of her footsteps on the stairs he heard her say, "Vito, Oh, Vito. Please wait I'll come and open the door for you."

The Wolves Of Brooklyn

Candida came into view through the glass panels of the inside door. She wore only a sheer negligee which accentuated her forty-two year old, but still full and curvaceous, figure. Vito eyed her up and down almost by instinct, now. She immediately noticed his eye movements and she was pleased.

"Hello, Vito, hello. Come on in," she said and embraced him tightly pressing her bosom to his and flexed her knee between his legs. Vito's passion stirred.

"Hi, Didi, how have you been?" asked Vito, gently pushing her away. "Is Chico home? He's not at work is he?"

"Well, to answer your first question, I'm as good as ever, as you can plainly see. At least, that's what Chico used to say when he used to live here."

"You mean he doesn't live here anymore? Have you two had a spat? How long as he been gone?" asked Vito.

"Chico moved out about two weeks ago. No, it's not just a spat, this time it's for keeps. We're legally separated and I've filed for a divorce."

"Why? What happened between you two? There's not another woman, is there?" he asked.

"No . . . I mean, yes, I guess you could say that. It's that stupid construction business of his. That's his mistress. All he ever does is work, day and night, weekends, holidays, birthdays, every day. He even missed our wedding anniversary party because of some trouble with some dumb job he was doing."

"I'm sorry to hear that, Didi. What are you going to do now? Are you going to keep this house?"

"I don't know for sure yet, Vito. I can't be alone like this all the time. I'm still a young women, Vito. I have needs, passionate needs," she said as she moved from her chair and slipped onto Vito's lap pressing her buttocks firmly into Vito's groin. Vito flushed but hesitated.

"Don't, Didi. You're my sister-in-law, my brother's wife, you're family," he said.

"Not anymore I'm not. And besides you're not really brothers by blood. Even if you were it's all the same blood so it's okay," she said as she untied her robe and unbuttoned the front of her negligee. She pressed her open mouth against his as she reached down picked up his hand and placed it against her breasts.

The nearest bed was on the third floor, two flights up in the old Brooklyn brownstone. Neither one of them could wait that long. Didi led him into the living-room where she spread out the sofa cushions on the floor to form a bed.

"Oh, Vito, I knew you'd be a terrific lover and you were magnifico."

"You, too, Didi. You too."

Click, click, click, unexpectedly, they both heard the tumblers turning in the front-door lock. They jumped to their feet and quickly wrapped their clothes around themselves. Chico walked into the room to find them frozen as they both stood by the cushions.

"You good-for-nothing, animale, you disgrace your family again," said Chico trying to control his anger.

"What did you expect Chico? You're never home to be a husband to me, anyway," said Didi.

"Not you, you cheap whore. I expected no better from the likes of you. I was talking to him, Vito. First my sister, Angel, and now my wife. You ain't got no shame at all, do you?"

"Now wait a minute, Chico, this wasn't all my fault. Didi came on to me. I'm only human, you know. I ain't made of stone," said Vito.

"I know that, Vito. Didi's been trying to seduce every man in pants for years. That's only one of the reasons I walked out on her. She's tried it with my business partners, my friends, my workers, and even some of my family but they all walked away, until now."

"How did you know that, Chico? You been spying on me, ain't you?" she said.

"I didn't have to. I know because they all told me about you but at first I didn't believe them," he said as he pushed her aside and stepped close to Vito.

"But not you, Vito. You ain't got enough respect for anything or anybody to do that. All you care about is yourself and your pleasures. You don't love anybody but yourself. You never have and you never will."

"That ain't true, Chico. It was different with Angel. I loved Angel and I still do. But your crack-pot father won't let me see her, or Mama neither."

Chico stepped even closer to Vito so that they were nose-to-nose. "You'd better get out of here, Vito, before I kill you here and now." Then he ran to his desk in the adjoining office and searched the drawer feverishly for his 38-caliber Police Special. In the meantime, Vito had quickly put on his slacks and shirt without wasting any time with shoes and underwear. He dashed, bare-footed, toward the front door, shirt tails flying behind him as he tried to zipper up his fly.

Chico stepped out into the hall just as Vito opened the front door trying to exit quickly. Chico's first shot struck the door frame and lodged deeply into the thick, oak molding. He was steadying his arm for another shot when Didi swung the living room door open vigorously and knocked the gun from his hand with a crack, The blow most certainly fractured one or two of Chico's fingers. Vito bolted out the door and dashed up the street as Chico gripped his throbbing right hand in severe pain.

"I'm gonna kill you, Vito," shouted Chico up the street after Vito. "If you ever come near my wife or me again I'll kill you, Vito. So help me God, I will."

Chico decided then and there that he would call his brother, Mario, in the morning to ask him to help him keep track of Vito's activities and whereabouts. Since Mario was as Assistant District Attorney, Chico knew he had many contacts in the underworld and police department.

"Hello, Mario. It's me, Chico, your big brother."

"Oh, hi, Chico. How's everything going?"

"How's everything going? You want to know how's everything going? I'll tell you how everything is going. Everything stinks, including that son-of-a-bitch, Vito."

"Oh, no, not more trouble from him? What did he do now?"

"You'd think he would have learned something when Mama threw him out of the house for what he did to Angel? But, oh no, not that pig. So, now he takes my wife to bed."

"Why, the man has no morals at all. How's Didi taking it? Was she real upset? Is she all right?"

"All right? Her? She's an animal, too, a rotten whore that's what she is. She enjoyed every minute of it. I blame her as much as Vito."

"Were you two having marriage troubles?"

"Yeah, Mario. I left her a few weeks ago. We were legally separated. Then when I caught them together, I moved out for good that same day. She was never any good. And I want you to help me file for a divorce, too."

"Well, Chico, I only do criminal law but I know a good divorce attorney. I'm sure he'll help me with it. But you know, you'll need some substantial, concrete evidence of infidelity?"

"That ain't going to be too tough to get, now," said Chico.

"Why? What do you mean, Chico?"

"My neighbor called me and told Vito moved into my house with my wife just hours after I moved out. I should have killed him when I had the chance," said Chico slightly

The Wolves Of Brooklyn

choked with emotion on the words. He deliberately did not tell Mario about the attempt he had already made to shoot Vito.

"Now don't talk that way, Chico. If there are any witnesses to those kind of threats you could get in real trouble if anything does happen to Vito. But, you're right, that is good evidence in a divorce suit, especially if we can get some pictures of the two of them together. We'll hire a private detective to stake out the house for a few days. He'll record all of Vito's and Didi's comings and goings, take a few choice photos and we'll have plenty of evidence in no time at all," said Mario.

"Yeah, sure, that should nail down the divorce but what about getting even with Vito. I'll need that to keep from going crazy."

"I think I can understand that but you'd better quit that talk about killing Vito. . ."

"No, I didn't mean that. Can't we have the private 'Private Dick' keep track of his Mafia stuff, too? I'd like to see the little punk behind bars for a long time."

"Yes, we might be able to manage that, too," answered Mario. "I have some good friends in the DA's office. They owe me quite a few favors. Now might be the time to call some of them in. I'll find out what parts of the operations Vito's involved in and pass the word along to the Private Investigator."

"So, let's get started. I want him nailed real quick," said Chico.

"Now, hold on Chico. The divorce thing we can do in a few months, that's no problem. But the criminal charges are something else again. Vito's no dummy, you know. It'll take quite some time to accumulate all the evidence we'll need. Then there's the indictment, apprehension and arrest, and probably a long trial with the usual delays. . ."

"So, how long are we talking about, here? Maybe six months?"

"Oh, Chico, I can see you know nothing about the American legal system. We're probably talking about years."

"Years? How many years? One, two? How many do you mean?"

"Yes, at least. Maybe even more."

"What the hell kind of system is this anyway? The victims get robbed or killed or raped right away and the criminal walks around a free man for years. A bullet or a sharp stiletto blade would be a lot faster and cheaper too," said Chico.

"It doesn't work that way, Chico. This is suppose to be a democracy. The wheels turn very slowly," said Mario.

And, indeed, several years were to pass before Vito would get his just punishment for all his crimes.

The Wolves Of Brooklyn

CHAPTER FIFTEEN
A PAIR OF CEMENT SHOES

Four and a half years had transpired and there was still not enough evidence to convict, or even arrest, Vito for any crimes except some minor misdemeanors. He had long since left Chico's wife, Didi. But he had had many live-in, female companions.

In the interim, Vito had progressed up the ladder in his criminal career. He had replaced Sal and Georgio and was now Louie Lupo's number one bodyguard. Louie also put him in charge of the policy-numbers racket, a branch of the gambling operations. Vito was delighted with this new duty, especially since it increased his access to large sums of cash, and his opportunity to skim some big cash off the top for himself.

Chico had divorced Didi but his construction business had continued to grow making him one of the most powerful building contractors in Brooklyn. His bitterness toward Vito had mellowed but he still craved revenge.

Mario's brilliant legal career blossomed and he was appointed as an Assistant District Attorney for Kings County in Brooklyn.

The Wolves Of Brooklyn

"Hello, hello, Mario, it's me, Chico. I need to talk to you about you-know-who but I don't think we should do it over the phone. Where can we meet in private?"

"I think it would be best to meet somewhere outside our own turf. I got it. There's a small pizzeria in the Red Hook section called 'Enzio's Pizza Parlor'. It's on President Street right off Vanderbilt Avenue. I'll meet you there tonight at 8:00 o'clock. Is that okay? Chico."

"Yeah. Sounds okay to me. I'll see you tonight at eight," said Chico and he hung up the phone.

***

Mario sat nervously awaiting Chico in the pizza parlor. He was anxiously nursing a glass of homemade (and illegally sold) Chianti wine which he had ordered in the hope it would calm his anxiety. It didn't. Intentionally sitting at a table in the rear with his back to a wall and facing the door, he continually looked over his shoulder. The back door which was only a few yards away from where he sat did mildly comfort him.

"Come on, Chico, I don't have all night," he muttered to himself.

"Excuse-a-me," called the owner from behind the bar. "You want something?"

The sudden sound startled Mario who partially jumped up from his seat.

"What?" said Mario.

"I thought you said something, mister. You want some more Chianti?"

"No, no thanks. I was just thinking out loud."

"What? What did you say . . .?"

"Oh, never mind," said Mario, obviously irritated.

The old man shrugged his shoulders, mumbled some Italian swear words and went back to polishing his glasses. Mario gulped down a large swallow of the wine as Chico strolled in the front door.

"It's about time, Chico. Where the hell have you been? It's almost 8:20."

"Hey, hey, calm down, will you. I got tied up in traffic on the Ft. Hamilton Parkway. There was a big accident with . . . "

"Okay, okay, already. Forget it. What's up? What did you want to talk about?"

"It's about Vito," said Chico.

"Keep it down will you. Don't talk so loud," whispered Mario.

"What the hell is wrong with you anyway? How come you're so jumpy?" said Chico

"Nothing, nothing's wrong. I just got a lot of things on my mind. And besides, Vito has made a lot enemies around here. You never know where and when someone's going to look for revenge."

"That's just what I wanted to talk to you about," said Chico.

"Oh, really. What do you mean?"

"I mean Vito's been missing for about three weeks now. Nobody has seen him or heard from him for quite a while. He usually sends Mama and Papa a couple of hundred bucks every week. Even my ex-wife, the bitch, hasn't heard from him. We're worried something might happened to him."

"Who do you mean, we? asked Mario.

"Yeah, we. Papa, mama, me and even Angel. We've been worried a lot."

"But why? He's a no good creep. He has hurt everyone of us very deeply. Why should we worry about him?"

Mario was sweating profusely, now, and his hands were visibly shaking.

The Wolves Of Brooklyn

"Two more Chiantis, Enzio, please. Larger glasses this time," Chico called out.

"You gotta pull yourself together, Mario. Slow down a little. You're working too hard. Here, drink your wine. It will steady your nerves. We gotta find Vito," said Chico.

"Yeah, I guess you're right. But I'll only help because you and the others want me to," said Mario.

"Now, where to begin? I figured your office must have some files on Vito since he's been with the Mafia. Maybe we could find out where he hangs out, who are his friends and such," said Chico.

"Well, that might be a problem," said Mario. "Those files are only for official use. I can't just go into them without a very good legal reason. My job could be jeopardized."

"Oh, I didn't know that, Mario."

"I have an idea, though. I can quietly launch a low level investigation into Vito's Mafia activities for tax fraud, or something. That will make it look official. Then we extract whatever information we can use. It'll mean some extra paper work for me but I'll handle it."

"Good" said Chico, then that's settled. You let me know what you find out and I'll go to try to find Vito, or find out what happened to him."

"Okay, Chico. I'll call you as soon as I have something. Oh, and sorry I blew up at you, Chico. I didn't mean anything by it."

"Yeah, sure, that's all right. You call me as soon as you got something we can use," said Chico as he departed the Pizzeria.

***

"Hello, Chico, this is Mario. I think I have some useful information on Vito but I don't think we should discuss it on the phone," he said.

"Okay, I can meet you somewhere. How about Enzio's Pizza Parlor? You know, the place we met before."

"No, no, I don't want to go there. That's Mafioso territory. We had better go someplace more remote, more secluded. You know the Staten Island ferry dock down at the battery? There's a seven o'clock ferry to Staten Island every night. I'll meet you on the boat, top deck, outside, tonight," said Mario.

"How come out there?"

"It's safer, Chico. No chance for electronic bugs, hidden cameras and all that stuff."

"Okay, sounds crazy to me but whatever you say. See you tonight at 7 o'clock," said Chico and hung up the phone.

***

Chico arrived just as the gangplank was about to be lifted and after the last passenger had boarded.

"Wait, wait for me," shouted Chico. The gangplank was again lowered and Chico scrambled aboard very short of breath and he gasped,

"Thank you too much. I just had to get this boat."

He rested several minutes before attempting to take the sixteen steps to the upper deck. Scanning the inside area of the upper deck he could see no one. And there was no one on the outside deck either.

"Mama mia," he said, throwing up his hand and the slapping them together. "I do all this running for nothing, he's not even here."

Consequently, he sat down in frustration to wait for the boat to make the round trip, alone. Ten minutes later a clicking sound awakened him, with a start, from a nap he had decided to take. Quickly standing up, he looked around the still empty deck.

The Wolves Of Brooklyn

"Who is it? Who's there?" he said peering into the darkness toward the men's restroom door which had just clicked closed. A man in a gray trench coat, dark glasses and gray hat approached him.

"Relax, Chico, it's just me, Mario," said the shadow as he removed the hat and glasses.

"Santa Lucia, Mario. What are you trying to do scaring me like that? You want me to have a stroke or what?"

"Calm down, calm down, will you. I'm just being cautious, that's all," said Mario.

"You been in that john all this time while I've been sweating, and cursing you out here?"

"Yes, I wanted to be sure you were not being followed."

"Why would anybody follow me, Chico Mastrangelo? I'm just a construction worker, nobody important."

"Yes, I know but you're also the half brother of Vito Vitale, and the brother of an assistant district attorney who does Mafia cases. The family wouldn't hurt you but they could use you to trap one of us," said Mario.

"I guess I'm going to have to learn to be more careful from now on. I no like this stuff. How can you live this way, Mario? Always looking over your shoulder and sneaking around like this--your job can't be worth all that trouble."

"That's why I'm not planning to do this for the rest of my life. Once I get a reputation and a big chunk of money I'll quit and go into private law practice, or maybe a whole different business."

"Oh yeah? And how do you plan to make this great reputation and, especially, a big chunk of money?"

"Don't worry, Chico. There are ways and I've got some plans already made to get me there," said Mario.

"So what's this information you've got about Vito, Mario?"

"Oh, yes, I found this file on one of Louie Lupo's bodyguards, a nobody named Joey 'Wheels' Ciclio. Do you know him or ever hear of him?"

"No, I don't think so," said Chico.

"Well, anyway, Louie assigned him to be Vito's tail. He followed Vito and recorded every move Vito made. All of his rendezvous with women, to the movies, his visits to Mama and Papa, everything."

"Is my wife's name mentioned in that record?" asked Chico tightening the muscles in his jaw.

"You don't want to know, Chico. Anyway, I thought you had her out of your system by now."

"I do, I do. Never mind then, go on with the rest of the file," said Chico.

"So, this 'Wheels' character follows Vito to upstate New York to a resort in the Catskills, and guess what?"

"I don't know, what?" said Chico.

"Well, Vito is there at Grossinger's shacking up for the weekend with Louie's new, young, vivacious wife, Tina. They're registered under assumed names, of course, but there are these Polaroid photos in the file of them together in bed ."

"So what's our next step?" asked Chico, "to find this 'Joey Wheels' guy?"

"Yes. Once we find Wheels maybe we can scare him into telling us what's happened to Vito," said Mario.

"Or maybe he had something to do with whatever has happened to Vito. Is that what you mean?" said Chico.

"I see you are having the same fears that I am about Vito," said Mario.

"What else? What other way does the 'family' use to get revenge but by getting rid of it's trouble-makers and traitors?" asked Chico.

"Well, I was kind of hoping, just this once, they wouldn't go that route and . . .and that Vito might still be alive."

"Not much chance of that, Mario. Not much chance of that kind of luck even for Vito--who usually has all the good luck."

"Let's go try to locate Joey 'Wheels', Mario."

"I have an old address of one of Joey 'Wheels's' favorite hangouts. Let's go see if anyone has seen him lately," said Mario.

"Let me see that paper, Mario. Oh, yeah. Kelley's Bar and Grill on Jouralemon Street. I know that place. It's over near the old post office, right off the Borough Hall."

They flagged a taxi and arrived at Kelley's in 20 minutes with Chico giving precise directions.

"How come you know so well where this place is, Chico?"

"I get around a lot . . . in my construction business. You know, you do a lot of leg work trying to find the big jobs, the subcontractors and construction workers. You know, stuff like that," said Chico.

They found Kelley's Bar and Grill practically empty since it was a week night.

"Hey, hi ya, Chico," said Kelley from behind the bar. "I didn't expect to see you again so soon. How's it going?"

"Hi, Kelley, comé sta? How's business? This here's my brother Mario." Kelley leaned across the bar to shake Mario's hand. "He's a lawyer, a big assistant DA for the county," said Chico. Kelley suddenly stopped before reaching Mario's hand and withdrew his own.

"Relax, Kelley, he ain't after you, you big, dumb Mick. He's just after big time stuff, not small potatoes like you," said Chico laughing.

"Oh, okay, then I will shake his hand," said Kelley quite visibly relieved. "What can I serve you gents?" he added.

"We just want some information. We ain't thirsty," said Chico.

Kelley frowned and looked around the empty saloon.

Mario interjected, "Change that order, Mr. Kelley, we'll have two sniffers of brandy and make it your best imported stock."

Kelley smiled and said, "Sure thing, coming right up, counselor. I'll have to get it from the back room. The bums I get in here don't usually order that good booze. It's real expensive you know."

"That's all right, Kelley, Chico's got lots of money. He can afford it," said Mario chuckling.

Chico waited until Kelley left the room before he said to Mario, "Why did you order that swill? You know I don't like brandy. I'm strictly a-Chianti- and-Grappa-man."

"Because you don't get information for free in places like this and especially from men like Kelley. You should know that, Chico."

"Oh, yeah, sure, I forgot."

"And you better leave him a big tip if he gives us what we want to know."

"Me leave a tip? What about you, Mario? You don't make peanuts for a salary."

"Quiet. He's coming back in," said Mario changing the topic quickly.

"Here you go, Gents, the best brandy in stock. Now, what else do you need?"

"We need to know where we can find Joey 'Wheels' or if you have seen him lately," said Mario.

"Joey 'Wheels'? I don't think I know him," said Kelley as he casually continued cleaning glasses.

Mario nudged Chico with his elbow. Chico responded by removing a large roll of bills from his pocket. Then he peeled off a twenty-dollar-bill and place it on the bar.

Kelley looked at the bill, smiled and said, "Oh, yeah, you must mean Joey Ciclio. No, I don't know where he lives, or anything. And I ain't seen him lately---not that I can remember, anyway."

Mario nudged Chico again. Chico peeled off another twenty dollar bill.

"But, now that I think about it, I guess I did see him in here about a month or two ago," said Kelley.

"Was he alone?" asked Chico.

"It's funny, you know, I can't quite remember if he was or not. It must be old age creeping into my brain."

Chico didn't wait for Mario's nudge this time. Instead, he quickly peeled off another twenty-dollar-bill and placed it on the bar.

Kelley glanced at it, frowned and shrugged his shoulders. Chico added another twenty. Kelley frowned again but this time Chico picked up all the money off the bar and started to leave.

Kelley grabbed his hand and said, "Wait, yeah, now I remember. He was with another guy I didn't recognize. Must have been a new guy in town."

Mario opened his file folder and produced a photo of Vito, "Was this the man who was with him?"

Kelley blanched and began to sweat because printed on the bottom border of the photo was the name, Vito Vitale.

"So that's what he looks like," said Kelley. "He don't look as tough as his reputation makes out. In fact, he kind of looks like a pretty-boy type. If you get my drift," he added.

"Don't let his looks fool you. And you better not let him ever hear you say that, not if you like living," said Mario.

"Yeah, I heard that about him, too."

"Did they leave together?" asked Mario.

"Yeah, they did. It was about closing time, 2 am."

"Did they happen to say where they were going next?" asked Chico.

Suddenly Kelley was mum again. Chico placed another twenty-dollar-bill on the bar, put the rest of his roll of bills back in his pocket and said, "And that's the last of the doe, no matter what."

"No, they didn't say but Joey's girlfriend don't live to far from here. That would be my best bet. Her name's Lucille DeMello. She lives over on DeGraw street just two blocks from here. Number 73, I think it is."

Mario was surprised at this last flood of free-flowing, unsolicited information. 'Oh, well, I guess he just figured we would ask anyway,' he thought.

"Thanks, Kelley," he said.

"Yeah, thanks, Mr. Kelley. I don't think there's any change coming back from all those twenties, do you?" said Chico smiling.

Kelley didn't answer, didn't even look up from his polishing beer glasses.

A few minutes later Mario and Chico arrived at number 73 DeGraw Street. It was a second story walk-up flat over an abandoned store. There were no lights in the windows facing the street.

"Looks like nobody's home, Mario. Let's come back tomorrow."

"No, wait, Chico. Let's go up and knock, anyway."

"Why? It's all dark and there's no noises coming from inside. Nobody's home, I tell you."

"I know it's just a hunch, Chico, but I get some good ones once in awhile. Trust me on this one, will you?"

Chico nodded as they cautiously climbed the one flight of stairs, up to the unlit hallway, and to the apartment door. Chico knocked but there was no response. Mario put some pressure on the door knob with his hand. The door swung open with a squeak.

"Wait, Chico, look it's unlocked."

"Hey, ain't it illegal to just go in like this, Mr. Assistant D. A.?"

"I won't tell on you, if you promise not to tell on me," said Mario smiling.

"Very funny," said Chico.

"Whew! What is that rotten stink coming out of this place? I haven't smelled that stink since I worked at the slaughter house many years ago," said Chico as he moved through the door opening.

They looked at each other, momentarily startled, and then they pushed the door all the way open, hurried inside and turned on the wall switch.

"Oh, God! Would you look at them," said Chico.

Mario gagged, tried unsuccessfully to restrain himself, and then vomited.

"Oh, I forgot, you never worked in the slaughter house, have you?" said Chico, smiling.

Joey 'Wheels' Ciclio's and Lucille DeMello's bodies were lying face down and naked on the the blood soaked bed. The ten to twelve knife wounds in each body spewed foul smelling, purulent material from the decaying corpses. Chico leaned over and checked each body for a pulse. Of course, there was none.

"It's no use, Chico. They have been dead for days, maybe even weeks."

"Yeah, Mario. I'll just cover them up with a blanket or something. Then let's get out of here. I think I'm going to be sick myself."

"You go ahead without me, Chico. I have got to notify the police and call my office. Wait for me out front. I'll be down in a few minutes."

Chico left the apartment, gladly. He waited out in the welcomed fresh air for Mario. But a half hour passed and Mario didn't come out. Chico decided to go back in to check on him. He hurried back up the stairs and went inside with his handkerchief covering his nose and mouth.

"Mario, Mario, where the hell are you?" he called out.

"I'm up here, Chico, in the attic," said Mario as Chico looked for a stairway but saw none.

"There's an opening in the kitchen ceiling," came Mario's muffled words.

Chico went into the kitchen, found the ceiling opening and the kitchen chair Mario had used to climb into the attic. It was immediately apparent to Chico that he wasn't tall enough to reach the opening. He didn't try.

"What the hell are you doing up there, anyway?" he yelled through the opening while standing on the chair.

"I think I found something that might help us find Vito," he answered.

"Oh, yeah, What is it?"

"Wait a minute, I'll be right down. Stand clear of the opening and I'll toss them down to you."

"What the hell is he talking about? And how did he find that attic?" Chico muttered to himself.

Suddenly some clothes and a pair of boots fell through the attic-ceiling opening.

"Here, Chico, grab these tools. They'll make too much of a racket if I dropped them."

"Okay," said Chico as he took hold of the business ends of two shovels and the handle of a mason's trowel.

"Hey, this stuff is really all grubby. There's dried cement all over them," said Chico.

"Yes, I know, Chico. Help me down, will you?"

Chico guided Mario's feet to the chair then grasped his waist and eased him down the rest of the way.

"What is all this junk? And how did you know it was up there, Mario?"

"I . . . ah, I came in for a glass of water to wash the puke-taste out of my mouth. Then I heard these pieces of dried concrete crunching under my shoes. I looked up to the ceiling and there it was, wide open."

"Just like that, heh?"

"Yes," said Mario, "just like that."

"So what is all this stuff and what does it all mean?"

"Don't you see, Chico? These coveralls and boots covered with concrete, and the tools, too? I mean it's obvious, 'Wheels' was making a pair of cement shoes for someone. Maybe for Vito."

"You don't know that. Maybe he was just doing some repairs around here," said Chico.

"Look around, do you see any fresh concrete work anywhere? There's no backyard and the city sidewalk, maintained by the city, runs right up to the front door. Nobody repairs the city's property, sometimes not even the city," said Mario.

"Yeah, I guess you're right. Boy, being an Assistant DA teaches you how to be a detective, too, don't it?"

"Here, Chico, you search the pockets of the coveralls. I'm going to get some scrapings of the concrete and mud off the boots for the lab."

"Okay," said Chico and he began to go through the pockets as instructed. "Oh, oh," he said "I think I found something important, Mario."

"What is it, Chico?"

Chico slowly withdrew his hand from the left hip pocket of the dirty coveralls. Suspended from between his index finger and thumb was a long ice pick. Its handle and blade were covered with dried blood.

"A typical Mafia murder weapon. Try not to smudge any fingerprints on the handle, Chico. Here, let me hold it by the point and you get one of those large manila envelopes to put it into."

They were washing their hands in the kitchen sink when they heard the police cars pull up outside the apartment house. Two homicide detectives rushed up the stairs and into the flat with their revolvers drawn.

"Raise your hands over your heads and lean against the wall, both of you," said one of the detectives.

"Easy detectives, I'm an Assistant District Attorney for this county. My name's Mario Mastrangelo," he said holding his hands up.

"Oh, yeah. Can you prove that?"

"I've got some identification in my wallet in the inside pocket of my coat," said Mario as he began to reach for it.

"Freeze, Mister, right where you are. Don't go for it," said the detective as Mario stopped his motion mid-air.

"Just slip off the jacket, nice and easy like and toss it to my partner. And don't put your hands into any of the pockets or you'll have as many holes in you as those two corpses we got called about."

Mario followed the detective's instructions and tossed the jacket to his partner. The partner reached in and found the wallet with the identification.

"He's legit, Dave. He is an Assistant DA just like he says. Here's his ID card, photo and all."

"Okay, Mr. Assistant DA, you can put your hands down. Sorry for the trouble but you know you can't be too careful these days."

"It's all right detective, we understand. In fact, that was very good police work. I'll have to let your chief know how well you follow procedure."

"Yes, sir," he said as he walked over to the bed and pulled back the blanket covering Joey and his girlfriend.

The Wolves Of Brooklyn

"Oh, Christ. Look here, Pete, will you. He looks just like the guy we pulled out of the East River this morning. The same mob-like M. O."

"What guy?" said Mario.

"We don't know who he is yet. We haven't identified him yet. But he was a young fellow--probably about your age. The body had undergone a lot of decay being under water for several weeks."

"Did he have a big block of cement on his feet?" asked Chico.

"Yeah, that's right. How did you know?"

"And you say he was full of pick holes just like these two bodies?" asked Mario.

"Yeah, that's right, too. Say, maybe you guys are more involved here than we thought," said the detective.

Chico flushed and felt weak in the knees. He looked at Mario and shook his head in disbelief that the body in the river might be Vito.

Mario shrugged it off and said, "We might be able to help you identify the guy from the river. We think he might be our . . . our half, I mean adopted brother, Vito Vitale. He disappeared a few weeks ago."

"Yeah, sure, I've heard of him. Wasn't he one of Louie Lupo's mob?"

"That's right. He was into the numbers racket and other gambling operations for Louie. Plus, I hear he was into Louie's women, too, especially Louie's new, young wife," said the second detective.

"What makes you think the guy from the river might be Vito? Mr. Assistant DA," said the first detective.

"Well, you see, that man under the blanket there, he worked for Louie, too. His name's Joey 'Wheels' Ciclio. And the last time they were seen alive they were seen together at Kelley's saloon. We have a statement to that effect from Kelley himself. It seems to add up to me," said Mario.

"Makes sense, doesn't it? But there's still the matter of identifying that river corpse. Is there any other family members that could help with that?" said the first detective.

"Yeah, there's my mom and pop, and my little sister. But I would rather not put them through that if we could help it. Mario and me can identify him. Right Mario?" said Chico who was clearly shaken by the entire matter.

Mario put his arm around Chico's shoulder to steady him. "Of course, Chico, you and I can do that. They won't have to see him that way." Then he hesitated a few seconds to allow Chico to compose himself. "But, you know Chico, we are going to have to tell them, eventually," he added.

"Yeah, sure, I know that. Oh, madonna mia, Mama's going to go plain crazy with grief," said Chico.

"Why?" said Mario, "after all the rotten things Vito has done to us and to her over the last few years . . ."

"So what!" said Chico, "you think she has ever stopped loving him like her own son? Like you and me? Mama don't hate nobody. That's why she's a saint," he added.

"Yes, of course, you're right, Chico. I'm sorry I said that," said Mario with a small but real remnant of jealousy still festering deep within his soul. He cursed himself for allowing Vito to still get to him even after he was dead. 'Damned his black soul,' he thought.

"Well, that's up to you two to decide how you tell your folks. If you could come down to the city morgue tomorrow morning, I would appreciate it. Oh, and see if you can find out who Vito's dentist is. The dental records might be useful," said the first detective.

"Certainly, we will be there around 10 am," said Mario.

"Come on, Chico, I'll go home with you to Mama and Papa's. We'll tell them the news together. Maybe that will make it easier, although, I doubt it."

***

Chico and Mario pulled up in front of the same three story, wood frame tenement apartment house where the Mastrangelos had lived since arriving in America in 1901. The same tenement where Vito's parents had perished in a fire in their third floor flat. A fire started because of Vito's careless, but accidental, kerosene spill. An accident that caused Vito to carry an inappropriate feeling of guilt inside himself for his entire life.

"Maybe we ought to wait a little while before we tell them, Mario. What do you think?" said Chico.

"No, I don't think so, Chico. It won't make it any easier later. Besides, would you rather they hear about it from a friend or on the radio?"

"Nah, of course not, you're right, Mario. But I'm shaking inside already just thinking about it. You feeling that way, too?"

"Yeah, sure I am," said Mario trying to look nervous. "But I'm not as bad as you. I'll tell them just as long as you're there to help me."

Mario walked up the front steps at a normal pace but Chico lagged behind at half his usual speed.

"Come on, Chico. How bad could it be?"

"Oh, you don't know Mama and Papa. You weren't old enough to be at the wake or the funeral when they buried Vito's parents."

"No, we kids weren't' allowed to view the body or attend the burial in the old days," said Mario.

"Well, it's a good thing you didn't'. When Mama went up to the open grave to throw in a rose she through herself in the hole, instead," said Chico climbing the stairs slowly.

"No! You're joking," said Mario.

"No, I'm not joking," said Chico, as he finally reached the top step and then paused to catch his breath.

"And then the whole damned place went crazy when Papa jumped in, too, to get Mama out. You should have seen it."

They approached the door to the flat and knocked as they simultaneously opened and called out, "Mama, Papa, it's us, Mario and Chico."

'Nunciata Mastrangelo sat at her small Singer sewing machine showing Angel how to hem a dress. Papa was sitting in the parlor in front of his small nine inch, black and white TV set watching the Dodgers getting trounced by the Giants, again.

Mama looked up from her work and immediately sensed, as she always could, when there was trouble, big trouble.

"What's the matter? What is it? Chico, Mario, what's wrong?"

Papa heard the tone of urgency in his wife's voice and came into the kitchen.

"What's-a-matter, 'Nunciata?" said Papa.

Angela stood up, put her hands to her mouth and began to tremble.

"I think you should all sit down," said Mario. "I have something to tell you. Chico go get the Grappa and some Anisette for the women."

"Oh, my God, it is something terrible, isn't it?" said Angela.

"I'm afraid it is," said Mario who was relatively calm and composed. "It's about Vito . . . we . . . that is, the police think they have recovered his . . . his body from the East River."

"Dead body! You mean his dead body? My Vito is dead? No, it can't be," said Mama 'Nunciata as she slumped back into her chair.

Now Angela began to sob uncontrollably. Papa just stood motionless and somber not knowing what to feel or how to react. Mama sat frozen in her seat as if she was experiencing a bad dream from which she would soon awaken.

Chico filled three shot glasses full of Grappa and Anisette in two others. Papa took one immediately and knocked it down quickly. Angela refused the glass Mario offered her and Mama sipped hers slowly while Chico held the glass to her lips.

"Who did this terrible thing? I must know who brought this pain on my family?" said Papa, more out of anger at his family being violated than over the loss of Vito.

"We . . . the police don't know yet. But Joey Ciclio was the last person to be seen with Vito alive," said Mario.

"Then it must have been Louie Lupo who gave the order to kill Vito. Joey is one of Louie's torpedoes, ain't he? We gotta find Joey and make him tell us it was Louie," said Papa.

"But we can't do that, Papa. Joey's dead, too, along with his girlfriend. We just found their bodies in her apartment. They've been dead for days."

Mama still sat motionless and mute. Then she stirred and said, "Where's my Vito? Where is he? We must bring his . . . him home."

"We can't do that yet, Mama," said Chico. "Mario and me have to go down to the city morgue tomorrow to identify it . . . him," he added.

Suddenly Mama came to life again and she said, "then you mean, maybe it's not Vito? Maybe it's a mistake and it's somebody else? Oh, madonna mia, let it be so," she cried, clasping her hands to heaven as in prayer.

"But the corpse had on Vito's jewelry and clothes. Vito's wallet and car keys were in his pockets. There's not much doubt that it's Vito but his dental records should settle it," said Mario.

"Who was Vito's dentist, Mama?" asked Chico.

She didn't know, so she said, "Papa, do you know?" But he didn't know either.

Then Angela spoke up, hesitantly, and with some difficulty, "Dr. Vincent Lupo, Dr. Lupo was his dentist."

"What?" shouted Papa. "Another Lupo mixed up in this thing with Vito. I knew it. It has to be Louie that gave the contract on Vito. I'm gonna get a gun and kill him myself for bringing this grief to my family," he added as he ran around the kitchen frantically.

"Papa, don't talk like that," yelled Chico trying to physically restrain his father. He finally subdued him and forcibly sat him down and poured him another Grappa. "Now, cool down, will you. You're not going to kill anybody. Do you want to go to jail or the electric chair? How would that help Mama and Angel or Vito?"

"Chico's right, Papa. If Louie Lupo is behind this the law will take care of him and he'll go away for a long time or get the death penalty," said Mario trying to appease and calm everyone.

"No," said Mama as she struck her breast with her clenched fist. "No law, no trial, no jail."

"What do you mean, Mama?" said Chico stunned at her strong reaction.

"Just-a-what I say," she said, suddenly reverting to her almost defunct broken English accent which only surfaced now in times of real anger or stress.

"Mama, don't talk that way. I've never heard you talk like that before. What's come over you?" said Angela.

"I mean, we gonna settle this thing like in the old country, in Italia. This is a great country, my country, this America but so many criminals get away with too much here. Louie has committed many crimes, killed many innocent people and got away with it. He cannot, he must, not get away with these things any more."

The Wolves Of Brooklyn

"Come on, Mama, Papa. You can't do anything that foolish," said Mario. "You both should know better than that."

"What are we going to do with the two of them, Mario, Chico?" asked Angela. "They're talking crazy."

"Oh, they're just upset over Vito's death. Don't worry Angel, they'll get over it, you'll see. They won't do anything crazy. Just give them some time," said Mario.

Angel, Mario and Chico stayed up all night with Mama and Papa trying to console them and calm them down. Finally, at 4:30 am they fell asleep when the Grappa and the emotional exhaustion had worn them all down.

"Mario, Mario," Chico whispered and shook his brother so as not to wake the others.

"Yeah, what?" said Mario still groggy, grubby and unshaven.

"It's 9 o'clock, Mario. We have to go to the morgue, don't you remember? And we have to stop on the way to get Vito's dental records, too."

"Oh, yeah," said Mario as he removed his stiff legs from the kitchen chair he had them stretched out on all night.

"Where is everybody? Are they still asleep?" he asked.

"Yeah. Mama and Papa are in the bed and Angel is asleep on the sofa," said Chico.

"Good. Leave them a note then we'll go out quietly and down to the city morgue," said Mario.

***

Mario and Chico arrived at the morgue at 10:30 am because, initially, Dr. Vincent Lupo had refused to surrender the dental records. But Mario threatened him with a subpoena for all his records, including his financial and tax files if he didn't comply. Dr. Lupo then surrendered Vito's dental records.

"I don't like doing these things, Mario," said Chico.

"What things do you mean, Chico?"

"Looking at dead bodies, going to the morgue and that kind of stuff. It just gives me the creeps."

"I know, I know, Chico. But death is a fact of life, there's no getting away from it. Besides in my line of work you get used to it."

"Sure, but this time it's one of your own family. It's gotta be different. I mean, it's gotta effect you in a personal way."

"Yes, I suppose you're right. This will be my first identification of somebody close," said Mario.

'I don't know about Mario,' thought Chico. 'He seems awful cool about this whole Vito thing.'

The morgue attendant showed them down the corridor passed the long row of gleaming, steel, refrigerated drawer compartments. Mario, the attendant, and a detective walked three abreast but with Chico a safe, quiet, five paces behind them, bringing up the rear. Mario glanced back over his shoulder at Vito and smiled. The detective and attendant remained stoic.

'Look at that Mario,' thought Chico, 'he almost looks like his enjoying this whole business,' as a cool chill passed through his entire body.

"This is it," said the attendant. "Are you ready to make the ID?"

They waited until Chico caught up with Mario and was standing at his side to the right of the slab drawer. The detective stood on the left. Mario and Chico nodded, the attendant pulled out the drawer and then Mario and Chico flushed in anticipation. Chico then turned ashen gray and grabbed onto the drawer to maintain his balance. Mario gripped him under the arms to steady him.

"I don't know, I don't know if it's him," said Chico. "His face is so swollen, and with all those cuts and bruises. It looks like they beat him up pretty bad before they . . . finished him. I have to sit down somewhere," he added, looking around for a chair as his knees began to buckle.

Mario and the detective helped him to a bench against a wall ten feet away. Chico sat and leaned back against the wall but was instantly recoiled by the bench's icy cold, marble surface. The chill again knifed through his body right down to his toes. He quickly leaned forward placing his face in his hands.

"I can't be sure, either, detective," said Mario. "There's so much distortion and edema. He's the right size, the head is shaped the same and the hair cut is right but I just can't say for sure."

"Did you bring his dental records?" said the detective.

"Yes, they're right here," he said handing them to the detective.

"Good, let's go across the street to my office. I'll have our forensic pathologist check them while you wait. And I've got some whiskey in my desk. It looks like your brother can use some right now."

Mario nodded his head in agreement.

***

Ten minutes later Chico threw back his had and downed his shot glass of Seagram's quickly. Mario filled his glass again.

"You all right, Chico?"

"I will be in a minute or two," he answered as he bolted down the second ounce-and-a-half of the sharp liquid. A warm sensation bathed his entire stomach and the color returned to his face. He shook his head to clear it.

"I'm okay, now. You know, Mario, I don't think that was Vito now that I think about it."

"Yeah, I think it was him, Chico. Even though the face is distorted everything else seemed to fit," said Mario.

"Except the hands," said Chico. "Them wasn't Vito's hands."

"Well, but don't forget, Chico, they took off all the jewelry. That makes a big difference, you know."

"No, I don't mean that. That guy's hands were all calloused and full of small cuts, like he did heavy work all his life."

"So?"

"So, don't you remember how Papa was always on Vito because he never did any hard labor? He always called him 'a lazy bum' for that, don't you remember?"

"But his hands could have been swollen and distorted, too. After all, Vito was in that cold, dirty river for a long time," said Mario.

"Maybe so but Vito was proud of those hands. He used to get a manicure every week. Remember how he used to say that he wasn't going to earn his living doing donkey work, like Papa, and have his hands spoiled, like Papa's? Don't you remember that?" said Chico.

"No, I guess I don't. But the dental records will settle the issue," said Mario making every effort to change the direction of the conversation.

"Yeah, unless Dr. Lupo messed them up or even switched them."

"Why would he do that?" said Mario clearly irritated by Chico's persistence.

"Hey, don't bite my head off, Mario. I was only thinking out loud. After all, he is Louie's brother, you know. So he could do anything, if Louie asked him to."

By now, Chico was feeling calmed but lightheaded from all the whiskey. He sat calmly, quietly now, awaiting

The Wolves Of Brooklyn

the forensic pathologist's report. But Mario was nervously pacing back and forth across the room.

"Why don't you sit down, Mario? What are you so nervous about? Here, have another shot of whiskey."

"No, no thanks, Chico. I want to keep a clear head."

"What the hell's the matter with you, anyway?" said Chico.

"Nothing's wrong with me. I just want to get this whole messy business over with. I have a job to worry about, you know. And then there's Mama and Papa to take care of. They're going to need our support, and a lot of it."

"You don't have to worry about them. They know we'll always be there for them. But, I don't like the way Mama was talking about revenge. That's not like her," said Chico.

"But she's not herself. That was just her grief talking," said Mario.

"And Angel? What about her? I ain't never seen her fall apart like that," said Chico.

"Well, she and Vito were pretty close as kids. She idolized him. He was her hero," said Mario.

"Yeah, but I think it is more than hero worship or brother-sister love," said Chico.

"You mean you think there was something . . . romantic between them?" asked Mario.

"Could be, you know. We don't really know what happened when Mama and Papa found them together half undressed. We only have their word that nothing happened," said Chico.

"You know, if Papa was convinced that something did happen he would . . . kill Vito himself," said Mario suddenly realizing the timeliness of this remark. His eyes darted back and forth, beads of perspiration appeared on his upper lip. He licked them dry.

"Yeah, wouldn't that be something. I thought about that, too. But, nah, I'm sure it was Joey Wheels who did it under Louie's orders," said Chico, only half convinced.

"I hope you're right, Chico. Jesus, this family is going completely bananas and all because of Vito."

"I still don't see how Mama and Papa can love a guy like Vito who was nothing but trouble for them," said Mario.

'Wow,' thought Chico, 'I guess Mario really hated Vito. I wonder why.'

The forensic pathologist came back into the office appearing glum and perplexed.

"Well, was it a match, Doc? It is Vito's body, isn't it?" asked Mario.

"I'm afraid it is not. The dental records, xrays and charts are not even close. This dead guy didn't have half the teeth this Vito had. And those he did have were full of cavities. Whereas, Vito's xrays didn't show a single cavity.

"What? That can't be right. You must have screwed up the examination," said Mario jumping to his feet. "It's gotta be Vito."

Then Mario stopped, composed himself and then realized that Chico and the pathologist were stunned and confused by his outburst.

More calmly and coolly he said, "I mean . . . it's got to be Vito. He looked like him, had on his clothes and jewelry, didn't he? Who else could it be?"

"We don't know the answer to that, yet. But I think we will soon. We are checking all the missing-persons-files now."

"Come on, Mario, let's go home and tell the family," said Chico.

"I'll call you, Mr. Assistant DA, when we make a positive ID," said the detective.

The Wolves Of Brooklyn

CHAPTER SIXTEEN
A REAL FAMILY

"Let's use my car, Chico. I've got a two-way radio in case they want to reach us about the corpse's identity," said Mario.

Traffic was heavy on the Flatbush Avenue Extension which was a feeder to the Manhattan Bridge. They moved at a snail's pace which was typical of rush hours. The street was so jammed it looked like a mile-and-half long, ten lane wide parking lot.

Chico broke a long silence, "You know, little brother, there's something funny about this whole business with Vito and Joey Wheels and . . . and you, Mario."

"What do you mean? 'funny' . . . and me?" said Mario.

"Well, for instance, you were so sure the corpse was Vito's you almost looked surprised, no, disappointed that it wasn't."

Mario flushed but said nothing.

"I mean," Chico continued, "I know you and him didn't get along but I didn't think you hated him or wanted to see him dead. You didn't, did you?"

There was a few seconds of uneasy silence.

"Yes," Mario said finally, and hesitated.

The Wolves Of Brooklyn

Chico flushed with shock and anger.

"Yes, if you meant did I hate him," added Mario, "but, no, if you meant did I want to see him dead."

"But, why? Mario. Why did you hate him?"

"Because he was always hurting those who gave him the most and loved him the most. He hurt you, me and Angel, and your ex-wife. And he was always doing something to upset Papa, and always going out of his way to defy and disobey him."

"I don't think Papa loved him too much, not as much as he loved us," said Chico.

"No, but he always provided for Vito even though he didn't deserve it," said Mario, as his anger and frustration grew. "And attention, Vito always got all the attention from the minute he moved into our apartment as a kid. It was always, 'Vito is so handsome, Vito is so smart.' And, 'isn't Vito good at sports'; and 'all the girls think he's such a *dream boat*.' Vito this and Vito that, I got pretty sick of it, I'll tell you," said Mario concluding abruptly when he realized that all his jealousy and envy of Vito had finally surfaced.

"Wow, you really wouldn't cry if he was dead, would you?"

Mario tried to calm and control himself and said, "I didn't say that but, look, even Mama finally got fed up with him and threw him out of the house after he tried to seduce Angel. She always used to forgive him and cover up for him, like the time he stole money out of the coffee can and Papa caught him."

As they now sat in silence the traffic began to dissipate and now they were only a few minutes away from the tenement on High Street.

"Oh, so he really did steal that money, heh?" said Chico.

"Of course, he did. He was rotten through and through."

"Yeah, but Mama, and even Papa had a change of heart when they heard he might be dead. They even vowed revenge on Louie Lupo. You were there, you heard them."

"Yes, but that was all talk, they were just over emotional and irrational," said Mario as he pulled up to the curb outside the tenement.

Angela who had seen them pull up from the second story window of the flat came running down the stairs. Mario and Chico were getting out of the car.

"You've got to stop them," she yelled.

"Stop who, Angel? From doing what?" said Mario.

"Mama and Papa, they got Papa's old 32 caliber revolver from his tool cabinet and they went to Louie Lupo's barber shop to kill him."

"Oh, my God, no," said Mario.

"Only a lot of talk, heh? They're over emotional all right, emotional enough to go crazy and kill Louie," said Chico.

"Quick, get in the car Angel, we've got to catch them. Which way did they go?" said Mario.

"They took Gold Street toward the Navy Yard and then turned left when the came to Sand Street."

The tires of Mario's car squealed as he made a high speed U-turn and went down High Street to Gold and made a sharp left.

'Mr. Mastrangelo, this is the city morgue calling, Mr. Mastrangelo, Assistant DA,' the two way radio crackled. Mario picked up the microphone, and said, "This is Mr. Mastrangelo, assistant DA, over."

"We have identified this corpse with his dental records. This body is not, repeat, *is not* the remains of Vito Vitale, over."

Mario was dazed and unable to speak.

"Mr. Mastrangelo, do you read me? Please reply and confirm transmission, over."

Angela and Chico gazed at each other, with there mouths limply open.

"Yeah," said Mario, "I mean, I copy. Repeating transmission, 'body is not, I repeat, *is not* that of Vito Vitale, over."

"Message correct, Mr. Mastrangelo, over."

"Do you know the true identity of the corpse? over."

"No, sir, not yet. Will label as a John Doe and inform you when an ID is made. Over and out."

The microphone slipped out of Mario's hand and onto the car seat next to him.

"That means Vito is still alive, don't it?" said Chico.

"No, not necessarily. It just means that that wasn't his corpse," said Mario again eerily calm.

"You are awful quiet, Angel. How come you ain't upset or at least relieved to know it wasn't Vito?" asked Chico.

"Because I knew all along it wasn't Vito," she said.

"You knew? How could you know that for sure?" said Mario.

Angel tried to recover herself quickly, "I didn't mean I actually knew--"

"What did you mean then?" asked Mario raising his voice.

"I meant, I knew in my heart it wasn't him. I just could feel it in my heart, I just knew he couldn't be dead," she said.

"Knew it in your heart, heh? You and Vito were really close, then, weren't you?" asked Chico.

"Yes, we *are*, very close," she said.

"You 'are'? Don't you mean you were close?" said Mario pressing the issue. "Just how close were you two, anyway? Would Mama approve of how close you really were?" he added.

"That's none of your damned business, Mario. Why don't you just shut up and drive faster. We still have to stop Mama and Papa," she said.

Mario slammed the accelerator to the floor in anger, Chico's and Angel's heads jerked backwards. Within a few minutes he brought the vehicle to a screeching halt in front of Louie Lupo's so called 'club house'. They ran toward the store and they could see Papa pointing the revolver at Louie and one of his bodyguards through one of the storefront's large windows. They found the front door locked, however.

"Papa, Papa, open the door. Don't do this", shouted Angel while she vigorously knocked on the plate glass window with the knuckles of both hands. "Please, please, Papa, don't shoot. Mama, unlock the door, please, I beg you," she added crying, sobbing and now screaming.

Chico and Mario were trying to force the door with their shoulders. It wouldn't budge.

"Watch out, Mario," said Chico, as he pushed Mario aside. Then he stepped back ten feet, ran full speed and leaped off the ground feet first at the door. The flat bottoms of both his work-boot-covered feet struck the door just below the lock. Wood and glass splinters flew in all directions and the door slammed open with a crash.

Mario ran into the club while Chico recovered himself from the sidewalk. He and Angel then soon followed Mario into the store.

Mama and Papa were so stunned that Mario was able to wrench the revolver away from his Papa easily.

"What the hell has gotten into you two, Papa?" said Mario holding the gun on Louie and his goon.

"And you, Mama," said Angel, "I've never known you to seek revenge on anyone, ever."

The two women embraced and sobbed softly. Papa slumped into a nearby chair, emotionally drained.

The Wolves Of Brooklyn

"I'm-a-so sorry, Angel," said Mama making the sign of the cross and crying. "But me and Papa work so hard to raise all of you kids. And this scum lives like a king and then he takes away one of the only treasures we have. I could think of nothing but revenge on him."

Chico sat on the arm of the chair and tried to comfort his father, "It's okay, Papa, it's all over now."

"Yep, it's all over," said Louie smiling. "Carmine, you can pick up your gun now. Mario, you keep an eye on them, I'll close the door and draw the curtains over the windows. Now, don't anybody move a muscle. If they move, Mario, you shoot."

Carmine picked up his gun and pointed it at them. Mario hesitated uncertain of his next move.

"Mario," shouted Louie, "I told you to keep them covered. Do it!"

Mario slowly turned the gun on his family. Carmine stepped next to Mario and motioned for Angel and Mama to join Chico and Papa near the chair.

"Madonna mia, Mario, what are you doing?" cried Mama.

"Jesus Christ, Mario, what's wrong with you, anyway? Stop pointing that thing at us, will you," said Chico.

"Mario!, No, please don't," said Angel.

"Shut up and sit down, all of you," shouted Louie.

Mario stood motionless, but clearly committed.

"Now what, Louie?" asked Mario obviously quite tense.

"Now we get rid of them just the like we got rid of Vito. Carmine, you go get the truck and some bags of cement. You know, all the usual stuff," said Louie.

"Now wait a minute, Louie, isn't there some other way?" said Mario. "They won't talk, I'll see to that. I'll make them promise--"

"Forget it, Mario, this is the only way to silence a witness, any witness," said Louie.

"But this is my family, Louie, I can't, I can't do it."

"Shut up, Mario," yelled Louie, "unless you want to go with them for that swim in the East River."

Mario fell silent.

"Now, give me your gun, Mario. And go in the back room and get some rope to tie them all up, both their hands and feet. Now get moving and be quick about it," said Louie waving his 45 automatic at Mario.

Mario handed Louie his revolver and went into the back of the store. When he started for the back room, suddenly, Mama tried to stop him saying, "Mario, filio mio, you cannot do this terrible thing."

"Shut up, you old witch," shouted Louie brandishing his gun. "Get back over there or I'll shut you up permanently."

But she ignored his threats and held her hands to Mario's face saying, "Dio mio, Mario, you are no murder, no scum like this one. We taught you to be a good boy, a good son."

Louie hesitated firing on the old woman.

"Oh, yeah," said Louie, "that's what you think. Who do you think killed Joey and his girlfriend?"

"No, not my son. Tell me you did not do this terrible thing."

"Sure he did. And he gave the contract to Joey to get rid of Vito. When he thought the deed was done he had to kill the only witnesses who could finger him. Just like I taught him. And he did that all on my orders. Orders I've been giving him since he's been in the DA's office," said Louie laughing.

"You no good, rotten, slime-ball," said Chico as he rushed at Mario. But Louie intervened and struck Chico in the back of the head with his heavy automatic pistol. Chico dropped to the floor, unconscious.

"Now, the rest of you stay put. Mario go get that rope," said Louie.

Mama tried to go to Chico's aid but Louie stopped her and forced her back beside Angela. Mario docilely went to the back room as the truck Carmine had retrieved pulled up outside the clubhouse. Papa remained strangely calmed and controlled throughout the ordeal, thus far.

Louie, who mistakenly perceived Papa's inaction as cowardice, pointed a gun at the old man's head saying, "Now, old woman, your old man gets it first, right between the eyes, if you move again. Capicé?"

Mama just nodded and stepped back next to Angela. Carmine, for some unknown reason, still sat behind the steering wheel of the truck.

Louie noted this and yelled to Carmine just as Mario reappeared with the rope, "Carmine, what the hell are you waiting for? Get your ass in here, now."

Carmine still hesitated and paused for a few more seconds until Mario was back into the center of the room and binding Chico's hands and feet. Louie watched, intently, to make sure Mario tied the knots securely.

The front door of the clubhouse clicked open and then shut behind Louie and Mario. They could hear Carmine's footsteps approach them slowly.

"Carmine, you stupid Calabrese, get the lead out . . ." said Louie.

But then Louie stopped when he felt the cool steel of a gun barrel behind his right ear and then heard the hammer click back into the firing position.

Mario looked up from his task and said, "Vito, it's Vito."

Mama and Angela gasped a sigh of relief.

"Just drop the gun, Louie, right down between your feet," said Vito. "Mario, you stay right down there where you are. And don't bother waiting for Carmine to rescue you. He's sleeping it off in the back of the truck."

But Louie hadn't yet relinquished his automatic. When he still didn't move, Vito thrust the barrel of the revolver more forcefully against Louie's skull.

"Do it, Louie, now, or you will soon join Joey, his girlfriend, and that innocent derelict you sunk into the river."

Louie dropped the weapon. But as he did so he quickly whirled around to try to rush Vito. Vito didn't fire and then, at the same instant, Mario stood and also rushed Vito. Papa, however, swiftly threw his still muscle-bound-body over Chico and tackled both Mario and Louie to the floor. Vito came to his aid and subdued Mario as Papa held Louie in a head lock.

"Nice going, Papa," said Vito, "you're still as strong as a bull and as quick as a salamander's tongue, aren't you?"

"Yep, still strong enough to whip you and all your brothers and your friends at the FBI all at once," Papa answered smiling.

"Vito, you bastard, where did you come from? You're supposed to be dead," said Mario.

"Well, that was your plan, yours and Louie's, not mine."

Angela rushed to Vito's side, threw her arms around his neck and kissed his cheek saying, "Vito, Vito, my darling, you are alive."

"Wait just a minute, sweetheart, until we tie up these two, then I'll explain everything."

Mama, and especially Papa, were amazed and embarrassed at this display of romantic affection Angela and Vito revealed. After all, they were brother and sister.

The Wolves Of Brooklyn

Vito securely bound Mario's hands and feet while Papa did the same to Louie. When they were done Angela ran over and kissed Vito passionately on the lips and Vito responded in kind. Now stunned, Mama and Papa, stood and watched dumb founded with their mouths agape.

"Angela, Vito!" said Mama, "brother and sister should not kiss in such a passionate way. Should they, Papa?"

"No, no, it is a sin. You will both burn in hell," said Papa.

"But that's only if you were truly blood relatives, Mama. Isn't it? And Vito and I are not really, are we? But we are . . . we are . . ." said Angela hesitating to utter the next word.

"We are married," said Vito, "and we have been for these past three years, now."

Suddenly Mario shouted, "I knew it. You did seduce her as a young girl, you lecherous son-of-a-bitch."

Vito didn't respond but Angela did.

"No, that never happened, Mario, except in your dirty, suspicious mind. But, that was when we fell in love."

"Married?" said Mama, "you two are married? But why didn't you tell us? We would have understood and supported you, wouldn't we Papa?"

Papa didn't answer.

"Here, honey," said Vito handing Angela a business card, "call the FBI at this number, ask for the chief, while I explain this to them."

Angela took the card and called the FBI office.

"So, here's the way it happened, Mama and Papa. About four years ago, when Angel and I knew we loved each other but not as siblings, I knew I had to straighten out my life if I wanted to make a new start with her. So, I went to the FBI and volunteered to be an undercover agent for then inside the Mob if they would grant me immunity from any prosecution."

"Too bad," said Mario, "because we had just accumulated enough evidence to nail your ass."

Vito ignored him and went on, "The FBI agreed and I have been working for them ever since, gathering proof against Louie and his bosses, the Mafia."

"But what about the corpse in the river? Who was he and how did he die?" asked Chico.

"Yeah, well, he was a derelict who apparently got drunk, fell in the river and drowned. Since he looked a lot like me, and when we knew about Mario's contract with Joey, we put the body in my bed in my apartment just before Joey came to kill me."

"Oh, so, Joey didn't know it wasn't you in the bed?" said Papa.

"Yes, Papa, that's right. And Mario and Louie didn't know, either. Only the FBI knew. I couldn't even tell Angel, to be safe and to protect her. I'm sorry I had to deceive you, honey," he said.

"I forgive you now but I was worried sick for awhile," said Angela as she took hold of Vito's arm.

"So, what happens now?" asked Chico.

"Now we wait for the Bureau guys and the cops to come to take Mario, Louie and his goons to jail," said Vito.

"But what will happen to my Mario?" said Mama with soft tears tumbling down her cheeks. "He is still my son and your adopted brother, Vito, and Angela's full brother."

"I know he is, Mama. And I still feel something for him in spite of everything. But . . . I don't know, I just don't know," said Vito.

"No, but I know," said Papa flattening his brow and hardening his face.

Just then the FBI and the NYPD arrived, put shackles on Vito, Louie, and Carmine and took them away.

It took four hours for everyone to give their statements to the authorities. Then Mama, Papa, Chico,

The Wolves Of Brooklyn

Angela and Vito solemnly accompanied Mario to his arrest and arraignment.

As a court officer led him away, Mario turned and said to his family, "I'm sorry, Mama, Papa, and everyone. Please don't hate me, just don't let them kill me."

Now it took two officers to drag the sobbing Mario away to his cell.

"No, my son, we no hate you. We still love you," called out Mama 'Nunciata.

"And we no gonna let them kill you, either, ain't that right, Chico, Vito?" said Papa.

"Yes, that's right, Papa," said Chico.

Vito added, "I'll do everything I can, Mario."

***

Three months later Louie Lupo, and many other Mafia mobsters, both big and small, were convicted on multiple felony counts for which they received the maximum penalty allowed by law. Their sentences amounted to several decades each and many would die in prison, as old men.

Mario Mastrangelo was charged with murder on two counts with a strong recommendation in favor of the death penalty by the county prosecutor. He was tried and convicted on all counts and sentenced, by the judge, to death in a federal penitentiary.

Vito and Angela had to go into the witness protection program under new identities.

"Don't worry, Mama, Vito and I will keep in touch with all of you, somehow," said Angela.

"No," said Mama, "you cannot go until you help us to stop them from killing my son Mario."

"No forget, he's still your brother and you promised," said Papa.

Angela looked into Vito's face as she held his arm saying, "Papa's right, Vito, you did promise."

Vito hesitated but only because he thought of the potential, but real, danger for himself and his now two month pregnant wife.

"Sure, Mama, I didn't forget. Certainly, we will help you. We will do all we can to get an appeal and the sentence reduced to imprisonment only. No death penalty," said Vito as Angela nodded in agreement.

***

It took four years, three appeals and three stays-of-execution but Mario's sentence was eventually reduced to life in prison with a chance at parole after ten years served. But the Brooklyn District Attorney did not support the recommendation for leniency because of Mario's violation of his oath as a former office of the court. The Governor of New York state, however, approved the leniency recommendation for Mario. Therefore, the sentence was reduced.

Vito and Angela took on new identities, moved somewhere in the New England area but less than a days drive away from Brooklyn, his family and Mario's prison. The Mastrangelos visited their imprisoned son at least once a month, on holidays and on other special occasions.

And, as many times as they can manage it, the Vitales with their two children, Charles and Amelia, visited Mario to offer support despite the risk to themselves. But Vito and Angela would often go in disguise or in secret with the warden's approval. The children viewed this as a fun-game.

When asked by a fellow FBI agent why he would expose himself to such danger, Vito Vitale answered, "Because we are family, real family---not like the Mafia family."

THE END

About The Author

Ron Aigotti has been freelance writing, fiction and non-fiction, since 1982 after taking his first writing class at Indiana University. His works to date include twenty-seven short stories, six of which have been published in a small, national magazine called, *GOOD OLD DAYS*. In addition to his short story collection he has written, to date, seven complete novels.

He has also completed and self-published a non-fiction work of 110,000 words related to his primary profession, i.e., medical oncology. The work entitled, *THE PEOPLE'S CANCER GUIDE BOOK,* has met with moderate success with sales of approximately 3000 copies. This work also received two favorable reviews: one by the library magazine, *CHOICE*; the second by *THE MIDWEST BOOK REVIEW*.

Printed in the United States
111449LV00001B/40-60/A